CRY WOLF

(THE EMPIRE'S CORPS - BOOK XV)

CHRISTOPHER G. NUTTALL

Cover By Tan Ho Sim
https://www.artstation.com/alientan

http://www.chrishanger.net
http://chrishanger.wordpress.com/
http://www.facebook.com/ChristopherGNuttall
All Comments Welcome!

DEAR READERS

I must apologise for the long delay between this book being announced as a forthcoming project and its appearance. However, as I'm sure you'll agree, I have a good excuse.

As you may know, if you follow my blog, my health began to deteriorate in November 2017 and, after a brief period when I thought the problem was behind me, started to collapse again in April 2018. The doctors tried several possible approaches before discovering, thanks to a private MRI/CT scan my wife insisted I take, that I had lymphoma. Chemotherapy was prescribed. This may just have been in time to save my life. I collapsed when I went for the first set of treatments, allowing the doctors to realise that I *also* had a nasty chest infection.

I ended up spending three weeks in the hospital, having antibiotics fed into my system and my lung drained of fluid. This was not a pleas-ant experience and I found myself being moved between the haematology ward and the high-dependency care unit, depending on my exact condition. Eventually, they gave me the first treatment in two sections and—after my health started to improve—allowed me to go home. I was not, however, in a good condition for some time afterwards. The side effects made it hard to eat, at first, and then I caught a cold because my immune system had been badly weakened by the treatments. It was some time before I was able to muster the energy to finish this book.

Obviously, I hope to regain full health once the treatments have been finished. I have a backlog of story ideas I want to write, including the start of a new *The Zero Enigma* arc and a couple of completely new universes that need developing. (I spent a lot of time thinking of ideas while lying in that hospital bed.) If you want to pray for me, please do.

I hope to finish the *Invincible* trilogy sooner rather than later, too, but I cannot guarantee anything. Please bear with me.

Thank you.
Christopher G. Nuttall
Edinburgh, January 2019

PS—If you liked this book, please write a review. It's growing harder to make a living as an indie author these days and every little helps.
CGN

CONTENTS

PROLOGUE I

FROM: *The Death Agonies of Empire*. Professor Leo Caesius, Avalon University, 46PE.

AS WE HAVE SEEN IN PREVIOUS VOLUMES, the Fall of Earth managed to surprise nearly everyone within the Core Worlds, save for a handful of far-sighted visionaries. Earth had been the centre of human civilisation for centuries, the cradle of the human race and the heart of the Empire itself, for so long that there was a *permanence* about Earth that seemed...well, permanent. It was almost impossible to grasp the fact, intellectually as well as emotionally, that Earth was gone. The core of the Empire could *not* be gone.

But it was.

Earth's significance did not *just* lie in sentiment alone. Earth was the home of the Grand Senate and, thanks to the presence of hundreds of interstellar corporations, the heart of the Empire's economy. It is literally impossible to estimate just how many billions of credits passed through the Solar System each day, nor how many trillions had been spent on the system's vast industrial base. Nor was Earth insignificant in other ways. The naval presence alone—and its support system—cost millions of credits every year. Every element of the Empire's military might had its HQ on Earth—even the Imperial Marines were formally based on Earth—and no officer could be truly said to be going places unless he'd served a term on the homeworld. And, of course, the endless stream of immigrants to newly-settled colony worlds came, by and large, from Earth.

And now it was gone.

It took time, perhaps longer than many people realise, for word to spread. When it did, when it reached the rest of the Core Worlds, people were disbelieving. Earth could not be gone, they told themselves. It took time for understanding to arrive and, when it did, it brought terror in its wake. Love it or hate it, Earth was gone. And it had taken the core of the Empire with it. Planetary governments—and governors—awoke to the fact that they were on their own, corporations realised that vast amounts of money and assets had simply vanished, naval units realised they would never get orders from home—they would never get orders again—and independence movements across what had once been the Empire took heart. Their prospects for gaining their freedom had never been better.

The chaos was not long in following. A handful of unpopular governors fell, only to be replaced by governors who could no more handle the crisis and calm the chaos than their predecessors. A handful of ambitious naval officers declared themselves warlords, only to discover that ruling a vest-pocket empire was nowhere near as easy as they'd believed. And others, seeking stability, found that there was none to be found in the ruins of empire. It truly seemed like the end of times. It was no surprise that radical religious factions, some old and some new, spread like wildfire. The people wanted hope. It was hard to find as the madness gripped the remnants of a once-great civilisation.

But, even during the darkest days of the Fall, there were some who were trying to bring back the light…

PROLOGUE II

TARSUS WAS DYING.

It was not, the man in the dark suit mused, a quick death. There was no fleet of angry starships preparing to scorch the entire planet, no giant asteroid on its way to strike the surface with the force of a million nukes, no dread disease steadily working its way through the population and killing everyone it touched...no, it was the slow death of economic collapse. The men and women below didn't realise it, not yet, but the Fall of Earth had done immense harm to Tarsus and the remainder of the sector. They simply couldn't grasp that things had changed. How could they? There had been economic downturns before—the man in the dark suit owed his position to the previous downturn—but nothing so drastic. The Empire had seemed immortal...

...Until it was gone.

He stood at the window and peered at the streets below. It was near midnight, but the city was still humming with life. The men and women hurrying up and down the streets didn't understand the new reality, not yet. They didn't believe what had happened. Earth was hundreds of light years away. They didn't understand that Earth was—that Earth had *been*—the core of an economic system that covered thousands of light years, nor did they realise that its absence meant utter chaos. The man had seen the reports, the ones his political enemies had tried to hush up. No one *really* knew what would happen when reality finally hit the population. It was so utterly unprecedented.

And yet, there was a twinge of fear running through the air. People knew that *something* was wrong, even if they couldn't put a name to it. The smarter ones were already hoarding food and fuel, something that was technically illegal…the dumber ones were flocking to the entertainment complexes, trying to forget about the shadow looming over the city. They tried to close their eyes to the steadily-growing signs of decline—businesses closing, banks calling in loans, hundreds of thousands already out of work as the economy contracted—even though it was an exercise in futility. If a rising tide lifted all boats, as the finest economic theorists asserted, what happened when the tide was *receding*? The man didn't want to admit it, not even in the privacy of his own head, but he knew the truth. There was nothing to be gained by trying to hide from it. The wealthy and powerful would be the last to fall, perhaps…but they would fall. It was the end of the world.

He turned his eyes towards the distant Government House, where the First Speaker and his cronies were trying to find something—anything—that would save their bacon when the population realised just how thoroughly screwed they were. The man admired their determination to blind themselves to inconvenient facts, even as he held them in utter contempt for their failure. They'd built their system on the assumption that nothing would ever change, although everyone knew that change was the only universal constant. They simply didn't have the determination to do what needed to be done. They were weak when they needed to be strong and strong when they needed to be weak. The man rolled his eyes in disgust. The First Speaker gave the population what they wanted, but not what they needed.

His eyes sought out the distant spaceport, half-hidden in the darkness. The police and security forces were already rounding up the Forsakers, preparing to deport them to…the man didn't know where they were going, let alone when. No one did. All that mattered was getting rid of them. But the man knew it was an exercise in populist pointlessness. The Forsakers might be a drain on society, but deporting them wouldn't solve anything. They weren't *that* big a drain on society. The whole thing was nothing more than a desperate bid to win approval from a population that was about to discover that it had bigger things to worry about than the wretched Forsakers. The government *might* see a blip in its approval ratings, for a day or two, and then reality would assert itself once again. And Tarsus would continue her slow slide into chaos.

But chaos brings opportunities, the man thought. *Who knows what the future may hold?*

He smiled, coldly. He was a popular man—and his party was a popular party—but they had been deprived of *real* power. They'd won enough of the popular vote to be included in government, yet the governing coalition had successfully blocked *any* of their proposed legislation. It was maddening—the man knew his party would share the blame for mistakes that were none of their doing—but it could not be helped. The party structure that had governed Tarsus for over two thousand years was almost impossible to change. And yet, it was based on an economic system that no longer existed. It was dead. It just didn't *know* it.

Not yet, the man told himself. In some ways, the government's refusal to face up to facts worked in his favour. *Let them exchange worthless favours for a few more weeks. Let their promises be exposed as worthless. Let them thoroughly discredit themselves. And then, we can take over and put the world to rights.*

He poured himself a drink, then turned back to the window. A shuttle was taking off from the spaceport, the twinkling lights vanishing in the cloudy skies. A storm was brewing. The man could feel it in his bones. He raised his glass in a silent toast to the future and took a single sip. The wine was worth savouring. He had a handful of bottles, locked away for special occasions, but once they were gone they were gone. There would be no more Rose Picard from Marseilles or scotch from New Aberdeen until someone rebuilt the interstellar economy from scratch. The man doubted he'd live to see it. His projected lifespan was over two hundred years, but rebuilding the Empire would take thousands.

But I can start the process, he thought. Tarsus wasn't a *bad* place to be, if one happened to have ambition. The planet was close enough to Earth to maintain valuable links, both with the homeworld and the other important worlds, yet far enough from the centre of power to be relatively safe. *There is opportunity here, for the man who dares to reach out and take it.*

His intercom pinged. "Mr. Secretary, the First Speaker requests your presence at the cabinet meeting tomorrow."

The man smiled. "Does he indeed? How nice of him."

It was not, he knew, a request. He'd be expected to rubber-stamp a decision made by the First Speaker's inner circle. There was no point in trying to object, not now. But—in time—he would avenge every humiliation the wretched ruling class had inflicted upon him and his supporters. The rulers had thought their position unchallengeable. They'd certainly sealed up all the normal avenues to power. But the Empire was gone. Who knew how far an ambitious man could go?

He took another sip of his wine. "Inform the First Speaker that I would be deeply honoured to attend his meeting," he ordered, dryly. "And tell my wife I will be leaving the house early tomorrow."

"Yes, sir."

The man finished his drink, then took one last look at the streets below. They were still brightly lit…that was going to change. The man had no illusions about just what would happen when the truth finally slammed home. Tarsus, one of the most stable worlds in the sector, was about to undergo a massive shock. The wildfire sweeping over the once-great Empire would burn the planet to ashes.

But we will rise from the ashes, he told himself. He silently catalogued his plans and preparations, reassuring himself that he'd covered all the bases. There was a certain element of risk, of course, but he'd minimised it as much as possible. *And we will build a better world.*

CHAPTER ONE

It will come as no surprise that the single most distrusted entity within the Empire, from the moment the decline began to Earth's final collapse into madness, was the media. It is difficult to say for sure, but it seems unlikely that many people believed what they were being told.
—Professor Leo Caesius
Crying Wolf: The Media and the Fall of the Empire.

IT WAS A DARK AND STORMY NIGHT, Clarence Esperanza narrated to himself, as he surveyed the chain-link fence between him and the dark industrial estate. *It was a dark and stormy night, damn it!*

He smiled—white teeth flashing in a dark face—as he looked for an easy way to get over the fence. He'd always enjoyed adding little flourishes to his work, even if half of them were gleefully stolen from ancient writers hardly anyone—and certainly none of his readers—had heard of. It wasn't theft, not really. It was...all right, maybe it was a kind of theft, but it was in a good cause. Clarence knew, without false modesty, that he was no writer. He lacked the skill to string words together in a manner that would comfort the powerless and afflict the powerful. Whatever skill he'd had in writing, once upon a time, had been ground out of him by a creative writing course

1

and ten years as a reporter. It was no comfort to know that everyone else had the same problem.

An aircar flew overhead, heading north towards the spaceport. Clarence glanced up at it, then returned his attention to the fence. The estate had been abandoned two years ago, according to the city files, but *someone* had taken precautions to make sure that no one could get in or out of the massive complex without going through the gates. Clarence had expected to find a whole string of holes in the wire—cut by the homeless, looking desperately for somewhere to sleep that wasn't damp and cold—but there was nothing. Gritting his teeth, he checked his gloves and started to scramble over the fence. It was harder than it looked and he nearly fell twice before he got over the wire and landed on the far side. The sound of his feet hitting the ground was terrifyingly loud in the silent night air. He ducked down, expecting to see a night-watchman heading towards him. The estate was certainly large enough to merit *someone* on duty at all times.

And my press pass probably won't be enough to spare me a night in jail, Clarence thought, as he listened for the sound of approaching footsteps. The watchman *might* show him the door or he might call the cops. There was no way to know how the cops would react. They wouldn't risk abusing a journalist, but a night in the cells was hardly *abuse. And the editor will give me hell for being caught.*

He smiled at the thought. The tip-off had been vague, but it *had* come from a trustworthy source. *Something* was going to happen tonight, in the vast industrial estate. Clarence would have preferred more details, particularly a clear idea of precisely *what* was going to happen, but his source had gone silent. That wasn't uncommon, in a world where talking to the media could get a source fired and blacklisted...he shook his head. The risk of getting caught was high—press pass or no press pass—but it had been a long time since he'd done *anything* worthy of the great reporters of the distant past. He'd spent the last five years taking official statements and trying, desperately, to put his own spin on bland pap. One might as well add spice to fried mush. No matter how much spice one used, it was still mush.

His smile grew wider as he stood and slipped further into the industrial estate. A chunk of it, according to the files, had been turned into living space for the Forsakers, but the remainder was still empty and cold. He glanced into a giant warehouse as he passed the door, seeing absolutely nothing inside. The building itself was designed to survive everything the planet could throw at it, but the owners had declined to turn it into a homeless shelter. Clarence snorted in disgust as he took a quick snap of the interior, then resumed his walk into the estate. It hadn't escaped his notice that the number of homeless camps—and beggars on the streets—had been increasing recently. There was probably a good human interest story in there, somewhere. And perhaps a story asking precisely *why* the estate had been abandoned when it could be turned into a homeless shelter.

He walked around another warehouse and stopped, dead, as he saw the second fence. The owners might have deeded part of their territory to the Forsakers, willingly or not, but they'd clearly been determined that the Forsakers would not leave the handful of warehouses that had been put aside for them. *This* fence was even newer than the last one, with barbed wire on the top. Clarence wouldn't have cared to bet that it hadn't been electrified, if not alarmed. The owners looked to be selfish bastards. *They* probably wouldn't give a damn if some poor hobo touched the fence and got a nasty shock...

Wankers, Clarence thought.

He put the thought aside as he peered into the semi-darkness. Nothing was happening, as far as he could tell. A small fire burned merrily outside one of the closer warehouses—a handful of people clearly visible in the light—but little else. It looked like a homeless camp, not...he tried to decide what it looked like, then gave up. It didn't matter. It didn't look as if *anything* important was happening within the darkness, certainly nothing demanding his attention. Shaking his head, he walked over to the nearest abandoned warehouse and scrambled up a ladder onto the roof. The air felt colder, somehow, as he lay on the rooftop and looked towards the Forsaker camp. Nothing was happening.

3

Waste of time, he thought, as the cold started to seep into his bones. *I should have stayed in bed with my wife.*

He allowed himself a moment of irritation, then reminded himself to be patient. The *really* great reporters didn't sit in their offices and wait for someone to bring them the news. No, they went out and *got* the news. Sometimes, it went badly wrong and then they *were* the news...Clarence shook his head, again. Nothing was going to go wrong. He was just going to wait a few hours and see what happened, then sneak back over the fence, call a hovercab and go home. His editor would have a few nasty things to say if Clarence turned up at the office without a story—or hopped up on stims—but he'd understand. It wouldn't be the first time a tip had turned into a giant waste of time. Clarence reached into his pocket, produced his recording spectacles and placed them on his nose. They were a pain in the ass to wear, but their recordings had saved his bacon more than once. If nothing else, they'd prove he hadn't been doing nothing in the dead of night.

Although I am doing nothing, he thought, silently starting to compose his latest story for the newspaper. *I'm lying on my chest on a freezing cold rooftop when I could be having naked time with my wife.*

Another aircar flew overhead, lights flickering in the darkness. Clarence did his best to ignore it, telling himself that the aircar wasn't looking for him. It wouldn't take military-grade sensors to pick him out on the rooftop, but who would give a damn? He looked like a hobo himself—he'd been careful to dress as a dockyard worker, rather than a flashy reporter—and it was unlikely that anyone would care about a hobo in an abandoned estate. It wasn't as if there was anything worth stealing...not really. The only thing of any value within the estate was the buildings themselves. It wasn't as if a small army of hobos could pick *them* up and carry them away.

Which won't stop the police chasing the hobos out if someone makes a fuss, he thought, grimly. There was another human interest story there, he was sure. *The homeless simply want a roof over their heads when they sleep, just like the rest of us.*

It was nearly an hour—and he was on the verge of giving up—when he heard the faint sound of engines. He tensed, peering into the darkness. A small handful of trucks were pulling up at the distant gate. Were they coming for him? He silently calculated a handful of ways to get out of the estate in a hurry, although—as policemen started spilling out of the trucks—he had a nasty feeling that there would be no way out. It looked as if the police had arrived in force, ready for war. He could see men wearing helmets and body armour, carrying shockrods and neural whips in the foreground, while others—armed with real weapons—hung back. They looked ready to intervene at any moment.

His blood ran cold. This was wrong. The police did not come in the dead of night, certainly not to a harmless estate. It was hard enough to get them to come out when one lived in a middle-class estate in the heart of the city, let alone the homeless camps and ghettos along the edge. But now...a shiver ran down his spine as the policemen moved forward in eerie silence. He tapped his spectacles, making sure they were recording the scene. The policemen moved through the gates and straight towards the warehouses...

Someone shouted. A handful of men appeared, carrying makeshift weapons. Clarence winced, unsure if he should laugh or cry. The Forsakers were carrying baseball bats and iron rods, nothing *really* dangerous to a man in body armour. They didn't even have a chance to try before a flurry of stun bolts left them lying on the ground, twitching helplessly. The policemen marched over them, abandoning all pretence at stealth. Clarence covered his eyes as the policemen turned on the lights. The estate was suddenly bathed in brilliant white light.

"ATTENTION," a voice boomed. The warehouse seemed to shake with every word. "COME OUT WITH YOUR HANDS IN THE AIR!"

Clarence covered his ears, a fraction of a second too late. He couldn't help thinking, as he turned his head to capture as many details as possible, that half the city had been awoken by the racket. The warehouse district was large, but it wasn't *that* large. He watched, feeling a twinge of sympathy, as dazed Forsakers stumbled out of the warehouses. The policemen grabbed them, male and female alike, and snapped on the cuffs before forcing them to lie on the ground and wait. Clarence made sure to record it all. The public wouldn't be sorry for the Forsakers unless they saw the poor bastards being made to suffer.

And it is so pointless, he thought, as a crying child was made to sit next to her mother. *What does it matter?*

He shuddered, helplessly. The Forsakers had a bad reputation. They were lazy and arrogant beggars, walking around in their traditional clothes as if the world owed them a living, utterly unwilling to abandon their primitive culture and join the mainstream. Everyone knew the Forsakers were a drain on the planet's public funds...until they actually ran the figures for themselves. Clarence had, more out of curiosity than anything else. The Forsakers *weren't* draining the planet dry. They weren't even claiming a percentage point of a percentage point of the government's budget. The government spent more on bureaucracy than it did on public aid.

A scream rent the night air. Clarence scanned the scene before him, then zoomed in on a young girl who was being harassed by two policemen. One of them was holding her, the other had his hand up her dress...Clarence shuddered again, as a senior officer marched over and rebuked the two coppers, who didn't look remotely repentant. Clarence wasn't really surprised. The news file in the office contained lots of stories about policemen who abused their powers, stories that the editor had killed on the grounds they'd incite social unrest. And some of the stories had been a little hard to believe...Clarence swallowed. It was clear, now, that the stories had some basis in truth.

But that doesn't mean they're true, he thought. The poor girl, crying silently, had been dumped with her fellows. *Just that they could have happened.*

The dreadful night wore on. Clarence watched, helplessly, as the policemen stripped everything out of the warehouses and piled it up in the trucks, then marched the prisoners to the gate. He filmed everything, from the crying children to the broken spindles and other primitive tools that were part of the Forsaker heritage. The policemen seemed to take an unholy delight in breaking things, although it was nothing but spite. There was certainly nothing to be *gained* by smashing tools the Forsakers would need…

It hit him in a moment of insight. *Dear God*, he thought. *They're deporting the bastards!*

Clarence swallowed, hard. It couldn't be true, could it? There was nothing to be gained by shoving the Forsakers on a starship and tell them never to come back. He ran the calculations in his head and scowled. It would probably cost the government more, in the long run, to deport the Forsakers than to keep them. Hell, there was no reason the Forsakers couldn't be given land and told to farm it if they wanted to stay alive. But they'd already been evicted from lands they'd held for generations. The big farming corporations had wanted the land for themselves and the government hadn't had the will to say *no*. Who cared about a bunch of weirdoes in outdated clothes when there was money to be made?

Not that the price of food went down, Clarence thought, coldly. He made a decent living, but even *he* had noticed that the cost of living was steadily inching upwards. God alone knew what was *really* happening in the countryside. *The Forsakers were evicted for nothing.*

He looked towards the spaceport in the distance as the rest of the pieces fell into place. The Forsakers were easy targets. Harmless, by and large; unarmed, certainly. And easily demonised by radical politicians. The pressure to do *something* about them was overwhelming…no, had *been* overwhelming. It was clear the government had decided that deporting the Forsakers was a concession they could afford to make, although it was pointless. Clarence hoped, in a moment of naked horror, that the government actually *was* deporting the Forsakers. There were nastier things that could happen…

This will not stand, he promised himself, as the police started to drive away with their prisoners. They were heading towards the spaceport, at least, although he knew that proved nothing. There was plenty of room for a mass grave in the wastelands beyond the spaceport complex. *I'll tell the world.*

Clarence rolled over and stood, hurrying back towards the ladder. The show was over, as far as he could tell. He had to get his story out before the Forsakers were actually loaded onto a starship—or sold into slavery or whatever other horrible fate the government might have in mind for them—and deported forever. He'd make sure the people knew what was being done in their name. He silently reviewed the footage he'd recorded as he slipped down the ladder and ran towards the fence. The Forsakers weren't popular, but the *right* footage—carefully chosen—would change that. He'd have the entire population shouting in outrage by the time he was done.

Scrambling over the fence, he fled into the darkness. There was no sign of anyone on the streets, not even a handful of homeless or a patrolling police car. It was easy to believe that he'd imagined everything, he thought, as he reached a diner and called a hovercab. If he hadn't had the footage, it would have been hard to convince anyone that it had really happened. It was so unthinkable that…it was unthinkable. The government was harsh, at times, but it wasn't monstrous…

Hard times make people do monstrous things, he thought, as the hovercab dropped him off outside his apartment. *And people who think they cannot be called to account can be the worst of all.*

Clarence allowed himself a tight smile as he sat down in front of his terminal—his wife had long since gone to bed—and started to review the footage and write the story. It would make his career, he was sure. Every reporter yearned for something that would make him famous, something that would change the world. The truly great reporters had been household names, once upon a time. They'd exposed corruption, they'd caught criminals…a couple had even had flicks made of their lives. Clarence wanted that kind of fame for himself. And he would have it…

He finished writing the story, uploading it and the footage to the newspaper's server, then went to bed. His wife shifted uncomfortably as he climbed under the sheets, but otherwise didn't move. Clarence didn't really blame her. She'd been up for most of the day, first taking their son to nursery and then handling her job. Clarence would have liked to be the sole breadwinner—he didn't like the tired look in his wife's eyes—but there was no alternative. He simply didn't bring in enough money to ensure a good start in life for his son.

Things will be different, he silently promised his wife. *And they start from tomorrow.*

And he was right. The following morning, he received an email that told him he'd been fired.

CHAPTER TWO

That, too, should be no surprise. The difference between what the general public was being told and reality, what they were actually seeing, was too great to be wished away. People refused to believe— and quite rightly too—that their eyes and ears were lying to them.
—**PROFESSOR LEO CAESIUS**
Crying Wolf: The Media and the Fall of the Empire

CLARENCE STARED AT THE EMAIL IN SHOCK.

It was hard, so hard, to process what he was actually *seeing*. He'd expected praise, not...he hadn't expected to be fired. His thoughts ran in circles as he read the email again and again, trying to make some sense out of it. He'd been fired. He'd been fired. He'd been...

He swallowed hard, unable to believe what he was seeing. He'd been fired...it was the end of the world. He was jobless...he'd never get another job, not if he'd been fired. His heartbeat was suddenly very loud, pounding in his ears. He'd been fired. There was no hope of finding another job, not in the cutthroat world of the reporter. Every news service on Tarsus would blacklist a reporter who'd been fired. And even if they didn't...he was all too aware of just how few jobs there actually *were*. A reporter—a man who wasn't qualified to be anything else—had no hope of finding another job. He wouldn't even have a hope of becoming a street-sweeper. The union would make sure of *that*. He didn't even have the right qualifications.

Clarence's fingers shook as he made himself a cup of coffee, his head spinning. It was the end of the world. He found himself looking around the apartment numbly, silently cataloguing just how many things had been bought on account. It wouldn't be long before the bank started talking tough, demanding to know how he intended to pay his mortgage, let alone his credit chip debts. They'd be right, too. Clarence didn't have *that* much in his savings account. It wouldn't be long before he couldn't pay his debts and everything would be repossessed. What little he owned that was *his* would be taken away and sold to offset the debts…

He took a long breath, forcing himself to calm down. Perhaps it wasn't as bad as it looked, he told himself. Perhaps…he sat down in front of the terminal and tapped a key, bringing up the email again. It was hard, so hard, to concentrate. How long would it be before they cancelled his datanet account? It didn't cost *much*, in the grand scheme of things, to have access to the datanet, but if he'd been fired…he tried to imagine life without the datanet and shuddered. He wouldn't even be able to file stories to the media networks without datanet access…if, of course, the networks accepted them. The union would bitch and moan about an independent reporter trying to make a honest living. And no one would risk speaking up in his favour.

The email stubbornly refused to change, no matter how he stared at it. Clarence sipped his coffee, forcing himself to read through it once more. It was a masterful piece of bureaucratese, he had to admit, claiming that he'd been fired for a handful of unspecified offences…he cursed, savagely, as the truth dawned on him. Whoever had fired him had set out to do him a favour…no, it just *looked* as if whoever had fired him had set out to do him a favour. In reality, they'd stuck a knife in his back. There was no way he could disprove the claims against him, no way he could defend himself from charges that were maddeningly undefined…there was no way anyone would *hire* him, when they didn't know what he'd done. Clarence found himself shaking in horror. His life was over. A petty thief had a better chance of getting another job than him, now. He was going to starve to death. His wife and son were going to starve to death beside him.

A surge of helpless anger ran through him. He'd been screwed. He'd been thoroughly screwed…and why? What had he done? He couldn't understand it. He'd been a good reporter, damn it! He'd written stories covering everything from politics to flower arranging, as his bosses had decreed. And now he'd been fired. He stood, pacing the room as he tried to understand what had happened. Why had he been fired? And why had he been fired in such a manner? He'd never heard of anyone being fired in a manner that made it impossible for them to get another job!

He grabbed his coat out of habit, keying his terminal to call a hovercab before remembering—too late—that he could no longer afford to waste money on indulgences. His finger hovered over the cancel button before he decided that there was no point in trying to claw back half the taxi fare. It was only ten credits…he shook his head as he pulled on his coat and snapped his terminal into his belt. He couldn't take the time to *walk* to the office, not when he needed to see Alistair Allrianne before the man's daily routine of meetings began. The Chief Editor would understand, surely, when Clarence explained that he needed his job. He'd tell Clarence that he hadn't been fired…wouldn't he? Clarence knew he was clutching at straws, but…he had to *try* to get his job back, somehow. He'd do *anything* to get his job back.

The terminal bleeped, informing him that the hovercab was waiting downstairs. Clarence took one last look at the apartment, wondering just how long it would be before he and his family would have to move out, then hurried downstairs to the door. The hovercab driver waved cheerfully at him as he clambered into the vehicle. Clarence barely heard the man's attempts to chat, even though normally he would have enjoyed bandying words with the driver. The man wouldn't be so friendly if he knew Clarence had been fired. An unemployed man had no friends or family, for fear that unemployment might be catching…somehow. Clarence felt his heart sink as he remembered a handful of his fellow students who'd never managed to find good jobs. He hadn't shunned them, not really…

You did, his thoughts mocked them. *You could have stayed in touch. But you didn't.*

He sagged into the seat as the hovercab passed a pair of aircars and headed north, towards the bustling heart of the city. The sight normally took Clarence's breath away, but now…he could hardly think straight. He wondered, morbidly, just how hard it was to live on the streets…it wasn't a pleasant thought. There were already hundreds of thousands of homeless people on the planet. Would he and his family be allowed to join them? Or…he shivered helplessly. How could he do anything for his family without a job?

His terminal bleeped. He glanced at it in sudden hope, then felt his heart sink—again—as he realised it was just a piece of spam advertising a fancy aircar he wouldn't have been able to afford even when he'd had a job. *That* was going to stop, he told himself, once the spammers realised he was unemployed. There was no point in trying to get money out of an unemployed man. Clarence had never had *that* much money in his life. And when he was cut off from the datanet…a bleak vista opened up in front of him, dragging him down into the depths of despair. If he wasn't a reporter, what was he? He didn't know.

Useless, he thought. *I'm a useless bastard without my job.*

He touched the terminal, one finger lingering over Minnie's icon. He could call his wife…he *should* call his wife. And yet, the thought was somehow unbearable. He couldn't tell his wife that he'd been fired, not yet. She'd be shocked, then horrified, then finally angry at him for losing his job. *She* didn't bring in enough money to keep them off the streets, if she managed to keep her job. Clarence cursed his boss under his breath as he realised that Minnie might get fired too. *Her* boss wouldn't know what her husband had done to get fired either.

Go to work, he thought, desperately. *Get your job back. Somehow…*

"Here we are," the driver said, with maddening cheer. "The front entrance, sir?"

"Yes, please," Clarence said.

He pressed his credit chip against the reader as the hovercab landed, half-expecting the transaction to be declined. God knew what he'd do if it *was* declined. He didn't carry much cash on him, no one did. Easier and safer to carry a credit chip, unless one had been fired and one's creditors were breathing down one's neck. The bank might place a hold on all transactions until he worked out a new payment plan...if he *could* work out a new payment plan. He hadn't realised just how tense he was until the machine bleeped, informing him that the transaction had been accepted. The door clicked open. Clarence wondered, as he scrambled out of the hovercab, just what would have happened if it had been declined. The driver might have flown him straight to the nearest police station.

Which would have been the perfect end to the day, he thought, sourly. *Lose one's job, get arrested...all in the space of a few hours.*

The *Daily Truth* lived in a colossal building, a steel and iron monstrosity that had been the height of architectural fashion a few hundred years ago. Clarence had admired the design hugely when he'd first started to work for the newspaper; it had, he'd felt, the right attitude for a media company that prided itself on asking the tough questions and giving answers to the public. Fifteen years as an employee, from cub to senior reporter, had soured him somewhat on the ideals of journalism, but...he still admired the building. Now...he sucked in his breath and marched towards the door, steeling himself to face the stares of his former colleagues. They'd been his friends, once upon a time. Now...he told himself that he had to keep going, somehow. He tried not to think, as he stepped into the lobby, that *once upon a time* had been only yesterday.

He passed through the lobby, silently grateful that it was almost empty. The thought of being *seen* as he came to plead with his boss—for his job, for answers, for...he wasn't sure any longer—was horrifying. And yet...when he pressed his fingers against the inner door, it bleeped in warning. His access to the upper floors, where the actual work was done, had been cancelled. He wondered, as he turned to look around the lobby, just why it surprised him. There was no shortage of horror stories about disgruntled former employees turning up at their former jobs and opening fire. It had never occurred to Clarence that he might, one day, be one of those poor bastards.

The secretary looked up at him, her eyes widening—slightly—as she saw his face. Clarence felt a surge of sudden hatred that surprised him in its intensity, even though the poor girl had done nothing to him. She was just window dressing, chosen more for her looks than any actual *competency...* she had a job. It wasn't much—there was no shortage of young women willing to sit at a desk and look pretty—but it was a job. Clarence gritted his teeth, telling himself to calm down. The secretary was powerless. There was nothing she could do to help or hurt him. And yet, she had a job. She was a cut *above* him, now.

And perhaps we shouldn't have mocked the wretched girls so badly, he thought, with a twinge of shame. *If this one remembers me...*

He kept his face impassive, silently grateful that his dark face hid his feelings. The secretaries, receptionists and interns came and went, sometimes so quickly that no one outside Human Resources knew their names. They were terrifyingly vulnerable to predators in the office, Clarence knew. He hadn't taken advantage of any of the young girls himself, but he hadn't stopped any of his friends from doing it themselves. Journalism's dirty little secret was that it was easy to exploit people for personal gain. And not just sexually. He'd intended to turn the Forsaker tragedy into his personal story, the expose that would transform him into a celebrity and catapult him into the major leagues. He'd thought it would secure his place in the history of journalism.

"I need to speak to Mr. Allrianne," he said, suddenly unsure what to say. Allrianne had always insisted his reporters call him by his first name, but...now, Clarence *wasn't* one of his reporters. "Please could you buzz me through the doors."

The receptionist gave him a bland smile, but he could see the tension in her eyes. "I'm afraid Mr. Allrianne is busy, sir," she said. "If you leave your name, address and contact details, he'll get back in touch with you as soon as possible."

Clarence felt his temper fray. "You know damn well who I am," he said, sharply. "You can call him and..."

He caught himself, knowing it was already too late. The receptionist was *young*, barely out of her teens. She didn't deserve to be shouted at by... by what? What was he, now he was unemployed? There was nothing to be gained by shouting at her. She couldn't do anything, up to and including going to the toilet, without permission from her superiors. She could no more buzz him through the security doors than she could wear something that actually made her look like a respectable employee. He found it impossible to believe she actually *wanted* to wear a ridiculously over-sexualised dress.

"I'm afraid Mr. Allrianne is busy," the receptionist repeated. "If you leave you..."

"He knows who I am," Clarence said. He felt as though he was bullying a child, but he couldn't stop himself. "Call him. Tell him that..."

He heard someone behind him, too late. A strong arm slammed into his back, forcing him over the desk. Clarence barely had any time to react before his arms were yanked back and cuffed behind his back. He twisted, but he couldn't break free. The security guard—he kicked himself, silently, for looking down on the security guards too—searched him roughly, then pulled him to his feet. Clarence knew he'd seen the man before, but...he didn't know the man's *name*. He really *should* have learnt their names before he needed their help. They might have been more willing to help him.

"I'll take care of him," the guard growled. "You don't worry about a thing."

The receptionist gave him a brilliant smile. "My hero."

Clarence tugged against the cuffs, even though it was futile. "Let me go!"

"Quiet, or I'll use the shockrod." The guard sounded as though he *wanted* to use the shockrod. "You're under arrest."

"I need to see the editor," Clarence protested. "Let me go and..."

The guard hefted his shockrod. Clarence shut up. The guard smirked, then half-dragged him to the elevators and shoved him inside. Clarence swallowed, hard, as the elevator headed downwards. He'd heard whispered rumours of...*things*...under the building, but it had never occurred to him that the newspaper might have a *jail*. A shopping mall might have a holding cell for shoplifters to hold them until the police arrived, yet…he found it hard to believe there was a jail under the building. It was far more likely that any miscreants would be summarily fired.

Like you, he thought, as the guard shoved him into a small office. His own thoughts came back to mock him. *You got fired and now you got arrested.*

"Sit," the guard grunted, shoving Clarence onto a bench. "Stay."

"Woof," Clarence said, sarcastically. "I know my rights and…"

The guard shrugged. Clarence wondered, suddenly, what his rights actually *were*. His press ID was in his pocket, but it had probably been cancelled by now. The police weren't likely to be *gentle* with a former reporter, not when they realised he'd fallen from grace. The only people who hated reporters more than the police were soldiers…Clarence cursed under his breath. He had enemies, of course. Every reporter had enemies, from people who thought they'd been slandered to people who'd been exposed by the press. And now he was as naked and vulnerable as he'd been the day he was born.

He tried to force himself to relax, but it was futile. He'd fucked himself. The police were going to come and…and he was going to go to jail. There was no way he could afford bail, not now. Minnie certainly couldn't raise the money to get her husband out of the lockup, not when their savings were likely to be seized to pay their debts. And the police probably wouldn't offer him the chance, even if he *could* pay. A former reporter in gen-pop… the police could probably make money selling the recordings of him being shanked by an inmate who hated the press. Clarence could name a dozen people who'd pay to see him humiliated.

And yesterday seemed such a great day, he thought. Yesterday, he'd been at the top of his game. Now, he was cuffed in a cell, waiting for the police. He wondered, morbidly, if the police would bother to inform his wife. They might walk him past a tame judge and sentence him to deportation without further ado. *What the hell do I do now?*

CHAPTER THREE

Indeed, to paraphrase an old saying, "they only pretend to
tell us the truth and we only pretend to believe them."
—**PROFESSOR LEO CAESIUS**
Crying Wolf: The Media and the Fall of the Empire

IT FELT LIKE HOURS BEFORE THE DOOR FINALLY OPENED.

Clarence looked up, expecting to see a leering policeman or—perhaps—a security services officer. Instead, Alistair Allrianne stepped into the office. The Chief Editor of the *Daily Truth* looked tired, as if he hadn't slept all night. His eyes flickered from side to side, sweat shining on his brow as he nodded to the security guard. The man touched his cap, stood and walked out of the office, leaving Clarence and his former boss alone. Clarence wondered, sardonically, if Allrianne felt *safe*. Clarence was cuffed and helpless—and the guard wouldn't have gone very far—but the editor had never been renowned for his bravery.

"Clarence," Allrianne said. He sounded tired, too. "I wish you hadn't come here."

Clarence studied him, thoughtfully. Allrianne had always been overweight, his hair thinning because he couldn't or wouldn't pay for treatment, but it looked as though he'd put on considerably more weight in the past few hours. He might well *not* have gone home last night, Clarence thought. Normally, Allrianne was a great deal more dapper than *this*…although it was hard for him to look handsome. The older man had let himself go a long time ago. Indeed, there was something faintly unpleasant about his jowly cheeks. Clarence asked himself, sourly, if there had *always* been something *wrong* about his boss. He just wasn't used to being so…so what? Powerless? In hindsight, he'd always been powerless.

He forced himself to think. Was he really that powerless? Allrianne hadn't *had* to come see him. No one would have questioned the Chief Editor ignoring a former reporter's attempt to see him. No one would wonder if Clarence was unceremoniously handed over to the police and unpersoned, completely wiped from the records. And if they did, they wouldn't dare to question. Who knew who would be the *next* to be fired?

"What happened?" His voice sounded more plaintive than he cared to hear. "Alistair…sir…what happened?"

"You were fired," Allrianne said. There was no trace of vindictiveness in his tone, no gloating…Clarence could almost believe that Allrianne hadn't *wanted* to fire him. "You were sent an email…"

"An email full of lies," Clarence snapped. He rattled his cuffs, loudly. "You didn't have the nerve to come out and say *why* I was fired."

A sense of bleak despondency overcame him. "*Why* was I fired?"

Allrianne said nothing. Clarence stared at him for a long moment, then lowered his eyes, finally giving in to despair. If he'd been fired for insubordination, for disagreeing with his superiors, that would have been one thing. The union would have defended him, even if they hated him. They wouldn't have had a choice. There was no way they'd allow a reporter to be fired in a manner that set a precedent for firing other reporters without due process. And if he'd been fired for criminal behaviour, he could have forced them to *prove* him guilty or…he knew someone who'd won severance pay, even though he'd been caught stealing office supplies, because he'd threatened a lawsuit. But Clarence? The charges against him were so vague that they couldn't be disproved. He would never be able to find another job.

"I need my job," he mumbled. He was begging and he hated it, but he had no choice. "Sir...*please*."

"I can't," Allrianne said, softly. "Clarence, you were fired!"

"Why?" Clarence knew he was shouting, knew the guards might burst in at any moment, but he didn't give a damn. "Why was I fucking fired!"

He lifted his head, glaring at his former boss. "I did good work, you know it. I was the one who exposed the sentencing racket in the manpower commission, I was the one who found proof that..."

Allrianne held up a hand. "Clarence, listen to me," he said. "You have to..."

Clarence snorted. "Do what?"

He started to giggle, hysterically. Oh, he had his enemies in the manpower commission all right. Even the ones who hadn't been involved in the sentencing racket itself hated his guts for the scrutiny they'd had to endure. They were going to shit themselves laughing when they found out Clarence had been fired. Who knew? They might be glad of the chance for a little revenge. No one would give a damn about a reporter who was *accidentally* sentenced to a hellworld. Even a relatively decent stage-one colony world would be hard on its indentured labourers. And his wife wouldn't want to come with him.

"I did good work," he repeated. "I wrote a good story, didn't I?"

"Yes," Allrianne said, tonelessly.

"And now I'm fired," Clarence said. He looked down at the tiled floor. "What am I doing to do?"

Allrianne's voice didn't change. "I don't know."

"We'll lose everything," Clarence said. He was starting to panic, again. "Why? Why did I get fired?"

A thought struck him. "This is about the Forsakers, isn't it?"

"Perhaps," Allrianne said. "Clarence..."

"What?" Clarence glared at him. The older man didn't meet his eyes. "What can you do to me *now*?"

He rattled the cuffs, again. "Perhaps I should go to the union anyway," he snapped. "They would take the case, even if they don't know *precisely* why I was fired…"

Allrianne stamped his foot. "Clarence, listen to me. Who do you think fired you?"

Clarence blinked. The question had honestly never occurred to him. Allrianne was the only one who could hire and fire, wasn't he? Sure, every prospective candidate had to jump through a dozen hoops crafted by Human Resources dickheads who needed to justify their salaries *somehow*, but Allrianne had the final word. The man was a micromanager in the worst possible sense, when it came to hiring reporters. He wouldn't accept anyone he hadn't interviewed personally.

"You," he said, finally.

"No." Allrianne let out a heavy sigh. "The orders came from high up."

Clarence stared. "The stockholders?"

"Higher than that," Allrianne said. He still wouldn't meet Clarence's eyes. "The orders came all the way from Simon Goldwater himself."

"What?" Clarence couldn't believe it. He would sooner believe that water had been turned into wine. "Goldwater? *The* Goldwater? Simon Goldwater fired me *personally*?"

"Him, or someone in his office," Allrianne said. "We got the orders within an hour of you filing the story. The paperwork was already completed by the time they deigned to inform me. And Clarence? Rest assured that the union isn't going to say *anything* about this particular firing."

Clarence was still having problems with the concept of Simon Goldwater even knowing Clarence's *name*. The man was—perhaps—the richest person on Tarsus, owner of a tangled web of corporations so complex that it was hard to say where his power and influence truly ended. Clarence hadn't known that Goldwater owned the *Daily Truth*, but…he had to admit it was possible. He certainly owned a sizable media division of his own. And it would be just like Goldwater to imply that Allrianne had a certain independence, even though it wasn't remotely true. What sort of idiot would bite the hand that fed him?

Me, apparently, Clarence thought.

His thoughts ran in circles. It made no sense. He could understand the government getting pissy about the story—expelling the Forsakers was pointless and everyone knew it—but *Goldwater?* What was *his* involvement? Had someone from the government brought pressure to bear on Simon Goldwater? *That* was hard to believe. The man was so rich that everyone knew he had hundreds of representatives in his pocket. Very few government officials would dare to try to bully him. It was easier to believe that Goldwater had fired him personally.

"I can still go to the union," he said, putting the thought to one side. It didn't matter right now, not when his entire *life* was at stake. "Sir, if I go…"

Allrianne cut him off. "It will be rejected. Clarence, I've seen the paperwork. The union isn't going to say *anything* about this firing. If you go to the union, you'll just get kicked out."

"The union leadership might refuse to get involved," Clarence said. "But what about the actual members—what about them?"

"What about them?" Allrianne echoed. "Do you really think the union gives a damn about the rank and file?"

Clarence swallowed, hard. The union leadership was composed of professional activists, not…not the people they were supposed to represent. It had been meant to make the union more efficient, if he recalled correctly. Union membership was pretty much mandatory in journalistic circles. But… it also meant that the leadership had lost touch with the people below them. There was a good chance that they'd be more concerned about ruining their personal relationships with the big bosses than defending their people. Clarence had a nasty feeling that the fix was firmly in. The union might be able to come up with a good case for *not* defending him.

"Fuck," he managed.

"Quite," Allrianne agreed.

He shook his head. "I wasn't given a choice. I had to sign off on your termination. If I hadn't…"

Clarence could guess. If Allrianne balked, he would be fired too. The stockholders would be furious if Allrianne put their investments in jeopardy. Simon Goldwater—assuming it really *was* Simon Goldwater and not some underling trying to please the big boss—wouldn't have to pull many strings to get rid of a particularly foolish editor. In hindsight, Clarence wondered just how he'd *ever* thought that Allrianne enjoyed a certain degree of independence. How quickly would *he* have folded if he'd thought his livelihood was at stake?

"I understand," he said, softly. "I *need* my job."

"I can't give it back to you," Allrianne told him. "I can't even give you a reference, not now."

"But it's so fucking pointless," Clarence said. "How does *anyone* benefit from expelling the Forsakers? Or by abusing them or…?"

Allrianne let out another sigh. "You should know by now that what someone *believes* to be true may not *actually* be true," he pointed out. "And you should *also* know that it doesn't always matter if someone believes something that isn't true. The only thing that matters is that they *believe* it to be true."

Clarence made a rude sound. "They'll find out soon enough," he muttered. "I'd bet good credits that it cost more to expel the Forsakers than it would have done to keep them in that estate for a hundred years."

"You might be right." Allrianne looked as if he didn't care. "But it doesn't matter."

Clarence met his eyes. "I need my job back," he said. "I…I'll do anything. I'll…"

Allrianne looked away. "I *can't*! Get that through your head. I cannot employ you in *any* role. There is *nothing* I can do to get you a job."

"Fuck it," Clarence said. "I…I don't know what to do."

"I know," Allrianne said. "And I'm sorry."

"Yeah," Clarence said. "I *bet* you're sorry."

24

"There's only *one* thing I can do for you," Allrianne said. Clarence looked up, hopefully. "I can ensure that this little…*incident*…doesn't get included in your file. The guards will kick you out of the building, then wipe the recordings. You won't have to explain your stunt here to prospective employers. That's about the only thing I can do for you."

"Gosh," Clarence said, sarcastically. "That is *so* generous of you."

"Yes," Allrianne agreed. "It is."

Clarence looked down. The hell of it was that Allrianne was right. It wouldn't be easy to convince *anyone* to hire him, not now, but it would be impossible if prospective employers knew he'd gone straight to his former workplace and made a scene. They wouldn't want to take a chance on *him* when there was no shortage of others willing and able to work who *didn't* have blots on their records. Clarence knew he *should* be grateful, that he *should* be on his knees thanking his former boss. And yet, it was hard to feel any gratitude. When push came to shove, he'd been betrayed so rapidly that he still hadn't come to terms with it.

"Thank you," he managed.

"You're welcome," Allrianne said. "Good luck."

"Hah," Clarence muttered.

It was a bitter thought. He didn't have a hope of getting another job as a reporter. *That* was as clear as day. But what other job could he get? A shopping mall wasn't going to hire an older man when they could hire a young and pretty girl instead. Besides, they'd think Clarence was overqualified for just about any post. They wouldn't realise that he desperately needed the money. No, they would realise it. They just wouldn't care.

And that was my mistake, he thought. *I started to care.*

He shivered, remembering the Forsakers who'd been abused and molested before they'd been unceremoniously deported to some godforsaken rocky planetoid on the edge of explored space. They hadn't deserved to be uprooted from their homes, they hadn't deserved to become the playthings of corrupt police and security officers, they hadn't deserved to be sent into an exile that would probably force them to either embrace technology or die…

they hadn't deserved anything. And if Clarence had realised that reporting on an atrocity would cost him everything, he knew—to his eternal shame—that he would have killed the story before it was even written. What does it profit a man to expose injustice, he asked himself, if it costs him everything?

And the injustice hasn't even been exposed, he told himself. He hadn't had a chance to look at the latest bulletins, but he'd bet every last credit in his savings account that his story hadn't even reached the editors before being killed. It had probably been replaced by a collection of lies about how much money had been saved by expelling the Forsakers, even though no one in their right mind would believe it. *No one knows what really happened last night.*

Clarence looked at his former boss, feeling too tired and beaten to be angry. How could he call Allrianne a coward when he knew, even if he didn't want to admit it, that he would have killed the story in a heartbeat if he'd known what it would cost him? It wouldn't have been hard to write a puff piece about how wonderful a Forsaker-less world would be. He would have written the story and…and done his best to forget that *real* people had had their lives torn apart, for nothing. It was true. He didn't want to admit it, but it was true. He was just as much of a coward as everyone else.

And they'll make sure everyone knows why I was fired, he thought. *It would keep them from rocking the boat themselves.*

"I hope you find *something*," Allrianne said. "And if you don't…you can always emigrate."

"Perhaps I can follow the Forsakers," Clarence growled. The government had no qualms about buying starship tickets for anyone who wanted to leave, provided they were heading to a stage-one colony world. "Who knows where they're going?"

"They might be better off than you think," Allrianne pointed out. "They'd know how to survive on a colony world, wouldn't they?"

Clarence had to admit it made a certain kind of sense. Stage-one colony worlds were almost always low-tech, at least for the first hundred years. It was cheaper to give the colonists primitive gear, equipment they could repair or replace for themselves, rather than keep them supplied with modern technology that would cost a great deal to replace. He wanted to believe his former boss was right. It would be nice to think that the Forsakers had been exiled to a world they'd consider paradise.

And how long would that last, he asked himself, *when they truly had to live without modern technology?*

He shook his head. It was hard to believe the government had *bothered.* It was far more likely that the Forsakers had been sold into indentured slavery or simply dumped on the nearest world…if they were lucky. There were quite a few nearby worlds that depended on high tech to survive. The Forsakers would hate them. And…he cursed, once again. It didn't matter. He'd tried to help them and it had cost him everything. There was nothing more he could do for anyone. He didn't even have the nerve to kill himself.

"Good luck," Allrianne said. The editor sounded sincere, although he'd sounded sincere when he'd been extolling the virtues of a free press too. "The guards will escort you out."

Clarence nodded—he wasn't going to *thank* the man, even though he knew he should—and watched him leave the office. His wrists were starting to ache uncomfortably. The guard returned a moment later, his face grim. Clarence said nothing as he was hoisted to his feet and marched down a long corridor to the rear entrance. Thankfully, he wasn't about to be taken through the lobby again.

"If I see you again, you'll be taken straight to the police," the guard growled as he unlocked the cuffs. "Do you understand me?"

"Yes, sir," Clarence grated. There was no point in trying to say anything else. No one would make a fuss if the guard zapped him with a shockrod. He concentrated on trying to massage some feeling back into his wrists. "I won't see you again."

"Good," the guard said. He opened the door and pushed Clarence into the alleyway. It was bitterly cold outside, despite the coat. "Fuck off."

CHAPTER FOUR

*It was, however, incredibly difficult for the average person to either
get their hands on accurate information or, for that matter, to start
their own media business. The regulatory nightmare created by the
Empire's bureaucrats—all for the population's own good, of course—
bore down particularly hard on independent media producers.*
—PROFESSOR LEO CAESIUS
Crying Wolf: The Media and the Fall of the Empire

CLARENCE HONESTLY WASN'T SURE what to do with himself as
he hightailed it away from the *Daily Truth.*

It was hard, so hard, to walk down the street and *know* he didn't have a
job. The hundreds of suited professionals walking past him, heading to the
shops for lunch or simply taking a break before they returned to the office…
they were all so *secure* in their lives. They had jobs, they had lives…he knew,
intellectually, that their positions were no more secure than his had been,
but he didn't believe it. He felt a surge of hatred as he passed a group of
chattering women, bragging openly about their latest outfits…didn't they
know they were wasting the money? Didn't they know they could lose their
jobs at any moment? But how could he blame them when he knew *he* hadn't
thought about it either?

I thought I was secure until I wasn't, he told himself. The grim awareness that he would have been a coward, if he'd realised that there was a reason to be scared, gnawed at him. He didn't want to look at himself in the mirror. *And now it's too late.*

He stopped outside a small cafe and had lunch, a sandwich, a drink and a packet of crisps. It occurred to him, a moment too late, that he might not be able to afford it…and, even if he could, perhaps he *shouldn't* afford it. The kind of meals he'd been allowed to put on his expense account were suddenly out of reach. It was all he could do to force himself to put a tip on the table when the time came to pay. God knew if he could afford a handful of credits for a girl who was probably trying to work her way through university. He wanted to scream at her, to tell her that she would never be able to pay back her loans, but it was completely pointless. He'd done his best for the Forsakers and look how *that* had ended up.

At least she's not opening her legs for money, he thought, sourly. Years ago, the *Daily Truth* had run a shocking expose on students who'd sold their virginity for the money to pay off their student loans. He'd mocked and sneered, both at the girls themselves and the bastards who'd paid them, but now…now he understood all too well. Student loans just kept growing bigger and bigger with every passing year. *The poor bitches had no choice.*

The girl thanked him as he left the cafe. Clarence nodded in return, silently grateful that she didn't know he was unemployed. He'd have had to pay in advance if she'd *known* he was unemployed. There was no shortage of stories about people being denied everything from a seat reservation to a banking loan because they were unemployed. It carried a terrible stigma that no one wanted to face. Clarence knew it was only a matter of time until the news leaked out. None of his friends—his former friends—would want to know him once they knew the truth. Unemployment might be catching.

Literally, in my case, Clarence thought. Many of his friends worked at the *Daily Truth.* They would be wise to avoid him, just in case Simon Goldwater noticed them too. *How can I blame them for pretending that I don't exist?*

He reached for his terminal, intending to call a hovercab, then forced himself to start walking home instead. It wasn't *that* long a walk. Besides, he knew he might need ten credits for something more serious. He thought hard as he made his way down the street, trying to plot out the future. Minnie didn't make anything like enough money to cover their expenses, let alone the interest on their loans but…he could talk to the bank, try to work something out before it was too late. Who knew? Maybe he *could* get a job as a toilet cleaner or street-sweeper or something—anything—else. And he *did* have his degree in journalism. It might just give him a toehold somewhere else.

Unless I've been completely blacklisted, he thought. He'd heard rumours about what happened to people who were unpersoned. They couldn't get a job anywhere, anywhere at all. And, if the rumours were true, they never knew for sure what had happened. They just kept applying for job after job, always being rejected. *And if I can't get a job, what then?*

He nodded politely to his neighbour as he entered the apartment block, trying to look as if nothing was wrong. Mrs. Douglas was a gossip, plain and simple. If she knew what had happened to him, everyone else would know within the day. The tenant's association would start demanding that they paid their dues within a week or…or what? Clarence wasn't sure *quite* what would happen, but he was certain it wouldn't be pleasant. He hadn't liked anything that had happened over the last few hours and he was pretty sure the rest of the week would be worse.

Henry was sitting on the sofa when Clarence entered the apartment, looking scared. "Dad? What's happening?"

Clarence stared at him in shock. It was only three o'clock in the afternoon. Henry should *not* be home, not yet. The nursery should have kept him until five, when he should have been collected by Minnie on her way home from work. He heard someone moving in the bedroom and felt his heart sink. Minnie was home. Minnie had come home early…he swallowed, hard. If Minnie had been fired too…

"Stay there," he said. Minnie would have called him if she'd been fired, wouldn't she? He didn't *think* she would have taken Henry out of nursery if she'd been fired. She would have gone home and...and what? "I'll be back in a moment."

"But Dad…"

Clarence ignored his son as he slipped into the bedroom. Minnie was sorting through her drawers, tossing a handful of clothes towards a single suitcase sitting on the bed. For a moment, Clarence just stared. Minnie had been beautiful when he'd first met her, over ten years ago, and she was still beautiful. She'd worked hard to regain her figure after they'd had a child— she'd refused to bear a second child—and it had paid off for her. Clarence could easily believe she was younger than her real age.

Minnie straightened up and turned to face him. Clarence felt breathless. She was a dark-skinned vision of beauty, even when she was angry. Her almond eyes sat within a heart-shaped face, her long dark hair framed her face...she could have been a supermodel, Clarence thought. He was still surprised, at times, that such a vision of beauty had agreed to marry him. Minnie's face darkened…

…And then she slapped him, hard.

Clarence stumbled backwards, more shocked than hurt. They'd had arguments in the past, great screaming rows that had brought complaints from the neighbours, but she'd never *hit* him. He found it hard to believe what had just happened. She couldn't slap him...Minnie drew back her hand for another slap, lashing out at him as hard as she could. Clarence caught her hand instinctively.

"Let go of me," Minnie snapped. She lifted her knee, ready to go for his groin. "You bastard…"

The red rage rose up. Clarence shoved, hard. Minnie fell back on the bed, her mouth going wide with shock. He'd never hit her either, not even when they'd been struggling to make ends meet. Those days...he'd wanted to forget those days. He'd thought they were over when they both finally had good jobs. Anger surged through him. How could she turn on him at the darkest hour? The urge to hit her, to beat her into submission, was almost overwhelming. He had his fist raised before his conscious mind caught up with what he was doing. She was his *wife*! He didn't want to hurt her. And yet, his cheek was a throbbing reminder that she'd hit him first.

Minnie sat upright and glared at him. "What did you do?"

She knows, Clarence thought. Minnie knew he'd been fired. He'd hoped to get at least one or two interviews lined up—even for dirty underpaid jobs—before she came home and he had to tell her the truth. But instead… she knew. Who'd told her? They had friends in common, including some who worked at the *Daily Truth*, but he found it hard to believe that any of *them* had told her. *She knows and…*

He found his voice. "I fucked up!"

"You're damn right you fucked up," Minnie snapped. "What did you do?"

Clarence glared at her. "Who told you?"

"I got an email saying you'd been fired," Minnie said. "No name. No ID header. Just an email saying that my fucking *husband* had been fired for some stupid shit and…"

She leaned forward, glaring at him. "What did you do?"

"I wrote a story," Clarence said. His head was starting to pound. He knew, intellectually, that she had every right to be angry…but, emotionally, he wanted her to shut up and support him. It had been a bad day and he wanted, he *needed*, her comforting arms. "And they gave me the sack."

"For writing a story?" Minnie crossed her arms under her breasts. "Are you sure that's the whole story?"

The rage boiled up again. "Of course I'm fucking sure that's the whole story," Clarence snarled. "That's what I did. I wrote a story and they fired me!"

"And you didn't think," Minnie demanded, "about what would happen to *us*?"

"I didn't know *anything* would happen to us," Clarence said. It was true. Journalists had been fired for a great many offences, ranging from stealing office supplies to sexual harassment, but he'd never heard of anyone fired merely for writing a story that had been killed before it could be published.

He'd certainly had stories killed in the past—without consequence—simply because he hadn't been able to prove his assertions. "Minnie…"

"Don't you talk to me," Minnie snapped. "I…I would sooner come home to find you in bed with a fucking whore than get fired. I…"

She covered her eyes. "Clarence, what are we going to do?"

"We have enough money to last a couple of months, if we're careful," Clarence said. He made a mental note to check for severance pay. The email had suggested that there wouldn't be any, but he might be able to force *something* out of the *Daily Truth* in exchange for not going to the union. Who knew? It was certainly worth a try. "And I can interview for other jobs…"

"And when you go to the interviews," Minnie snapped, "what then? What are you going to tell them?"

"The truth, or as much of the truth as they can handle," Clarence said. If he told them about Simon Goldwater, they'd think he was mad. Or had a persecution complex. He rather suspected that would be preferable to them actually *believing* him. "There aren't any clear charges against me…"

"Which means they won't know what you did," Minnie said. She uncovered her eyes and glared at him. "And why the fuck should they believe you?"

"It would be the truth," Clarence said, weakly.

"And even if they *did* believe you, what then?" Minnie stood and paced towards her dresser. "Do you think they'd give you a decent job?"

Clarence said nothing. His career had been long enough for him to apply for a senior reporter's position at another newspaper, without working his way up the ranks, but…he knew, all too well, that his application would be deleted unread. Anywhere else…he'd probably have to start at the bottom, assuming he got the job in the first place. He forced himself to think how he could present his skills in a desperate bid to improve his standing, but nothing came to mind. A reporter's skills couldn't be used outside the media, could they?

Perhaps I should become a private detective, he thought. *Or a stalker.*

"Of course they won't," Minnie said. "They'll pay you minimum wage. And then sack you when they discover you're totally incompetent."

Clarence balled his fists. "I'm not incompetent!"

"You just got yourself fired," Minnie thundered. "What would *you* call yourself?"

"I can make money," Clarence pleaded, although he wasn't sure which of them he wanted to convince. "Even if I get minimum wage…"

"We'll lose the apartment in two months," Minnie said, remorselessly. "That's when our savings will run out. Henry's nursery will start talking tough about his fees in two months too…you *did* have to send him to a fee-paying nursery, didn't you?"

"That was *your* idea," Clarence snapped.

Minnie ignored him. "The banks will probably start calling tomorrow, demanding to know how we intend to repay our loans. They're *our* loans, aren't they? If you get paid minimum wage, our collective earnings will be too high and we'll have to keep repaying the loans; if you get paid nothing, we won't be able to afford the apartment and food and everything else we need anyway! What are we going to do when Henry needs new clothes? He's not going to fit into *your* old trousers, is he?"

"No," Clarence said. "But…"

"But what?" Minnie resumed packing her suitcase. "We are doomed. Get that through your thick skull. We. Are. Doomed."

Clarence took a long breath, forcing himself to unclench his fists. "What are you doing?"

"I'm packing a bag," Minnie said. She picked up a bra and hurled it into the suitcase. "What does it *look* like I'm doing?"

Clarence sat down on the bed. "You're leaving me."

"I don't have a choice," Minnie said. "I'm taking Henry back to my mother's house. She can take care of him while I go to work and…and try to earn enough to keep us both afloat."

"We can get through this," Clarence said. "Minnie…"

"How?" Minnie's voice rose until it was almost a scream of pain. "You have destroyed our family! What's going to happen when we drown in debt?

What will happen to us when we don't have any money left? What will happen to us if I stay?"

She looked, just for a moment, if she wanted to slap him again. "Do you expect me to go to the spaceport and spend my nights turning tricks for sailors? Ten credits to go down on my knees and suck him? Fifty credits for letting him bend me over a smelly rubbish bin and fuck me? Hey! Maybe he'd give me a hundred credits if I let him take me up the arse! What do you expect me to do to clean up this awful fucking mess you have created?"

Clarence straightened. "Don't say that..."

Minnie rested her hands on her hips. "You know as well as I do what happens to women who become homeless," she said. "They don't have many options left, do they? What is it to be, Clarence? Take a one-way ticket to a colony world I've never heard of and hope for the best? Or spend the rest of my shortened life on the streets, begging for change? Or selling the only thing I have left"—she grabbed her breasts—"in the hopes that I can earn enough money to stay alive one more day? No. I won't. I'll leave now and I'll take Henry and I'll thank you to keep out of our lives in the future!"

Clarence stared at her. "He's my son!"

"What kind of father puts a fucking story ahead of his son?" Minnie slammed the suitcase closed and clicked the lock. "I don't know what you were writing about, but tell me...was it worth it?"

"...No," Clarence said. "I didn't think..."

"That could almost be the story of your life," Minnie said, bitterly. Tears glittered in her dark eyes. "You're not eighteen any longer, Clarence. You're not a single man with...with the nerve to do whatever it takes to challenge the establishment. You have a family, a family you have destroyed. I won't have Henry growing up with a whore for a mother and I won't have him go into care while his father...oh, fuck it. Just get out of our lives and stay out."

She picked up the suitcase and marched out of the room. Clarence wanted to go after her, but something—despair, perhaps—kept him rooted to the bed. He heard her snapping at Henry, telling him to pick up his bag and follow her down the stairs. Clarence lay back on the bed, lost in his despair. He had lost everything. His wife and child had left him…

…And, in truth, how could he blame her? Minnie was right. He'd destroyed their life.

He staggered to his feet and walked into the kitchen. It looked homey, as if Minnie had only stepped out for a minute. But he knew she would never come back. Shaking his head, he opened a cupboard and found a bottle of expensive wine. He'd intended to save it for his birthday, but now…he doubted that birthday would ever come.

Lifting the bottle to his lips, he took a long swig.

CHAPTER FIVE

It was literally impossible for a media producer to exist without breaking at least a hundred different laws and regulations. A producer that ran a story without—for example—getting written permission from everyone involved would technically be in breach of the law, although it was unlikely that such permission would be forthcoming. Why would someone accused of a crime grant permission for their name to be mentioned in print?
—PROFESSOR LEO CAESIUS
Crying Wolf: The Media and the Fall of the Empire

"FUCKING COLONIALS," SOMEONE SAID, as he raised his glass high. "Damnation to the bastards!"

"Damnation to the bastards," Colin Simpson echoed. He took a long swig of his beer, savouring the taste. It was thinner than he liked, thinner than the beer one of his wretched stepfathers had brought home years ago, but it was alcoholic. "And death to the shitters!"

"Death to the shitters," the small group echoed.

Colin allowed himself a cold smile as he looked around the bar. It was heaving with young men like him—women and older men knew to give the bar a wide berth—all angry at the lack of anything *meaningful* in their lives. Or even a hope of supporting themselves. Colin had graduated from

39

college with a decent degree, and excellent prospects, but the jobs he'd been promised had been nowhere to be found. He'd hoped to be a starship pilot, once upon a time; he'd discovered, rapidly, that there was no hope of turning his degree into a practical high-paying job. He hadn't even been able to switch to the technical schools when he'd realised the scale of the problem. Instead, he was competing with immigrants and worthless countrymen for jobs that didn't require any education, but didn't pay very well. The handful of credits in his pocket was all he had. And his mother was nagging him to get a better job.

Stupid bitch, he thought, as he took another mouthful of beer. It had been easier in her time, if she was to be believed. Young men had walked out of school and straight into jobs. Good jobs. Colin's never-to-be-sufficiently-damned stepfather had a *very* good job, although Colin had a sneaking suspicion that it wasn't as good as the bastard claimed. *It isn't easy to get a job any longer.*

He felt a surge of bitter anger. It wasn't fair! He'd worked his ass off in school, struggling desperately to keep his grades up…he'd known, they'd all known, that high grades were their only hope of getting somewhere in life. But it had grown harder and harder as the classes had grown bigger and bigger, as children and teenagers from the countryside or orbital settlements crowded the classrooms. Colin gritted his teeth, remembering how little time the overworked teachers had had for the locals. They'd spent so long trying to help the country boys—the shitters—that Colin and his peers had been left alone. It just wasn't *fair*!

Why couldn't they have stayed home? He'd asked that question once, which had earned him a detention and a nasty slap from his stepfather. But it was a fair question, wasn't it? Why was Tarsus being flooded with outsiders when there was little enough for the locals? *They're taking everything from us!*

The hatred had started to curdle as he'd grown older, as he'd watched their once-nice district of the city go downhill. He'd been told that it wasn't the fault of the newcomers, that they were fleeing problems back home, but…they weren't *his* problems. Why did they have to disrupt and destroy *his* life? The streets were dirty, the schools were crammed, there were fewer jobs…Colin's sister didn't dare go out after dark for fear of being attacked. Colin hated it, *hated* it. He wanted to have a decent life, the sort of life he saw on the viewer every day. But he couldn't climb the ladder when he couldn't even get on the first stair!

He glanced at his friends and nodded to himself. They'd grown up together. They'd played together in the park, when they were younger; they'd chased girls together, when they were older. And they were all in the same sinking boat. They knew, all too well, that they didn't have a hope of climbing the ladder. There was no chance of moving to a better area. The costs were too high, even for Colin's stepfather. The only hope was finding a way to fight back before it was too late.

"It's time," he said, quietly.

The alcohol felt warm in his belly as they slipped out of the bar and onto the darkened streets, heading down towards the edge of the estate. There were supposed to be streetlights driving back the darkness, but they'd failed long ago. Some had been broken by vandals—immigrant vandals, Colin was sure—while others had simply failed and never been replaced. Colin gritted his teeth as they stopped at Parker's shed to pick up their supplies. There had been a time when it had been safe to walk the streets. He'd had no qualms about walking from one end of the estate to the other when he'd been a child. Now, even a lone man would hesitate to go out after dark. He looked up, feeling a stab of envy when he saw the gleaming towers in the centre of the city. The people who lived there didn't give a damn about people like him, did they? They kept mindlessly babbling on about duty and honour and obligation while—somehow—never having to sacrifice their peace and security to appease the nagging crowds.

If they wanted to house the shitters in their towers, he thought, *no one would say a word of complaint.*

He cursed under his breath as he saw the small cluster of houses at the edge of the estate. They'd belonged to his people, once upon a time, but the banks had foreclosed and the owners—the rightful owners—had been evicted. And *then* they'd been given to the intruders, as casually as someone might throw meat to a dog. Colin had no idea just how many immigrants lived in those houses—he'd been told there were five or six families living in each of the buildings—but it didn't matter. There were plenty of other people on the estate who owed the bank money. It was just a matter of time before the wretched bastards started talking tough to them too. Colin had heard the stories. The locals would be evicted to make room for the newcomers unless they took a stand.

Not that anyone listens to us, he thought, savagely. The handful of people who'd dared protest had been destroyed. They'd lost their jobs, they'd lost their homes…they'd been ripped to shreds by the media, painted as irredeemable monsters rather than men and women who'd been trying to defend their homes. *We have to make them listen.*

They stopped in the shadows and opened their bags. It hadn't been *easy* to get their hands on a canister of gas, then use it to produce a handful of makeshift grenades. He'd looked around for contacts who might be able to help them get their hands on *real* weapons, but even the drug dealers were reluctant to use anything more dangerous than baseball bats and kitchen knives. The police would come down on anyone with firearms like the hammer of God Himself…Colin suspected, and he knew others who felt the same, that the government was more concerned with keeping the population under control than allowing them a chance to defend themselves. How many people would be evicted if they were armed and able to shoot the bankers when they came to claim the house?

"One each," he muttered, as he passed out the bottles. It hadn't been easy to design a trigger either. His education had been lacking in anything *practical*. He was uncomfortably aware that he'd come far too close to blowing himself up several times when he'd been filling the bottles with gas. The slightest spark would have been enough to set off an explosion. "When I throw mine, throw yours."

He watched his friends hurry down to their positions, then surveyed the houses. They'd been nice once, when their owners had felt pride in their estate. Colin remembered a friend from his younger days who'd lived there, before he'd been evicted and gone…gone where? No one asked *what* happened to people who lost their jobs and their homes, as if the mere act of asking would bring bad luck down on their heads. Colin couldn't even remember the boy's *name*. The poor boy had had an older sister, if Colin recalled correctly. She'd been pretty enough to draw attention from all over the estate, before she'd been evicted. Was she selling herself to survive?

Hatred surged in his breast as he braced himself. His friends had lost the houses they'd worked to earn, while the newcomers merely had to arrive to be *given* houses. He lifted the bottle, took aim at the nearest window and threw it with all the strength he could muster. The window shattered as the bottle struck home, smashing through the glass. A second later, the gas exploded. Colin heard someone scream—and remembered the story about five or six families crammed into each house—as the flames spread rapidly. The houses hadn't been very well designed. It was quite possible that they'd burn to the ground before the fire department arrived.

Or before they can put the fire out themselves, he thought, as he turned and ran down the street. Flames were coming from all six houses now, crackling merrily as they devoured the stolen buildings. He could hear people shouting inside, trying to get out…he grinned, savagely, as he picked up speed. *They won't have anywhere to go now.*

He wished, suddenly, that he'd dared recruit more friends. They could have lurked in the darkness and attacked the bastards as they ran out of their home, striking a far harder blow for freedom. But that was folly. It had taken weeks to sound out his closest friends, knowing that even *one* traitor would be enough to nip his plan in the bud before it even got off the ground. He'd just have to hope that others decided to emulate him, now the first blow had been struck. They'd have no choice. The newcomers would form gangs of their own and start pushing back.

He heard a crashing sound behind him, but didn't look back. Instead, he nodded to his gang and commanded them to head home. It was unlikely that anyone would call the police—no one on the estate liked or trusted the police—but the firemen would probably take care of that when they arrived. Fire was a real threat, particularly if it spread to the other houses. Colin wondered, suddenly, just how careful he'd actually *been*. The dramas on the viewer had shown the police effortlessly solving an endless series of crimes, arresting the masterminds and evicting the foot soldiers within half an hour. But if the police were really *that* good, why were so many criminals still on the streets? Colin knew drug dealers, petty thieves and drug dealers—everyone knew them—who could have been rounded up in less than an hour, if the police had wanted to do it. *Everyone* knew who they were.

The police in the dramas have a friendly scriptwriter, he thought, as he reached his apartment block and hurried through the rear entrance. The security system was broken at the back, although no one cared enough to try to fix it. For once, the estate's condition worked in his favour. There'd be no record of him leaving the apartment and returning. *The police in real life don't have anything like as many advantages.*

He snorted to himself, despite the cold lump in his stomach. No one gave a damn if an oldster was mugged, or a woman was raped, or a child was snatched off the streets...but he was sure it would be different now. The government had been resettling immigrants for months now, driving out the locals and replacing them with strangers. Colin couldn't imagine them turning a blind eye to open violence. The government was no different to a street gang. It couldn't allow its authority to be challenged openly or it would lose it.

It will lose it, Colin told himself. *No one in the estate will betray me.*

He hoped—as he stepped into the apartment—that that was true. There were hundreds of poor and desperate people on the estate. One of them might be tempted by a reward, particularly if it included a transfer to a better estate on the other side of the city. A person who spoke to the police would be lucky if they were merely beaten up, but...Colin shook his head. There wasn't a person on the estate who wouldn't approve of what he'd done.

"You're back early," Angelina said. His sister was sitting on the crumbling sofa, watching a romance drama. "Did you have enough beer?"

Colin winced at the resentment in her voice. His sister, three years younger than him, was already a beauty. He'd drawn a knife on a boy who'd whistled at Angelina once, threatening to cut off his penis if he ever so much as *looked* at Colin's sister again. But he was all too aware that he couldn't protect her forever. The wolves were already gathering. What would happen if the estate were to be overwhelmed with newcomers? Or if Colin's stepfather lost his oh-so-important job?

"I couldn't afford to stay," he said. He couldn't risk telling Angelina the truth. He trusted her, but…she was a girl and girls gossiped. "And the beer really should have been poured back into the horse."

Angelina scowled. She didn't *want* to go to the bar and get drunk, he thought, but she resented not having the freedoms he took for granted. Colin didn't blame her for wanting to go out at night, rather than sharing the apartment with their mother and stepfather. Their stepfather wasn't *that* bad, he supposed, but he wasn't good company either. Angelina would be a great deal happier if she could go out of the building—and out of the estate—every so often. But it wasn't an option.

And the swimming pool was closed down months ago, he thought. He wasn't quite sure of the details, but he was certain it had something to do with the newcomers. *And people would ask questions if we went out of the estate.*

Colin nodded to her and walked into their bedroom. Having to share with his sister was a minor indignity—they'd spent hours rigging up blankets so they could each have some privacy—but one he'd learnt to endure. It wasn't as if he'd be bringing anyone back home in a hurry. His mother would start cooing at the merest hint her son was getting married…Colin shook his head as he undressed and climbed under the sheets. He couldn't afford a wife. There was certainly no way he could afford to get married. They'd have to share an apartment with their parents…

And it isn't fair, Colin thought, as he closed his eyes. *There's no way out of the trap.*

The next thing he knew, Angelina was shaking him. "Colin? Colin, wake up!"

Colin jerked awake, unsure of what was happening. Last night... had it been a dream? Or...he forced himself to sit upright. "What... what happened?"

Angelina looked away, granting him what little privacy she could. "There's a man here to see you," she said. She didn't sound as if she believed her own words. "He says he's a head-hunter."

A cold lump settled in Colin's chest. The police? Could they have tracked him down already? No, the police would have crashed into the apartment and handcuffed everyone inside before he had a chance to shake off his slumbers and run for his life. But a head-hunter? It sounded like something out of one of Angelina's stupider dramas. People with degrees, experience and connections got headhunted. Colin was all too aware that he was utterly worthless, easily replaceable. No one would bother to hunt *him*.

He stumbled to his feet, glanced at the clock and dressed rapidly. Ten o'clock. His stepfather would be at work, his mother would be drinking tea and washing clothes with her friends. Angelina...he told her to stay in the bedroom and walked into the living room. A tall dark-skinned man was standing there, wearing a black suit. He looked completely out of place, as if he'd stepped out of a drama and into the real world.

"Colin Simpson," he said, calmly. There wasn't even a *hint* of doubt in his voice. "Last night, you and your friends burnt down three build-ings on the edge of this estate. Fifteen people were killed, nine more were badly wounded."

Colin felt cold. "I was here all night," he said, quickly. He hadn't expected to be caught *this* quickly. And he'd killed...it hadn't really dawned on him that people would be killed, even though he'd prepared the gas grenades himself. But...who *was* this man? "You can't prove otherwise..."

The man smiled. "You misunderstand," he said. "I'm not with the police. I'm here to offer you a job."

"A job?" Colin repeated, stupidly. He felt completely off-balance. "You're offering me a job?"

"You could say I'm with the resistance," the man said. His smile sharpened. Colin couldn't help thinking of a tiger advancing towards its prey. "And you joined us last night."

CHAPTER SIX

This was not—perish the thought!—done out of any intent to suppress the freedom of the press. Indeed, every media-related law and regulation existed to defend the rights of the individual over the media juggernaut. Each and every one of them—and the bureaucrats could cite case law to prove it—had come into existence after the media overstepped itself.
—**PROFESSOR LEO CAESIUS**
Crying Wolf: The Media and the Fall of the Empire

SOMEONE WAS KNOCKING AT THE DOOR.

Clarence lay on the sofa, barely caring. It didn't matter who was at the door. They could wait. He wasn't sure *how* long he'd been in a drunken stupor, but he didn't care. The last week had been an utter nightmare. He'd gone to the bank, only to be told that there was no way they could renegotiate his loans; he'd gone to the job centre, only to discover that there were no jobs that would allow him to salvage *something* from his life. And then the creditor notices had started pouring in. They wanted their money back or else. Clarence had no idea what the 'or else' was, but he didn't care about that either. He'd simply started to pour alcohol down his throat until he'd started to lose track of time.

The knocking came again, louder. A bailiff, Clarence thought. Someone who thought he could pick up a few items from the apartment to pay Clarence's debts. Or…someone who wanted to evict him. No, they'd have been sent by the apartment's owners. They would have had a keycard. Clarence coughed loudly, his fingers searching for the bottle. Whoever it was could wait. There was very little in the apartment that was worth anything, save perhaps for the viewer and Clarence's terminal. The thought of losing *that* gave him a pang. He would be completely isolated from the rest of the world…

He shook his head, bitterly. He *was* isolated. Everyone knew what had happened to him, how he'd been fired, how his wife had left him…he'd felt eyes following him every time he'd left the apartment. People on the *streets* knew he'd been fired. None of his old friends, damn them to hell, had bothered to reach out to him. Clarence wondered, bitterly, if any of his friends had truly been friendly, back when he'd had a job. Or had they merely been tolerating him? He wanted to scream in frustration. It was only a matter of time before the bank evicted him and…and then what? There was no one who would give him a place to crash, even for a night or two. Unless…he wanted to scream. His mother-in-law wouldn't give him a place, not when he might bring misfortune on her head. She'd always felt that Minnie had married beneath herself.

Bitch, he thought, nastily. The knocking grew louder. *Go away, whoever you are.*

He blinked, shocked out of his daze, as he heard the outer door open and someone step into the apartment. They had a keycard? He felt, just for a second, a flash of hope. Minnie? She'd come back to him? The footsteps sounded feminine…no, there was something *hesitant* about them. *Minnie* wasn't hesitant. Besides, her mother would have been chewing her ear off about getting a divorce before the remainder of Clarence's life crashed and burnt. She wouldn't come back to him if it meant picking a fight with her mother.

"Well," a voice said. "You *do* look a mess."

50

Clarence twisted his head and blinked in surprise. A redheaded woman was standing in the door, looking down at him. Her body looked oddly fragile, a sign that her parents had been born on a low-gravity world. Clarence swallowed hard, remembering her. Claudia Sorenson was not the kind of person it was easy to forget.

"Claudia," he managed. It had been nearly eight years since they'd last seen each other—and ten since they'd been lovers—but she hadn't changed much, if at all. Her face looked just as he remembered. "What…what are you doing here?"

"I heard you could use a job," Claudia said. She wrinkled her nose at him. "But first I think you need a shower and a change of clothes."

Clarence felt a flash of shame. He'd always been a dapper dresser, even when he'd been a student struggling to make ends meet. His father had always told him that the key to being treated as a respectable man was *looking* like a respectable man. Now…he lifted his head and looked down at himself. His shirt was stained with beer and vomit and he'd lost his trousers sometime during the last bender. Claudia could see his pants…the nasty part of his mind insisted that she'd seen them before, but not like this! He forced himself to sit upright, despite the alcohol flowing through his system. He hadn't drunk himself so senseless since he'd been a student!

And I was senseless back then anyway, he thought, as he rubbed his forehead. He could feel a headache coming on. *How many stupid things did I do when I was an idiot who thought he knew everything?*

"You need a sober-up," Claudia said, mercilessly. "Do you have one in the apartment or do I need to fetch one?"

Clarence had to think hard before remembering the answer. "There should be one in the kitchen cupboards," he managed. He *thought* there was a small bottle of sober-up pills in the kitchen cupboards. Neither he nor Minnie had ever drunk enough to make them more than slightly tipsy. "Look at the back."

He tried to stand as Claudia hurried into the kitchen, looking around frantically for his trousers. They were nowhere to be seen. His legs refused to work properly, forcing him to sit back down again. He swallowed a number of very nasty words as another wave of dizziness overcame him. He'd drunk far too much for his own good.

"Swallow this," Claudia said, holding out an innocuous white pill and a glass of water. "And then drink *all* the water."

"Thanks," Clarence said, sourly. He'd taken enough sober-up pills, in his student life, to know that they were thoroughly unpleasant. "Bottoms up."

He swallowed the pill, then chased it down with the water. Moments later, he felt his entire body begin to sweat as the alcohol was forcibly purged from his bloodstream. He stumbled to his feet and staggered into the bathroom, shutting the door behind him a moment before he vomited into the toilet. Claudia made no attempt to follow him into the bathroom, for which he was uncommonly grateful. He didn't want her to see him in such an awful state. She deserved better.

"Go for a shower," Claudia called, from the other side of the door. "And then get dressed."

As if you'd want to see me naked now, Clarence thought. His body was shaking, but—thankfully—the effects of the alcohol were gone. He pulled off his remaining clothes and dumped them in the sink, wondering how the hell he was meant to wash them. It wasn't as if he had the money to use a laundry. *I've made a right mess of my life.*

He clambered into the shower and turned on the water, silently grateful that it hadn't been cut off yet. He'd paid the last water bill, if he remembered correctly; there was at least a month before he had to tell the water board that he couldn't afford to pay them. Unless they already knew…he'd discovered, time and time again, that nothing moved faster than names on an electronic blacklist. The water board might send someone round to demand payment at any moment if they thought there would come a time when he couldn't pay.

"Better hurry," Claudia called.

Clarence sighed, then washed and dried himself before donning a dressing gown. He could change into something more suitable if she convinced him to leave the apartment. He didn't *think* she'd try to trick him, but he'd heard horror stories of people going out and coming home to discover that the locks had been changed. God alone knew what would happen to his possessions. Sold off to recover what little they could, he supposed. Feeling marginally human again, he opened the door and returned to the living room. Claudia was seated on a chair, her hands resting in her lap. Clarence hesitated, remembering when they'd been lovers, then sat facing her. She really *hadn't* changed all that much.

"So," he said, finally. "What happened? The last I heard, you were with the *Solarian*."

"They wanted someone to shake her tits in front of the camera, not a serious reporter," Claudia said, tartly. "And the editor was a perverted... bastard. I would have quit on the spot if I hadn't needed to line up another job first."

She shook her head. "Clarence, I need to know. What—*exactly*—happened?"

"It's a long story," Clarence said. He explained about the Forsakers, and about the story he'd written, *and* about how he'd been fired. "And now I don't have a hope of finding another job."

"So it would seem," Claudia said. "You don't have anything to lose, do you?"

Clarence looked around the apartment. It wasn't *his*, not really. Nor were most of the furnishings. Only a tiny handful of things could be said to be truly *his* and none of them, absolutely *none* of them, were immune to being seized in lieu of debts. He doubted he'd be allowed to keep even a handful of clothes when the bailiffs finally appeared. His wife had gone, taking their child with her. What did he have to lose?

"Not really," he said. "Are we going to rob banks?"

Claudia had to smile at his weak joke. "Since I left the *Solarian*, I've been having trouble moving up the ladder. The editor didn't do anything *obvious* to my record, but I was more of a freelance reporter than someone with an actual *job*. I'm pretty sure the bastard badmouthed me to all and sundry."

"Bastard," Clarence agreed. "What did he want you to do?"

"You don't want to know," Claudia said. "I've done a lot of things to pay the bills, but there are limits."

She met his eyes. "And then I got a rather unusual job offer. A group of people are setting up a new media…*organisation*. They were looking for experienced reporters."

Clarence frowned. Claudia wasn't an experienced reporter, not if her story was true. He certainly couldn't recall seeing her by-line at any point since they'd lost touch. And yet, she'd been hired on the strength of her experience? Something about the story didn't quite add up. Her new employers would know how inexperienced she was, wouldn't they? She would have problems showing them a portfolio of work if she didn't *have* one.

"They were rather desperate," Claudia admitted. "They hired me."

"I see," Clarence lied. That *still* didn't make sense. Claudia was hardly the only freelance journalist. There were thousands of them, all with stronger portfolios than hers. "Why did they hire you?"

It struck him, a moment later, that that was the wrong question. "Who *are* they?"

"Students," Claudia said. "They're setting up a new media organisation from scratch."

Clarence blinked in shock. "Students?"

"Students," Claudia repeated. "They don't want to go to work for the *Solarian* or the *Daily Truth* or even the *Blabbermouth*. They want to work for themselves. They've actually got a workable business model."

"A student newspaper," Clarence said. He shook his head. He'd worked on the student newspaper when he'd been a student—it was where he'd met Claudia—but it hadn't been very exciting. There were so many rules and regulations about what the reporters could and couldn't say that practically every *interesting* story had been cancelled before it could even be written. "And they can afford to hire us?"

"It isn't a student newspaper." Claudia sounded as though she'd given the same explanation time and time again. "It's a newspaper run by students."

She held up a hand before Clarence could say a word. "They've practically established themselves already, as a workable business. Their business model is relatively healthy, even in these times. They certainly *should* be able to make money. Hell, they don't have the massive overhead of running a big institution like the *Blabbermouth*."

"Or the celebrity access of the *Blabbermouth*," Clarence said. Everyone read the *Blabbermouth*, particularly the people who said they didn't. It had taken him longer than it should to realise that nine-tenths of the celebrity newspaper's scoops were not dug up by its reporters, but deliberately handed out by publicity agents. Very few of the scoops actually *hurt* a celebrity's career. "They're going to have problems getting off the ground."

"That's why they need us," Claudia said. "They have a technological base, Clarence, but not experienced reporters."

Clarence sucked in his breath. "And this is real? They're actually going to do it?"

"They're determined," Claudia said.

"They'll have to be more than *just* determined," Clarence pointed out. "This could go spectacularly wrong."

He looked down at his hands. There was no law against starting a new media organisation, any more than there were laws against writing blogs or founding datanet sites. But only a large organisation could afford the compliance and legal departments that were required to keep the newspaper from running afoul of the law. It would be very easy to step on a legal landmine and get blown up, if one didn't have money and connections. Clarence remembered Simon Goldwater's intervention and shuddered. The students might wind up in *very* deep shit indeed.

"Yes, it could," Claudia said. "But do you have anywhere else to go?"

"…No," Clarence said. "Do you think they can pull it off?"

"Perhaps," Claudia said. "They're certainly going to *try*."

Clarence frowned. The students would face a hell of a lot of problems. The *Daily Truth* had hundreds of reporters under its banner, from senior journalists to junior muckrakers and interns who would only be hired permanently if they brought the editor a story. The *Solarian* and the *Blabbermouth* weren't *that* different, even if they relied more on connections than a nose for stories. But a small student-run newspaper wouldn't be able to field hundreds of reporters, let alone cover every story that demanded media attention. The students would have real troubles building up something that could challenge the big guys.

"Look," Claudia said. "Come with me. Meet the students. See what they've got and…and get some money. Maybe it will be enough for you to live on."

"I doubt it," Clarence said. "I'll be kicked out of this apartment by the end of the month, if I'm lucky."

"Exactly," Claudia said. "What do you have to lose?"

Clarence had to smile. "Nothing," he said. "But will they want me?"

"They're ready to give you a chance," Claudia said. "And if you do well, they'll be delighted."

"I see," Clarence said. "And now…"

"Money?" Claudia smiled. "You'll draw a salary of roughly two thousand credits a month, plus a number of stock options. If the business does well, you'll do well too."

"And if it goes bust, I go bust too," Clarence muttered. "And if someone brings pressure to bear against them, how long will it be until I get fired?"

Claudia snorted. "What happened to the demon boy reporter I met at journalism school?"

"He grew up and had a kid." Clarence remembered some of the things he'd done at journalism school and shuddered. What had he been thinking? He should have *known* he wasn't really immortal. "I think…"

He froze as he heard something rattling though the letterbox and falling to the ground. "What was *that*?"

Claudia gave him an odd look. "The postman?"

"The postman comes in the morning," Clarence said. Ice congealed around his heart. "I think…"

He stood and paced towards the door. A simple brown envelope, marked with the renting agency's sigil, lay on the mat. Clarence didn't want to open it—he already knew what it was—but he had no choice. He opened the letter and read it twice. The legal jargon was deliberately designed to be confusing, but the intent was all too clear.

Claudia cleared her throat. "What does it say?"

Clarence glanced back at her. "I have to pay six weeks rent, more or less, within the week or be evicted. I'm fucked."

"Then you can come work for us," Claudia said, briskly. "We can probably work out *something* about housing, if you do."

"Thanks," Clarence said. Would he share an apartment with Claudia? It had been a long time since they'd been so close together. Or...or would he have to sleep on the floor? He told himself, firmly, that he was being stupid. He should be grateful not to have to sleep on the streets. "I suppose you're right."

"Always," Claudia said, with a wink.

"I don't have anything to lose," Clarence said. "So I might as well take a gamble."

He went back into his bedroom, changed into a working outfit and packed a small bag. It wouldn't keep him going forever, but at least he'd have *something* outside the apartment if the bailiffs came early. There was no way he could meet the demand for money in advance and he suspected the landlord company knew it. It wouldn't be long before they foreclosed and he wouldn't have a hope of winning in court. Hell, he didn't have the money for a lawyer. The state certainly wouldn't allow him to speak for himself.

Isn't it funny, he reflected, *how something meant to help can become a hindrance in the right—or wrong—circumstances?*

Taking one last look around the apartment, and promising himself that he'd come pick up the rest as soon as possible, he followed Claudia out the door.

CHAPTER SEVEN

Individually, each and every regulation was justified. It was true enough that a person's reputation might be ruined beyond repair if a false story was run in the media, even if that person could prove that the story was nothing more than a tissue of lies from start to finish. However, the net result of all of the regulations was to put a serious dampener on press freedom.
—PROFESSOR LEO CAESIUS
Crying Wolf: The Media and the Fall of the Empire

"I HAVEN'T BEEN TO IMPERIAL UNIVERSITY," Clarence said, as the hovercab banked towards the landing pad. "I wouldn't have expected a new business to be born here."

"Technically speaking, none of the students here have been to Imperial University either," Claudia commented. "This is an offshoot of the *real* Imperial University, on Earth. A degree from here isn't worth *quite* as much as a degree from Earth."

"Assuming it is worth anything at all," Clarence muttered. He'd once read an article that claimed the only advantage that came from an Imperial University degree was that you knew not to be impressed with an Imperial University degree. "And your…employers live here?"

"In the student accommodation block," Claudia said. The hovercab landed with a dull thump. Claudia paid the driver, then hopped out. "They're working on opening offices off-campus."

Clarence kept his thoughts to himself as he looked around. The campus was a whole different world from the grimy towers and grim students of journalism school. The students—two-thirds of whom looked young enough to be his children—seemed happy and contented, running around the campus as if they didn't have a care in the world. His eyes lingered on a redheaded girl in a tight top for a long moment—few girls would have dared to wear something so revealing on his former estate—before he looked away, torn between embarrassment and envy. She was so *free*, so unconcerned about the world. He told himself, firmly, not to be silly as Claudia led him down the grassy path. A journalist had better reason than most to know that the face someone presented to the world might not be their *real* face.

Everyone lives a life of quiet desperation, he reminded himself, dryly. For all he knew, the girl was struggling to pay off her student loans. Imperial University—even a satellite campus—was not *cheap. And no one wants to admit they have a problem for fear the sharks will start to gather.*

And yet, it was hard to believe that the students *had* problems. Dozens of young students—it was hard not to think of them as boys and girls—sat in the park, chatting happily or eating ice cream. A handful were sitting by the lakeside, fishing with more enthusiasm than success; he felt a twinge of nostalgia as he saw a pair of young lovers kissing under a tree. It had been a long time since *he'd* been allowed to be romantic, since he'd dared broadcast his emotions to the world. But then, he *was* nearly twice as old as the young students in front of him. He found it hard to believe that they'd ever faced *any* problems in their lives.

"Earth is gone," he muttered. "And they're eating ice cream."

"They don't grasp what it really means," Claudia commented. "Do you?"

Clarence shrugged. He'd never really given much thought to Earth. Humanity's homeworld was the centre of civilisation, the birthplace of the sole intelligent race in the cosmos…but it had never really impinged upon his life. He had never really comprehended, at an intellectual level, just how important Earth actually *was* until the planet had collapsed into chaos. It was so *great* a loss that *everyone* was struggling to comprehend what it meant. Everyone was pretending that everything was normal because they didn't want to face up to the truth.

We're stunned, he thought, as Claudia stopped in front of a midsized frat house. *We're too stunned to understand what's happened.*

"This building is technically part of the university, but it's also technically *not* part of the university," Claudia explained. She pressed her fingertips against a scanner, which bleeped and opened the door. "The donor who endowed it was very clear on that point. He would only give the university a shitload of money if the university agreed to respect the frat's rights for the rest of time. One of them is the right to set up their own businesses without university oversight."

She grinned as she pushed the door open. "The university has plenty of legal ways to manipulate student newsletters, but here? They'd lose the endowment if the students complained to the donor's estate. The students can do pretty much anything as long as it isn't outright illegal."

It didn't strike Clarence as being very secure—he was all too aware how rules and regulations could be manipulated to make something impossible without ever *quite* forbidding it—but he reserved judgement. A cunning donor *might* have been able to manipulate the terms of the donation to ensure the safety of future students, although Clarence had no idea what would happen after the donor was dead. The frat house was in good state, but it didn't look *that* new. He could easily believe that the donor had died hundreds of years ago.

He lifted an eyebrow as they passed a handful of earnest-looking students, but kept his thoughts to himself. They were dressed surprisingly conservatively, for students; the men wearing loose trousers and shirts while the women wore long dresses and shirts that *didn't* draw attention to their breasts. Clarence was surprised they were dressed like that in public, although he had to admit that they looked old enough to attend job interviews. Student fashion might be to show as much flesh as possible, the men as well as the women, but it was hard to take someone seriously if they were barely covering their genitals. They might get the job, the cynic in him thought, yet…he doubted they'd enjoy it.

But everyone is desperate for a job these days, he reminded himself. He wouldn't be in the frat house if he didn't want a job himself. *I'd go to an interview wearing nothing more than shorts if I thought it would get me the job.*

Claudia led him up the stairs, then stopped in a small waiting room. "I'll be back in a second," she said, as she pointed to a comfortable chair. "Wait here."

"Understood," Clarence said.

He sat down and leafed through the magazines—*paper* magazines—as Claudia headed into the next room. The students seemed to have focused on serious publications rather than anything else—there wasn't a single magazine devoted to fashion or pornography—although there was something odd about the selection. Each and every one of them was an *upper-class* magazine, with an upper-class take on the world and the universe at large. He thumbed though a report of riots on Terra Nova, rolling his eyes at the conceit that anyone on Tarsus would *care* about Terra Nova. It was the first world humanity had settled, when the Phase Drive had been developed and the stars had opened, but it wasn't *that* important. But then, he supposed the magazine's editors knew their audience. They weren't trying to market to the proles.

And they're wasting vast amounts of money on putting out a paper edition, Clarence noted, as he returned the magazine to the rack. The *Daily Truth* was one of the oldest newspapers on Tarsus and it had *never* put out a paper edition. Clarence knew, even if he had never been able to articulate it, why that was true. It was a great deal easier to hide inconvenient facts and shove embarrassing mistakes down the memory hole if there was no hard copy. *How many stories were* corrected *before they were ever seen?*

Claudia returned, looking mischievous. "They're ready to see you now, Clarence. Good luck."

Clarence glanced at her, then stood, smoothed down his shirt and walked through the door into the next room. It looked like a standard interview chamber, with a handful of chairs, desks and jugs of water in strategic positions. Three people sat behind one of the desks—a young man who couldn't be older than twenty and two young women—and another man stood by the far door. Clarence glanced at him, wondering why he was there. A security officer? A bodyguard? It wasn't uncommon for job interviewers to be protected by security goons, but he'd seen nothing to suggest that anyone on campus feared for their lives. Did they think they had to have a security officer? Or was he something else altogether?

"Thank you for coming," the young man said. He had an upper-class accent that grated, faintly, on Clarence's sensibilities. "Please, take a seat."

"Thank you."

Clarence sat, reminding himself—sharply—that this was a job interview. The three youngsters facing him had the power to give him a job—or refuse him. He *had* to take it seriously, even though it was hard to accept that they wielded so much power. He wanted—he needed—a job. He'd crawl over broken glass if there was a promise of a job at the far side.

"I'm Jack Jackson, the lead editor and publisher of *Seeing Eye*," the young man said. He indicated the young women. "This is Elle Hartington, one of our top reporters, and Jessica Pierce, one of our administrators. We are, to all intents and purposes, the steering committee."

And you wouldn't have said that unless you were a little unsure of yourself, Clarence thought, wryly. He felt a flicker of warmth. Jack Jackson—the name was as upper class as the voice—was clearly less arrogant than most people of his class. *You wanted to make it clear that you were in charge, when no one should even have to question that you were in charge.*

"We heard about you from Claudia," Jackson said. He gave Clarence a warm smile that showed brilliant white teeth. "Why were you fired from the *Daily Truth*?"

"I told the truth," Clarence said. The question stung, more than he cared to admit. He could have saved himself a *lot* of trouble if he'd spoken to his boss before writing and publishing the story. "And that cost me my career."

Elle leaned forward. "We know the story," she said. "Why did you write it? Why did you take the risk of publishing it?"

Clarence found it hard to articulate his reasons. They seemed so weak and frail in the light of everything that had happened. If he could go back in time and change what he'd done, he knew he would without hesitation. He was ashamed of himself, but he knew it was true. But he had to try to put his reasons into words. He had the feeling that the question was more important than it seemed.

"It was wrong," he said, finally. "What happened to the Forsakers…it was wrong. They didn't deserve to be rounded up and shipped off to some godforsaken hellhole in the middle of nowhere. Even if one believes they would be happier on a stage-one colony world, they still didn't deserve to be uprooted and cast into outer darkness. Deporting them was a terrible thing to do. Abusing them as they were deported was even worse."

He took a long breath. "And even if one isn't concerned about the *morality* of deporting the Forsakers, even if one thinks it was the best decision for all concerned, it was still utterly pointless. Deporting the Forsakers probably cost the government more than *keeping* them. It will not solve any of the planet's problems. The economy will not magically get better because the Forsakers are gone. It is nothing more than a sop to public opinion that will produce a slight uptick in the polls, an uptick that will last only as long as it takes the people to realise that things have *not* gotten better."

"And you think they won't," Jackson said.

"I *know* they won't," Clarence said. He took a moment to put his thoughts into words. "From the point of view of the average citizen, someone who barely earns two thousand credits a month, the million or so credits spent on the Forsakers seemed a vast sum of money that could be better spent elsewhere. On him, for example. But, from the point of view of a government that has a gross income of *trillions* of credits, a million or two is nothing more than small change. We lose more in accounting errors and cost over-runs than we spent on the Forsakers."

He shrugged. "Maybe we save a couple of million. But we lose more than that elsewhere."

"Interesting argument," Jackson said. "And not one I've heard elsewhere."

"No," Clarence agreed. "The government doesn't want to admit that it has made an expensive and completely useless gesture."

Jackson shrugged, then started firing off questions about Clarence's career. Clarence replied, silently wishing he'd had more time to prepare for the interview. But then, he suspected it wouldn't have helped as much as he might have hoped. Some of the questions were reasonable, and fairly typical of routine job interviews, but others were completely out of left-field. It was impossible to tell if the questions were intended to make him think or if it was a sign that Jackson and his friends didn't really know what they were doing. He reminded himself, again, that he had to take it seriously. There was an earnestness about the students that he found a little appealing.

"Very good," Jackson said, after Clarence had fielded a question about his relationship with his former editor. "I believe that Claudia has told you a little about us, correct?"

"Just a little," Clarence said.

Jackson nodded. "We'll make sure you have a chance to read our business statement—we really should have given you a copy while you were waiting—but the basic outline is that we're creating a newspaper that will concentrate on *real* news. We want to tell people what happened, like all the other newspapers, but we also want to tell people *why* it happened; we want to encourage people to think about what they're being told, we want to put forward the pros and cons and..."

"He's making a speech," Elle said, with a wink.

An idealistic speech, Clarence thought. He liked the ideals, but he'd worked as a journalist long enough to know that ideals rarely survived contact with the real world. *Seeing Eye* was tiny, compared to the *Daily Truth*.

The idea that the student newsletter could compete with the *Daily Truth* was absurd. *He says the right things, but does he mean them?*

"Yes, I am," Jackson said. He gave Clarence another smile. "There is no way we can compete with the big boys, at least when it comes to grabbing scoops, but we can try to put our own spin on them. Your article about the Forsakers, explaining *why* deporting them is useless as well as immoral, will offer valuable depth to our readers."

"I see," Clarence said. He had his doubts, but…the idealist in him liked the ideals, while the more practical side noted—again—that he *needed* a job. "And you want me to put that spin on it?"

"Yes," Jackson said.

His face tightened. "We do have some other advantages," he added. "We won't be producing eReaders of our own. There's no way we can afford to produce an eReader dedicated to a specific newsletter. But we will be putting our material online for anyone to view through the datanet. Subscribers will receive *some* bonus content, but not as much as they might hope."

Clarence frowned. The *Daily Truth* had produced and marketed its own eReader, hoping to lock its readers into a single newsletter. Very few readers *wanted* to buy a dozen different eReaders, something that had caused a great deal of discontent over the years. He'd never considered it before—it was just the way things were—but he could see very definite advantages in the plan. *Seeing Eye* would have problems protecting its content—they wouldn't be able to keep readers from sharing their material—yet…in some ways, that would work in their favour. The only thing worse than having their articles pirated was *not* having their articles pirated.

And it will boost customer confidence if it's harder to rewrite an article after it's published, he told himself. The *Daily Truth* had never told its readers when an article was edited after publication. It had never *had* to tell its readers. *They'd have to be honest about their mistakes.*

"It sounds workable," he said, finally.

"Thank you," Jackson said. He glanced at his co-workers, who nodded. "I understand you need accommodation?"

Clarence blinked, then nodded.

"We'll put a room aside for you, if you want to live on campus," Jackson said. "If not…we can advance you a small sum towards your living expenses."

"Ah…thank you," Clarence said, honestly surprised. It normally took weeks for an interview committee to extend a job offer. The idea of someone extending an offer on the spot was utterly alien. "I…"

Jackson smiled and stood, holding out a hand. "Jessica will give you a copy of our employment contract," he said. "I think you will find it suitable. If so, welcome to the team."

"Thank you," Clarence said. He already knew he was going to take the job, unless the contract was *truly* appalling. "I look forward to working with you."

"And we look forward to publishing your article on the Forsakers." Jackson's eyes burned with passion. "It's time the people knew the truth."

CHAPTER EIGHT

It was also impossible for any such producer to survive the sort of fines that might be levied on them without powerful political patrons—and political patronage was not forthcoming without, effectively, selling the business's soul. Indeed, cynics referred to Interstellar News as Ingram News, because it was owned by Ingram Interstellar—a powerful corporation—and spent much of its time shilling for its corporate masters.
—**PROFESSOR LEO CAESIUS**
Crying Wolf: The Media and the Fall of the Empire

"SO," PATRICIA MILLER SAID. "WHAT DO YOU THINK OF YOUR ROOM?"

"I think I went to the wrong university," Clarence said. "This room is a dream."

Patricia gave him a sharp look, as if he'd started speaking in tongues. Clarence concealed his amusement with an effort. Patricia didn't have a *very* upper-class accent, but it was clear that she was used to far better accommodation than the tiny student bedsit. Clarence, on the other hand, thought it was wonderful. A room to himself, a comfortable bed, a desk for his terminal, a kitchen kept stocked by the staff…it was small, true, but heavenly. He would have sold his soul for a room to himself at journalism school. His roommate in first year had snored so loudly that Clarence hadn't been able to sleep comfortably.

"If you say so," Patricia said, doubtfully. She looked older than the rest of the students, although she was still considerably younger than Clarence himself. She was pretty, with short dark hair and a pale face, but there was a sharpness in her eyes that suggested she had *some* experience of the real world. "There are worse places to be."

"Yeah," Clarence agreed. He'd gone back to his apartment with Claudia, packed a couple of suitcases and left everything else for the landlord. There was no point in saving *everything*, even if he'd had the space to store it. The landlord could sell the remainder of Clarence's possessions if he wished. "You could be on the streets, selling yourself."

"True," Patricia agreed. "Have you come up with your next story yet?"

Clarence shook his head. His instructions, once he'd moved into the bedsit, had been clear enough. He had to find something that had happened fairly recently, then come up with his own spin on it. But little *had* happened, certainly little that had made the news. The media was doing its best to downplay the growing economic crisis—*that* was clear—but Clarence wasn't sure he *wanted* to write about it. He was no economist—he had his doubts about the economists who were regularly trotted out to reassure the public that everything was going to be fine—and he didn't think he could write a story that people would *read*. And even if he did…what then? It might start a panic at the worst possible time.

"There was an incident a few days ago on a ghastly estate on the other side of the river," Patricia said. She sat on the bed, swinging her long legs. "A group of thugs burnt down a handful of buildings, killing at least a hundred economic migrants. So far, none of them have been arrested."

"That's no surprise," Clarence said. "Anyone who grew up on an estate would learn the value of keeping their mouth shut, when the police start asking questions. If, indeed, the police even *bother* to ask questions."

Patricia cocked her head. "Why wouldn't they tell the police who to arrest?"

Clarence grinned. "You didn't grow up on an estate, did you?"

"No." Patricia eyed him, narrowly. "What does that matter?"

"An estate is usually dominated by a group of shitheads," Clarence said. He *had* grown up on an estate. "Most of them are no better than parasites, even the ones who are clever enough not to kill the goose that lays the golden eggs, but you know what? They're insiders and the police are outsiders, people who come in, shake everything up and then go away again, leaving the people who *live* there to cope with the consequences. The shitheads may be shitheads, but they're still part of the estate."

He scowled as he remembered his early life. "And even when the shitheads are *real* shitheads, what happens? What do the police do to them?"

"They get jailed," Patricia said. "Right?"

"Right, for a year or two," Clarence said. "And then they get released from prison and they come back, looking to kill the person who betrayed them. No one actually wants them around, but...what does it profit them to report the shitheads to the police when the shitheads will come back in a year or so, with blood in their eyes? Whoever killed those migrants is probably safe, because no one will dare betray them."

"I tried to investigate the story," Patricia said. "I got nowhere."

"I'm not surprised," Clarence said.

He glanced at Patricia, trying to see her as an estate-dweller would see her. It wouldn't be a flattering first impression. Too many people would see her as a remarkably *secure* young woman, safe and comfortable, even if they saw the hardness in her eyes. And others would see her as nothing more than a sex object, a vision of beauty walking down the street. They would find it hard to take her seriously. He was surprised Patricia had ventured into the estate. She would draw entirely the wrong sort of attention.

"Thanks," Patricia said, sourly. "Does the great and powerful and wondrously wise super-journalist have any advice for *getting* the story?"

"You'd have to interview people under strict conditions of secrecy," Clarence said. "And that would not be easy, because no one there will trust you to keep your word."

Patricia glared. "I would not betray my sources!"

"And the police can bring a *lot* of pressure to bear on you," Clarence said. "How long will you keep your mouth shut when they start threatening to jail you for withholding information?"

"I wouldn't talk," Patricia insisted.

Clarence shrugged. He had no doubt that Patricia *meant* what she said. But he doubted she *could* stick to it, when the police started turning the screws. She had grown up in a community where the police were polite and friendly, not in a place where the police were often as much a threat as the gangbangers. Her bravery might melt like new-fallen snow when she was hurled into prison and told she'd be staying there until she talked. And while the *Daily Truth* had a lot of influence it could bring to bear on the police, *Seeing Eye* didn't have anything like as much. It was unlikely that Jack Jackson could convince an overzealous policeman's superiors to call him off.

Although Jackson is clearly well-connected, Clarence thought. *Perhaps he can bring some influence to bear.*

He considered the incident for a moment, then dismissed it as a potential story. Incidents like it happened all the time, although the media generally ignored them or whined about hapless migrants being abused by xenophobic bigots. There was no room for nuance, no room for understanding the threat migrants posed to people who were already struggling for survival... Clarence had no doubt that Patricia would not understand, even if he tried to explain it. She simply could not comprehend the estate he'd—somehow—managed to leave behind. It was totally alien to her.

There was a knock at the door, which opened a moment later. "Hey, Patricia," Jennifer Turner said. She was another reporter, in fact if not in name. She'd certainly never gone to journalism school. "Do you have time to help me with my story?"

"Sure," Patricia said. She rose, brushing down her skirt. "Clarence, you'd better come up with something special, soon."

Clarence nodded, stiffly. A reporter was only as good as his last story. The comments on the Forsaker story—which he'd cunningly rewritten to ensure that the *Daily Truth* couldn't lay claim to it—suggested that it had made an impact, but that wouldn't last. The *Daily Truth* could afford to keep reporters on the payroll, even when they hadn't tracked down a good story in months; *Seeing Eye* didn't have that luxury. He watched the girls go, then locked the door and turned his attention back to his terminal. A handful of new story headings had already popped up in his inbox.

I'll need an eReader to read most of them, he thought. It was annoying to see something he wanted to read, but to be unable to read it without investing in an expensive piece of technology. There was no *technical* reason why the bigger newspapers couldn't put their material on the datanet for all to see. *But at least I can see what they're talking about.*

He scanned through the headings, one by one. There was no mention of an attack on economic migrants, suggesting that someone in the government had decided that it was better to cover it up than condemn it. Clarence wasn't too surprised. The government—and the well-heeled—might decry the attacks, but the people who were suffering as a result of economic migration were more likely to see the attacks as encouragement to engage in attacks of their own. It was as pointless, in its own way, as deporting the Forsakers—driving out migrants wouldn't solve the economic crisis—yet it didn't matter. People who were desperate would clutch at any straws.

And besides, it's her story, he thought. It would be easy enough to take her to the estate, after cautioning her to dress appropriately, but he doubted they'd dig up very much. Whoever had carried out the attack would be protected by the code of silence. *And it isn't one that will go very far.*

He shrugged and continued to skim through the headings. Thomas Wycliffe, the First Speaker of Tarsus, had announced a new economic summit to solve the sector's problems. It looked as if the Empire Loyalists—the current ruling party—was starting to realise that there wasn't much of an empire left to be loyal *to*, although there was no way to be sure. Earth was gone and the Core Worlds were starting to fragment. The Corporatists and the Rebirth Parties had announced their support, although in such vague terms that Clarence found it impossible to tell if they expected the summit to do any good or if they were merely humouring the Empire Loyalists. It was quite possible that they were trying to do *both*. If the summit actually produced an economic upswing, they would share in the reward; if the summit failed, no one would be able to blame them. But would it work?

They've been pretending that everything is normal ever since we heard about Earth, Clarence thought, coldly. *But there's no way they can keep the pretence up forever.*

He sucked in his breath. Tarsus had been remarkable stable, politically speaking, for well over a thousand years, but the government had never been designed to cope with a disaster that threatened to tear the Empire apart. Hell, it had rarely mattered *who* had sat in the big chair. The political establishment was designed to make it difficult for *anyone* to change things, no matter who they claimed to represent. Rebirth was the only party that preached reform and even *it* couldn't change things. But now...

Clarence shook his head. There was no point in writing speculative articles on the summit when so little information had been released. He doubted he'd be allowed to attend the summit, even as an observer. And even if he somehow managed to get his hands on a press pass, there was no way he'd be able to attend the *real* meetings. The public conferences would be nothing more than window-dressing. The *real* decisions would be taken well out of the public eye. He wondered, morbidly, just what those decisions would be. There was no easy solution to the planet's problems. He found it hard to imagine *any* kind of solution that might preserve something of the planet's former greatness.

Perhaps that's why they deported the Forsakers, even though they had to know it was useless, he thought, sourly. *They wanted to do something, but they didn't know what.*

He shrugged, then returned his attention to the terminal and resumed flipping through the article headings. A young girl had been crowned Queen Bee of her school's beauty pageant...he shook his head in disgust and moved on. Several popular designers were having a spat over who actually had exclusive rights to design for a handful of power couples...Clarence found it impossible to believe that anyone actually found it *important* when the planet was on the verge of complete chaos. An entertainment star in a poly-marriage had been caught cheating on her partners…pathetic. Clarence wondered, sourly, if he should grab his coat and go onto the streets. Perhaps he'd see something worth turning into a story if he walked a mile or two…

An article blinked up in front of him, one cleared for public access. Clarence clicked on it automatically and read it, line by line. It was a gushing piece about the planned redevelopment of an estate on the near side of the river, talking about how Maxima Corporation had purchased every house in the estate, paying enough money to allow *every* single inhabitant to move up in the world. The article was so sweet that he felt his teeth starting to ache. Clarence read it twice, feeling his instincts starting to twitch. There wasn't a single negative point, not one. Even by the standards of corporate boilerplate, press releases written by PR specialists and distributed without challenge, it was embarrassing. It *had* to be hiding something.

And Maxima Corporation has some excellent PR specialists, Clarence thought. His lips thinned as he remembered that Simon Goldwater, the CEO of Maxima Corporation, was the person who'd gotten him fired. He was *very* tempted to go see what he could dig up. *But why do they want to redevelop an entire estate now?*

It was an odd thought. The chances were good that the estate *needed* redeveloping—if it was anything like the estate Clarence had known as a kid, knocking it down would be doing the inhabitants a favour—but now? Why now? Maxima Corporation was unimaginably rich, but starting out on a redevelopment project when the economy was so fragile struck Clarence as dangerously absurd. Was it a make-work project? Clarence found it hard to imagine that redeveloping an estate would mean jobs for the unemployed. Maxima couldn't possibly employ enough people to make a difference, could they? The more he looked at it, the more unlikely it seemed.

He flipped through a string of articles, trying to find one—just one—that questioned the corporation's decision. But there were none. He wasn't too surprised. If Simon Goldwater had enough clout to get a reporter fired, he certainly had enough clout to keep negative stories from appearing in the mainstream media. Still, Clarence doubted that *everyone* supported the project. There had to be *some* people who thought it was a bad idea.

And everyone is talking about how generous Maxima is being to the people who are being relocated, Clarence thought. That struck him as odd. Corporations were not renowned for being generous. *It might be worth checking on that, just to see what they're hiding.*

He closed the terminal and stood, grabbing his coat and pulling it on. Jackson had hinted—and Clarence suspected that it was actually an order— that Clarence should try to include one of the student reporters when he went chasing a story. Clarence wasn't sure what he made of that—he couldn't help feeling that he was being asked to train his replacements—but there was nothing to be gained from picking a fight over it. He would have preferred to take Claudia, or someone with more experience, yet…he shrugged as he left the room, locking the door behind him. He would just have to put up with it.

I'll take whoever I see first, he thought, as he stepped into the common room. *Seeing Eye's* offices felt surprisingly informal, for the heart of a media operation. But then, they *were* in a frat house. *I wonder…*

He frowned, inwardly, as he saw Patricia sitting in a chair, drinking coffee and reading a datapad. She wasn't the person he *wanted* to take to the estate—he had a feeling that she wouldn't listen to him—but she *was* the first person he'd seen. And…he considered it for a moment, then shrugged. The only way to learn was by doing. Patricia would just have to learn from experience.

"I think I have something," he said, as Patricia looked up. "Interested?"

"Sure," Patricia said. She put the datapad aside and stood. "Where are we going?"

"Hellebore Estate," Clarence said. "There might *just* be a story there."

And even if there isn't, he added silently, *it will give us both some much-needed experience.*

"Sounds awful," Patricia said.

"Hellebore is a flower," Clarence said. He'd looked it up when he'd seen the name of the estate, more out of curiosity than anything else. "Get changed into something more suitable and we can go."

Patricia frowned. "What's wrong with my clothes?"

"You have to look professional," Clarence said, simply. "If you don't, people won't take you seriously. And then they won't talk to you."

He'd expected an argument, but Patricia simply nodded. "Fine. I'll do as you say."

"I'll call us an aircar," Clarence said. "Be ready to go in twenty or I'll go without you."

"A terrible fate," Patricia said. She headed for the door. "I'll be there, believe me. And I hope this will lead to something good."

"So do I," Clarence said. "So do I."

CHAPTER NINE

The core of the problem, therefore, was two-fold. The interstellar media corporations—themselves often subsections of far larger conglomerates, which had close ties to the Grand Senate—had a very strong interest in not rocking the boat. Stories that were unfavourable to their corporate masters—indeed, to the Grand Senate as a whole—were often killed before they could be published. It wasn't uncommon for a promising and idealistic young reporter to discover that his scoop had led him straight to the unemployment line. The smarter reporters wised up and focused their attentions on the party line.

—**Professor Leo Caesius**
Crying Wolf: The Media and the Fall of the Empire

"YOU SAID YOU GREW UP ON AN ESTATE," Patricia said, as the aircar dropped into Hellebore Estate. "Was it anything like this?"

"No," Clarence said. The aircar touched down with a bump. "It was worse."

Patricia looked as if she didn't believe him. Clarence didn't really blame her. Hellebore Estate was grey, utterly grey. The towering apartment blocks looked ancient, as if they should have been condemned years ago; the handful of shops looked deserted, as if no one had the money to spend to keep them alive. There were only a handful of people on the streets and they looked listless, as if they knew their lives were already over. The estate was a concrete nightmare…and yet, it *was* better than his birthplace. There were no visible signs of crime, prostitution or drug abuse.

He paid the aircar driver and looked around, trying to decide where to begin. There was always a housing office in an estate, but there was no point in starting there. The people who worked at the office would always toe the party line, knowing that they'd be fired in a heartbeat if they upset their superiors. He saw a tiny cafe, apparently deserted, and nodded to himself. It was as good a place to start as any. He glanced at Patricia, making sure that she was ok, then led the way towards the building. The dirt and grime on the shopfront wasn't remotely reassuring.

Patricia coughed. "They're watching us."

"We're strangers," Clarence reminded her. "Everyone on the estate probably knows everyone else. They don't know us."

He stopped in front of a streetlight, mildly surprised that it hadn't been vandalised and destroyed long ago. Another sign, if he'd wanted it, that this estate was better than his birthplace. A large poster had been wrapped around the streetlight, warning the locals that they had to be out of the estate in two weeks. The legal warnings at the bottom were far from reassuring too. Anyone found in the estate afterwards would be assumed to be a trespasser and treated accordingly.

If they're found at all, Clarence thought. He'd seen the immense vehicles that were used to knock down apartment blocks. They were intimidating even when compared to military tanks. There was a good chance that anyone hiding out in his former apartment would be killed when the building was knocked down, with his killers unaware of what they'd done until they found the body in the rubble. *The demolition squads might not bother to search the buildings before they knock them down.*

He put the thought to one side as he pushed open the door and stepped into the cafe. It had clearly started life as a diner, complete with colourful pictures and plastic furniture, but somewhere along the line it had turned into a cafe. An old man sat at one table, drinking a mug of tea; a couple of youngsters who really should be at school were sitting at another, looking bored in a way that made Clarence roll his eyes in annoyance. They were skiving from school and yet they looked bored? But then, there were worse places to be. The cafe might be ancient—and Clarence suspected that the food would be thoroughly unsafe—but at least it wasn't a gang. Or…the kids weren't *that* young. There were *definitely* worse places to be.

"Take a seat," the waitress said. She was sitting behind a counter, leafing through a magazine. Clarence didn't have to read any of the articles to know it was a fashion magazine. "I'll be over in a minute."

Patricia caught Clarence's eye as they sat down. "Shouldn't we be asking her questions?"

"Later," Clarence said. He picked up a menu and scanned it thoughtfully. "What do you want to drink?"

The waitress bustled over, her face somehow managing to convey the impression that she *wasn't* pleased to see them. Clarence studied her, thoughtfully. She couldn't be much older than him, he thought, but she *looked* older. A lifetime spent trying to keep a failing business afloat would put immense wear and tear on anyone. The cafe would be one missed payment away from failing. He understood, all too well, how she might feel.

"What can I get you?" The waitress's voice was rough, as if she'd smoked too many cigarettes. "Coffee or tea? Or hot chocolate?"

"Tea, for both of us," Clarence said. He suspected it would be the safest thing on the menu. "And we were hoping we could have a chat."

The waitress eyed him, sharply. "About what?"

"We're reporters," Patricia said. "We come in peace."

"Hah." The waitress didn't even smile at Patricia's weak joke. "Let me get your tea and then I'll be right with you."

Clarence shook his head wryly as the waitress hurried away. "You probably shouldn't tell *everyone* that you're a reporter," he said. "There are people here who regard reporters as their natural enemies."

"But we're on *their* side," Patricia protested, quietly. "Clarence…"

"They don't know that," Clarence said. He kept his voice low. "And you're not really meant to be on *anyone's* side. You're meant to serve the truth."

"Yes, sir," Patricia said.

The waitress returned, carrying two mugs of tea. "My name's Cindy," she said, as she sat down facing them. "What do you want to chat about?"

Clarence took a sip of his tea. It was unpleasantly weak, more like milky water than tea. But it was drinkable. He'd had worse.

"We read the stories about the estate being demolished," he said, after he keyed his terminal to record the conversation. It struck him, suddenly, that most of the estate's population might have already left. "We wanted to find out if they were true."

Cindy eyed him. "And what will you do if you discover that they are lies?"

"Tell the truth," Clarence said.

"Hah," Cindy said. "You know this place? It's been in my family for the last three generations. Granddaddy bought the entire building when the estate was built, then daddy turned it into a cafe when people stopped eating here. He left it to me when he shuffled off this mortal coil. It's mine. I own it."

"I understand," Clarence said.

"And now I've been told to leave," Cindy said. "This place is being taken from me, if I like it or not. And where am I meant to go?"

Patricia leaned forward. "I thought you were being rehoused? And compensated…"

"Hah." Cindy laughed, bitterly. "I've just been told to get out of my house and fuck off, bugger off, don't bother to write…a new house? They haven't given me anything!"

"But if you own the house," Patricia said, "surely…"

"I do own the house," Cindy said. She waved a hand in the air. "I own the entire block. And you know what? It's just been taken from me. Where the hell will I go?"

"You weren't paid anything," Clarence said. He kept his feelings under tight control. "On what grounds?"

"Some legal bullshit." The bitterness in Cindy's voice was palatable. "I own the building, you see. But I don't own the *land*. They'll be quite happy for me to take the building somewhere else, it seems, but how am I meant to do *that*?"

Clarence sucked in his breath. He'd heard of similar tricks, but nothing quite so blatant—certainly, nothing on so big a scale. Someone could reasonably ask the owner of an aircar to move it, if it had landed on private property, yet…how could someone move an entire *apartment block*? It was impossible. There was no way it could be dismantled and rebuilt elsewhere, not easily. How could Cindy even afford to…he shook his head, dismissing the thought. It was absurd.

"That's not what it said in the articles," Patricia said. She sounded honestly outraged, even though no one with any sense should have expected the writers to confess to something most of the population would consider a thoroughly dirty trick. It was technically legal, but outrageous. "They said you were being compensated."

"Well, I'm not being compensated," Cindy snapped. "And even if I was, I wouldn't want to go."

Clarence nodded in understanding. Cindy's cafe might not look impressive, to him, but it gave her a life above the ordinary. She was her own boss, something he almost envied even though he knew there were downsides. Would she want to go work for someone else? Could she go work for someone else? If she had no savings, and it was unlikely she had *anything*, she might not be able to find somewhere to stay, let alone a new job. The more Clarence thought about it, the more he knew Cindy had been screwed. How could she sell the apartment block when it was going to be knocked down in two weeks?

"I've lived here all my life," a gruff voice said. Clarence looked up to see the old man inching towards them. "And now I've been told to go…go where?"

Patricia moved aside to allow the man to sit down. "Can we quote you on that?"

"Why not?" The old man snorted, rudely. "I'm Ted, by the way. You'd better spell my name right."

Clarence had to smile, although he knew it wasn't *really* funny. It wouldn't be the first time the editor had thought he'd known better than the writer, even when the writer had been the person to take the interview. Having his spelling corrected was irritating, but understandable; having it *uncorrected* was impossible to stomach. And there had never been anything to gain by arguing with the editors. Their fancy degrees made them utterly secure in their own intellectual superiority.

"We'll be happy to mention your name," Clarence said. "And yours too, Cindy."

Cindy laughed, humourlessly. "What do I have to lose?"

Quite a bit, perhaps, Clarence thought. Long experience had taught him that anyone who spoke out of turn—anyone who could be proven as having spoke out of turn—could be crushed by the corporate juggernaut. *But you really have nothing to lose.*

He listened to Ted's story, occasionally dropping a question into the mix. The estate had hovered on the brink of anarchy for years, but—somehow—it had never quite turned into a gangbanger's paradise. Ted claimed that Hellebore Estate had a personality of its own, an understanding that there were lines one did *not* cross…Clarence found it hard to believe, but he made a note of them anyway. It would help sell the story if the people looked like harmless victims of corporate tyranny, rather than sinners who deserved to be driven out of their homes and onto the streets. No matter what they said publicly, very few citizens would shed a tear if one of the *really* bad housing estates was to be knocked down, along with its inhabitants. The gangbangers were not good neighbours.

"Do you think anyone will listen?" Cindy asked, when they'd finished recording the stories. "Do you think anyone will care?"

"Of course they will," Patricia said. "What's been done to you is… is *unjust!*"

Cindy looked at Clarence. "Is that true?"

84

"Perhaps," Clarence said. The blunt truth, he suspected, was that the vast majority of people wouldn't care. They had too many other problems. *And* they had too many reasons to despise people who lived on poor estates. The nastier stereotypes about estate-dwellers were about as accurate as the stereotypes about reporters, but it hardly mattered. All that mattered was that people believed them. "But I can tell you that people *won't* care if they don't know they *should* care."

"Hah," Cindy said. "Good luck. And I'll keep on making preparations to move out anyway, because I don't think things will change."

"We shall see," Clarence said.

He finished his tea, paid the bill and led Patricia back onto the streets. There were more people visible now—a glance at his watch told him that school had finished for the day—and he made silent estimates of how many were still living on the estate as they walked down the road. A cluster of abandoned factories and warehouses sat at the rear of the estate, mute testament to the days when everyone living on the estate had the prospect of good jobs and a living wage. It was quite likely, Clarence thought, that whoever had owned the estate—or at least the ground under his feet—had gone out of business long ago, their assets passed through a number of hands until Maxima Corporation had picked them up for a song. He could see the logic and yet…the more he thought about it, the less sense it made. There was no way Maxima Corporation would ever be able to recoup its expenses.

Perhaps that's why they're stiffing the inhabitants, Clarence thought. It did make a certain kind of sense, but no matter how he ran the figures through his head it still seemed as though Maxima had no hope of making a profit. He'd seen the condos on the far side of the city that sat empty, for lack of anyone willing to pay the cost of moving in. *But very few people are evil for the sake of being evil.*

He put the thought to one side as he spotted a mother with seven kids and waved to her. The mother eyed him suspiciously and only relaxed, slightly, when he showed her his *Daily Truth* press card. Technically, he should have returned it to his former boss—he was entirely sure it would show up as cancelled if someone ran a check—but no one had bothered to send a demand for its return. He couldn't help wondering if that was an oversight or someone trying to give him a hand. Very few people bothered to run the card through a processor unless they were trying to buy time.

"You're a reporter," the woman said. "What do you want?"

Clarence let Patricia ask the questions—he had a feeling the mother would be happier with another woman asking the questions—and listened, quietly. The story was the same, more or less. The mother didn't own her house, and her landlord didn't want to kick her out, but she was being forced to leave anyway. She didn't know *where* she and her children—the oldest was twelve—would go. Their father lived in Gamma Estate, on the other side of the river; she didn't think they'd be welcome there. Clarence had a nasty feeling they would be all *too* welcome. The oldest son was just the right age to join the gangs. He didn't want to think about what could happen to the daughter.

"Thank you for your time," Patricia said, finally. "I'll be in touch."

"And I want paid," the mother said. "I gave you some good stuff."

Clarence slipped her a handful of credits, then led Patricia down the street. "Not bad," he said, once they were out of earshot. "That will help put a human face on the tragedy."

"I thought the government had to provide housing for mothers," Patricia said. "It's a human right. I heard about it in school."

"Perhaps, technically," Clarence said. "But there's no rule stipulating where they have to be housed. They might be denied housing if there is a prospect of them living with their father…and there *is* a chance they could live with him. But they won't *want* to live with him."

"Why?" Patricia looked puzzled. "She didn't say he was a monster…"

"He lives in Gamma Estate," Clarence reminded her. "That's one of the worst estates in the city. The police don't go there unless there's a small army at their backs. I wouldn't give a bent credit for their chances once they move into their father's house."

"You don't know he'll mistreat them," Patricia protested. "He might be a good man."

"A good man living in a cesspit will still smell," Clarence said. He shook his head as he spied another interview candidate. "You don't get to live in a place like that unless you're tough or prepared to knuckle under to the gangs. That daughter, the twelve-year-old girl? What's her father going to do when the local thugs come sniffing around her?"

"She's *twelve*," Patricia said, horrified.

"Do you think it matters?" Clarence met her eyes. "The gangs won't care. And you know what? No one else will care either."

"You should write about it," Patricia said. "*Make* them care."

Clarence laughed, humourlessly. "Back when I was writing for the *Daily Truth*, there were ladies who would write endlessly about social issues. They said we should care about…well, everyone who was different from us. Everyone was just the same, under the skin; everyone could be understood, if you tried. And you know what?"

He nodded at the grey buildings. "None of them would have walked through this estate after dark. Or Gamma Estate. They knew, even if they didn't want to admit it, that it would be suicidal. All they were doing was making excuses for people who were caught in a bind."

Patricia looked pale. "Really?"

"Oh, yes," Clarence said. He shrugged. "Let's do a few more interviews and go home."

CHAPTER TEN

The second problem, however, was that the media had simply lost touch with the needs of its customers. This was not out of any actual malice, but an inevitable side-effect of the vast layers of bureaucracy between the reporters, the editors and the publishers who decided what actually got published.

—PROFESSOR LEO CAESIUS

Crying Wolf: The Media and the Fall of the Empire

"THIS IS A VERY GOOD STORY," JACK JACKSON SAID, looking down at the datapad. "Are you sure you have the facts in order?"

"I checked as best as I could," Clarence said. Beside him, Patricia nodded eagerly. "There's no indication—beside the stories planted in the media—that anyone within the estate was actually compensated, let alone given somewhere else to live. Maxima Corporation seems to have been lying through its collective teeth. They just laid claim to the ground under the buildings and told the inhabitants to get out or die."

Jackson read the story again. Clarence watched him, wondering if the younger man would actually have the nerve to run it. Maxima Corporation could be a dangerous enemy. Simon Goldwater had practically unlimited resources to fight and win a court battle. Truth was no defence in court, not when so much money was involved. It was quite possible that the story would be buried under a mountain of lawsuits. Clarence had studied the history of journalism. The truth did not always set one free.

"And there's a definite moment of human interest," Jackson mused. He looked up, smiling warmly. "We'll run it."

And take a flying leap into the dark, Clarence thought. The nasty side of his mind wondered just what would happen when Maxima Corporation started demanding a retraction. It would be all too easy for Jack Jackson to stand on principle and be destroyed by the corporate juggernaut. Or would his parents demand that he retract the story before the corporation found a way to hurt them? *There are so many ways to bring pressure to bear on people these days.*

He scowled, inwardly. The hell of it was that he could hardly have blamed Jackson for blinking, for deciding *not* to run the story. *Seeing Eye* didn't need to make so many enemies so quickly. It might be better to build up a reputation first before running the more controversial stories, the ones that would plunge them into a life-or-death fight for survival. Clarence knew, better than anyone else on the team, just how easy it was to have one's career destroyed. He was more afraid of losing his new job than he cared to admit.

"Well done, both of you," Jackson added. "I'll have the story uploaded tonight."

"Yes, sir," Clarence said, automatically. He suddenly felt very tired. "If you don't mind, I'd like to hit the sheets."

Jackson lifted an eyebrow. "You don't want to go out drinking tonight?"

Clarence hesitated. He'd learnt, sometimes the hard way, that failing to make connections with his co-workers—by going drinking or golfing or whatever they considered important—could be detrimental to his career. If Jackson wanted to take everyone out for drinks, it might be a mistake to refuse. But he was in no state to go out drinking, not now. He wanted—he needed—to go to bed.

"Maybe later, sir," he said, reluctantly. Students were renowned for heavy drinking—Clarence had to admit he'd been a heavy drinker himself in journalism school—but he was at least a decade older than the oldest student on staff. "I need to go to bed."

Jackson nodded. "Check in with Frank tomorrow morning, then start looking for your next story." He met Clarence's eyes. "You've got good instincts, by the way. You found a story where no one else would think to look."

"He is good," Patricia said.

"Yeah," Jackson agreed. "Why did you think to look there?"

Clarence hesitated, unsure how to put his feelings into words. "There were just too many puff pieces being written about the project," he said. He had no way to be sure, but he was fairly certain that all of the gushing media reports had been written by the same person. "It made me wonder what they were trying to cover up."

He shrugged. "It might have led to nothing, sir. Everything might have been exactly as it said on the tin. I had no way to be *sure* there was a story there."

"I understand," Jackson said. He winked. "Go to bed. And don't forget to take a cup of hot milk to bed with you."

Clarence had to smile at the weak joke, then sobered as he left the office. Jackson was being reasonable, *now*. But how long would that last if Clarence *failed* to keep bringing him stories? Clarence knew he'd been lucky to stumble across evidence of corporate misbehaviour. His luck might not hold out for long. The *Daily Truth* could afford to keep reporters on the payroll indefinitely, even if they weren't earning their keep. He wasn't so sure *Seeing Eye* could do the same.

"You gave me a lot to think about," Patricia said. She walked beside him as they made their way back to the bedrooms. "Do you think I'll make a good reporter?"

"You did okay, talking to those people," Clarence told her. It wasn't *easy* to encourage people to talk when they expected everything they said to be written down, taken out of context and used against them. There was a reason that most people considered journalists to be scum and he knew it. "And you asked some of the right questions."

Patricia looked pensive. "And I also asked some of the wrong ones. What if...what if I missed something because I lacked the context to understand it?"

Clarence felt a flicker of respect, if not admiration. He'd known too many reporters who had *never* had the self-awareness to realise that they lacked the context—or the experience, or the background knowledge—to understand what was *really* going on. It was easy to condemn someone for doing something when one didn't understand *why* someone was doing something. He'd once read an article on prostitution that had blithely assumed the prostitutes would have no trouble getting *real* jobs if they wanted. The writer had never been poor, or hungry, or completely lacking in skills, in her entire life.

"It will come, with experience," he assured her, finally. "Don't be afraid to ask questions. Or to read around a subject instead of simply regurgitating whatever you've been told."

"Thanks," Patricia said. They stopped outside his door. "Do you want to spend the night together?"

Clarence blinked in shock. He hadn't expected *that*. He'd certainly never thought that Patricia was attracted to him. The thought that she *might* be attracted to him was unexpectedly flattering. Clarence was at least ten years older than her, with few prospects...he swallowed, hard. He was also a married man. Minnie might not have contacted him since she stormed out, taking their son with her, but they were still married. He was tempted, more tempted than he cared to admit, to betray his wife by sleeping with another woman...he shook his head. That would destroy any hope he might have of reconciling with his wife...

"I'm married," he said, finally.

Patricia shrugged. "So?"

"I don't want to betray her," Clarence said. It was hard to know what to say. Students slept around as much as possible—Clarence himself had been a real horndog when *he'd* been at journalism school—but *he* was an older man. He liked to think that he was more mature than his teenage self. He also had far more obligations. "And besides, I really do need to sleep."

Patricia looked oddly put out by his words. Clarence wasn't sure what to make of it. Was she insulted he'd declined her offer? Why had she made it in the first place? Clarence liked to think he was stunningly handsome, a vision of male beauty, but honesty compelled him to admit that his six-pack was slowly becoming a keg. Patricia was hardly *ugly*. She would have no trouble picking up someone to warm her bed in the nearest bar. If Clarence had been younger, and unmarried, he wouldn't have hesitated.

Except I have to work with her, he reminded himself. *If we sleep together now, what will become of us?*

He shook his head. There was no shortage of horror stories about journalists who'd slept with their co-workers—or, worse, slept with their sources. Journalists could be quite bitchy at times, particularly when someone was noticeably doing better than everyone else. Clarence knew one female reporter who'd been accused of trading sex for stories. Her detractors had claimed they were upholding journalistic morals, but no one believed them. They were far more likely to be annoyed that she was getting stories and leaving them in the dust.

"Well, I'll see you in the morning," Patricia said. She sounded as if she couldn't quite believe that he'd rejected her. "Good night."

Clarence hesitated, then slipped into his room and closed the door behind him. Part of him couldn't quite believe it either. There was no reason to think that Minnie would ever come back to him. Clarence knew his wife too well to expect her to come crawling back, unless Clarence managed to re-establish himself. He was tempted, more tempted than he cared to admit, to open the door and call Patricia into the room. But he knew it would be a very bad idea.

He checked his terminal, noting the handful of emails from various staff members, then undressed and climbed into bed. The bedsit felt like home now, even if there wasn't enough room to swing a cat. He closed his eyes, silently wishing his wife was lying beside him. He was used to having her next to him. Now the alcohol was no longer numbing his thoughts, he missed her. He wondered, grimly, if he should take an aircar to his mother-in-law's apartment and try to patch things up. If nothing else, he should secure access to his son.

Except my failure cannot be allowed to taint Henry, he thought, glumly. Minnie was right about that, if nothing else. Henry could not be allowed to grow up as the son of a man who'd been sacked. It would be hard enough for him to get a job when he reached adulthood *whatever* he did. *It would be better for him if I stayed away for good.*

The thought brought him no peace. He tossed and turned for what felt like hours before the alarm finally rang, dragging him out of an uneasy sleep. His stomach growled as he sat upright in bed, reaching for his terminal to shut off the alarm. It was seven o'clock, but it felt much earlier. He felt as if he hadn't slept at all.

Bastards, he thought, as he stumbled out of bed and splashed water on his face. Someone was playing music further down the corridor, just loudly enough for him to hear the beat. He wondered, as he dressed himself, if he'd been quite that inconsiderate when *he'd* been a student. The thought made him smile. *I'll be telling those kids to get off my lawn in a few years or so.*

He strapped his terminal to his belt, then walked down the corridor and into a kitchen. Two students, a boy and a girl, were sitting at the table, both completely naked. Clarence looked away, silently glad that his complexion hid his embarrassment. He'd never walked around naked when *he'd* been a student, not at journalism school. He forced himself not to look at either of them as he made himself a large mug of strong coffee. They were both so perfect that it was clear their families had paid for genetic engineering or cosmetic surgery.

And they didn't grow up on an estate, Clarence thought. He found it hard to believe that his *sister* would be so unselfconscious when confronted with a strange man. He couldn't believe that his sister would have been walking around naked at all. *They're safe.*

He carried his coffee out of the kitchen and walked up the stairs to the offices. He'd been told that the WebHeads were on duty at all times, although he hadn't really believed it. The newspaper was too small an operation, he'd thought, to maintain a permanent staff. But, when he glanced into the monitor room, Frank Wong was sitting in front of his terminal, surrounded by holographic images. A faint smile flickered on his face as he looked up at Clarence. Like most WebHeads, he didn't seem pleased by the reminder there was a world outside the datanet.

"Sit," he said, quietly. "I'll be out in a minute."

Clarence sat, studying Wong with a reporter's eye. Frank Wong looked baseline oriental, to the point Clarence was fairly sure that Wong's family had come from one of the oriental-ethnic worlds. They'd had their bodies genetically engineered to maintain an oriental appearance, even though the vast majority of colony worlds were multiracial if not multiethnic. And yet, there was something about the way he held himself that suggested his body had been modified only a few short years ago. It wasn't uncommon for someone who'd had excessive cosmetic surgery to have problems growing accustomed to their new bodies. Clarence wondered, idly, just what had happened. But he was too polite to ask.

"Your story is trending," Wong said. He waved his hand, dismissing his holographic helpmates. "It has already been accessed thousands of times. There's also been quite a bit of dirty sabotage and cunning rewriting. I've managed to ensure that a locked copy of the story is available online, practically everywhere. Things are starting to move."

Clarence frowned. "Who's been trying to rewrite the story?"

"Oh, practically everyone." Wong shrugged. "So far, none of the big news organisations have picked up on it, but the little fellows have been...well, questioning the story. I've been following the underside of the datanet as copies are passed from email account to email account. Quite a few emails have...ah...*vanished* in transit."

"Shit," Clarence said. "Are people *reading*?"

"Of course." Wong snickered. "A lot of people don't realise how easy it is to evade censorship on the datanet without ever actually doing anything *illegal*. A lot of other people don't realise—or didn't realise—that their data-net providers can and do make their emails vanish in transit, but they do now. It won't be long before the sheep start making life hot for the idiots who made their interference a little bit too obvious…"

"I see," Clarence said. He didn't, not really. He'd never really understood how the datanet went together. "And is the story gaining momentum?"

"It's hard to say," Wong said. "We've gained a *lot* of subscribers over the last few hours, paid and unpaid. I'll probably have a story myself about how the online providers have been trying to censor emails, in the name of public safety of course. And there are lots of people discussing the story, so…"

He shrugged. "It may die down in a day or two. Something else will happen. A celebrity will die or put on a new dress or *accidentally* let someone snap a photograph of them in their birthday suit. And…it's hard to say how much the online world actually matters. The people who spend their time exploring the underside of the datanet are not the people who make actual decisions."

"You want to reach people who actually matter," Clarence said. He studied the screen for a long moment. "What's going to happen next?"

"I'll make sure the story keeps spreading through the datanet, despite their best efforts," Wong said. "There's no shortage of hackers who're willing to help me, just to give the finger to the big corps. But…I don't know how long it will last."

Clarence nodded, soberly. It was hard to say what sort of impact the story would have, if indeed it would have *any* impact. Maxima Corporation could simply afford to outwait any public protest…if, of course, there *was* any public protest. Or they might simply accuse *Seeing Eye* of libel and sue. Clarence was certain the story would hold up in any impartial court, but they'd never *see* an impartial judge. Maxima Corporation would make damn sure that the court was rigged from one end to the other before the judge took his seat.

And they might just ignore it, he thought, as he walked back to his room. *They might just carry on with whatever they're doing and to hell with us.*

He sat down in front of the terminal and brought up his email inbox. A handful of emails were waiting for him, ranging from a couple of comments from old acquaintances to a detailed breakdown of the story's first five hours. He snorted as he read the first set of emails, remembering how his old friends had shunned him in the days and weeks after he'd been fired. Who knew why they'd contacted him now?

They've probably been told to get in touch with me, he told himself. He tapped a button, deleting the emails. *Or maybe they want jobs here.*

He put the thought aside as he started to scan through the latest collection of articles, looking for another story. Nothing quite seemed to fit, he decided as he fell into the zone. There was certainly nothing that stood out, save perhaps for a report of gunfire on the other side of the city. *That* was odd, but meant nothing. It could have been anything from two gangs going at each other to the police shooting a criminal suspect.

There was a sharp knock on the door, dragging him out of the zone. "Come in!"

Patricia entered, looking disgustingly bright and cheerful. "You want to come for lunch?"

Clarence glanced at his watch. It was twelve o'clock. Where had the time gone?

"Sure," he said. "Let's go."

CHAPTER ELEVEN

It was obviously unlikely, for example, that the inhabitants of lower-class Rowdy Yates Block on Earth would give much of a damn about fashion in the upper-class Susan Beeves Block. However, stories about fashion were what they got. The publishers published material they considered important to them—and never considered, because they lived in a bubble, that others might feel differently.
—**PROFESSOR LEO CAESIUS**
Crying Wolf : The Media and the Fall of the Empire

"SO," PATRICIA SAID. They sat in the small student cafe, studying the menus. "Why did you become a reporter in the first place?"

Clarence considered the question for a long moment. "It was a difficult decision," he said, reluctantly. "I wanted something that would let me make a name for myself, something that would make me famous. I wanted to be the next...well, the next reporter who exposed the truth and was feted for it. And I'd grown used to asking questions as I grew older...reporting just seemed like the ideal career."

Patricia smiled. "And do you still feel that way?"

"It's hard to say," Clarence admitted. "I have never written a story so powerful, so universe-shaking, that I could dictate my own terms. I have never been a star who simply could not be fired because he could find another job at a moment's notice. And...a lot of the stories I did write were nothing more than boilerplate or otherwise useless. The closest I ever got to something controversial, before the Forsakers, was trying to track down compromising photographs of a political candidate who wanted to run for mayor. I didn't think I ever would become a superstar."

He snorted. "*God*, I was naive. It never occurred to me that I would be fired for chasing the truth. I knew the story could be killed, I knew the editor might insist on it being rewritten, but...I never thought I'd be fired. I must have stepped on a *very* sensitive bunch of toes."

Patricia cocked her head. "At least you weren't deported."

"I suppose," Clarence said. He wondered, not for the first time, why Simon Goldwater had ordered him fired. It seemed a bit of an overreaction. Neither Goldwater nor Maxima Corporation really benefited from expelling the Forsakers. It made him wonder if someone in the government had brought pressure to bear on the corporation. But it still seemed like pointless sadism. "But if I had been deported, at least I would have had a chance to set up home on a colony world."

He looked down at the menu, silently rolling his eyes. There was a long list of fancy dinners, ranging from seafood linguine to fancy chocolate cakes...all terrifyingly expensive, at least by student standards. Patricia hadn't even *blinked* at the prices when the waitress had put the menus in front of them. Clarence wasn't sure if he was more annoyed by the lack of any *real* food—there were no burgers, pizzas or anything else *he* might have eaten as a student—or by the unspoken assumption that he'd be able to pay for it. Jackson had given him an expense account, true, but there were limits. Clarence doubted Jackson would be amused if he blew everything on a fancy lunch.

"Perhaps," Patricia said.

Clarence ordered the cheapest thing on the menu, then looked at her. "Why did *you* decide to become a reporter?"

"It seemed like a good idea at the time," Patricia said. She let out an embarrassed giggle. "I was a reporter for the school newspaper, then a student newsletter...when I heard about *Seeing Eye*, I jumped at the chance to actually report on something *serious*. You know what they had me doing in school? Writing stupid interviews and asking dumb questions!"

"I can believe it," Clarence said.

Patricia flushed. "We had a visit from Gayle Horton—you know her? The superstar with the huge..."

"I know her," Clarence said. He'd never met the superstar in person, but every boy and half of the girls at school had had a huge crush on her. "You actually got to meet her?"

"I wanted to ask hard-hitting questions about her divorce from...from whatever her husband was actually called," Patricia said. She giggled, again. "I used to adore him, but I've forgotten his name! Anyway, they wouldn't *let* me ask her anything *interesting*. I was ordered to fawn on her and give her easy questions and generally treat her like a favourite auntie than a living person. I wasn't *that* young. They made me act like I was five!"

"Oh dear," Clarence said, amused. "And what happened?"

"It was a waste of time," Patricia said. "But that's why I wanted to get into real journalism. I wanted to be more than just a puppet. I wanted to ask the hard questions."

"Like why she was separating from her husband," Clarence said.

"I didn't understand it," Patricia agreed. "He was so handsome, like... so *cute*. And she was ditching him. I wanted to know why."

"Whatever answer you got would probably not have been the truth," Clarence said. He'd never worked as a celebrity reporter, but he'd heard stories. The world of famous film stars and singers bore little relationship to reality. Everyone talked about relationships, dropping titbits of information designed more to spur public interest than actually tell the truth. And *smart* reporters knew they'd better play along if they wanted more stories. "And she might have complained to your teachers."

"I could have coped," Patricia said. "Although, you know, they did often cancel stories at the last minute."

"I know," Clarence said, as the food arrived. "Believe me, I know."

He eyed his plate in dismay. The cheese might be fancy—the menu claimed it was imported from Nouveau Paris—but there just wasn't *enough*. The rolls looked to have been freshly baked, something he'd never seen outside high-class restaurants, yet—again—they were too small. He made a mental note to suggest that they eat outside campus next time, if there was a next time. It would give Patricia some insight into how ninety percent of the population ate.

"Good choice," Patricia said. "That cheese is supposed to be special."

"If you say so," Clarence said. He buttered one of the rolls, then covered it with cheese and took a bite. It tasted of garlic and cream. "But I could get five or six extra-large burgers with fries and drinks in a diner for the same price."

Patricia took a bite of her food. "So what?"

"So I'm going to have to go somewhere else to eat tonight, or cook something for myself," Clarence said. "This isn't going to last me for long. And you know what? There are people out there who couldn't afford to eat here."

"I know that," Patricia said.

"But do you really *understand*?" Clarence tried to put it into words. "You're used to seeing the world in a particular way. But not *everyone* sees the world like you."

"That's what I want to learn from you," Patricia said. "I want to learn how they see the world."

Clarence sighed, just as his terminal bleeped. He glanced at it and frowned. "Jackson wants to see us back at the office," he said. "Now."

"Better finish your dinner first," Patricia said. "He won't mind if we're a few minutes late."

"We should go now." Clarence felt cold. If they were being summoned... perhaps he was being fired. Again. Frank Wong had made it clear that *someone* had noticed the story. It wouldn't be *that* hard for Maxima Corporation to bring pressure to bear on the university or simply offer a colossal bribe. Whoever had sponsored the frat house would have far less influence if Maxima offered to make up the loss. "Come on."

He packed the remains of the cheese and rolls into a bag, then stood. Patricia followed him, looking annoyed. Clarence didn't really blame her, even though he found her calm immensely irritating. *She* was in no danger if she lost her job. Her family would take care of her until the day she died. Clarence, on the other hand...he paid the bill, slipped the waitress a tip and hurried onto the street. Patricia caught up with him as he made his way back to the frat house. Thankfully, for better or worse, the scanner on the door allowed him to enter the building.

"It might not be that urgent," Patricia said. They made their way up to the office, then tapped on Jackson's door. "You're overreacting."

The door opened. Clarence braced himself as he walked into the room. Jackson was sitting on the sofa, looking delighted. Claudia sat next to him, holding a small glass of sparkling wine in her hand. She winked at Clarence as he closed the door, then sat down on the chair Jackson indicated. The scene felt odd, as if Clarence had stepped out of one story and into another, but at least it didn't feel like disaster was looming over him. He wondered, morbidly, just what Jackson and Claudia had been discussing. Claudia would have all sorts of ideas for improving the business.

"We won," Jackson said.

Clarence blinked. "We won? We won *what*?"

Jackson held out a datapad. "Maxima Corporation confessed to wrongdoing," he said, delightedly. "They're going to be compensating everyone who got kicked out of Hellebore Estate."

"What?" Clarence couldn't believe it. "They *confessed*?"

He shook his head. Every corporate lawyer knew that *no one* could afford to admit liability, not when it would be taken as a confession of guilt. The sharks would scent blood in the water and come for their share of the loot. Maxima Corporation was huge, with immense resources, but even *it* couldn't stand up to a prolonged legal feeding frenzy. It would have to waste a great deal of time and money fending off spurious lawsuits that it wouldn't be able to have dismissed because it had already confessed. He found it impossible to believe that they'd done anything of the sort.

"Read it," Jackson said. "We won!"

Clarence took the datapad and read the brief statement. It wasn't *actually* an admission of anything, as far as he could tell. Maxima Corporation's spokesperson had merely stated that the corporation had been misled by estate agents and it would be compensating the homeowners and tenants directly. There were vague hints, carefully crafted, suggesting that the estate agents had embezzled the compensation without ever quite coming out and *saying* it. Whoever had written it, he decided reluctantly, knew what he was doing.

"That's good, isn't it?" Patricia clapped her hands. "We made a difference!"

"Perhaps." Claudia didn't sound convinced. "Or perhaps they're just hoping the whole affair will go away before they actually have to *pay*."

"They have two weeks to pay," Patricia said. "Less than two weeks, really. The affair isn't going to go away so quickly."

Clarence read the statement again, carefully. It did look as if *Seeing Eye* had scored a major victory. Maxima Corporation might not have admitted anything that would come back to haunt them, but they *were* compensating their victims. It was a victory. And yet...he glanced at his watch, silently calculating the time. The story wasn't even a *day* old. It was...odd.

"You're very quiet," Patricia said, nudging him. "What do you think?"

"I think it was too easy," Clarence said.

He wanted to believe that they'd achieved something. He *really* wanted to believe that he could affect social change by writing and publishing a story. It would be so great to go back to Allrianne and tell his former boss that the *Seeing Eye* had done something that the great and powerful *Daily Truth* hadn't been able to do. But...the more he looked at it, the more it puzzled him. It had been too easy.

"Too easy," Patricia repeated. "It wasn't easy to talk to all those people..."

"Yes, it *was*," Clarence said. "*Think* about it. The story has been online for what? Twenty hours, more or less? And in that time, enough has happened to convince one of the richest and most powerful corporations on the planet to cut its losses and surrender. They're going to take a lot of heat for that even if they manage to blame the estate agents for the whole affair. Why the hell did they surrender so quickly?"

"Protest movements were already forming," Jackson said. "There was going to be a student march—they're calling it the March Against Maxima—tomorrow. I dare say it'll be cancelled now that Maxima has backed down."

Clarence shook his head. The idea that a student protest could possibly convince Maxima Corporation to back down was absurd. They'd be more inclined to dig in their heels and fight to the death, rather than let people think that a handful of protests were all that was required to make them change their minds. They'd be *buried* in protests. A larger mass movement *might* have forced their hand, but it didn't look as if one was on the horizon. It had been *years* since the last mass movement—the Rebirth Party—had threatened to change the face of politics for good.

And they were absorbed into the political establishment, Clarence reminded himself. *None of their leaders stayed true to their principles.*

"There were going to be other protests," Jackson added. "Mass letter-writing campaigns, sit-in protests, public demands for an inquiry…"

"I don't think so," Clarence said. Maybe there would be a fuss, for a few days. And then the public would simply lose interest. "It's just too *easy*. Why would they give up so quickly?"

"They might be telling the truth," Claudia said. She tapped the datapad. "It's *possible* that compensation *was* paid to the estate agents, who refused to distribute it any further or simply stole it outright."

"If they could prove that, they'd have no trouble proving their innocence *and* putting the blame where it belongs," Clarence countered. "They wouldn't *need* to hint that the money was embezzled if they could come right out and *say* the money was embezzled."

"That's true," Claudia said. She had enough experience to see the oddities. "But it would still make them look bad."

"Careless and stupid rather than bad," Clarence said. "Some poor sap gets the blame and fired and…nothing else, not really. They have to be up to *something*."

Patricia cleared her throat, loudly. "Do you *have* to be so cynical?"

"Yes," Clarence said. "If there's one thing I've learnt in my years as a reporter, it is that everyone lies, that the first version of the story is rarely the correct one and that *someone* will come up with a pettifogging reason to dismiss a perfectly valid argument."

"That's *three* things," Patricia pointed out.

"I rest my case," Clarence said. He grinned at her. "Yes, you're right. I did list three things when I said there was only one. But does that make them wrong?"

He shrugged. "I mean, we're talking about a vast corporation here. It can take weeks or months to draw up the mission statement, which is a piece of useless bumph hardly anyone bothers to read. Every department has to sign off on the wretched piece of crap before it gets uploaded onto the datanet and ignored. And they decided to pay compensation to a handful of helpless people on an estate in less than a *day*? It normally takes longer to decide what drinks will be served at the corporate meetings discussing what decisions they're going to have to make, let alone actually *making* them."

"I can make decisions quickly," Jackson said.

"You've got a small organisation," Clarence said. "Maxima Corporation is *huge*. Even a simple decision like what to have for lunch can take hours. They acted quickly, too quickly."

"They might have had a contingency plan for *something* going wrong," Claudia mused. "It would be pocket change to them, wouldn't it?"

"They don't mention a precise amount," Jackson mused.

"The original puff pieces claimed that everyone on the estate was getting at least fifty thousand credits," Clarence said. "If we assume that the estate has a population of twenty thousand, we'd be talking about"—he tried to do the sum in his head and failed—"well over a billion credits. If they only paid households instead of individuals, the total would still run into the millions. That's not the sort of sum that can be paid out on a moment's notice."

"There weren't twenty thousand people on the estate," Patricia objected. "I don't think there could be more than three or four thousand at most."

"You might be surprised," Clarence said. He'd been in estates that had *much* larger populations. His birth estate had been considerably bigger than Hellebore. "You can fit thousands of people into each of those apartment blocks."

Jackson cleared his throat. "I understand your concerns," he said to Clarence, "but I think we can chalk this up as a victory. We changed the world. We brought a little justice into the whole affair. And we did well."

"Yeah," Clarence said. He wanted to believe it. "But it was still too easy. They didn't even *try* to challenge the story or demand evidence or *anything*."

"Perhaps we caught them by surprise," Patricia said.

"Then it should have taken longer for them to make a decision," Clarence said.

"I think we should have a celebration," Jackson said, firmly. "I think drinks all round, for starters. And then we can have a party. We won!"

"Yes," Clarence said. "But it still seems odd."

"Then you can look into it, *after* the party," Jackson said. He stood, reaching for his terminal. "Right now, *everyone* is going for drinks."

"Yes, sir," Claudia said.

CHAPTER TWELVE

Indeed, this disconnect helped propel Earth towards its final crisis. The media spoke, in glowing terms, of relief missions to distant planets and sang the praises of the people who donated to the 'save the [insert alien animal here] fund.' From their point of view, this was not a mistake. However, the vast majority of Earth's population felt differently. The billions of credits lavished on interstellar charity, they felt, could be better spent at home.
—**PROFESSOR LEO CAESIUS**
Crying Wolf: The Media and the Fall of the Empire

THE GYM, COLIN SIMPSON DECIDED, had seen better days. It had once been well-equipped, he was sure, but thieves had stripped almost everything out of the building shortly after it had been abandoned by the last set of owners. The walls were bare brick, the floors hard and wooden, the handful of light-fittings so dim that it was easy to believe that it was dark outside. He rubbed his mask, uncomfortably, as he joined the handful of other masked boys on the gym floor. They'd been warned, in no uncertain terms, to keep their masks and gloves on at all times.

"The police are deeply corrupt," he'd been told, when he'd visited for the first time. "They will spend more effort on tracking you down than on catching criminals from the shitter. So *don't* leave them any clues."

It had been an interesting, if terrifying, couple of weeks. He'd spent the first week expecting the police to snatch him and his friends up at any moment, but—apart from a handful of crime sweeps through the estate—the police had done nothing about the dead shitters. It made him think that all he'd needed to do—all the estate had needed to do—was make it clear that there *would* be resistance to any further outsiders being moved into their territory. It had emboldened him to consider more and more acts against the shitters, against everyone who had moved into the city and displaced the original immigrants. It had given him a sense that he wasn't alone and, more importantly, that he *could* make a difference.

The sergeant appeared out of a side door, looked them up and down and snapped out a series of instructions. Colin jumped to obey, trying his hardest to keep up with the tougher lads who had no trouble performing a hundred press-ups on command. He'd never realised just how much went into military training until he'd found himself in what was, effectively, a military training course. His body ached after every session—and after forcing himself to continue exercising at home—but it was growing easier by the day. The sergeant was a tough teacher—Colin had once seen him pick up a boy who'd talked back to him and shake him—yet he was also a *good* teacher. Colin had disliked all of his teachers at school, but he respected the sergeant. It helped that the sergeant clearly knew what he was doing. Most of the teachers at school had been useless.

"Very good," the sergeant said, finally. He wore a mask, like everyone else, but his voice wasn't muffled. "Relax."

Colin let out a long breath, trying to ignore the sweat trickling down his back. He'd thought the gym was cold, when he'd first visited, but now… now he was glad of the cold. His body ached, in places he hadn't known he had. He told himself not to rub the aches and pains, even though he wanted to find *some* relief. It wouldn't make things any better, he knew from grim experience. And besides, he didn't want to let the sergeant down.

"Follow me," the sergeant said.

He led them through the side door into what had once been a changing room. It stank of mildew and human sweat. The tiles had been left in place, but the plaster holding them together was stained with unpleasant-looking green muck. Colin didn't want to think about what it might be. A large table sat in the centre of the room, where young women had once changed their clothes; another, piled with household goods, had been positioned against the far wall. Colin found it hard not to laugh—some of his comrades weren't so lucky—when he saw the supplies. Cleaning fluid? Basic medicines? A clockwork clock? A toolkit right out of a set of children's toys?

The sergeant let them have their laugh, then clapped his hands for silence. "Tell me," he said. "Why did I bring *these* here?"

Colin took a guess. "Because you want to show us an alternate use for them?"

"Quite right," the sergeant said. His gaze swept the room. "You will know, of course, that it is quite difficult to obtain *real* weapons these days. Buying a weapons permit is impossible without both cash and connections. Illicit weapons are more likely to bring the police down on your heads than kill your enemies. I once saw an assault rifle, recovered from a gang, that was so corroded that it exploded when we tried to fire it on a gunnery range. Therefore, I will be teaching you how to *improvise* a number of weapons."

He lowered his voice until Colin had to struggle to follow. "This is probably the most dangerous thing I'll teach you," he added, "so remember this. Anyone who fucks around with this sort of stuff is likely to end up dead. And if you don't kill yourself, I'll kill you."

Colin shivered. He believed every word.

"First up, what do we have here?" He held up a bottle. "A standard floor cleaner, which you are meant to mix with water before using. Right? Now"—he held up another bottle—"what do you think you get if you mix this floor cleaner with *that* floor cleaner, then light a match?"

One of the bigger boys stuck up a hand. "An explosion?"

"Quite right," the sergeant said. He snickered. "Whoever designed these mixtures was very clever—and very stupid in the way only very clever people can be. In the interests of safety, they've separated most of the compounds that would produce a big explosion…but they haven't told anyone why. If you mix them together, you restore the explosive power…and no one can prove you meant to do it. How many policemen would question someone owning a bottle of each? How would they know *you* knew to mix them together?"

Colin nodded. They'd also been warned not to write anything down.

The sergeant continued, without pause. "You mix roughly equal proportions of both into a plastic container, leave them to blend and then strike your match. Or, if you don't want to blow *yourself* up, you rig a detonator. Again"—he pointed to the clock on the table—"you use something that is perfectly innocuous, until you turn it into a bomb."

He held up a self-heating dinner pack. Colin stared. He'd eaten more than his fair share of such dinners—and he had a suspicion they were poisonous, as they tasted thoroughly unpleasant—but he'd never thought of them as a potential weapon. He frowned, trying to figure out how they *could* be turned into a weapon. Perhaps they *were* poisonous after all.

The sergeant waited for someone to try to answer, then pressed on. "Quite harmless, right? Only really harmful to your digestion? Not quite."

He opened the pack, revealing the heating element. "You'll note that the heating element is wrapped in plastic, which is designed to degrade into nothingness the moment it is opened," he continued. "The *really* interesting thing about the wrapping is that exposure to certain kinds of chemicals starts the same reaction. If you put the heating element in your chemical mix, for example, the wrapping degrades rapidly, triggering the heating element. And then you get an explosion."

Colin hesitated, then stuck up a hand. "Sir…how can you tell *when* the device is going to explode?"

"You can't," the sergeant said, bluntly. "In theory, you'll have ten minutes from the moment the heating element is exposed to the explosion. In practice…the heating element may react badly to the chemical mix, triggering the explosion ahead of time. You need to use clockwork if you want a more precise detonation."

The lesson seemed to last for hours, but Colin barely noticed as the sergeant brought out item after item—from cleaning supplies to make-up and toys—and explained how they could be used to wage war against the intruders. One chemical mix would produce a very nasty gas that, in a confined space, could be lethal. Another would be blinding, if it got into someone's eyes. A third was harmless, but stank of *real* gas. The sergeant pointed out that it could be very useful if someone wanted to start a panic.

"If you're purchasing these supplies," the sergeant said, "make sure you purchase them separately. You don't want to raise eyebrows, not in these days. Who knows where it might end?"

Colin nodded. He'd had a neighbour, once, who'd been investigated for purchasing too many diapers for her infant children. The poor woman had been harassed for hours, simply because she didn't want to have to keep running back to the shop every time she needed a new box of nappies. It was spite, pointless spite. Colin was sure of it. He simply hadn't been able to work out how *anyone* benefited from the whole affair. Stealing food made sense, he supposed, but restricting nappy purchases? It was just another case of people being harassed because they lived on an estate.

The sergeant dismissed his students after another session of physical training, reminding them—again—to stay in the shadows as they left the gym. Colin did as he was told, only taking off his mask once he was out on the darkened streets. He'd been told that the security cameras had been destroyed—or spray-painted—long ago, but it was well to be careful. The big security cameras weren't the real threat. It was their tiny cousins, the ones that were too small to be seen with the naked eye, that were the true danger. The sergeant had made it clear that they weren't going to be able to find them without equipment they weren't going to be able to obtain.

Bastards, he thought, as he jogged back towards the bar. He'd arranged to meet his mates after the training session. *They don't miss a trick.*

His friends met him outside the bar. He'd told them about the resistance, but—as the sergeant had instructed—he hadn't told them anything specific. It was his duty to pass on what he'd learnt, without betraying the larger organisation. Colin hated the idea of keeping secrets from his friends, particularly the ones who were equally at risk from police sweeps, but he had no choice. What his friends didn't know they couldn't tell.

"Everyone talks," the sergeant had said. "You think you're tough. You think you can keep your mouth shut. Well, you're wrong. The police can make you talk, eventually. They will beat you up. They will pressure your friends and family. They will drug you. They may even wave a pile of cash under your nose. They will break you. It may take them some time, but they will break you. Be careful what you tell others. What people don't know they can't tell."

"I don't know where we're going to get all that shit," Magus said, when Colin had finished outlining the lesson. "We don't have the money to buy it."

"So we steal it," Gordon said, bluntly.

"They'd know what we stole, wouldn't they?" Magus glared. "They'd guess what we wanted it for…"

Colin considered it, then smiled. "No, they wouldn't. Not if we burn the store down in our wake."

They discussed the plan in hushed voices as they collected their tools and made their way out of the estate, into a slightly higher-class district. The row of shops, including a hardware store, were closed and shuttered, their owners knowing there was no point in keeping them open after dark. They looked intimidating—the shutters looked solid—but Colin knew better. He'd been shown how to open them days ago. No one would pay any *real* attention if the alarms went off, either. Alarms went off all the time.

And the police don't come here that often, he thought, as he carefully opened the shutters and led the way into the shop. It was dark and creepy. He shone his flashlight around, carefully locating everything they needed. *We can take what we want and destroy the rest.*

"Pass me a shopping cart," he muttered. He put two bottles of cleaning fluid aside, then dumped the rest into the basket. There were fewer bottles than he'd expected, all cheap brands. The shop wasn't as well-supplied as he'd hoped. "Get the…"

He froze as he heard someone shuffling their way down the stairs. Ice washed down his veins. It hadn't occurred to him that someone might live above the shop. He should have thought of it, but...the shutters had been designed to be opened from the outside. Gordon let out a curse and ran into the back, waving his flashlight like a madman. Colin followed him, just in time to see Gordon knocking a man to the ground. His head hit the ground with a sickening crunch. He was old enough to be Colin's father. Above them, a female voice cried out in alarm.

"Get up there," Colin snapped. They were committed now. The police might come, if they were called. He couldn't afford to be recognised. "Move!"

Magus ran up the stairs. Colin ran after him as the sound of fighting echoed down, almost tripping twice on the rickety stairway before reaching the top. A teenage girl was struggling desperately, fighting with all of her strength to escape Magus's grip. He knocked her to the ground, banging her head on the flooring. She let out a grunt and lay still, her terrified eyes staring up at them. Magus snorted and started to tug at her nightdress.

Colin caught his arm. "What do you think you're doing?"

"Having some fun," Magus said. The girl's breasts came free. She whimpered as Magus ran his hands over her bare flesh. "You want a go afterwards?"

"Fuck it," Colin said. He cursed himself under his breath. If he'd known someone lived above the shop...he might still have carried out the robbery, but he would at least have *thought* about what he would do with any prisoners. "Do you realise how much evidence you'll be leaving behind?"

Magus lifted himself off and finished removing the nightdress. "Does it matter? They rape our women, we fuck theirs..."

"Yes, it does," Colin said. He tried not to look at the girl as he hefted his flashlight and brought it down on her head, hard. "You don't want to leave a signed confession behind, do you? Now, get off her and help us get everything else out of the fucking store."

He checked the remaining rooms, silently relieved there was no one else in the store, then led the way back downstairs. Magus followed, grumbling under his breath. Colin ignored him as he finished piling up the supplies, then splashed cleaning fluid everywhere. The sergeant had taught him well. Once the flames reached the fluid, he thought as he struck a match, the shop would turn into a towering inferno. Both the girl and her father—or grandfather—would be consumed by the fire.

The thought cost him a pang. He hated the shitters, he hated the outsiders and the richer folk who sneered at everyone who lived on *his* estate, but the girl had been an innocent. She could only be a year or two younger than him at most. She had looked sweet and desirable and…he glared at Magus as he lit the fuse and fled the store. It had never occurred to him that Magus would try to *rape* someone either.

We had to kill them, he thought, glumly. The police might not come at once, or they might not come at all, but he dared not take it for granted. A witness statement might bring the police down on his head. *We had no choice.*

Colin silently promised Magus an ass-kicking he'd never forget as they fled into the night, a moment before the store exploded into flames. He glanced back once, silently praying that the girl wouldn't wake up before she died, then turned away from the fire and ran. Magus ran beside him, his long legs easily keeping up. Gordon brought up the rear.

"You didn't have to stop me," Magus said, once they were back home. "That was the first time since…"

"We have a fucking job to do," Colin snarled. What would the sergeant do? Probably snap Magus's neck like a twig. Colin couldn't do that. There was no point in appealing to Magus's sense of morality, either. Very few people on the estate could *afford* a sense of morality. "And we are not stopping, we are not risking being caught, just so you can have a quick fuck!"

"She was a shitter," Magus protested. "She was…"

"It doesn't matter," Colin said. He tried to channel the sergeant, as best as he could. "If you do it again, I'll fucking kill you. Do you understand me?"

Magus glared, then dropped his gaze. "Yes."

"Very good," Colin said. He pressed his advantage. "We have a cause now. And I won't let you throw it away."

He glanced down at their loot. There was enough cleaning fluid—and other supplies—to fuel a dozen explosions. He had the feeling they'd come in very handy. Thanks to the flames, no one would even know what they'd stolen. And then...

They may catch us, he thought. *But by the time they do, we will have made our mark.*

CHAPTER THIRTEEN

Practically speaking, they were wrong. It would have been very difficult to fix all of the problems with Rowdy Yates Block alone, even if all the charity money had been donated to that cause. That did not matter. The perception that Earth's money was being wasted, while large segments of the population struggled to survive, sparked an explosion that eventually sent the planet surging into chaos.

—**PROFESSOR LEO CAESIUS**
Crying Wolf: The Media and the Fall of the Empire

IT MADE NO SENSE.

Clarence rubbed his aching head, wishing he hadn't drunk so much alcohol before going to bed. He'd taken a sober-up as soon as he woke up in the morning, wishing he was dead, but it hadn't done wonders for his headache. His eyes hurt every time he looked at the terminal, yet he couldn't look away. He was *sure* the whole affair made no sense.

A whole string of puff pieces hovered in front of him, from press releases put out by Maxima Corporation to detailed articles published by the *Daily Truth*. They *looked* to have been written by different people—he'd done a style analysis to be sure—yet they all said the same thing, in many different words. Maxima Corporation was moving ahead with its project to demolish the estate, but it would be making sure that the inhabitants would be properly compensated. It *looked* wonderful. The press releases were still coy about what had actually happened, but the detailed articles placed the blame—bluntly—on the estate agents. They had no qualms about making it clear that the original compensation had been stolen in transit.

Clarence took a sip of his coffee, cursing his headache under his breath. It was still too good to be true. A powerful corporation did *not* change course overnight, not when there were vast sums of money involved. If it took weeks to get a corporate office to process a relatively tiny refund, as he'd discovered when he'd done battle with the bureaucracy as a young man, it should have taken *months* to convince the corporation to pay out millions of credits in compensation. He was sure there were corporate lawyers who would have urged the CEOs to fight to the death, relying on their vast coffers to keep the lawsuits at bay until the attackers ran out of money. Maxima Corporation could simply outwait its opponents.

And no one on Hellebore could afford to fight a lawsuit, Clarence thought. *And they wouldn't be able to delay the demolition unless they got a sympathetic judge and no judge would support them against Maxima.*

He shook his head. It just didn't make sense. More people read *Seeing Eye* than an outsider might expect—*Seeing Eye* practically gave its content away, much to his private shock—but its readership wasn't *that* large. And there had been no mass protests, no sit-ins…no crowd of well-connected students sitting in the condemned buildings daring the demolition teams to move forward and kill them as well as the buildings. Clarence could have understood Maxima Corporation climbing down if things looked bad, but…things had barely gotten started. Maxima had folded too quickly and it simply didn't make sense.

There was a knock at the door. Clarence started, then looked up. "Come in!"

Claudia entered, wearing a long nightgown. "This takes us back, doesn't it?"

Clarence looked down at himself. He was wearing boxers, but nothing else. He wasn't even sure what time he'd gone to bed, although he'd definitely been alone when he'd undressed and turned off the light. It *did* remind him of journalism school, when they'd been lovers…he shook his head. He'd learnt too much about the real world to pretend to be a carefree student, even if it *hadn't* been a little creepy. He was too old and too responsible to convince himself, for even a few seconds, that nothing he did would have any negative consequences.

"I suppose it does," he said. Claudia had been beautiful when she was a teenager. She was *still* beautiful. He looked away, trying not to imagine what she looked like under the nightgown. It was quite conservative, by the standards set by the younger students, but it still left little to the imagination. "But we're responsible adults now."

"Speak for yourself," Claudia said. She sat on the bed, close enough to touch. "Do you *really* feel that old?"

"Compared to the students, yes," Clarence said.

Claudia poked his arm, gently. "Do you remember some of the stupid shit *we* did when we were students?"

"It all seemed a good idea at the time," Clarence said. The sex, the drinking, the…he cringed at the memories. Some of the crap they'd pulled would have destroyed their careers, if they'd done it as adults. It still astonished him that some of his fellows had been allowed to graduate with bad habits that had probably gotten them fired. "I suppose they feel the same way."

"Probably," Claudia said. "There was an orgy downstairs, you know. It made our little games look tame."

Clarence believed her. He'd taken a course on psychology and the lecturer had explained that most humans were attracted by the forbidden, although they would never admit it to a soul. The more freedom they had—the more they could do without consequence—the more they'd be drawn to what little they *didn't* have the freedom to do. Jackson and his friends could do so much, without incurring the merest whiff of disapproval, that they'd keep pushing the limits until they ran into real trouble. He wasn't sure he wanted to know how far they'd go in pursuit of pleasure. The things he'd done as a teenager had been more than dumb enough.

"I don't want to think about it," Clarence said. He kept his eyes on the screen. "In hindsight, some of the games we played were *really* stupid."

"Tell me about it," Claudia said. Her voice darkened. "I heard from Willis a couple of years ago, you know? The very first thing he said to me was *do you remember playing the wheelie game*?"

"Ouch," Clarence said. Willis had been a dick. "And you said?"

"I told him to fuck off," Claudia said. "But you know…Willis could never keep his mouth shut. Or his pants on."

Clarence glanced at her. Her face was tight, angry. He'd never asked why she'd left her job—he'd certainly never thought that *she'd* been fired—but he could guess. Willis had been the worst kind of sociopath, a manipulator who'd somehow always managed to get authority on his side. Traits that had been admirable as a young student were despicable in the working world. Clarence had no trouble believing that Willis had made life uncomfortable for Claudia until she'd jumped ship at the first opportunity. It was funny how rules designed to protect people could be bent and twisted until they hurt people instead.

"You should warn Patricia and the others," he said. "What they do now will come back to haunt them."

"I doubt they'd listen," Claudia said. "Did *we* listen when we were kids?"

"No," Clarence said. He indicated the screen. "I've been reading all of the stories that have come out over the last twelve hours. Everything that happened…it just doesn't make sense."

Claudia leaned closer. "And you think there's still a story there?"

"I think there's *something* there," Clarence said. "But what?"

It had been a long time since they'd been study partners, as well as friends and lovers, but they fell into old habits with a comfortableness that surprised him. He supposed it shouldn't have done, as they crawled through newspaper articles and government archives looking for something they hoped they'd recognise when they saw it. They'd once been as close as it was possible for two people to be. Even now, even when they were no longer lovers or partners, they understood each other. And yet, there was no hint as to *why* Maxima Corporation had folded so quickly. It was enough to make him wonder if there was nothing more to the story than the press releases claimed.

And if I believed that, I'd also believe in Santa Claus and the Easter Bunny, he thought, as he took another sip of his coffee. It was cold. *They shouldn't have paid out so much money so quickly.*

The door burst open. "Clarence," Patricia said. "You'll never believe who's come to visit!"

Clarence made a mental note to keep the door locked in future. "No, who?"

"Simon Goldwater *himself*," Patricia said. "He's in the common room right now!"

"…The fuck?" Clarence couldn't believe it. Claudia looked as if she didn't believe it either. "Simon Goldwater himself?"

"Yeah," Patricia said. "He's asking to speak to all of us."

Clarence stood and grabbed his dressing gown. There was no time to shower or shave…he tossed another robe at Claudia as he donned his gown and tied the belt. It made no sense…none of it made any sense. Simon Goldwater wasn't the kind of person who made house calls without careful planning. The *Daily Truth* had once been visited by someone *very* high up the corporate ladder—someone far *below* Simon Goldwater—and the whole affair had been arranged weeks in advance. Simon couldn't believe that Goldwater's close-protection team had signed off on the visit. They'd want time to check out the situation first.

"We're coming," he said, as he headed for the door. "Did he say what he wanted?"

"He said he wanted to meet us," Patricia said. Her eyes were shining with excitement. "He just walked right up to the door and rang the buzzer."

Clarence exchanged glances with Claudia. It *really* didn't make any sense. Even here, even on campus, Simon Goldwater would hardly be treated as an ordinary visitor. The dean and the rest of the staff would be fawning on him, hoping for a contribution. A tiny amount of pocket change, for Goldwater, might endow the entire university for years to come. God alone knew where Imperial University was going to get the funding, now that Earth was gone. They couldn't expect Tarsus to pick up the slack.

I wonder if that's *the answer*, Clarence thought, as he led the way into the common room. Two bodyguards, both clearly enhanced humanoids, stood outside. *If the corporation is having economic problems, they might not have been able to risk a lawsuit that would have exposed their weaknesses...*

Simon Goldwater *looked* like an avuncular grandfather. He was tall, but not too tall; heavyset without actually being fat; his blue eyes twinkled with amused benevolence as he studied the students in front of him. Clarence felt the effect, even as he reminded himself to remain cynical. It was hard, somehow, to believe that the elderly man in front of him had a malicious bone in his body. But Simon Goldwater had not reached the top of the ladder without a great deal of both cunning and ruthlessness. His appearance was just another weapon in his arsenal to disarm opposition. Simon had no doubt that a hundred focus groups had helped to determine *precisely* how Goldwater should look at all times.

And no one would dare to impersonate him, Clarence thought. He'd seen enough photographs of Goldwater to be fairly sure they weren't dealing with a fake. Besides, even getting onto the university campus would be difficult without money or influence smoothing the way. *The bodyguards alone prove that this is the real Goldwater.*

"Thank you for coming," Goldwater said. His accent was upper-class, but not *too* upper-class. "And thank you for allowing me to speak to you."

"You are more than welcome." Jackson didn't quite stammer, but it sounded as though he *wanted* to. Goldwater was well above even *his* level. "It's a pleasure to have you here."

Yeah, right, Clarence thought. He had no idea *why* Goldwater had come, but he was sure it boded ill. Goldwater—or someone in his office—had ordered Clarence fired. *That* didn't suggest the charming older man was remotely benevolent. *Why did you even come here?*

"I owe you a great debt," Goldwater continued. He *sounded* as though he meant it. "If you hadn't stumbled across the…ah…*problems* with Hellebore Estate, we might have committed a great injustice. Thanks to you, the displaced *will* be compensated and the guilty punished."

Angeline Adams, one of the youngest reporters in the room, leaned forward. "What actually happened, sir?"

Goldwater's brow furrowed. "It seems that one of my junior staffers, in cahoots with an estate agent, came up with a plan to split the compensation between them," he said. His tone was one of firm disapproval. "They successfully convinced the accountants that the money had been paid, while actually keeping it for themselves. I have seen to it that they have both been fired and will be charged in criminal courts."

And that may or may not be actually true, Clarence thought. It was *possible*, he supposed, but surely *someone* would ask questions. The *Daily Truth's* accountants had questioned each and every one of his expenses, even when he'd been a senior reporter. *There might be more people involved than we see.*

He took a breath and asked a question. "Will the trial be public?"

Goldwater looked at him. There was no hint of recognition in his eyes. Clarence felt irked, and a little relieved, even though he supposed he shouldn't have been surprised. Goldwater hadn't had to know what Clarence *looked* like to have him fired. The whole affair had been life-shattering for Clarence, but Goldwater had probably considered it a very minor matter. He might not even have been *personally* invested in the whole affair. Firing Clarence might have been a favour for someone in government.

"It depends on how they plead," Goldwater said. "They may simply accept exile and be deported tomorrow."

Which will put them conveniently out of reach, Clarence thought. It wouldn't be the first time someone had been deported before they could answer questions. *And no one will bother to dig any further into the matter.*

Goldwater cleared his throat. "I was very impressed with your reporting," he said, addressing the room at large. "Your tiny operation uncovered a very big problem. None of the other newspapers bothered to look into the issue. They just wrote flattering nonsense that no one cared to read."

"We see ourselves as seekers of truth." Jackson sounded as though he was trying to be grave, but only made himself sound pompous. "We wanted to look for the story *under* the story."

And every big organisation knows precisely which side their bread is buttered on, Clarence added, silently. The *Daily Truth* wouldn't have run a story about Maxima Corporation refusing to pay compensation to the estate-dwellers, any more than it would have put the rumours about Adam Dent—the flicker mogul—into print. *They wouldn't risk an encounter with Maxima Corporation's lawyers, even if they could prove every word.*

"And I salute you for it," Goldwater said. "If you hadn't run the story, we wouldn't have known what was going on. And we wouldn't have been able to punish the guilty parties."

He managed to sound as though he actually *meant* it. Clarence was unwillingly impressed.

"We are glad to have been of service," Jackson said. "Both to you *and* to the truth."

"And I am glad that you were there," Goldwater said. "Glad enough to offer you a boon, as it were."

He looked around the common room, his expression unreadable. "You do good work, but you really don't have the budget—or staff—to continue seeking out stories. This office has its limits, does it not?"

"We are bringing in money," Jackson said, stiffly.

"Yes, but you're also living and working in—pardon me—a place where much of the work is done for you," Goldwater said. "This fraternity was *designed* to spark the entrepreneurial urge. It was never designed to house it permanently. Your expenses will skyrocket the moment you move out of the fraternity."

Clarence frowned. Could *Goldwater* have funded the fraternity? Or his corporation? The fraternity was older than Simon Goldwater, Clarence thought, but Maxima Corporation was older than Tarsus itself. Whoever had provided the original funds was hidden behind a small army of accountants and lawyers. It was certainly possible that Goldwater might be a silent party in the background...

"Let me make you an offer," Goldwater said. "I'll give you a helping hand. I'll purchase offices for you, right in the heart of the city. I'll give you the budget and resources you need to compete with the big boys. I'll make sure you have all the clearances and permits you need to operate without hindrance. You'll be able to *really* change the world."

Jackson swallowed, visibly. "And...and what would that cost us?"

"Nothing," Goldwater said. He smiled, reassuringly. "You would have complete freedom of operation. You could do whatever you liked."

"Oh," Jackson said. He *was* stammering now. "I...I'd...I'd have to talk about it with my friends."

Goldwater looked oddly disappointed. "That is quite understandable, young man."

He stood. "My office will be in touch within the next few hours," he said. "If you wish to accept my offer, tell them. If not...well, I wish you the very best of luck."

And we can believe that as much as we like, Clarence thought. It was easy to feel as though he'd disappointed a kindly old uncle, even though he was far from blind to the manipulation. *Why did you even come here?*

His gaze sharpened as Goldwater left the room. *And what are you trying to bribe us to do?*

CHAPTER FOURTEEN

But it should not be believed that the publishers alone were the problem. The reporters were trained in reporting, and they were often quite good at it, but not in anything they might need to interpret their observations. They simply lacked the experience to tell when they were being lied to.
—**PROFESSOR LEO CAESIUS**
Crying Wolf: The Media and the Fall of the Empire

"I THINK WE SHOULD HAVE DRINKS ALL ROUND," Jackson said, once Goldwater had left the room. "And then we need to make some decisions."

"There's nothing to decide." Patricia stood and walked over to the drinks cabinet. "We should take his offer and be glad."

Elle coughed. "And you don't think there will be strings attached?"

Patricia shrugged as she counted out the glasses, then picked up an unmarked bottle of white wine. "Technically speaking, we are only allowed to use this frat house for business until we either establish ourselves as a workable company or go bust. We *have* just established ourselves, so it is only a matter of time before the trustees tell us to move into the wider world and let someone else have a shot. And how many things will we have to learn to do—quickly—once we're no longer living on campus?"

"That's an unusual thing for you to say," Jackson said.

"Clarence taught me that life outside campus is different," Patricia said. She poured the wine with practiced ease, then handed out the glasses. "We may find it harder to make headway once we're in the real world."

Jessica Pierce looked up from her datapad. "Unless our earnings sky-rocket, we will *not* be able to afford offices in the centre of town for *years* to come," she said. "We're not doing badly—our income went upwards sharply after we broke the story and new subscribers are coming in all the time—but we're not making anything like as much as the bigger newspapers."

"There's no reason we *have* to have offices in the centre of town," Claudia pointed out, quietly. "We could find some quality accommodation in one of the middle-class estates without putting our staff in danger. It would be easier for people to reach us too."

Clarence was barely listening to the conversation. He was too busy trying to consider everything Goldwater had said—and *hadn't* said. It was quite possible that everything Goldwater had said had been the truth, but… Clarence didn't believe it. And then there was the offer to practically do *everything* for *Seeing Eye*. They were being offered everything they could possibly want on a platter. That *alone* would have made him suspicious. There was no such thing as a free lunch.

There's always a price, he told himself, firmly. *And that price might not be measured in money.*

"I've got three more years at university before I graduate in Mixed Gender Studies," Angeline said. "I don't want to move out of campus."

Clarence winced. Journalism School had been a four-year course—and everything useful could have been taught in a year—but at least it had been reasonably *practical*. There was nothing practical about Mixed Gender Studies, certainly nothing that would lead to a job outside academia. Angeline would find it impossible to do anything *meaningful* with her life after she graduated. He wondered, idly, why her parents were financing her studies. Did they think she could make something of it? Or was she just biding her time until she married someone who would support her for the rest of her life? Or…he'd heard enough stories about how the Very Wealthy got married to wonder if Angeline would be the one choosing her future husband. Her parents would have a say in who she married.

"You wouldn't *have* to move out of campus," Patricia said, in a tone that clearly added the word *idiot*. "You'd just take a hovercab from campus to the office."

"Being in the centre of town would certainly make it easy to shop," one of the girls Clarence didn't recognise said. "Right now, we have to take the aircar to the mall and…"

"You're not being paid to shop," Elle said, sharply. "And if you think that writing about the latest fashions will change the world…"

"We don't have time to argue," Jackson said. "You heard him. The offer won't be open indefinitely."

"That's not quite what he said," Patricia commented.

"But that's what he meant," Jackson insisted. "He might not be so impressed with us in a week or two."

"Try a few hours," Clarence said. He was impressed that Jackson had picked up on the unspoken threat. The offer, for better or worse, had to be accepted quickly or not at all. "The story—our story—will not remain headline news for long. We'll need to find another story quickly."

"And another, and another," Claudia muttered.

"Quite," Jackson agreed. "What are the advantages of accepting the offer?"

Jessica let out a long breath. "Budgeting and accounting *is* a valid concern." Her voice was very flat, completely toneless. "Right now, we do not have to pay for our power or our food or quite a few other things. They're supplied by the fraternity trust fund. If we move out of the frat house and go somewhere else, our expenses will rise. We will not be able to avoid those costs. If he offers to pay for them, it would make it easier to put our money elsewhere."

"We have money," Patricia said.

"We have an unpredictable income," Jessica said. "Our business model is based on a vast number of subscribers, each one paying a tiny amount. There is no way to be *sure* just how much money we will make this month, let alone the next month…and so on. If we find it impossible to meet the expenses we *cannot* defer, we will go out of business. It is as simple as that."

That was astonishingly practical for a student, Clarence thought. He made a mental note to check into Jessica's background. He'd assumed that she was a rich kid like Jackson and Patricia, but it was possible that she was a scholarship student instead. Someone from the middle classes would understand economics—and the simple fact that spending more than one earned was asking for trouble—better than someone who'd never had to worry about money.

"So you're in favour of taking the offer," Jackson said.

"I have no feelings," Jessica said. "I simply point out that yes, there are advantages to taking the offer."

"That's true," Jackson said. "And he *did* promise us considerable freedom."

"He said we could do whatever we wanted," Jessica pointed out.

"Unless we want to embezzle, I assume," Elle said.

Another student leaned forward. "If we take him up on his offer, would we not lose some of our other funding? The fraternity trust fund *does* state that we have to make our profits by our own efforts."

"We'll lose that anyway, when we get kicked out," Patricia said. "Either we make enough to satisfy the beancounters that we've formed a stable business or most of us graduate and leave the university anyway. We have to start planning for the day we move out now."

"If we have a year of stable income, which is *not* guaranteed, we should be fine," Jessica commented. "But things *will* wobble when we move out."

"It would also give us a great deal of clout," Frank Wong said. "Look how quick the university was to let him walk in the front door, *without* spending hours passing through security. His name could open doors for us."

"We wouldn't be working for him," Jackson said.

"But everyone would know we were funded by him," Wong pointed out.

"Yes, which may not work in our favour," Elle said. "They might see us as his attack bitches."

"He said we'd be independent," Jackson protested.

"And how many people," Elle demanded, "are going to believe it?"

"He's offering us everything we want," Jackson said. His gaze swept the room. "This isn't a hobby, not for most of us. We devoted ourselves to the truth. We knew the truth would be hard to find, but we swore that we *would* find it. And here he is, offering us the resources to find it. Do we not have an obligation to take his offer?"

"Strictly speaking, we have no obligations to him at all," Jessica said. "He can make all the offers he wants, but we are not obliged to take them."

"Yes, but we do *want* this, don't we?" Jackson said. "Or do we want to risk falling back into obscurity?"

"There will be other stories," Elle said. "I'm pretty damn sure of it."

Jackson frowned. "Clarence, you've been very quiet. What's *your* take?"

Clarence hesitated, trying to put his thoughts into words. "There are two problems with accepting his offer, a minor problem and a major problem. The minor problem is, as Elle said, that Goldwater's funding will make us Goldwater's attack dogs. We will go after people he *wants* us to go after or—worse—that is how we will be *perceived*. There's no shortage of newspapers that really *are* nothing less than attack dogs, who cheerlead for their owners and slander their enemies at every opportunity. They do not have any editorial independence at all."

"But that won't be fair," Patricia said.

"It doesn't matter," Clarence said. "The truth isn't as important as you might think. What is important is what people *believe*. And if the people come to believe that our *real* purpose is digging up dirt on Goldwater's enemies…well, it won't matter that we see ourselves as being devoted to the truth. They'll assume the worst of us, because that's the rational thing to do."

He took a breath. "But the major problem is considerably more serious."

"Joy," Jackson said, sarcastically.

Clarence hesitated, picking out the right words. "Pretend...pretend you're a chaste young woman. You don't want to have sex before marriage, as alien as that sounds. You're so keen on remaining chaste that you *tell* everyone that you're going to remain a virgin until your wedding night. Anyway, along comes a wealthy man who offers you a billion credits in exchange for having sex with him. You don't want to do it, but hey! A billion credits is a billion credits."

"Anyone with a billion credits will have no trouble finding someone to fuck," Elle muttered, darkly.

"So you say *yes*," Clarence said, ignoring Elle's injection. "A billion credits...you'll give up your virginity for *that*. It's only a little thing, at the end of the day. And a billion credits is a billion credits. Except...instead of handing over the money, the wealthy man asks if you'll sleep with him for a *single* credit. And you demand, in horror, to know what sort of woman he thinks you are."

He paused, dramatically. "And he says *we've already established what sort of woman you are, we're just haggling over the price.*"

"The point is this; once you compromise your principles, for anything, you've compromised your principles. You can no longer claim the moral high ground. No one will take you seriously if you try. Why should they? You've already shown that you are quite happy to throw your principles out the airlock if someone makes you an offer. And in this case, the woman has compromised her principles for *nothing*. She doesn't have to sleep with the wealthy man to be thoroughly screwed."

"Ouch," Jackson said.

"On the face of it, Goldwater's offer is a good offer—great, even." Clarence conceded that point, even though it cost him. "And yet, there is a nasty sting in the tail. Once you become dependent on his funding, and you *will* become dependent very quickly, he will have complete control over you. He won't need to tighten your leash very hard to make you uncomfortable, if you annoy him. You'll surrender the moment he points out that you have to pay the landlord and you can't pay without Goldwater's funding.

"And even if Goldwater has absolutely no intention of manipulating you, and he really doesn't do *anything* to interfere with you, he still makes you look bad. You claim that you are funded by subscriptions, that the only people who pay you are your customers. That will no longer be true if you take money from Goldwater. You will look like his lapdogs even if he doesn't do anything. That might even be his plan. He does nothing anyone can blame him for, but you get discredited anyway."

Elle snickered. "Are we really that important?"

"We caused Maxima Corporation some embarrassment," Clarence pointed out. "At best, Goldwater looks like a fool who hired a thief. That's not going to do wonders for his reputation. His rivals will be making fun of him for years. And at worst…well, we interfered with *something*. I still don't know why they surrendered so quickly. Discrediting us might be worth a few million credits. It's pocket change to them."

Jackson shook his head. "Can you really be sure?"

"If your principles mean anything to you, you shouldn't let yourself be pushed into a position where you either have to compromise your principles or *appear* to compromise them," Clarence said. "Either way, you are discredited. My strong advice—my *very* strong advice—is to politely decline the offer."

"But surely Goldwater wouldn't want to discredit *himself*," Patricia said. "If he threatened us…"

"He wouldn't do anything *too* overt," Clarence said. "But yes, he *could* tell you to kill a story and you'd do it, because otherwise he'd cut your funding. And you could scream about it all you liked and no one would give much of a damn, because…why should they care about you? You're just another bunch of people who sold out their principles for money."

"Ouch," Jackson said.

"And maybe—just *maybe*—Goldwater would blame it on someone else, someone who could take the blame and a slap on the wrist"—Clarence shrugged, expressively—"and you'd still know that he could knock you down at any moment, if you didn't toe the line. He could keep his hands clean and *still* put you in your box."

He tapped the table. "I was expecting this, sooner or later," he admitted. "And now you have to make a choice. Do you take the money, and turn yourself into yet another small media outlet, or do you stand up for your principles even if you have to fight for funding on a regular basis? What do you choose?"

It wasn't an entirely abstract question. Clarence had no doubt that Maxima Corporation had dug into the story's background, if only to figure out if the story was actually true. He would have been surprised if they hadn't realised that the 'Clarence Esperanza' who'd written the story was also the 'Clarence Esperanza' who'd been fired at Goldwater's command. The name wasn't *that* uncommon, in the estates, but Clarence couldn't recall meeting *another* Clarence who'd been a reporter. It was quite possible that Goldwater would press for Clarence to be either fired or otherwise neutralised once he had a firm grip on *Seeing Eye's* finances. Claudia might be fired too.

"Fuck," Jackson said. "Are there any strong arguments in favour?"

"We don't *know* that Goldwater will pressure us," Patricia said.

Jessica kept her eyes on the floor. "I once got into trouble with a man," she said. "And I screamed for help. And it was hard to convince the floor warden that I'd been in real trouble because I'd taken my top off willingly. He kept asking why I'd undressed myself, why I'd made myself vulnerable. I hadn't realised how far the bastard wanted to go. It wasn't until he started to tug down my panties that I…but I couldn't convince anyone to believe me. I'd made myself vulnerable and…"

Her face was burning red. "We'll be in the same boat, if we take Goldwater's money," she said. "There'll be no way we can claim complete innocence. It will look like we were willing victims, even though we were nothing of the sort. We cannot afford to look as though we willingly put ourselves in his power."

Clarence felt a flicker of respect. Jessica was brave. Braver than he'd realised. To say that, to *admit* that, in front of a crowd that would *not* understand...

"Point taken." Patricia looked and sounded as though she'd bitten into a lemon. "I withdraw my comments."

"Then we vote," Jackson said. "All those in favour of telling him to go fuck himself?"

"I'd tell him something a little politer that that," Claudia said, dryly.

Jackson counted the hands. "Seventeen in favour," he said. "Anyone against?"

"I second Claudia's objection," Clarence said. "We don't want to give him an excuse to go after us."

"We'll be polite," Jackson said. "But I think we have agreement not to take the offer."

Clarence allowed himself a moment of relief. "Things are going to get harder from here," he warned. "We caught them by surprise. No one expected us to actually look into the story, let alone make a difference. Next time...it will be a little harder. We have to bear that in mind."

"And we have to find the next story," Jackson said. He grinned. "Go get changed into something you can wear outside and go get me a story."

"Yes, sir," Clarence said. He'd had a couple of emails from former colleagues. It might be worth seeing what they had to say. "I shall see what I can find."

"And the rest of you, sober up," Jackson added. "We're playing with the big boys now."

And we may get knocked down, Clarence thought. *Goldwater alone could crush us, if he wanted. We have to remember that too.*

CHAPTER FIFTEEN

The lighter side of this was quite obvious. One young reporter filed a story about an Imperial Navy mobile planetoid (yes, you read that right) that could travel at a million times the speed of light, possessed weapons that could take out an entire star and was so huge that it could throw a whole planet into shadow. Needless to say, the 'top secret' planetoid did not exist. The Imperial Navy could not have hoped to build anything remotely as immense, even at the height of its power.
— **PROFESSOR LEO CAESIUS**
Crying Wolf: The Media and the Fall of the Empire

"IT'S GOOD TO SEE YOU AGAIN, CLARENCE," Johan Darling said, as Clarence took a seat in the crowded bar. "It's been a long time."

"You could have called me at any time," Clarence said, although he understood better than he cared to admit. The unemployed had no friends or family, for fear that unemployment might be catching. "I would have welcomed a call, you know."

Darling looked embarrassed. "I know. But you know…"

"Yeah," Clarence said. "I know."

"You've made quite a splash," Darling said, indicating the two mugs of beer. "Your story had one hell of an impact. I heard people discussing it at the water cooler until word came down from on high that we *weren't* to discuss it. Even here"—he glanced around, then put a scrambler on the table—"you never know who might be listening."

Clarence nodded. It was almost pathetically easy for the boss and his cronies to monitor conversations within the office. The staff had no right to privacy. Their contracts suggested that they could be watched at any moment, even when they were in the bathroom. It was something he'd tried not to think about when he'd been at the *Daily Truth*. Even now…he eyed the scrambler warily. He'd always had his doubts about the devices when they'd been issued. It was quite possible that they'd been tampered with to ensure that the boss could *still* hear every word they said.

And our sources take them for granted, Clarence thought. *They think that they're not being recorded. What if they're wrong?*

He shrugged. "What have they been saying?"

Darling smiled. "Some of the reporters have been admiring your balls," he offered, rather ruefully. "Others…others think it's just a matter of time before you get sued and spend the rest of your lives paying back a hopeless debt. They think you're doomed."

"I got the picture," Clarence said. So far, nothing *Seeing Eye* had done had been illegal, but that might not matter if they couldn't afford the legal fees. "What do *you* think?"

"I wish I was ten years younger, without a wife and three appetites to feed," Darling said. "I would join you in a shot."

"We all thought we were immortal when we were young," Clarence said. He took a swig of his beer. "We learned better as we grew older."

"Still, sexy university girls," Darling said. "Should your wife be worried?"

"My wife is none of your business," Clarence said, more sharply than he'd meant. "Why did you invite me for a drink?"

"I missed you?" Darling tried a smile. It didn't work. "I wanted to see you again?"

Clarence lifted an eyebrow, sardonically.

"I've been doing the economy column," Darling said. "And I've been given some pretty strict orders to basically take everything I'm hearing from the government economists as hard fact. The editors aren't even keen on me putting it in my own words. It's got pretty odd."

"Do tell," Clarence said.

"On the surface, everything is absolutely fine," Darling continued. "But, just below the surface, a lot of people are scared. The economy has been declining over the past twenty years or so, but…when people *really* realise that Earth is gone, the economy is going to go into free-fall. Lots of cash is simply going to vanish."

Clarence leaned forward. "How much?"

"I don't know," Darling said. "And…well, I've been discouraged from asking questions. I think the government has been trying to stabilise things, but there are simply too many valueless assets—and toxic assets—for them to have a hope in hell of actually succeeding. Do you know how much money our corporations have invested in Earth?"

"No," Clarence said. "Billions?"

"Try *trillions*," Darling said. "Everything from investment in Earth's orbital industries to outright loans to the Imperial Government. The government—our government—actually *encouraged* the loans for some reason. And all of that money has just evaporated. No one is going to be paying the interest, let alone repaying the original loan. What's going to happen when the truth finally gets out?"

Clarence frowned. "And you want us to tell the world?"

"I want to know the truth," Darling said. "You know what else? There's been a staggering rise in violent crime over the past two days. Robberies, murders…there was even a police car blown up when someone hurled a makeshift grenade through the window. And practically *none* of it has been reported. I don't even know *why*."

"Curious," Clarence agreed. It would be fairly simple to verify the economic problems, but harder to decide if the story *should* be told. Starting an economic panic would be grossly irresponsible. He tried to imagine what would happen if the entire system collapsed and fell flat. It was beyond his imagination. "If someone is concealing the crime rate...why?"

"I don't know," Darling said. "They *are* closing down a number of asteroid settlements, though, and bringing the populations down here. Maybe *that's* why they're suppressing any mention of the crime rates."

Clarence considered it. It had been generally agreed, on the estates, that migrants produced crime, although no one was entirely sure if it was because migrants were criminals or because their arrival provoked resistance. There were certainly plenty of estate-dwellers who resented having to share their territory with newcomers, particularly newcomers who were too different to be assimilated easily. He'd heard enough horror stories about the police backing the newcomers over the original residents to know that the story was rarely so cut and dried. And yet, actual *assaults* on the police were rare...

"I'll look into it," he promised, although he wasn't sure where to begin. The police wouldn't talk to him, probably. He'd known a couple of talkative policemen, but that had been when he'd been with the *Daily Truth*. They might not be so free with their opinions now. "Anything else?"

"I'll keep my ears open," Darling assured him. "But, you know, we're watched carefully."

"Quite," Clarence agreed. "Did you hear anything about the Forsakers?"

"The official government line is that they've gone to a better place," Darling said. "I felt quite envious when the spokesperson finished outlining all the advantages the Forsakers would have when they reached their new home. Unofficially, the government doesn't particularly care *what* happens to the Forsakers. I'll tell you *something*, though. Guess who owns the estate where they used to live?"

Clarence took a guess. "Maxima Corporation?"

"Precisely," Darling said. "And you know that the Forsakers were actually billeted quite close to *Hellebore* Estate?"

"...Oh," Clarence said. He could have kicked himself. Hellebore really *wasn't* that far from the spaceport, and where the Forsakers had been, even though there was no reason to think they were connected. "Are you saying that the Forsakers were evicted because *Maxima Corporation* wanted the land?"

"I'm not saying anything," Darling said. "You said it. But—you know—there's a disused industrial estate *between* the other two estates. And guess who owns *that*?"

"Maxima," Clarence said.

"Yep." Darling grinned, savagely. "Maxima just got control of three estates, pretty much for a song. Probably more, too. The estates are scattered like squares on a chessboard and I *think* Maxima could lay claim to more of them."

"Why?" Clarence finished his beer and put the mug on the table. "What does it profit them to secure the estates now?"

"I don't know," Darling said. "Right now, practically *every* long-term project—government or corporate—has been suspended. I don't think Maxima really has the resources to turn the three estates into anything more than a pile of rubble. Even if they did, who'd buy them?"

"There are people who would go hugely into debt to live in a gated and secure community," Clarence said, quietly. "What does the size of your bank account matter when the lives of your family are permanently at risk?"

"Yes, but are there enough people who can afford it?" Darling didn't sound convinced. "I want it, but I can't afford it. How many banks are going to loan *me* a million credits?"

"You're obviously a terrible investment risk," Clarence said, mock-seriously. It hadn't been *hard* to get a loan when *he'd* been working, although that had been almost ten years ago. He'd heard it was harder to get a loan now. "If they're not going to turn the estates into condos, though, what *are* they doing?"

"Good question," Darling said. He winked, then looked down at his tanned hands. "I have no idea. Let me know when you figure it out."

He stood. "I have to be back at the office before you-know-who comes back from lunch," he said. "Good luck."

"You too," Clarence said. He watched his friend—his former friend—pick up the scrambler and put it in his pocket. Darling was in for an unpleasant shock if they *had* been monitored by his superiors. The mere act of turning on a scrambler suggested that someone had something to hide. "I'll see you soon, I hope."

He stayed at the table long enough for Darling to leave the bar and hide himself within the crowds of workers heading back after lunch, thinking about what he'd been told. It *still* didn't make any sense. Maxima had nothing to gain by taking control of three estates, rather than just one; it certainly didn't have any *real* prospect of turning a profit. Unless...no, no matter how he ran the figures, it simply didn't make sense. Not as a corporate project, not as a government makework project...not as *anything*. And that meant the corporation had to be up to *something*.

I'll find out, he thought. Simon Goldwater had gone to a lot of trouble to suborn *Seeing Eye* and its reporters. That suggested there was *something* rotten in Maxima Corporation, something they were so desperate to conceal that they'd folded without a fight. *And when I find out, I'll know what to do with it.*

He stood, feeling an odd twinge of nostalgia as he walked out of the bar. It had once been a favoured meeting place for reporters, who would drink beer and swap lies about their profession and—sometimes—share stories none of their superiors would touch. He'd wondered if he would be welcome when he'd walked in, but no one had said a word. Maybe they thought he was still one of them. He was certainly still a reporter. It struck him, suddenly, that they might even *envy* him. *Seeing Eye* had given him a genuine scoop. It was what he'd wanted as a cub reporter, before the reality had dawned on him.

The streets felt colder, somehow, as he walked through the shopping mall and down towards the campus. It was hard to be sure, but there looked to be fewer luxury goods on the shelves even though the window displays were full to bursting. The handful of staff he saw looked revoltingly cheerful, as if they were putting on an act. It was easy to believe that their superiors had ordered them to *smile, smile, smile*, even if they were deeply worried about their futures. The junior staff, the ones who actually interacted with customers, were disposable. Clarence had no doubt that they'd be the first to be fired if the company fell on hard times.

And it probably won't make much of a difference, Clarence thought. A high-class outlet might pay good wages, but the combined wages of everyone in the store wouldn't come to *that* much. *What happens when the entire company collapses into chaos?*

He considered it thoughtfully as he passed a pair of grim-looking policemen. Tarsus could feed itself—by law, all planets had to be capable of feeding themselves—and it *did* have a sizable industrial base, but there were limits. How much did the planet actually *import*? It was easy to believe that imports were restricted to luxury goods—there were import tariffs on just about everything—yet…was that actually true? He found himself wondering, for the first time, what *else* the planet imported? What did Tarsus import because it was cheaper to import something than manufacture it on the planet itself?

And what might we lack, when interstellar shipping falls apart, that will bite us on the behind? It wasn't a pleasant thought. *No one will die because they can't purchase a million-credit handbag, but what about medicines? Or fusion cores? Or starship components?*

He passed through the security gates and onto the university campus, still lost in his thoughts. Someone was shouting in the distance—no, hundreds of people were *chanting* in the distance—but he paid it no heed until he realised that the chanting was coming from the frat house. He tensed as he snapped back to himself, suddenly very aware that some students were hurrying past him and heading in the opposite direction. *Something* was happening, but what? He forced himself to slow down, painting a casual look on his face as he rounded the corner. It might be wise not to draw attention to himself until he knew what was actually going on.

A small crowd of students—thirty or forty, he estimated—were standing in front of the frat house, making a protest. They were keeping their distance, not blocking any of the routes in and out of the frat house, but… it would have looked laughable, Clarence thought, if it hadn't sounded so *threatening.* The students were protesting *Seeing Eye*, demanding that the newspaper shut down at once. Clarence shook his head in disbelief as he glanced at his watch. Simon Goldwater clearly didn't believe in letting the grass grow under his feet. It had taken him only a couple of hours to organise a protest movement and point it at its target.

Unless the movement popped up spontaneously, Clarence thought. It was possible, but unlikely. Things just didn't *happen* that quickly unless someone was using money and power to *make* it happen. Besides, the protest would have had to be cleared with the university authorities. *That* wouldn't have happened so quickly unless someone had called in a favour or two. *Better to assume the worst than hope for the best.*

He ignored the deafening chant—the protesters seemed to assume that Hellebore Estate was now *worse* off than it had been a day or two ago—as he walked past the angry faces and strode into the frat house. The noise level dropped rapidly the moment he closed the door, although he could still hear the racket pounding through the walls. Whoever had designed the frat house simply hadn't made it soundproof. They probably hadn't expected angry protesters at the doors.

Jackson was standing by the window when Clarence walked into the common room, looking disturbed. "They just came out of nowhere."

"Someone splashed out a great deal of money to make the protest happen," Clarence corrected. "They're trying to intimidate you."

"Goldwater?" Jackson didn't look away from the window. "Or someone else?"

"Perhaps," Clarence said. He didn't *know* it was Goldwater, but there weren't many possible suspects. "What do they think we've done?"

Jackson turned to face him. "They're arguing that we have made life worse for the people on the estate because we made sure they got compensation," he said. "These people, being poor, cannot *possibly* be prepared for a sudden windfall and will get into trouble when they try to spend it. Apparently, this is all our fault."

"If they managed to say that with a straight face, colour me impressed," Clarence said. He'd heard plenty of insane troll logic in his career—his editors had been particularly good at it—but that took the cake. "Do they really *believe* it?"

"It's arguable," Jackson said. "Every single person who got compensation will have to pay taxes on it—and the compensation alone will kick them into a higher tax bracket. Some of them may not even have *been* in a tax bracket before and they…"

Clarence shook his head. "Some of them will know it," he said. It was something they probably had to address in a future story. "Others will… others will learn. Just because they're poor doesn't mean they're stupid. Believe me, they'll *hate* you if you start implying they're stupid."

"But what if they're right?" Jackson asked. "Did we do the wrong thing?"

"No," Clarence said. He swallowed the response that came to mind. This was no time to pick a fight with his boss, even if he—like most rich kids—was unable to imagine life without wealthy and powerful parents. "If you hadn't run the story, Maxima wouldn't have paid the compensation and those people would have been far worse off. You've given them a *chance*, at least. Some of them will screw it up, yes. The others are far better off because of you."

He jabbed a finger at the window. "And those protesters need to know it," he said. "I could put it into words for you."

"I want it by the end of the day," Jackson said. He tapped his palm, meaningfully. "We'll run it tonight."

Clarence grinned. "Sure thing, chief!"

CHAPTER SIXTEEN

You would think, of course, that such a story would raise eyebrows—and convince the editors and publishers to take a more careful look before approving the story for publication. Instead, the story was actually published. It was not until the Imperial Navy itself questioned the story that the media executives realised that they'd been conned.
—PROFESSOR LEO CAESIUS
Crying Wolf: The Media and the Fall of the Empire

IT WAS NOT EASY TO BE A POLICEMAN.

It had never been *easy*, Senior Constable Peter Quigley told himself, but it had grown harder in the weeks and months since the Fall of Earth. Policemen had been booed in the streets, or attacked in the streets, or even... convinced...to leave some parts of the city strictly alone. No one *feared* the strong arm of the law any longer, not even the chattering sheep that made up most of the city's population. They preferred to whine and moan about the police rather than obey the law and stay out of trouble.

He kept a wary eye on the streets as he drove the police car towards the scene of the crime, silently cursing the dispatcher under his breath. Procedure stated that policemen should operate in pairs, but the department was so desperate to have as many cars on the streets as possible that

Peter and dozens of others had been sent out alone. It was one hell of a risk, Peter thought, even in a middle-class part of the city. Who knew *what* would happen if the sheep scented weakness. Peter had considered resigning more than once, as the job got harder and the rewards fewer, but where else could he go? Ex-policemen weren't welcome in the job market. He'd heard of a few who'd left the force, only to be unable to find a job elsewhere and come crawling back. It was discrimination, plain and simple.

"Turning into Rally Street now," he said, keying his intercom. In theory, an emergency team was on standby to respond to any *real* trouble. In practice, the team might already have been called out to an emergency on the other side of the city. There just weren't enough cops to police the streets. He'd heard rumours that the Civil Guard was going to be called up to patrol the streets. "No sign of any trouble yet."

He rolled his eyes as he glided down the line of cookie-cutter houses and mid-sized apartment blocks. No one was in sight, but that meant nothing. The kids would be in school—or playing truant somewhere else—while the adults would be at their jobs. And yet...*someone* had made a whiny little call to the police station, claiming that a *prostitute* was working the streets. Peter snorted in disgust. It was probably some ancient crone offended that a young and prettier woman was walking around. Or some wife, scared her husband would be tempted. It wasn't as if the poor bastard couldn't find an excuse to go to the red light district, or the row of bars and brothels near the spaceport. The whole affair was a waste of police time.

But at least it's safer than dealing with armed robbers, he reminded himself. He knew two policemen who were in hospital, after catching a gang of thieves in the act, and a third who was in the morgue. *They can't say I'm not doing my duty.*

A movement caught his eye as he passed one of the larger apartment blocks. He peered into the darkened alleyway and smiled, coldly, as he spotted a young woman...*servicing*...a young man. The call hadn't been a hoax after all. He called it in, then clambered out of the car, making no attempt to hide his presence. There was nothing to be gained by putting the prostitute's client in jail. The people who lived on Rally Street were rich enough to afford decent lawyers. Peter had no doubt the john would go free and *he'd* be reprimanded for wasting his time. He heard the sound of running feet as he strode into the alleyway. The john was already on the run. Peter hoped he'd thought to pull up his pants first.

And the pimp is probably running too, Peter thought, as he saw the prostitute cowering against the wall. It was rare for pimps to be arrested, but a smart pimp wouldn't take the chance. *He'll wait and see what happens to the girl.*

He studied the prostitute for a long moment. She was in her early twenties, although it was hard to be sure. Her face already bore the marks of a harsh life on the streets and constant abuse. The ragged outfit she wore would have marked her out as a prostitute even if it hadn't been pulled down, exposing her breasts. Her bright red hair was clearly dyed. Peter felt a flicker of disgust. He had no idea if she was unable to find a job or if she'd simply been sold into prostitution, but it didn't matter. She had no hope of a normal life. Not now.

"I can arrest you right now," he said, sternly. The girl flinched. She wouldn't last a week in gen-pop. "Or…"

He started to unbuckle his pants. The girl lowered her eyes in silent submission, then knelt in front of him and reached for his member. Peter was already hard. Free fucks from prostitutes was one of the benefits of being a policeman. He'd tell the dispatcher that the prostitute had fled when he'd arrived. Everyone would know the truth, but no one would really give a damn. It was the police force against the world. And besides, there was nothing to be gained by arresting the woman anyway. There were always more prostitutes on the streets.

The girl took him in her mouth, then froze as Peter's wristcom bleeped an alert. Peter swore out loud, then tapped his lips as he checked the sender. Sergeant Grozny, damn it. Most sergeants were all right, but Grozny thought he was supervisor material, the fool. He'd give Peter a chewing out—or worse—if he thought for one moment that Peter was getting his knob serviced and ignoring him. And Peter didn't need the hassle. Grozny would have no hesitation in sending him to the other side of the river if the sergeant thought he was being disrespected.

"Riot on Cavendish Street," Grozny's thick voice said. "Report there at once."

Peter snorted in disbelief. Cavendish Street wasn't *that* far from Rally Street, but…there *had* to be someone closer. And who the hell was rioting there anyway? It was an upper-middle-class district, not some housing estate on the other side of the river. The people who went there hired lawyers to do their rioting for them. But there was no point in wondering about it, not now. Grozny would make his life hell if he wasn't on Cavendish Street in five minutes or less.

"Yes, Sergeant," he said.

His member was already going limp. He pulled out of the girl's mouth and buttoned up his pants, then—in a moment of unaccustomed pity—slipped her a ten-credit note before turning and hurrying back to the police car. She wasn't going to have an easy time of it either, when her pimp caught up with her. The bastard would be demanding to know if she'd satisfied her unwanted customer or if he'd have to be shelling out bribes to stay on the streets. She'd probably have to give up the money to avoid another beating. But there was no time to worry about that either.

He slipped behind the wheel, turned on the siren and picked his way rapidly towards Cavendish Street. There were more people on the streets, mainly upper-class women who could afford to stay at home—and go shopping—while their husbands were at work. But there was no sign of an actual emergency. People either fled riots or ran towards them, hoping to join the crowd, yet…there was no hint of anyone doing either. The shopkeepers weren't pulling down the shutters…it was as if they saw no reason to panic.

"Turning into Cavendish Street now," he said. There was still no visible call for alarm. Had Grozny been fucking with him? It was hard to believe. The man was so straight-edged, without any eye for the main chance, that his subordinates joked they could use him as a ruler. "I…"

A small crowd—an angry crowd—had gathered outside Aisyah's, a prominent fashion store that imported much of its stock from Earth. Peter had had a girlfriend once who'd dreamed of an expensive handbag from Aisyah's, even though there was no visible difference between imported handbags and locally-produced handbags. It had struck him as thoroughly silly, if only because there was no way she could have afforded it on a nurse's salary. She would have had to work for decades, saving every last penny, to buy the cheapest thing in the store.

He put the thought out of his mind. A riot consisting of teenage girls... all probably just a year or two too old to be in school. Students, then. It wasn't really a riot, either. No windows had been smashed, no cars had been set on fire...someone had probably made a panicky call to the station and demanded action. No wonder only one policeman had been dispatched to deal with it.

A handful of girls scattered, running down the street, as he parked the car beside the store and climbed out. They'd probably be scared for hours, if not days; they'd probably assume the entire police force had nothing better to do than track them down and arrest them for...something. It was absurd. The police were so overstretched that Peter, at least, would count it as a victory if the entire crowd ran for its life. There was nothing to be gained by chasing them down.

He walked towards them steadily, his eyes sweeping the crowd. A middle-aged man was standing in front of the shore, sweat beading on his face. The manager, Peter guessed. He'd probably made the mistake of showing weakness in front of the crowd. A mob was only half as smart as the stupidest person in it and teenage students weren't renowned for their intelligence. If they were smart, they wouldn't be students taking useless degrees. Another girl, probably a year or two older than the others, was standing against the wall. She looked to be part of the mob, yet there was something about her pose that suggested she considered herself apart from it. The whole affair seemed to bore her. Peter felt a hot flash of anger as she met his eyes languidly. He'd bet good money that she'd helped to start the whole affair.

She smiled at him, faintly. Peter glared back at her. She was tall, with long brown hair, wearing tight clothes that showed off her curves. She was the sort of girl who'd never looked twice at him in school, the sort of girl who never faced any consequences for her words or deeds because her father was always there with his chequebook. He hated her on sight.

"He's here," one of the girls said. "You have to let us in!"

Peter blinked. What?

"There's nothing left," the manager protested. He was pressing so hard against the storefront that Peter thought he was going to break the glass and fall backwards into the store. "We don't have anything left!"

"Let us in," another girl shouted. The mob was rediscovering its courage. "Let us in!"

The manager shot Peter a pleading look. Peter cursed him—and everyone else—under his breath. He'd be the laughing stock of the entire police force if he called for reinforcements to handle a bunch of teenage girls...and *that* was assuming that reinforcements were on hand to be sent. Cavendish Street was normally crime-free. The police force rarely bothered to have more than a handful of policemen deployed to the district when they were desperately needed elsewhere. By the time reinforcements arrived, matters could have *really* got out of hand.

"They have money," the brown-haired girl said. Her voice was low, but intense. It cut through the babble like a knife through butter. "Why won't you let them in?"

Peter acted on instinct. He moved forward, caught the wretched girl's arm and yanked her forward. She let out a little sound of shock as she found herself bent over the car, her hands pulled behind her back and cuffed. Peter held her firmly in place as he turned to look at the other girls. They were backing away hastily, their eyes wide with sudden fear. Clearly, no one had ever stood up to them before. Peter allowed himself a smile, feeling—for the first time—that he was finally in control of the situation.

"If you're still here by the time I finish processing this silly girl, you'll be arrested too," he warned. "Go."

He turned away, deliberately exposing his back as he searched his captive. She wasn't carrying anything, apart from a terminal and an old-style pencil that had seen better days. Peter allowed his hands to linger on her bottom as he checked her rear pockets, silently admiring its firmness before he moved on to check that she wasn't hiding anything under her breasts. The girl tensed under his touch, but said nothing. She'd already realised that he could do *anything* to her. The thrill ran through him. It was suddenly hard to remember that they were in public.

"Up," he grunted. He pulled her upright, then opened the rear door and shoved her into the car, taking care to bang her head against the frame. "Stay there."

He closed the door and turned to the crowd. It was gone. A pair of girls were at the far end of the street—they ran further as soon as he met their eyes—but otherwise the street was completely empty. Even the manager had fled inside his store. Peter snickered, then walked around the car and climbed into the driver's seat. The girl was whimpering quietly in the back. It was pathetic. She'd probably never met a *real* man before.

"You're on your way to jail," he informed her, as the car hummed into motion. "Unless, of course, you'd like to make a deal."

He smiled at the thought. It was astonishing what some people would do to stay out of jail, even if—rationally—they wouldn't be staying long enough for tea. He had fond memories of his days as a private security guard, where shoplifters would do *anything* to be allowed to go free. One upper-class girl had been so terrified of her parents finding out that she'd been arrested that she'd...his smile grew wider at the thought. The silly bitch had never realised that her parents could get her out of trouble with a single word in the right ear.

It's good to be a cop, he thought.

The girl said nothing, even when he made the invitation a little more explicit. Peter was tempted to pull over and give her a final chance, but he knew better. He was already running late. He kept up a cheerful commentary on everything the girl could expect once she was in jail as he steered the car through the security gates and parked outside the holding centre. A pair of female correction officers were already waiting outside. Peter was almost sorry for the girl, even if she *had* managed to get under his skin. He'd heard *plenty* of horror stories about female correction officers. She would probably have been better off with the men.

He handed the girl over to then, signed the paperwork and took the car back onto the streets. His shift was almost over, thankfully. He'd have to do more paperwork when he returned to the station, but...he could probably spin the whole story into a masterful tale of how a brave policeman, completely alone, stopped a riot in its tracks. It would be a masterpiece. Sergeant Grozny would not be amused, let alone convinced, but it was just possible that his superiors would think otherwise. Grozny was just too street-smart to be a good officer.

The man himself summoned Peter as soon as he entered the station, his face grim. Peter followed him into his office, wondering what had happened. Even *Grozny* knew to let an officer who'd just come off-shift have a cup of coffee or two before discussing something—anything—that had happened during the patrol. But Grozny's face was too hard for Peter to risk objecting. Clearly, *something* had happened. But what?

Grozny slammed the door closed and turned to face him. "Do you have any idea what you've done?"

Peter blinked. He'd failed to catch the john, and the pimp, but no one gave a damn about them. He'd stopped a riot...who would complain about him stopping a riot? But...

"You arrested a girl," Grozny said, sharply. "Did you have any idea who she was? Or *what* she was?"

"...No." Peter felt ice trickle down his veins. Had he made a terrible mistake? Anyone with *real* connections would have said so the moment he'd grabbed her, wouldn't she? "I..."

"You arrested her," Grozny said. "You *groped* her and then you made indecent offers to her and…"

"Sergeant," Peter protested. Groping suspects was one of the perks of the job. Everyone did it. Even *Grozny* did it. "I…"

"*Be quiet*," Grozny snapped. "That girl, the one you mistreated, was a reporter."

"Bullshit," Peter said, without thinking. Reporters *always* identified themselves. They waved their press cards as soon as there was the slightest hint they might be in trouble. The bastards thought they were little tin gods. "Sergeant…"

"For *Seeing Eye*." Grozny cut him off. "You may have heard of them, eh? The ones who broke the story about Hellebore Estate? That girl was wearing a recorder. Everything, and I mean everything, has already gone live. It's fucking *trending*!"

Peter felt his legs buckle. "It was barely an hour ago and…"

"It doesn't fucking matter," Grozny thundered. "Oh, and lest I forget, that girl comes from a wealthy family. Your name isn't out there yet, but it will be. You are in deep shit!"

"Fuck," Peter said. He was going to be thrown to the dogs. He knew it. "Sergeant, I…"

"Shut up," Grozny said. "You are suspended. I don't want to see you anywhere near this station until the word comes down from on high. There'll be a fucking public inquiry about this, I just know it. Go home and stay home and if you want to eat a bullet, feel free!"

Peter turned and stumbled out of the station, too shocked to be angry. He hadn't done anything wrong. He hadn't done anything that everyone else hadn't done. But he was fucked. He was really—really—fucked. He'd be lucky if he wasn't deported to some godforsaken planetoid by the end of the day. Or maybe that would be too kind. He'd probably be skinned alive to appease the girl's family.

A man met him as he wandered down the street. "Peter Quigley?"

"Who gives a fuck?" Peter asked. It struck him, an instant too late, that he'd been foolish to leave the station in his uniform. "And why?"

"I heard about what happened," the man said. "Would you like a job?"

Peter laughed. "Are you kidding me?"

"No," the man said. He passed Peter a card. "If you want to do something useful, be at this address tonight. If not, good luck with the inquiry."

"Thanks," Peter said, sourly. He already knew the outcome. Everyone knew what the inquiry was going to decide, before it had even begun. "I'll think about it."

But he already knew, deep inside, that he was going to go.

CHAPTER SEVENTEEN

Further investigation revealed that the young reporter had been told a tale by a handful of Imperial Navy crewmen and simply lacked the experience to realise that he was being bullshitted. He might have been embedded with the navy, but he had done nothing to make himself popular amongst the naval officers and crew. It isn't clear if they meant to embarrass him—the navy's own investigation suggested that they thought the reporter wasn't that gullible—yet it didn't matter. The reporter's career was at an end.
—Professor Leo Caesius
Crying Wolf: The Media and the Fall of the Empire

"THAT," CLARENCE SAID, "WAS ONE HELL OF A RISK."

He told himself, firmly, not to stand too close to Jennifer Turner—let alone loom over her—as he spoke. Jennifer *looked* as calm and unharmed as one could have wished, but her hands—clasped in her lap—were shaking slightly. Red marks were clearly visible on her wrists, where she'd been cuffed. She hadn't been raped, and the correction officers had been very polite as soon as they realised who she was, but it hardly mattered. The idea of deliberately letting herself be arrested had probably sounded better before it had actually been put into practice.

"Yeah." Jennifer sounded shaken, even though she was clearly pleased with herself. "But I got the story, didn't I?"

Clarence wondered, sourly, if Jackson had signed off on the plan before Jennifer had put it into action. There were so many ways it could have gone wrong. Jennifer probably didn't realise it, not completely, but she'd run into a comparatively *kind* policeman. Clarence had heard plenty of horror stories—from his days on the estate—that had ensured he always viewed the police with a jaundiced eye. Jennifer, on the other hand, was probably used to regarding the police as friends and allies. She'd thought she was safe until it was too late.

And a damn good thing the prison wardens believed her when she told them her name, Clarence thought. They hadn't had a chance to put Jennifer through the usual ordeal reserved for anyone unfortunate enough to be entering prison. *They're the only ones who come out of this with a shred of credit.*

"It worked," Jackson said. "And we have one hell of a story."

Clarence wondered, sourly, if he should be grateful that no one had consulted him before the story had gone live. He wasn't sure what he would have said. No newspaper had ever drawn attention to the topic of police brutality before, even though everyone knew it was a serious problem. Clarence had heard horror stories during his time as a mainstream journalist too, stories where journalists had been abused—and sometimes jailed—just for being in the wrong place at the wrong time. Jackson might have struck a blow for police transparency, but he'd also made a whole bunch of dangerous enemies. The police wouldn't take it lightly.

Of course not, he told himself. *What are they going to do? They can hardly punish one officer for doing something every other officer does without risking a mutiny in the ranks.*

He glanced at his terminal. Frank Wong had excelled himself. The story was more than just *trending*, it had actually *already* leaked into the mainstream media. It probably helped, the cynic in him noted, that Jennifer was young, beautiful and had rich parents. The media outlet currently commenting on *beauty and the beast* had never had anything to say about estate-dwellers who'd been taken into the back of police cars and raped… he shook his head in irritation. It was possible that the story would provoke real change. But it was also possible that it would do nothing more than make new enemies.

"There are students already protesting police brutality," Elle said. "And their parents are becoming involved. They'll be taking protest marches onto the streets within the day."

Clarence rather doubted it. Protest marches generally took longer to organise. And they wouldn't get moving at all if the police denied the marchers a permit. The optics would be terrible—the police denying the marchers the right to protest police brutality—but they wouldn't give a damn. He wondered, absently, if the *parents* would give a damn. They were amongst the richest people on the planet. The police would have to be absolutely insane to push them around.

But will they do anything for the people who have been victimised all along? Clarence doubted that too. *They only cared when one of their own children was swept up in a police raid.*

He studied the latest set of reports thoughtfully. So far, the police department had confirmed that the officer in question—carefully unnamed by the story—had been suspended pending an enquiry, but nothing else. Clarence had a feeling that the officer in question would be *encouraged* to quietly accept deportation, if he simply didn't wind up being helped to commit suicide. The police couldn't afford a public trial. Who knew what else might come out if the officer sang like a bird? He was hardly the only guilty soul. Clarence knew, all too well, that abusing prisoners was the least of it.

But we should see how the story settles before we write more, he thought, as Elle helped Jennifer out of the room. The younger girl was smiling now, although she still looked a little shaken. *We don't want to make them even madder.*

Jackson caught Clarence's eye once they were alone. "What a scoop!"

"Perhaps," Clarence said. "Did you *order* her to take the risk?"

"No," Jackson said. "She thought she'd be doing a story on the handbag shortage."

Clarence—barely—resisted the temptation to roll his eyes. *Seeing Eye's* readership, it seemed, spanned all classes, from the very lowest estate-dwellers to the richest aristocrats on the orbiting halo. It was hard to imagine that *all* of them would be interested in a handbag shortage, even though it said worrying things about the interstellar economy. He rather suspected that some of their lower-class readers would give up in disgust. And yet... it had worked out in their favour. For the first time, a serious problem had been dragged into the light.

He met Jackson's eyes, willing him to believe. "Jennifer took an *awful* risk," he said, very clearly. "If they hadn't believed her when she'd given them her name...Jack, she could have been raped—or worse. She could have been sent directly to a transport and deported before anyone knew what had happened to her. And if they'd realised she was recording and transmitting everything...Jack, this could have gone badly wrong."

Jack paled. "It wouldn't have been that bad..."

"Yes, it would," Clarence said. He picked his next words carefully. "Jack...when you grew up, you were safe. You lived in a gated community. Your guards protected you. The uniformed police officers were kind and friendly. You were protected by an invisible aura of wealth and power that hung over you and your parents like a shroud. I bet none of the teachers ever hit you when you went to school."

"That's illegal," Jack protested.

"Tell that to *my* teachers," Clarence said. "I got smacked a few times when I was a kid."

"Write it up," Jackson said. "Turn it into a story."

Clarence shook his head. "You don't understand," he said. "The vast majority of people *don't* live in gated communities. They have *no* protection. They get hit by their teachers because no one gives a damn about them. Hell, by the time those kids become teenagers, they're hitting the teachers and no one gives a damn about *them* either. There are no private security guards.

The police, who are meant to keep people safe, are just another bunch of predators. A girl like Jennifer, someone who grew up on the other side of the river, would be taking her life in her hands if she climbed into a police car."

"But…" Jackson didn't understand. "They let her go."

"Yes, *after* they knew who she was," Clarence said. "How would anyone know that you were Jack, Son of Jack, if you didn't tell them? And why would they believe you if you didn't carry ID?"

He nodded towards the wallscreen, which was replaying the footage time and time again. "If things had gone differently, you'd be mourning her. This is a dangerous game. All of that"—he jabbed a finger at the screen—"is not a patch on what *could* have happened. This could have gone very badly wrong."

Jackson looked as if Clarence had hit him with a baseball bat. Clarence understood, although he was in no mood to be particularly forgiving. Jackson could no more empathise with someone from the other side of the river than he could imagine what it was like to…to be a responsible adult. It wasn't entirely fair, Clarence conceded, but he was in no mood to be fair either. Jackson and his friends were children playing an adult game, challenging the powers-that-be without any regard for the consequences. It was high time they grew up.

And that's how newspapers start letting stories slip through their fingers, he reminded himself, sourly. *Once they start worrying about offending people, or provoking an angry response, they start forgetting their obligation to the truth.*

"I don't know what to say," Jackson said. "What would *your* former editor have said if you'd wound up dead?"

Alas, poor…whatever his name was again, Clarence thought. *I knew him.*

"I knew the risks, when I took the job," Clarence said. Press pass or no press pass, he'd been beaten bloody more than a few times when he'd gone looking for stories. Too many people saw the media as the enemy, from the police to the poorest estate-dwellers. "I don't think Jennifer *really* knew them."

"I'll discuss it with her, afterwards," Jackson said. "Maybe arrange for her to have some counselling…"

"Do you think," Clarence demanded, "that the people on the other side of the river have any counselling?"

"No." Jackson stood straighter, showing a hint of backbone. "But that doesn't mean I shouldn't offer it to Jennifer."

"I suppose not," Clarence said. He had no faith in the *value* of counselling—the counselling sessions he'd been offered at the *Daily Truth* had been composed of pop-psychology, with a side helping of suspicion that the counsellors were reporting back to the bosses—but Jennifer's parents could probably afford the best. "Be careful what you say."

"Of course," Jackson said.

"And if you want a word of advice," Clarence added, "tell everyone else that, if they're going to do a demented stunt like that, they're to make sure they warn you first."

"Definitely," Jackson agreed.

Clarence grinned. "I've got something I want to check out," he said. "I'll see you later?"

"I'll probably need you to write a follow-up story," Jackson said. "Come see me when you get out."

"Yes, sir," Clarence said.

Patricia was standing outside the office when he walked out. "Do you have a moment to chat?"

"I've got somewhere to go." Clarence hesitated, then grinned. "Do you want to come with me? I'm checking out a hunch."

"Your hunches are always good," Patricia said. She slipped her arm through his as they walked down the stairs and out onto the grounds. There was no sign of any protesters outside the frat house. "Where are we going?"

Clarence called a hovercab. "Back to Hellebore," he said. "I have something I want to check out."

They climbed into the hovercab as soon as it arrived and gave directions to the driver, who frowned. "I can't take you all the way to Hellebore, mate," he said. "ATC declared a no-fly zone over it."

"That's awkward," Clarence said, thoughtfully. The estate *might* have been declared a no-land zone, particularly if it was being demolished, but a no-*fly* zone? That was more than just *awkward*. It was quite possible that ATC had barred aircraft and shuttles from flying over the estate too. "How close can you get us?"

"I can put you down in Remington Estate," the driver said. "That's quite close to Hellebore."

"That'll do," Clarence said. "We should be fine."

He leaned back into his seat as the hovercab took off, tapping his lips for quiet when Patricia started to speak. It was all too easy to forget that the driver had ears too—and that conversations could become public quite easily. His lips quirked into a faint smile. The copper who'd arrested and groped Jennifer had clearly forgotten that too. But then, what did he have to worry about recordings when his superiors would cover everything up?

I'd better start looking up the legalities of the situation, he thought, as the hovercab crossed the river. A faint plume of smoke was rising up in the distance, suggesting a fire within one of the poorer estates. *We might face all sorts of challenges in the next few weeks.*

He made a mental note to suggest that Jackson hired a decent—and well-connected—lawyer, then leaned forward as the hovercab banked right and dropped into Remington Estate. It was slightly richer than Hellebore, if he recalled correctly, although most of the inhabitants were still poor. A handful of shops, a couple of diners…there was slightly more variety in Remington Estate, but the apartment blocks were still made of featureless grey stone. He shivered, despite himself, as the hovercab landed. A small group of dark-skinned teenage girls watched them from the other side of the road.

Patricia nudged him. "Did you grow up here?"

"No," Clarence said. He paid the driver, then looked around to get his bearings. "This way."

Remington Estate had probably not been *designed* as an estate, he decided as they walked down the street. There was no clear line of demarcation between the estate and the outside world, no fence that kept the population in almost as much as it kept the riffraff outside. The city maps might show estates lined up like squares on a chessboard, but Remington Estate seemed almost...*free*. Hellebore, on the other hand, was fenced. There was a metal barricade in place, blocking access. A large sign warned that TRESPASSERS WOULD BE PROSTITUTED.

"That might not be a simple spelling error," Clarence commented. "They might mean it."

Patricia snorted. "You think?"

"You never know," Clarence said. He'd received plenty of official government documents that had been filled with spelling mistakes, but God help anyone who made even a *minor* typo on the forms they had to send to the government. The double standard had always enraged him. They could make mistakes, and get away with it, while the slightest mistake on *his* part was seen as *prima facie* proof of criminal activity. "But it would probably be a good idea not to get caught."

He peered through the fence, thoughtfully. Maxima Corporation had set a deadline for evacuation, a deadline that had come and gone, yet...the estate was still intact. No demolition crews moved from building to building, no monster trucks waited to cart away the rubble...the estate was as dark and silent as the grave. No lights shone in the windows, no people were visible in the streets...he felt a chill run down his spine as they walked slowly along the fence. Every entrance to the estate—to *all* of the estates the corporation had claimed—were solidly blocked.

A shuttlecraft flew overhead, heading towards the spaceport. Clarence watched it go, thinking hard. The ATC's no-fly rule didn't apply to shuttles, then. He would have been surprised if it did, but...even just blocking aircars and hovercabs from flying over the estate would be quite awkward. *Someone* would ask questions. The taxicab unions would protest...he wondered, absently, if there was a story in it somewhere. Why would someone block the quickest route to the spaceport?

They wouldn't, he thought. *Unless there was something going on, inside the estate, that they don't want people to see.*

Clarence peered through the fence again. There was nothing inside, just a handful of empty apartments and warehouses. He shook his head in disbelief. Hundreds of thousands of homeless people on the streets and… and all of this living space was just closed off? He couldn't believe the corporation was *really* going to turn the land into condos. They would have started demolition work by now, just to make sure that squatters didn't have a chance to move into the buildings.

"Those girls are following us," Patricia said. "Should we be worried?"

"Probably," Clarence said. He glanced back. The girls were shadowing them. "I'll call a cab."

He tensed, wishing he had a weapon. Or *something*. He knew from bitter experience that a teenage girl could be just as dangerous as a teenage boy, if she'd been born and bred on the estates. And there were at least seven girls following them. Thieves? Gangbangers? Or simply people who wanted to drive strangers out of their estate? There was no way to know.

"They won't hurt us, will they?" Patricia sounded plaintive. Her breath came in fits and starts. "Clarence?"

"Walk faster," Clarence said, sharply. This was no time to be politically-correct. "If they want to hurt us, they'll hurt us."

The hovercab landed. He opened the door, helped Patricia to clamber inside and followed her. The girls made rude gestures as the hovercab took off, heading back to safety. Clarence let out a breath he hadn't realised he was holding. They might have been in very real danger.

And we might have been overreacting, he thought. It was possible. Of *course* it was possible. *But at least we didn't have to find out the hard way.*

CHAPTER EIGHTEEN

The darker side, however, was far more dangerous. It was unfortunately true that the desperate attempts to maintain some semblance of order, during the waning years, produced a high rate of collateral damage. Uprisings against the Empire came at a high cost, both when the rebels rose up and when they were brutally put down. It cannot be denied that many counter-insurgency deployments resulted in hundreds of thousands of dead civilians.
—**Professor Leo Caesius**
Crying Wolf: The Media and the Fall of the Empire

"HEY, CLARENCE," CLAUDIA SAID. "YOU GOT A MINUTE?"

Clarence shrugged. He'd been spending the last four days researching the legalities of recording the police—and a number of other charges he suspected would be hurled at *Seeing Eye*—and covering the protest marches against police brutality that had brought the city to a halt. Jennifer's parents had done a remarkable job. Tarsus hadn't been so united since the planet had been cheated out of the Allston Sector Capital title by New Samos, something that still rankled hundreds of years later. Clarence doubted it would last—the poor would be put back in their place as soon as the rich lost interest—but he'd take what he could get. It would be harder for *anyone* to do anything about *Seeing Eye* while the streets were boiling.

Unless they decide to charge us with provoking a riot, he thought. The protests had been largely peaceful, but he'd heard reports that a handful of policemen had been attacked on the streets. *They might try to blame us for that as well as everything else.*

"Jackson wants to see you," Claudia said. "Coming?"

"Yeah," Clarence said. "I'm on my way."

The frat house *seemed* busier, now that *Seeing Eye* was growing into a real business. Jackson had hired several more experienced reporters, along with a number of inexperienced but keen students. Clarence wasn't sure how he felt about that, although he had to admit that the newspaper had to keep expanding until it reached critical mass or shrink back into insignificance. He'd read a handful of reports that suggested that most small businesses collapsed within the year, unless they sold their souls to the bigger corporations. He could believe it.

Jackson was waiting in his office. "We just got word," he said, without preamble. "The First Speaker is on his way."

Clarence blinked. "The *First Speaker*?"

"He's going to be addressing a gathering of students in response to the latest incident," Jackson said. "You're going to be listening to the speech."

"Yes, sir." Clarence was still astonished that the First Speaker was coming at all. The planetary leader had better things to do with his time, surely. But the protest movement was already getting out of hand. "Do we not have a press pass?"

Jackson looked as if he had bitten into a lemon. "Our permit to send reporters to the speech has been *unaccountably* delayed," he said. "They have no right to deny us a pass, but…"

"I understand," Clarence said. He looked down at his causal shirt and trousers. "Do you think I can pass for a student?"

"You're a little *too* well-dressed to pass for a student," Claudia said, wryly.

"You'll be fine, as long as you look like a mature student," Jackson said. He held out a terminal. The details of the speech were clearly visible. "And you're *already* inside the perimeter. If they say you can't watch the speech, just come straight back here."

"Yes, sir," Clarence said.

"Watch yourself," Claudia warned. "If there's anyone on our staff they're watching for, it's you."

"Or Jennifer," Clarence said. "She's probably right on the top of their *deny access* list."

"Her parents would have something to say about that," Claudia said.

Clarence nodded in agreement, then collected his recording gear before heading down the stairs and out onto the campus. The sound of chanting struck his ears as soon as he opened the door, even though the protesters were nowhere in sight. They were marching up and down the front lawn, daring the campus wardens to evict them. Clarence had to smile. The protests against police brutality were considerably larger and far more enthusiastic than the protests against *Seeing Eye*. Anyone would think the latter had been staged at a moment's notice.

He mulled it over as he walked down to the stadium. He'd never met the First Speaker personally—he'd never been senior enough to gain automatic access to political meetings and speeches—but he'd always had the impression that the man was *bland*. Thomas Wycliffe was an Empire Loyalist, a party that stood for nothing more than loyalty to an empire that was starting to collapse. Perhaps Wycliffe's position was weaker, Clarence considered, than the media suggested. What was the point in being loyal to an empire that no longer existed?

The Loyalists will have to find a new raison d'être pretty soon, he mused, as he joined the line of students waiting to pass through security. *What will they do once the shock wears off and everyone realises that nothing will ever be the same again?*

Clarence tensed, despite himself, as he saw the pair of policemen standing next to the security officers. They were studiously ignoring the waves of hate coming from the students, but…Clarence had a feeling it was only a matter of time before they slipped and *something* happened. Policemen were generally recruited from the lower middle class, sometimes right from the lower class itself, and they rarely *liked* rich boys and girls. The nasty side of Clarence's mind wondered if the policemen were privately cheering their disgraced comrade, whatever their superiors said or did. He'd managed to discomfit a rich bitch...

He pushed the thought aside as he reached the gate. The guards scanned him, but ignored or overlooked his recording gear. They didn't even ask to see his student ID. It made Clarence wonder if the guards were trying to be as gentle as possible or, perhaps less likely, if they thought Clarence wouldn't be on campus if *someone* hadn't already cleared him through security. Clarence grinned as he found an uncomfortable seat and settled down to wait for the First Speaker. He had half a mind to write a very sharp note to whoever was in charge of security, afterwards.

Maybe the guards didn't care about the recording gear, he thought, although it would have been a little unusual. Politicians *liked* being in sole control of what was released to the media. But then, it wouldn't be easy to keep the journalists from bringing their own recording gear. *Or maybe the First Speaker and his staff have too many other things to worry about.*

He tapped his terminal, bringing up the press release from the police force. It was a masterpiece of vague misdirection, somehow whitewashing the police of all crimes while simultaneously promising that the suspended police officer would face a full inquiry and disciplinary measures if he was found to have acted badly. Whoever had written it was a PR genius. Clarence rather admired his skill, even if he thought the skill could have been better used elsewhere. Writing novels, perhaps. The writer had a great talent for blending fact and fiction.

Let's see, he thought. *The opinion of the officer was that the person arrested was the instigator of the riot—wrong, but not unreasonable. The reporter clearly expected to be arrested—and provoked her arrest—because she was carrying a disguised recording device. The officer frisked—not groped—the reporter in a manner designed to ensure that she wasn't carrying any weapons at all. And so on. And so on.*

He had to smile. The *Daily Truth* had written a long opinion piece that stated that Jennifer had tricked the officer into searching her—on the grounds that she'd not given him her name, let alone any reason to think she was a reporter—and then retracted it, after receiving a threat of legal action from her parents. The story had already been memory-holed, but Frank Wong and his fellows had saved copies and continued to distribute them around the datanet. The *Bright Sunbeam* had gone so far as to say that the officer was merely trying to make Jennifer as uncomfortable as possible when he'd tried to pressure her and, of course, would not have gone through with it if she'd agreed. *That* story was still up, although Clarence was sure it was just a matter of time before it went down. The protests outside *Bright Sunbeam's* offices were something to behold.

The crowd started to chant. "FOREVER LOYAL! FOREVER LOYAL! FOREVER LOYAL!"

Clarence leaned forward as the First Speaker walked up the stairs and onto the podium. The chanting grew louder, until the racket was almost deafening. Clarence resisted the urge to cover his ears as he studied the First Speaker thoughtfully. In person, Thomas Wycliffe looked handsome, but weak. His face was perfectly sculpted to convey trustworthiness—and everything else the Empire Loyalists wanted in their leader—but there was no sense of actual charisma, let alone competence. It was hard to believe that this man could be elected dog-catcher, let alone planetary leader. But then, he hadn't won a popular vote. Thomas Wycliffe was the First Speaker because the Empire Loyalists controlled most of the seats in the Hall of Representatives. It was a wonder, Clarence sometimes thought, that anything got done. He knew political reporters who'd argue that *nothing* got done. It was an insight they were never allowed to put into writing.

Of course not, Clarence thought. *They'd be fired on the spot.*

The First Speaker lifted his hands, calling for silence. The chanting stopped, on cue.

"Thank you," the First Speaker said. His voice was perfectly pitched. "I thank you."

Don't make it sound rehearsed, Clarence thought, cynically. He'd bet half his pay for the month that at least a third of the students had been paid to attend. There simply hadn't been enough time for word to spread, unless someone was quietly calling students they *knew* would cheer on cue. *I wonder...*

He scanned the silent crowd, trying to pick out possible ringers. A number looked to be genuine fanatics—the Empire Loyalists had a presence on campus, as did most of the other political parties—but others looked rather less interested. Clarence had to smile as he spotted a girl carrying a placard, one that *had* to have been produced by the political staffers and distributed before the students went into the stadium. The girl looked so disinterested that he *knew* she was a ringer. It was just impossible to tell if she was there because she'd been paid or because her parents had insisted she go.

And two-thirds of the seats are empty, Clarence thought. The stadium was huge. There was room for everyone in the university to attend, if they'd wished. *Perhaps they should have given us more warning.*

"A very great wrong has been done," the First Speaker said. "At a time when tensions are running high, at a time when we all have to consider our role in the future, a very great wrong has been done. A policeman has overreacted and someone has been hurt."

And the only reason you're even giving this speech is because it was all caught on video, Clarence thought. The entire world had seen the police officer stick his hand up Jennifer's shirt. *You wouldn't give a damn if it was someone from the other side of the river.*

"I feel your pain," the First Speaker said. "I hear your concern..."

He was interrupted by a series of cheers and chants. Clarence snorted under his breath, then looked around the crowd. A number of students were *definitely* ringers. They looked surprisingly unenthusiastic, even as they cheered lustily. It probably hadn't occurred to them that the entire stadium was being filmed. The First Speaker's staffers would go through the recordings with a fine-toothed comb—afterwards—to see who was reliable and who did as little as possible.

They should have hired people from the slums, Clarence thought. *They'd have done anything for the promise of a hot meal and some ready cash.*

He dismissed the thought as the First Speaker droned on and on. His speechwriter was probably paid by the word. And he simply wasn't very good. The First Speaker dropped a ton of mindless bromides, as if he expected his word—his personal promise that things would change—to be enough to stop the protests in their tracks. Perhaps he did, or perhaps he was stalling…Clarence shook his head. The First Speaker had few other tools at his disposal. If he declared martial law, all hell would break loose.

It was nearly an hour before the First Speaker finally stopped living up to his name and left the stage, followed by enough cheering and chanting to shake the massive structure. It was a powerful sight, enough to make it clear that the First Speaker enjoyed the support of the student population. And if it wasn't clear enough, Clarence thought, a little creative editing would deal with *that* little problem. His lips twitched. How were they going to account for all the empty seats?

That's something we'll have to mention, he thought. The chanting finally died away and the audience started heading for the exits. *And now…*

He spotted the girl as she dropped her placard in the trash and walked towards the door, ignoring the attempts of two of the stewards to speak to her. Clarence followed, trying to keep at a distance. The stewards ignored him as they gathered up the placards and banners, piling them into bags for shipment back to the politician's office. Clarence couldn't help thinking that the girl had the right of it. The placards *deserved* to be in the trash.

The girl walked straight back towards the student accommodation, rather than heading down to the bars or the giant library. Clarence followed her, trying to catch up without seeming threatening. The last thing he needed was to be arrested by Campus Security. They could ban him from the campus at will, destroying his new career. Jackson would have no choice but to fire him…

"Hi," he said, when he caught up with the girl. "Can I ask you a few questions?"

The girl turned to face him. She was pretty enough, he supposed, but there was something *sharp* in her face that reminded him of Patricia—and Minnie. Her clothes were cheap and practical, rather than expensive and fancy. The wary look in her eyes, something that bothered him more than he cared to admit, suggested she knew more than her fellows about how dangerous the world could be. Clarence was *sure* she'd won a scholarship. There was no way *she* was from the upper classes.

"I'm Clarence," he said. "I'm a reporter for *Seeing Eye*…"

"I know who you are," the girl said. "I read your report on Hellebore."

And you were born somewhere nearby, Clarence guessed. The girl was good at hiding her accent, but she wasn't perfect. He felt a stab of pity. She'd probably been mocked relentlessly for being from the other side of the river. *You're just like me.*

"Thanks," he said. He allowed a little of his original accent to sink into his voice. "Were you paid to attend the speech?"

The girl hesitated. "Are you going to use my name?"

"You haven't told me your name," Clarence said. "And we don't have to use either your name or your face."

"You mustn't," the girl said. "Do you understand me?"

"Yeah," Clarence said. "I understand."

"You reported on Hellebore," the girl repeated, more to herself than to him. "You…"

She cleared her throat. "I won the Goldwater Prize…ah, *one* of the Goldwater Prizes. I…they said I could have a scholarship to attend Imperial University. But I have to do well."

Clarence frowned. Goldwater *again*?

"They said I had to attend the speech and cheer loudly, or else my scholarship would be called into review," the girl told him. "Others…others were simply paid to attend. I can give you their names if you like. They said…"

"I understand," Clarence said, again. He did. A girl who had won a scholarship would be in a good position to climb out of the estates, if she managed to get her degree. If, of course, the degree was in something *useful*. "When did they tell you?"

"Yesterday," the girl said. "They had us practicing all afternoon. I had to skip two of my classes to be drilled in cheering and"—her accent grew stronger—"do I look like a fucking cheerleader?"

"No," Clarence said, flatly. "You look like a sensible girl."

"Thanks," the girl said, sarcastically. "Do you know what my tutors are going to say? They're going to drop my GPA because I didn't attend their lectures. And what will this do to my ranking?"

Nothing good, Clarence said. Imperial University was supposed to be free of politics. That was about as true as the old story about the planet's moons being made of green cheese and inhabited by giant mice. *You might have lost your chance to get straight-As.*

"I won't mention you by name, nor will I show your face," he said. He wouldn't have been so accommodating to a rich girl, but a scholarship student could be destroyed on a whim. "How many others can you identify?"

"Too many," the girl said. "And thank you."

"You're welcome, Nameless Girl," Clarence said. He could find out her name easily, if he wished, but he had no intention of trying. "You have made a difference."

"You made a difference already," the girl said. "And it's Kinsey. My name is Kinsey."

"I'll try to forget it," Clarence promised. "Good luck."

CHAPTER NINETEEN

This was made worse, however, by the media often swallowing
enemy propaganda hook, line and sinker. It was generally believed,
at least by the military, that the embedded reporters never heard
an enemy lie they didn't repeat. Indeed, it wasn't uncommon for
the military to discover—after emerging victorious from a hard-
fought battle—that the media had branded it a defeat.
—PROFESSOR LEO CAESIUS
Crying Wolf: The Media and the Fall of the Empire

"WELL, EVERY MEDIA OUTLET ON THE PLANET is calling
the First Speaker's speech a great success," Jackson said, when Clarence
finally returned to the frat house. "The crowds went wild, they say; they
cheered the First Speaker for hours. Is that true?"

"Not really," Clarence said. He shrugged, elaborately. "They paid students to cheer."

He unbuckled the recording gear and passed it to Frank Wong, then
sat down and started to review the footage. It was pretty much as he'd
expected. The footage hadn't *precisely* been doctored, as far as he could
tell, but it had been carefully shot and edited to hide all traces of the empty
seats. The stadium had been full to bursting, apparently. The editors were

too ignorant to realise—or assumed that their audience was too ignorant to realise—that there were more uncomfortable seats in the vast stadium than there were students and staff in the entire university. If the stadium had been full, it would have been a clear sign that outsiders had been bussed into the university for the speech…

"You'll be able to download the footage and put it online," Clarence continued. "I'll write you a story in an hour or so."

Jackson nodded. "Did you have something to eat?"

"I had a sandwich at the bar," Clarence said. Kinsey had been reluctant to talk to him, let alone allow her to use her name and face, but the other ringers hadn't been anything like so discrete. They'd openly bragged about taking money for cheering, making jokes about being cheerleaders even as they'd spent their ill-gotten gains. Clarence had eaten and listened to everything they'd said. "I'll have something a little more solid later."

"Good idea," Jackson said.

Clarence nodded, then walked back to his room and sat down at the terminal. A handful of emails were waiting for him, responses to queries he'd filed with a couple of government offices. There was no dispute that Maxima Corporation had the right to demolish the estates—they had all the permits in order, which probably meant they'd paid out a great many bribes—but they hadn't started yet. Reading between the lines, Clarence had the odd feeling that Maxima wasn't *going* to demolish the estates. They seemed to have got all the paperwork in order, but there was a strange lack of actual *action*.

He put it aside for the moment and turned his attention to the story. Frank Wong had already uploaded the footage and included two transcriptions of the speech, one taken from Clarence's recording and one issued by the First Speaker's office. They were almost completely identical, save for a couple of minor stumbles. Clarence glanced at them briefly, then decided they'd probably been accidents. The First Speaker had given the speech without notes.

Without visible notes, Clarence reminded himself. Everyone would mock a politician who used a teleprompter—if he couldn't remember his lines, how could he be trusted to govern a planet?—but there were plenty of ways to keep an eye on the script without making it obvious. *He might have had the words beamed to him through an implant.*

He shrugged, then started to write. It was easy enough to detail the speech—and note all the questions it hadn't answered—before pointing out that a speech, no matter how good, was not *action.* The First Speaker had promised much, he told his readers, without actually *doing* anything. He hadn't even promised specific reforms. Clarence had to admit that actually *reforming* the police would not be easy—and he admitted as much to his readers—but the First Speaker didn't seem inclined to *try.*

The core of the problem is not police procedure, but abuse of police authority. The police have been allowed to go too long without any form of supervision, save for what little they offer themselves, ensuring that they have developed a culture of being fundamentally unaccountable to anyone, from the planet's elected leaders to the public they are supposed to protect. Worse, perhaps, when this is challenged—however weakly— they close ranks around the offender and offer excuses that either do not stand up to scrutiny or reveal worse issues the police would—per- haps—wish to conceal.

The police have stated, more than once, that the unnamed officer would not have arrested and frisked—their term—this newspaper's reporter if they'd known who and what she was. This may be true. But it cannot be denied that it implies that they would have mistreated someone who lacked the advantages of being both a reporter and upper class. That the officer made no attempt to find out who the reporter actually was is worrying. It suggests that he was more interested in mistreating her than in doing his duty. Even if he genuinely believed that she was behind the mini-riot, he should still have acted like a responsible officer.

181

It is not an attack on the police to say that a culture of unaccountability leads to abuse. It is, however, a clarion call for urgently-needed reform. The police have lost the public's trust. It was gone, in many places, well before our reporter was arrested. They will have to work long and hard to convince us, their people, that they can be trusted once again.

Clarence studied the text for a moment, carefully re-reading every line, then allowed himself a tight smile. It wasn't perfect, but it would do. He tapped a key, sending the first draft to Jackson, then returned to working through his inbox. A number of spam messages had arrived—he was surprised it had taken so long—but also a couple of possible tip-offs. He made a note of the details, then felt his stomach growl. It had been too long since he'd eaten that sandwich.

Jennifer was sitting in the kitchen, eating something that looked like soup and smelled like curry. Clarence glanced at the pot on the stove, then investigated the communal food store for anything edible. It still astonished him that the students were happier heating up a precooked meal rather than trying to cook themselves, although he supposed they did have the money to afford it. Personally, he thought it was cheaper to cook his own food. It certainly helped him to think while he was cooking.

"I was wondering," Jennifer said, as he stuck the burger in the microwave. "Should you or someone be interviewing me?"

"It might be a good idea," Clarence told her. The microwave bleeped. He took the burger out of the heater and put it on the table. "On the other hand, you don't want to personalise things *too* much. You're not the only victim."

Jennifer smiled, rather thinly. "Jackson said so."

He was listening, Clarence thought, amused. *And he did take it to heart.*

"I wasn't expecting...well, *that,*" Jennifer said. "I thought I'd asked him a question. I wasn't expecting..."

"That's the reality of the world for a *lot* of people," Clarence said, flatly. He took a bite of his burger. It tasted suspiciously like cardboard. "You were lucky. Remember that. You were lucky."

"Jackson said that too," Jennifer said.

Which makes Jackson the first boss I've had who actually listens to me, Clarence thought. It was a pleasant thought. None of his other bosses had treated him as anything more than a subordinate who could be fired at will. *And he isn't even saying that it was a splendid idea of his that I just happened to have.*

"Yeah, we can do an interview," Clarence told her. "But we should probably work on bringing other victims to light."

"They've been coming forward to my parents," Jennifer said. "Now there *is* a protest movement…"

"Just remember to keep their identities under wraps as long as possible," Clarence said, firmly. "Not *everyone* has wealthy parents."

Jennifer blinked. "Really?"

"Yes," Clarence said, flatly. His wristcom bleeped. The story had been accepted and uploaded, along with the footage. "You were lucky."

"So you keep saying," Jennifer said.

Clarence shrugged. "Female reporters come in for a lot of harassment," he said. "Ask Claudia if you don't believe me. There are thousands of stories. None of them ever got into print. The editors killed them all."

He shrugged as he finished his burger. It really hadn't tasted very nice. He wondered, as he wiped his lips, if the students liked it…or if they were simply too accustomed to weird-tasting food to care. He'd tried some of the fancier meals in the kitchen over the last few days and some of them had tasted *really* strange. What sort of mind liked the idea of eating fish eggs? They'd been disgusting.

A mind that knows it will be starving if it doesn't eat them, he told himself. *And over the years the idea just became fashionable.*

He met Jennifer's eyes. "Are you feeling alright? I mean…"

"I've been better," Jennifer said. "It helps that I've been fighting back, you know. Telling everyone what happened, speaking at the protest marches, doing everything in my power to make sure it never happens again…"

"Very good," Clarence said. "Just remember, most of the victims are poor. They don't have wealthy parents to speak for them."

Jennifer nodded in understanding. Clarence nodded back, then left the room. The purist in him was angry that it had taken such an incident to make Jennifer and her parents understand what life was like for people on the other side of the river, but the practical side of his mind insisted that it didn't matter. They'd realised the truth. Maybe their daughter had had to be groped—and threatened with all kinds of abuse—before they'd realised the truth, but they'd realised the truth. And they were doing something about it.

Let's just hope that it keeps going after the abusive shithead hangs himself or something, Clarence thought, as he walked down the corridor. *It will be easy for them to forget once Jennifer has her justice...*

"Hey, Clarence," Wong called. "Come and take a look at this!"

Clarence stepped into the WebHead's new office and looked around. Frank Wong had hired a handful of new WebHeads over the past few days, taking advantage of their presence to move himself into another room. A handful of computer terminals were mounted on the tables and linked together by a complex mass of wires. Two of them had their outer casings removed, revealing their innermost secrets. Clarence glanced into the mass of datachips and...*thingies* and shook his head. He knew more about computers than the average person—he'd spent so long fiddling with his terminal that it was practically part of him—but he knew when he was out of his depth. He'd thought that opening a terminal and messing around with the innards was strictly forbidden.

"Not forbidden," Wong said, when he asked. "Just very ill-advised unless you know what you're doing."

"And you do?" Clarence had no doubt of it. "What are you doing?"

"Trying to boost the capacity," Wong said. He snickered. "And reverse the polarity of the neutron flow."

"...I see," Clarence said, who didn't. "What does that have to do with anything?"

"One day," Wong said grandly, "I will meet a girl who understands that without having to be told. And on that day, I will have met my bride."

"Right," Clarence said. He took one last look inside the terminal—it didn't seem to be doing *anything*, as far as he could tell—and then sat down on a beanbag. "What did you want to talk about?"

"Your next story," Wong said. "You do realise that your *last* story has been vanishing from the datanet?"

Clarence wasn't particularly surprised. "That was quick." His watch insisted that it had only been an hour since the story had been filed. "From our site or everywhere?"

"Not from our site, not precisely." Wong's voice became pensive. "There *has* been a considerable increase in the number of pointless pings from unknown servers to our site, but nothing we can really point to and say *this is a deliberate attack*. Each ping on its own is harmless, naturally. It's when they get added together that we have to start getting worried."

He smiled. "But my systems are more than capable of handling the pings, for the moment. I will get more concerned when our enemies resort to tougher measures."

"Like viral attacks," Clarence said.

"Yeah." Wong smiled. "I've got some of the best WebHeads in the world helping us—and we've become quite popular in the wider world of hackers—but it's only a matter of time before we get *really* tested. And then… well, we'll see how good I really am."

He cracked his knuckles in anticipation. "Game on."

Clarence leaned forward. "There's a hacker community?"

"Always has been," Wong said. "Hardly anyone seems to know about it, unless they're interested in computers. Thing is, they built the datanet when the planet was colonised and then they built another datanet on top of the first and *then* they built lots of little datanets that they linked together into what was effectively a *third* datanet. There are lots of little nooks and crannies within the system, places where hackers can meet and chat and tell lies about which systems they've penetrated and…oh, there are lots of little secrets just buried away, waiting to be found. If you knew how easy it was to break into a bank's ultra-secure system and change a few digits, you'd shit yourself."

"I never heard anything about this," Clarence said. "Why not?"

"I blame the schools," Wong said. He tapped the terminal on Clarence's belt. "You went to a basic school, right? Kids who go there get taught how to use a standard user interface, but they're never told anything of how it actually works. They're taught more about the inner workings of their own bodies than they are about computers. They never realise, unless they're lucky enough to be very insightful, just how much there is under the surface. The hackers are the ones who *did* realise and devoted themselves to learning for themselves."

"I see," Clarence said, disturbed. "And the government just lets it happen?"

"Most WebHeads are harmless," Wong said. "And most of the ones who *aren't*...well, sometimes they get taken down by the community, sometimes they get caught by the government's own WebHeads and sometimes they just get paid off. I know a guy who was paid off by one of the largest banks in the system. They really wanted him to leave them alone."

"Fuck," Clarence said.

Wong smirked. "So, I've been fighting back on your behalf. You know the really big news corporations have access codes? It's what allows them to drop messages into your inbox, no matter how many times you add them to the list of spammers. Did they ever tell you that when you worked for the *Daily Lie?*"

"I never thought about it," Clarence admitted.

"I rest my case," Wong said. "You never gave it any thought, did you? But anyway...point is, a message with those codes cannot be wiped from the server automatically. There's probably a historical reason behind it somewhere, but I don't know what. I've copied the codes and affixed them to our newsletters. Everyone who signed up is now getting a copy without having it wiped before they even see it."

Clarence felt cold. "They can wipe messages out of someone's inbox?"

"Of course," Wong said. He winked. "I used to know a guy—one of those even-tempered dudes, mad all the time—who had a habit of sending outrageous messages to people, then hacking their inboxes to delete the messages before they saw them. It used to give him a thrill. And then someone saw the message first…"

"Oh shit," Clarence said.

"There's no diplomatic way to tell someone you want to fuck his mother," Wong agreed. He smiled. "I have all the data, if you want to look at it. You might get a story out of it."

Clarence's eyes narrowed. "Will they know what we've done?"

"Of course," Wong said. "They'll know when the messages refuse to vanish. The bastards will need to erase them all manually, which will take years. But…how can they complain without openly admitting what they're doing? What they've *been* doing for decades—centuries, really? How can they punish us without telling everyone that the oh-so-reliable datanet has more holes in it than my underwear?"

"I wish I was so confident," Clarence admitted. He shook his head. "I'll go back to researching the legal precedents."

"Once the truth is out, it cannot be put back in the bag," Wong said. "Hey, you know politicians do the same thing? All those wretched robocalls? They cannot be blocked because they have emergency priority."

"Everyone knows about it," Clarence pointed out. "And no one has complained."

"They might have done," Wong said. "How many complaining emails vanished in transit?"

"That's paranoia," Clarence objected, weakly.

"It isn't paranoia if they're out to get you," Wong said. "And you know, better than I, how easy it is to stop someone complaining."

"True," Clarence agreed. "There must be a story in there too."

"I bet you anything you care to put forward that they've already been interfering with the protest marches," Wong said. "Why would they use extreme force when they can just minimise the number of people who've heard about it?"

"No bet," Clarence said.

CHAPTER TWENTY

This was not the only problem. The reporters—and their publishers—rarely bothered to assess what they were being told. A handful of civilians who had been killed in the crossfire—often having been used as human shields by insurgents—would, by some curious alchemy, have been deliberately killed by the time the story was released. It was no surprise, therefore, that soldiers often regarded reporters as enemy combatants.
—**PROFESSOR LEO CAESIUS**
Crying Wolf: The Media and the Fall of the Empire

THE HELL OF IT, COLIN SIMPSON THOUGHT, was that the protest marches had started too late.

He would have liked to join them, to raise his voice with the hundreds of other young men and women protesting police brutality, but it was already too late. The sergeant had warned him—and the other trainees—not to have *anything* to do with the marches, even though many of the marchers were wearing masks to hide their faces. It wasn't *fair.* Colin loathed the police. He would have done anything to force them to leave the estates alone. He'd seen too many coppers abusing their power to want to have anything to do with them.

And the idiots who join the police get shunned in the streets, he thought, as he waited on the street corner with his friends. It felt odd to be out in the daylight, even though there was nothing separating them from yet another band of teenage layabouts. *They're nothing more than traitors.*

He pushed the thought out of his mind as the bus rattled into view. It was nothing more than an old school bus, dating back to the days when children on the estate were transported halfway across the city to attend an upper-class school where they'd fitted in about as well as a square peg in a round hole. Colin scowled at the memory, silently glad that *he* hadn't been one of the unfortunate children who'd been sent to the hellhole. The poor kids had been sneered at by the wealthier children and mocked at home. He didn't think that any of them had made *anything* of their lives.

The bus crashed to a halt. The smell of burning rubber and hydrocarbons assailed his nostrils as the door hissed open. Colin tensed, all too aware that they might be walking into a trap. He trusted the sergeant, insofar as he trusted anyone, but they'd been warned not to have too much contact with the rest of the resistance. What people didn't know they couldn't tell. It felt odd, to say the least, to gather his friends and bring them to the meeting place. He'd had second and third thoughts about doing it at all.

He looked into the shadowed interior. The sergeant stood there. Behind him, the driver was hidden behind a veil. Someone had draped cloths everywhere, making it impossible to see who was in the vehicle. Colin hesitated, then climbed into the bus. The sergeant nodded to him, then met his eyes. His voice, when he spoke, was very hard.

"This is your last chance to back out," he said. "If you want to go, go now."

Colin shook his head. He was committed. He'd been committed from the day he'd thrown a makeshift firebomb into a shitter household. The sergeant had taught him that he would never achieve anything on his own. Sooner or later, he'd be caught. The police would deport him, if they didn't hang him; the shitters would kill him. He had no choice. He *had* to stay with the resistance.

"Take an uncovered seat," the sergeant said. "And keep your mouth shut."

Colin heard him giving the same warning to the rest of the gang as he made his way down the aisle and sat on the nearest seat. It was uncomfortably hard. Someone had scribbled KILROY LUVS KILNY on the metal backrest. He forced himself to relax as Magus joined him a second later, his face slack with anticipation. Magus had been the most eager of all to get involved with the protests, coming up with hundreds of schemes to attack or embarrass the police. He'd even dreamed up a plan to ambush a police car and lure any police reinforcements into a trap.

The sergeant walked past them as the bus lurched back into life. "Keep the cover in place until I tell you to remove it," he said, as he pinned the cloth into position. "We'll be there soon."

Colin sighed, inwardly, as he looked at the window. It was opaque, denying him any chance to see the outside world. He wondered, absently, if the windows had been modified when the resistance obtained the bus or if they'd always been useless. School buses had been regularly attacked, once upon a time. Perhaps whoever had designed the buses had thought that concealing their passengers was a wise move. Typical bureaucratic stupidity, Colin figured, if that were true. The bus itself was a pretty clear indicator of what it carried.

Unless it does double duty as a prison bus, Colin thought, dryly. It was remarkably uncomfortable. His imagination supplied handcuffs and shackles to keep the prisoners in their seats. *It would make an excellent prison bus.*

It felt like hours—and countless stops and starts—before the windows went completely dark and the bus lurched to a halt one final time. Colin felt his heart starting to race as he heard the sound of footsteps, of voices asking questions before the sergeant told them to shut up and get off the bus. The cloth was torn away a moment later, revealing dozens of other teenagers scrambling out of their seats. Colin followed the sergeant's pointing finger and headed for the door. Outside, two men in orange jackets were pointing the teenagers towards the wall. It looked as though the bus had driven straight into a massive gym hall and stopped.

"It's a warehouse," Magus said, from behind him. "Just *look* at it."

Colin sucked in his breath. The building was *huge*, immensely huge. It was so large that he felt like a fly crawling across a windshield. He'd thought his school was big, back before he'd been given his worthless exam results and told to leave, but the warehouse could have held the entire school population and still had room for more. It was bigger than a football stadium, bigger than...

"Over to the wall," one of the jacketed men snapped. "Move it!"

"Yes, sir," Colin said, automatically.

He hurried over to the wall, feeling oddly unsure of himself. It was hard not to respond to the man's commanding tone—and the implicit threat of violence. He pressed his back against the wall, studying the jacketed men with interest. They held themselves with the same kind of quiet assurance he'd come to expect from the sergeant, men who saw no reason to assert themselves because they *knew* they were in charge. They were a stark contrast to the drug dealers and gangbangers he'd known on the estate. *They'd* always cracked down hard on anyone who dared defy them. But then, their positions were never as secure as they seemed.

A shock ran through him as he realised that the jacketed men were carrying *guns*. He'd seen countless guns on the viewscreen, hundreds of action movies where the hero had mown down his enemies in a spray of hot lead, but he'd never seen a *real* gun. It was rare for gangbangers to carry actual *weapons*, not when the police would ruthlessly hunt down anyone who did. Colin had once heard a friend bragging he owned a real gun, but he'd never shown it to anyone. It was next to impossible to get any sort of *real* weapon on the estate.

And they're carrying guns, openly, Colin thought. It occurred to him that the guns might be fake, but...he shook his head. They *looked* real. *What have I got myself into?*

He wanted to ask for shooting lessons, to have a gun put in his hand and fire it...he wondered, hopefully, if they *would* be taught how to handle guns. A gun was power. The flicks had made that clear, time and time again. A lone man could dominate a crowd with a gun in his hand. Bullies wet themselves and fled in terror, girls swooned at his feet...Colin *wanted* that sort of power. Beside him, Magus was practically *panting*. There wasn't a boy on the estate who wouldn't sell his soul for a gun. A gun would give him the power to finally assert himself.

The sergeant strode forward. "Quiet," he snapped. His voice wasn't very loud, but it *carried*. "The Captain will address you now."

Colin looked up as one of the jacketed men cleared his throat. "Our planet is at risk," he said, coldly. "For decades, we have been dominated by a government that doesn't give a damn; for decades, we have had to watch helplessly as the elitists make decisions to benefit themselves and to hell with the rest of us. They have made it impossible for us to get jobs, they have forced us to accept and integrate large numbers of migrants, they have ruthlessly crushed all resistance. There was no prospect of any of this changing."

His voice hardened. "But now, Earth is gone. Tarsus stands alone. And—finally—things can change."

Maybe, Colin thought. He agreed with the Captain's words, but he wondered—sometimes—if there was any hope of change. The estate ground people down. Even if he avoided the gangs, even if he tried to get a job, there was little hope of anything in his future. He knew men and women who were grandparents by thirty. *Can things really change?*

"You young men are the hope of the future," the Captain said. "You have already proven that you are willing to fight. You have already proven that you are willing to learn *how* to fight. And now, you will have the chance to show the world that you want change—that you *demand* change—and that you are willing to fight for it. Can the police stand against you?"

He smiled, rather sharply. "Alone, none of you can accomplish anything," he said, his words echoing Colin's earlier thoughts. "But, as a group, there is *nothing* you cannot do. We will teach you the *true* history of Tarsus. We will show you how you were stripped of your birthright—and we will show you how to get it back. And, by the time the shit hits the fan, you will be ready."

Colin watched, unsure what to say or do, as the Captain turned and walked through a side door. The Sergeant stepped forward.

"You are here because you have proven your willingness to fight and *learn*," the sergeant said. He was repeating the Captain's words. Colin didn't know why. "I don't know how long you will *have* to learn, but we will teach you as much as we can before the shit hits the fan. You will be drilled, extensively, in everything you need to know. I don't want you to be all spit and polish. I want you to be ready to inflict violence on the enemies of our world."

He paused. His voice took on a warning tone. "This is going to be very different to anything you've done before. There are rules, which I will expect you to obey. Anyone who disobeys will regret it. You all volunteered to be here, so don't come complaining to me if you don't like the rules. There is no place here for someone who is not completely committed to our cause."

Colin listened, carefully, as the rules were outlined. Obey orders at all times, without question. Do not fight your fellow trainees, no matter what past history you share. Do not attempt to leave the warehouses without permission, whatever the reason. The sergeant repeated that order twice, then warned them that the guards had permission to shoot first and ask questions later. Anyone who tried to cross the fence would be shot. It made Colin wonder, as his thoughts started to wander, just where they were. They couldn't be *that* far outside the city, could they? The bus had been slow as well as uncomfortable.

We might be still in the city itself, he mused. *But won't the police hear the gunfire?*

"If you follow orders and *listen*, you will learn," the sergeant finished. His face split into a nasty grin. "And, for your first order, follow me. We're going on a jog."

Colin had thought he was reasonably fit—weak men didn't last long on the estate—but he still found himself sweating like a pig after two laps around the giant warehouse. The sergeant led the way, somehow managing to stay ahead of his charges, while the jacketed men brought up the rear. Colin couldn't help noticing that they were carrying sticks, which they used to poke and prod the unfortunate trainees who couldn't keep up. He forced himself to keep running, silently relieved when the sergeant finally called a halt. His legs were aching and his heart was pounding like a drum.

"Very good," the sergeant said. "And now…"

It felt like hours before they were finally given something to eat, then assigned a bedroll and told to bed down in the warehouse. Colin knew he had never been pushed so far, not even when he'd first met the sergeant. He'd run, he'd marched, he'd practiced fighting…his cheek still ached from where one of his fellow trainees had landed a punch…he'd enjoyed himself, but he also felt drained. It was hard, so hard, to think straight. The only upside, as far as he could tell, was the food. It hadn't been very good, but he'd been encouraged to eat as much as he could.

Magus bedded down next to him. "What do you think we'll be doing tomorrow?"

Colin was too tired to shrug. "More of the same, I suppose," he said. It struck him, suddenly, that he had no idea when he'd be going home. Or if he ever *would* be going home. It wasn't the first time he hadn't gone home at night, but still…his sister was going to wonder what had happened to him. "Goodnight."

He closed his eyes. Sleep came rapidly.

• • •

"So," Constable Mallon said. They stood on duty outside Hellebore Estate, far from the maddening crowd. "What's it like being the most hated cop on the planet?"

Senior Constable Peter Quigley glared. That damned reporter. Why the hell couldn't she have told him who and what she was when he'd arrested her? Most reporters would have waved their press passes at him the moment he even glanced in their direction. Instead, the wretched bitch had kept her mouth firmly shut. She'd let him make an utter fool of himself and recorded it all, live. He hadn't even seen the goddamned recorder!

"Fuck off," he said, finally. He was still—technically—suspended. The only reason he was on guard duty, he suspected, was because his apartment was under siege by maddened protesters. Goddamned bitches. There was nothing about them that a damned good thrashing wouldn't cure. "I…fuck it."

"At least you got to put your hand on her ass," Mallon jibed. "What was it like? Was it firm? Or…"

Peter met his eyes. "How do you know this conversation isn't being recorded?"

Mallon blanched. Peter would have smirked, if he'd had the energy. His career was in the shitter, no matter how much the union bitched and moaned. He'd made too many powerful enemies to avoid being shit-canned, even if he wasn't officially fired. And the hell of it was that he might be better off getting fired. There wasn't a senior officer on the force who'd want Peter anywhere near his team. Peter would be lucky if he wasn't told to go out—alone and unarmed, wearing his dress uniform—and patrol the worst estates. They'd pull his body out of the river a few days later and everyone would pretend to be very sorry…

He turned away, eying the silent streets. Why were they even *here*, anyway? The estates were empty. There was nothing to be gained by assigning a handful of street cops to man the barricades when they could be employed elsewhere. Maybe Sergeant Grozny had convinced his superiors that it would make a convenient place to stash Peter until the police force decided his fate. Or…he shook his head. Grozny had been raging. He wouldn't bother being subtle when he could have broken Peter's neck like a twig.

And no one would have complained, either, he thought, as a shuttlecraft flew overhead. *He would have been given a medal for getting the police force out of a jam.*

He sighed. What had he done that was so wrong, really? He'd frisked the bitch, in accordance with procedure…he'd done his best to make her uncomfortable…it was what he was supposed to do. And even if he wasn't, even if he had gone too far, what had he done that countless *other* policemen hadn't done? Everyone knew that everyone did it. The bastards who were condemning him had their own dirty little secrets to hide.

Another shuttle flew overhead, heading to high orbit. There seemed to be fewer shuttles these days, Peter thought. It was hard to tell, but...he thought so. Perhaps they weren't deporting so many people, now that Earth was gone. Maybe he'd spend the rest of his days in a work camp instead of being dumped on some godforsaken rock along the Rim...

Sure, he thought, as he resigned himself to a long and bitterly cold night. *And maybe pigs will learn to fly.*

CHAPTER TWENTY-ONE

Indeed, it was privately estimated—by the military's internal assessment teams—that practically every media assessment of civilian casualties was almost completely inaccurate.
—**PROFESSOR LEO CAESIUS**
Crying Wolf: The Media and the Fall of the Empire

CLARENCE HAD BEEN NERVOUSLY EXPECTING the hammer to fall for several days, after Seeing Eye had reported on the First Speaker's speech. Their story—and the accompanying video footage and commentary—had been more accurate than anything the mainstream media had published, but he was grimly aware that truth was no defence when powerful people felt blindsided by the media. The longer it took for the hammer to fall, he fretted, the harder it would hit when it finally struck home. It was almost a surprise when Jackson had summoned him into his office and, instead of telling him that all hell had finally broken loose, sent him and Patricia to interview a new businessman. The aircar flight had taken longer than the briefing.

"He must have contacted us and asked for an interview," Clarence said, as he flicked through the handful of files on Neil Harran, CEO of New Technology Inc. There wasn't much, save for a handful of highlights. Harran had gone into business with a handful of university friends and made enough money—in his first two years—to draw attention from the big corporations. "What do you think he wants?"

"Us to tell the world how wonderful he is," Patricia guessed. "And is he?"

"We'll see," Clarence said.

The aircar banked and descended into a decidedly middle-class estate. Clarence allowed himself a moment of surprise that Harran had set up shop *here*, although he could see some advantages. One could purchase an entire factory in the middle-class estate for the price of a small apartment—or a tiny office—in the centre of town. Harran might not be *close* to the government, but there was nothing stopping him from taking an aircar to the towers or sending a representative in his stead. And he could actually bring jobs to the estate.

Clarence braced himself as the aircar landed on the pad. A pair of security officers—looking surprisingly friendly for corporate security officers—waved cheerfully as Clarence and Patricia climbed out of the aircar, then scanned their bodies with portable sensors. They made no move to carry out a physical search, something that surprised Clarence more than he cared to admit. Perhaps the expose of police misbehaviour had had a salutary effect on corporate security forces too.

A young woman wearing a well-tailored business suit met them as they were escorted through the doors. "If you'll come this way, Mr. Harran is waiting for you."

"We would be delighted," Clarence said.

The woman took them up an elevator, then through a series of nicely-decorated corridors and into an office. New Technology looked to be a better place to work than the *Daily Truth*, Clarence thought, although he was all-too-aware that appearances could be deceiving. They hadn't been shown the factory floor or anywhere where people actually *worked*. A corporation could have a great office, but that meant nothing if its products were crap or it treated its employees like slaves. *Seeing Eye* had pitiful offices, yet it was still the best place Clarence had ever worked.

Neil Harran was bent over a display when Clarence and Patricia were shown into the giant chamber. He straightened up as they approached and turned to face them. Clarence was fairly sure it wasn't an act. Harran didn't look the kind of person to *need* an act. He was younger than Clarence—only a year or two older than Patricia—but there was a kind of confidence in his movements that came from achievement, rather than old money and family protection. Clarence couldn't help being impressed.

"Please, take a seat," Harran said. His accent was decidedly middle-class. "I'll have some drinks and biscuits sent in."

Clarence sat on the sofa, studying Harran thoughtfully as a young maid brought a tea tray and left as silently as she'd arrived. He was definitely young, with curly dark hair, darker eyes, the first hints of a moustache and tinted skin that suggested there was probably a second—or third-generation immigrant somewhere in his family tree. Clarence wondered, absently, if that had opened his mind to new ideas. Tarsus had been staunchly conservative for centuries. The planet might have been relatively stable since the development corporation had transfigured itself into a government, but it hadn't produced anything new either.

"I've been trying to interest the media in our work for months," Harran said, as he poured the tea. "The really big outlets have all given us the cold shoulder. I would have been hurt if I hadn't known they were owned by the *really* big corporations."

Patricia took her tea and held it without sipping. "You think they've been ordered to ignore you?"

"I know it," Harran said. "Our money is good, right? But we can't put adverts in the mainstream channels, no matter how much we offer to shell out. No official explanation, of course, but I've been told—under the table—that we've been blacklisted. It's a pain in the bum, I tell you."

"I can understand," Clarence said. He believed Harran. The media would not refuse to run adverts, particularly if money was offered up front, unless they'd been given specific orders to do so. The only real question was who had issued the orders. "Why do you feel they've blacklisted you?"

Harran smiled. "That is a long story," he said. He made a show of looking at his watch. "But we have all morning, do we not?"

"Yes," Patricia said.

"Quite." Harran took a long breath. "The thing you have to understand, the thing you probably haven't realised, is that there have been no true advances in...well, *anything*...for centuries. About the only area in which there has been any *real* innovation over the last few hundred years has been medicine, specifically in life-extension and rejuvenation therapies, and that's only because powerful people have been funding intense research into medical science. And even *that* has been having problems. There is simply too great a demand for improvement—and too high a risk of failure—for anyone to carry out real research.

"Outside medicine...well, the terminal on your belt has a *lot* in common with a terminal from two hundred years ago. A computer? They haven't *really* improved in a hundred years or more. Starships? The Phase Drive has not been significantly improved for hundreds of years. Grief! The Imperial Navy has been using the same designs for hundreds of years."

"They work," Clarence said, quietly.

"Yes, they work," Harran agreed. "But there's no actual *innovation*. Why might that be, do you think?"

Clarence hesitated. He'd never really thought about it. Technological development had never really been an interest of his—he'd never been smart enough to be streamlined into the hard sciences at school—and he'd never had any reason to carry out background research. It had simply never been necessary.

"Perhaps we have run up against some hard limits," he said, finally. He tapped his chest, meaningfully. "Perhaps there is a point where technology simply *cannot* be improved."

"That was what I was told," Harran said. "But I didn't believe it."

He paused for effect. "I—and a few university friends—started digging into the *why* of it when we were supposed to be studying. We devoted ourselves to *really* understanding what was happening. And do you know what we found? Limiters. Things—social and legal—that hampered technological development."

Patricia frowned. "Someone has been *deliberately* preventing technological development?"

Harran looked thoughtful, just for a second. "I don't know if it was deliberate," he said, after a moment. "But it happened. You see…"

He stood and started to pace. "Take a basic terminal, for example," he said. "The user interface has been designed, not to put too fine a point on it, for dummies. There's no room for actual development. Then…then we run into legally-mandated limits. A standard terminal simply doesn't have as much memory as it should. Why not? Because there's a law dating back hundreds of years that forbids it. And do you know why? It took me weeks to figure it out."

"Go on," Clarence said.

"The people who were producing memory blocks—they were replaced with datachips, centuries ago—demanded laws to protect their market," Harran said. "Their market vanished long ago, but the laws are in place."

He shrugged. "And then there's the simple fact that most students don't learn anything of the hard sciences," he added. "They're not encouraged to dig into the underlying technology behind any major breakthrough, let alone understand how it works. The few that do…well, some of them *do* get picked up by the big corporations. But you know what happens to them? They find that the corporation's vast bureaucracy kills any innovations they might make. This has been happening on a *huge* scale. Between the universities and the corporations, innovation is practically dead."

Patricia sounded disbelieving. "But why? They'd make billions of credits if they brought out something new, wouldn't they?"

"Perhaps," Harran said. "Or maybe they'd damage themselves too. Suppose…Maxima Corp brought out a pocket terminal that could replace both your handheld *and* your home device. They'd sell billions. But they'd also torpedo several other product lines. Who would buy two separate devices when they could have just one?"

"I see," Clarence said.

"And they have a vested interest in not letting the customer perform any repair work," Harran added. "Basic self-improving and repairing software has been practical for centuries, but they don't want the customer deliberately extending the life of their products. They *claim* it is for safety, they *say* they want to help the customer, yet…do they?"

Clarence held up a hand. "And New Technology is doing…what?"

"Innovating," Harran said. "My friends and I developed ways to improve on existing technology, then started to market it. As you can see"—he produced a black terminal, slightly larger than Clarence's, and put it on the desk—"our terminal is handheld. But it can also replace a desktop system."

He pressed his finger against the scanner. A holographic keyboard and screen appeared in front of him. Clarence blinked, realising—for the first time—that Harran was right. No one had thought to work holographic technology into a handheld terminal before. And yet…it had been practical for centuries. Clarence had had a personal entertainment console that had turned his living room into a holographic gaming environment. The system in front of him was tiny by comparison.

"Our terminal is a little larger than the standard design," Harran said. "That's partly because we anticipate a market for repairable devices. A user doesn't have to be a skilled engineer to remove most of the components and replace them. Not everything, not yet, but…we anticipate a sizable market in spare parts. We're stockpiling them now."

His fingers danced over the holographic keys. "It does take a bit of getting used to, I should admit. We weren't able to slim down a solid-light projector and fit it into the terminal…well, not yet. We're still working on it."

Clarence picked up the terminal gingerly. "And this does everything a standard terminal does?"

"Pretty much," Harran said. "You can make calls on it. You can send emails on it. You can sit in an aircar and do your work on it while flying from place to place. You can even take pictures and record your life with it. The memory cell is about ten times larger than the average terminal's.

And"—he winked—"there's a way to leave the recording function on without making it obvious."

"I thought that was illegal," Patricia said.

"Not quite," Clarence said. It was a loophole the media had taken ruthless advantage of, over the years. "If someone asks if they're being recorded, you are legally obliged to tell them. But if someone doesn't ask, you don't have to tell."

He looked at Harran. "But are you allowed to expand the memory cell?"

"The laws in question came from Earth," Harran said. "Are they still legally binding?"

Clarence frowned. "Good question."

"That's not the only example of a stupid law," Harran added. "Earth produced nothing *but* laws. They're all still in the books even if they got superseded by other laws. And do you know how many of them are still followed? Too many."

"That's something to press for," Clarence mused.

"Yes," Harran said. He deactivated the terminal and pocketed it. "We are on the brink of a genuine technological and social revolution. Earth is gone. Yes, that's a disaster—and it is going to hurt badly when the economic shock catches up with us—but it's also an opportunity to change the world. No, the galaxy! Do you have any idea just how many ways we could innovate, once we escape the straitjacket? We could change *everything*!"

And that might not be a good idea, Clarence thought.

"You say you could change the galaxy," Patricia said. "What do you *mean*?"

"We are told that FTL communication is impossible," Harran said. "What if it *isn't* impossible? What if we found a way to send a signal from Tarsus to Terra Nova practically instantly? The galaxy would become a much smaller place. Or…what if we managed to find a way to make algae-based foodstuffs actually *tasty*? Starvation would become non-existent! And what if we managed to design a smaller and cheaper fusion reactor, one that *anyone* could buy? Energy shortages would become a thing of the past."

He paused. "You know something that would be funny if it wasn't so goddamned stupid—and tragic? We've known how to grow algae as a food source for centuries. It isn't exactly computer science either. So why doesn't *everyone* do it? Why are there people starving in the streets—here, on Tarsus—when we could be feeding them? Why is Earth the only world that was kept alive by algae bars?"

"There were rumours of people starving to death rather than trying to eat them," Clarence said, although he was more disturbed by the question than he cared to admit. That couldn't be true, could it? Earth had had eighty *billion* people living in the giant megacities before the skies fell. "Or...why? Why *don't* we feed ourselves?"

Harran laughed, humourlessly. "Because it's illegal," he said. "Farming combines pushed for algae-farming to be illegal on planetary surfaces. Earth passed the law, *after* writing an exemption to make sure it could keep feeding its own population. Yeah, sure, they taste worse than recycled cardboard. But who gives a shit if eating the bars is the difference between staying alive and starving to death?"

"I never thought about it like that," Patricia admitted.

"No," Harran said. "Neither did I, until I started to wonder *why*."

He stood. "Come on," he said. "I'll show you the factory floor."

Clarence kept his thoughts to himself as they took an elevator down to the production line and entered an observation room. He'd studied journalism law, back when he'd gone to journalism school, but he'd never thought to study the wider field of interstellar law. He had never even thought to question why it mattered. And yet...Harran was right. Earth had been setting precedents for human governance since before humanity had taken the first tiny steps into space. God alone knew how many useless—or outright harmful—laws were still on the statute books.

And anyone with enough wealth and power can afford to ignore them, Clarence thought. It wasn't hard to think of a handful of examples. The *Daily Truth* had broken the law at least seven times, to his knowledge; he'd be surprised if the total wasn't actually much higher. *But if you don't have the power to defy the law, watch out.*

He listened, silently making notes, as Harran explained how the production line actually worked. It involved a great deal of new technology and automation, apparently, although Harran was pushing to train new workers as quickly as possible. He had a *lot* of ideas, Clarence had to admit, from improving government to simply isolating the students who could think outside the box—and then nurturing that talent rather than allowing them to be ground under by the tutors and their fellow students. Clarence knew too many bright boys and girls who'd been mocked for taking their education seriously. If they could be given a new home, a place where they could actually learn…

"We're looking at apprenticeships," Harran said. "But they too are legally problematic."

"We'll make sure everyone knows about you." Patricia sounded as if she was very taken with Harran. "And things will change."

"I hope so," Harran said. "Earth is gone. Consider, for a moment, the implications."

"Everything will change, if we like it or not," Clarence said. He didn't blame Patricia for liking Harran—he found Harran admirable himself—but it was important to retain a certain degree of impartiality. They had to be neutral, to report the truth…whatever it was. He would have to make sure to look up the laws before he wrote anything. "And there's nothing we can do about it."

"Precisely," Harran said. "The Core Worlds have been stable for generations. Now…now that is going to change. And we have to be ready."

Patricia smiled. "We will be."

We shall see, Clarence thought. The optimist in him hoped she was right, but the pessimist feared the future. *We shall see.*

CHAPTER TWENTY-TWO

This was not always the fault of the embedded reporters. A number of editors and publishers, for various reasons, often saw fit to alter the original report until it bore (even less) resemblance to reality. This was particularly evident during the relatively minor insurgency on Palanquin, where a tiny skirmish that killed no one was turned into an immense week-long engagement that combined fast-moving tank battles with street-to-street fighting. The fact that no tanks were involved on either side—and, of course, the non-existent casualties—was never mentioned.

—PROFESSOR LEO CAESIUS
Crying Wolf: The Media and the Fall of the Empire

"WE HAVE A PROBLEM," JACKSON SAID, the following morning. "We have been summoned. Now."

Clarence felt his blood run cold as Jackson held out a terminal. He'd been expecting the hammer to fall for weeks now, but...it was still an unpleasant surprise. Perhaps it had been the story on Neil Harran and New Technology that had finally pushed the government over the edge. He took the terminal and read it, quickly. *Seeing Eye* was ordered to send three representatives to a government tribunal—a preliminary hearing—within two hours. It was the kind of move, he had to admit, that would terrify any small business. Two hours? It was barely enough time to *get* there.

He scanned the summons quickly, parsing out the bureaucratese. There was something mealy-mouthed about how the document was worded, with the consequences for defiance not quite spelled out, but he was fairly sure they would be dire. The government could just keep loading penalties on *Seeing Eye* until it collapsed into bankruptcy. There was no time to get a lawyer, let alone file for an injunction or anything else. They were going to have to fight the charges—whatever the charges actually were—in court.

"I'll be going, of course," Jackson said. "And Jessica is going to be accompanying me. Will you be the third?"

"Yes." Clarence silently thanked God that he'd spent days studying the precedents. "And you might want to call a lawyer too."

He dressed rapidly, feeling a yawning unease in his stomach. It was hard to force himself to eat, but he had no choice. He was pretty sure the judges—whoever they were—wouldn't be feeding them. Jackson and Jessica met him at the bottom of the stairs, both looking pale and wan. An aircar was already waiting outside. Clarence checked his terminal as they climbed into the vehicle and gave the driver his instructions. A handful of emails had arrived, mostly from people he didn't know, but none of them related to the hearing. He snapped the terminal shut and forced himself to relax as the aircar carried them towards the upper-class district. The looming towers—growing larger with every passing second—seemed to promise their doom.

Jessica caught his eye. "What do you think will happen?"

Clarence shrugged. There were any number of charges that could be brought against *Seeing Eye*, from the reasonable to the absurd. It was hard to imagine that any of them could be sustained in a fair and impartial court of law, but this was Tarsus. The government had plenty of ways to make someone's life utterly miserable without ever quite finding them guilty. They'd just have to play it by ear.

At least we got their attention, he thought, as the aircar landed in front of the courthouse and they clambered out. There were normally a handful of reporters outside the building—Clarence had done it himself, when he'd been a junior reporter—but there were none in sight today. *Did they get chased away or did the word come down from On High?*

He kept that thought to himself as they passed through a security screening—the guards were surprisingly professional, even as they systematically confiscated anything that could hide a recorder—and were directed into a waiting room. They were just on time, but Clarence wasn't surprised that they were made to wait anyway. It was nothing more than a power play, one he'd seen before from a dozen editors. Oddly, it reassured him. The judges wouldn't have hesitated to drag them into the courtroom—in chains, if necessary—if they had a solid case. God knew he'd had editors who'd *delighted* in chewing out their subordinates for the slightest mistake.

A door opened. "The judges will see you now," a young woman said. Her voice was completely professional. "If you'll come this way."

Jackson led the way into the courtroom. Clarence followed, looking around with interest. It was almost disappointing, more like an office than the gothic courtrooms he'd seen on the entertainment screen. Three people sat at a desk, facing them; a pale-skinned woman with short dark hair and two dark-skinned men, one who'd cut his hair short. They all wore judicial robes and matching poker faces. Clarence took his chair—*they* hadn't been given a desk—and studied the judges carefully. One of them looked surprisingly familiar.

"Judge Francisco," Jessica said, surprised.

Clarence blinked. Judge Francisco was a real judge, but he was the star of a reality program, where malefactors would be brought into his court and their guilt would be assessed before they were invariably sentenced to harsh punishment. His presence didn't strike Clarence as a good thing. Indeed, it made Clarence want to look around for hidden cameras. He saw none, but that was meaningless. The entire room could be wired.

"I am Judge Francisco," Francisco confirmed. "With me are Judge Seinfeld and Judge Hershey. You have been called before us to answer charges relating to owning and operating an illicit news organisation."

He paused. "How do you plead?"

Clarence sensed Jackson shifting uneasily. He spoke before his boss had a chance. "With all due respect, Your Honour, we don't know what the charges actually *are*."

"You *know* what the charges are," Judge Seinfeld snapped.

"No, Your Honour," Clarence said. He pressed on before his nerve could fail him. "By law, a court is required to present the accused—or even the summoned—with a list of charges or abandon the prosecution."

"This is not a prosecution," Judge Francisco said, smoothly. "It is merely a preliminary inquiry."

"You still have a legal obligation to present us with a list of charges," Clarence said. "Or else *we* will be obliged to declare the proceedings unlawful and withdraw."

Seinfeld gave him a nasty look. "You have no power to declare the proceedings unlawful."

"Yes, we do," Clarence said. "I can cite several court cases where the defendant's lawyers declared the proceedings invalid and *won*. Indeed, I might point to other cases where a failure to challenge the proceedings was regarded as a *de facto* and *de jure* acceptance of the unlawful proceedings. We would have no choice but to withdraw if you refused to uphold *your* obligations."

"You are not a lawyer," Seinfeld snapped. "You cannot argue in front of a court."

Clarence was tempted to point out that the summons hadn't given them anything like enough time to hire and brief a lawyer, but—instead—he concentrated on a different track.

"I am not a lawyer, Your Honour," he agreed. "However, as a Certified Journalist, I have the legal right to argue in front of a court. The right has not been *used* for over three hundred years, as most media organisations keep lawyers on staff, but it exists. I can defend myself—and my employers—in court if necessary. I can also declare the proceedings invalid."

Judge Hershey leaned forward. "Mr. Jackson, your friend is quite right. He does have the right to argue in front of a court. However, he is not a lawyer. Do you wish him to represent you?"

Jackson didn't hesitate. "Yes, Your Honour."

"Very well," Judge Francisco said. He tapped a terminal in front of him. "I'll have a print-out of the charges brought in at once."

The door opened a moment later, revealing the young assistant. Clarence kept his face expressionless as she handed out copies of the charge list, then departed as silently as she'd arrived. There hadn't been *time* to produce the copies. They'd already been printed out, just in case someone had the wit to demand them. It was just another power play. Clarence let out a long breath as he studied the list, comparing his copy to the other two. They appeared to be identical.

"As you can see, the charges against you are quite substantial," Judge Francisco said. "We believe, however, that something can be worked out."

Clarence read the list again, carefully organising his thoughts. "There are four main charges against us," he said. "Opening and operating an illicit news service. Interfering with the police in the lawful conduct of their duties. Taking a political stance by broadcasting commentary on the First Speaker's speech. And Grand Spamming."

"There are more charges," Seinfeld growled.

"They don't hold water," Clarence said. "For example, you have accused *Seeing Eye* of not paying taxes. However, there is no legal obligation to file a tax return until the end of the tax year. Paying tax itself comes later, once the tax authorities have processed the tax return and issued a demand for payment. *Seeing Eye* is simply too young to pay tax. You have also accused us of unsavoury business practices, such as underpaying our employees, but such issues have to be addressed through arbitration first. No one, to my knowledge, has filed a formal complaint."

"No one has," Jessica said, quietly.

"Furthermore, I can testify that *Seeing Eye* pays very well," Clarence added. "They are certainly not paying under the legal minimum wage."

Judge Francisco looked unhappy. "Very well," he said. "We will restrict our inquiry to the four main charges."

Clarence allowed himself a moment of relief. Every word he'd spoken was the truth, but...proving it would be costly. What did the law matter when powerful interests were at stake?

"But we reserve the right to reopen the other charges later," Seinfeld said. "They cannot be dismissed so easily."

But we could have tackled them without a kangaroo court, Clarence thought. *You're just trying to be an asshole, aren't you?*

He leaned forward. "Your first charge is that we opened and are currently operating an illicit news organisation," he said. Thank *God* he'd thought to look up the precedents. "It was clearly settled, seventy years ago, that *student* news organisations are—to all intents and purposes—legal news organisations, on a footing with *Daily Truth* or *Weekly Recording* or even *Brilliant Star*. The university handed out all the certification we need when it gave us permission to open and operate a student news organisation."

"But you are not *primarily* a student news organisation," Seinfeld said. "You do report *real* news, not shortages of canteen crap and how to achieve the perfect orgasm in ten easy steps."

"That does sound like most mainstream media outlets," Judge Hershey commented. "Self-help tips are all the rage these days."

Clarence concealed his amusement. "It doesn't matter," he said. "There is no requirement to report *solely* on matters of interest to students. And even if there was, we *could* argue that we have done so. Students need to be aware of the world around them."

He met Francisco's eyes. "The charge, in short, does not stand up to scrutiny."

"Perhaps," Francisco said. "We can certainly put it aside for the moment."

Clarence nodded and pressed on. "You have charged us with"—he made a show of reading from the paper—"interfering with the police in the lawful conduct of their duties. Again, this charge does not hold water. The recording—which we have made available to all interested parties—clearly shows that neither our reporter nor *Seeing Eye* as a whole made any attempt to interfere with the police officer in question. Our reporter was watching the story unfold until she became part of it. At that point…"

"You mean when she was arrested," Seinfeld said.

"When she was arrested, she offered no resistance," Clarence continued. "She allowed herself to be cuffed, searched and transported to a holding facility without making *any* attempt to resist."

"But she didn't identify herself to the policeman," Seinfeld said.

"She was in shock," Clarence said, bluntly. "The combination of being arrested and various lewd suggestions ensured she was in no state to speak until she reached the holding facility, where she was able to speak to a corrections officer. Furthermore, the officer never actually *asked* for her name. He made no attempt to identify her from the moment he laid hands on her until he handed her over to the holding facility's staff. Finally"—he took a breath—"she was in no way obliged to volunteer any information. I might refer you to a number of precedents…"

Judge Francisco held up a hand. "Perhaps," he said. "However, there is also the issue of you recording the policeman and releasing the recording, causing major disruption to the police as they try to undertake their duties."

"And releasing the policeman's *name*, which is flatly against the law," Seinfeld added.

Clarence braced himself. "Your Honour, with all due respect, we did not make the policeman act badly. We have testimonial from hundreds of women who have been forced to…ah…*endure* the attentions of police and security officers. That he acted badly—that he bent legal procedure as far as it will go—was not our fault. He had no right to expect *not* to be recorded, nor for the recording to be kept private."

"You should have taken it to the police complaints division," Seinfeld said.

"Your Honour," Clarence said, "would that have actually done any good?"

Seinfeld started to speak, but Francisco spoke over him. "You also released the police officer's name, which *is* illegal."

"No," Clarence said. "At no point did we reveal his name. We took all of the precautions we are legally required to take, including altering the footage to conceal his face. I do not know who revealed his name, Your Honour, but it wasn't us. We can prove it."

"Can you?" Francisco said. "We shall be checking on that, to be sure."

"Your Honour, our reporter was not the only woman to be molested by a thug in uniform," Clarence said. "We have drawn attention to a serious issue, one that needs to be fixed. And you are complaining that we did not follow proper procedure."

"Procedure exists for a reason," Francisco said. "Your actions led to countless attacks on the police."

"But those attacks are not our fault," Clarence said. "I might refer you to *His Imperial Majesty Vs Dunning*, where Dunning argued that he could not be held responsible for how people took his words or for their actions…"

"The details are not identical," Francisco said.

"No, but they're close enough," Clarence said.

Francisco snorted. "And the third charge?"

"That one is easy to dismiss," Clarence said. "We did *not* take a side. We merely reported the truth. Our commentary—our opinion—was clearly differentiated from our factual statements. Indeed, if you wish to complain about us reporting that the stadium was nearly empty, you must also complain about other media outlets telling the world that the stadium was packed to busting."

His lips quirked into a smile. The stadium had been huge, with nearly fifty thousand seats, but some media outlets had claimed that over a *million* students had stuffed themselves into the building to cheer the First Speaker. Didn't they know they were telling an absurd lie? Or were they too ignorant? He would have bet on the latter. An editor had probably added the line, without knowing or caring that it was obviously untrue. It was rare for an editor to gain the position without having his past experience somehow stripped from his mind. If, of course, he'd had any in the first place.

Seinfeld smirked, very faintly, but said nothing.

Francisco's lips thinned. "And the Grand Spamming?"

Clarence looked at the charge sheet again. "The charge can be separated into two sets," he said. He chose his next words very carefully. "First, you accuse us of obtaining the codes illegally. The codes in question are distributed to all regular news agencies, including the student ones. There is nothing illegal in us claiming the codes and using them. I might refer you to…"

"Yet another precedent," Seinfeld snapped. "I'm sure you might have a right to take something you're owed, but that doesn't give you the right to steal it."

"The codes are public knowledge," Clarence said. Frank Wong had explained it all in great detail. "We didn't *steal* anything."

"Hah," Seinfeld said.

"Second, we are not responsible for others copying our newsletters and forwarding them onwards," Clarence continued. "The people on our mailing list are the people who signed up for our newsletters. We cannot keep them from forwarding copies to their contacts."

"You should sell your own eReaders," Seinfeld said. "That would put a stop to your spamming."

It would also put a stop to our business model, Clarence thought.

He studied the judges carefully, trying to guess which way they'd jump. Hershey seemed friendly—or at least neutral. Seinfeld came across as an asshole; Francisco, by contrast, seemed to keep his thoughts to himself. It was hard to tell how *he'd* vote. But they'd still have to find a way to *legally* screw *Seeing Eye*. Their judgement would have to stand up to whatever challenges could be hurled at it…

"Thank you for your time," Francisco said. "Please wait in the sideroom. We'll call you back when we're ready to render our judgement."

And you're not pretending that this is a preliminary inquiry any longer, Clarence thought. *Is that a good or bad sign?*

"Thank you," Jackson said. He sounded tired, even though it was still early morning. "We will be waiting eagerly."

Clarence said nothing. His throat was parched.

CHAPTER TWENTY-THREE

It may seem curious that the media was allowed such freedom. As I have mentioned above, the corporate overlords dictated what the media could and couldn't say. This paradox has often puzzled my students. The answer, however, is quite simple. The overlords simply didn't care about damage to the military's reputation. They were far more concerned about threats to their own power.
—**Professor Leo Caesius**
Crying Wolf: The Media and the Fall of the Empire

"THAT WAS...NERVE-WRACKING," Jackson said, as he poured himself a glass of water. "I..."

Clarence tapped his lips. He'd bet every last credit he owned that they were under close observation. Whatever they said *would* be recorded and—perhaps—used against them. The panelled walls, decorated in a style that he thought was meant to be relaxing, could have hidden any number of microphones and video cameras. He wouldn't have been surprised to discover cameras in the washroom. A citizen had no right to privacy. *That* had been proven long ago.

"Take a drink and relax," he advised. "We'll go over everything later."

He sat, suddenly aware that his shirt was damp with sweat. They'd been lucky. The case against them hadn't been put together very well. They'd probably been expected to roll over and beg for mercy, rather than standing on their legal rights. Clarence had no doubt that the government would look for other ways to legally shut *Seeing Eye* down, if the young organisation refused to play ball, but…he shook his head. It would be hard for the government to find something—anything—that wouldn't incur the wrath of the mainstream media. They'd object—strongly—to a precedent that could be turned against them too.

But they have enough lawyers not to have to care about breaking the rules, Clarence thought, grimly. There were enough laws covering journalism to ensure that *no* newspaper could operate for long without unintentionally violating one or two. The mainstream media organisations kept lawyers on permanent alert to cover them if they *were* called out for breaking the law. *We don't have that luxury.*

He studied Jackson for a long moment, then turned his attention to Jessica. The youngsters looked tired and worn. They made no attempt to hide it. Clarence was fairly sure that they'd never experienced the coercive power of the state before, let alone felt as if they were one false move from plunging into the abyss. Jackson, at least, was from an immensely wealthy family. The odds were good that no one had ever forced him to do anything, let alone called him to account for his misdeeds. It was a minor miracle, Clarence considered, that Jackson had grown into a fine young man. And now…

They may think better of their project now, Clarence thought, feeling cold. *If they think they might be jailed—or worse—next time, what will they do?*

It was nearly an hour before they were summoned back into the chamber. The judges were still sitting at their table, as if they'd never left. Their faces were utterly unreadable, something that Clarence found a little reassuring. They wouldn't exactly have been gloating, he thought, if they'd found a legal way to screw *Seeing Eye*, but they would have shown a little hint of triumph. Clarence rather suspected they'd been given orders to shut the newspaper down, no matter what they did to the law in the process. The real question was who had issued the orders—and why.

It could have been the Justice Secretary himself, Clarence thought. The expose on police brutality had threatened the man's job. It still did, if the hints Clarence had received through his contacts were any indication. *The bastard hasn't realised that the scandal won't go away if we go away.*

He took his seat and rested his hands in his lap, waiting. Making them wait was a power play, one that suggested a certain insecurity. In hindsight, it was easy to realise that too many of Clarence's former editors had been strikingly insecure. They'd been one bad story away from being unceremoniously fired. No wonder Clarence himself had been fired without any protest from his editor. The poor bastard had known that any protest would probably end with him being shown the door too.

"We have consulted regarding your case," Judge Francisco said. His voice was completely flat. "It has become apparent that the charges against you do not hold water."

They never held any water, Clarence thought, hoping that his companions would have the wit to keep their mouths shut. The slightest word out of place would be used in evidence against them. *You threw mud at us to see what would stick.*

"Accordingly, we have no choice but to dismiss them," Francisco said, when none of the defendants said a word. "However, we must warn you against causing any further disruption."

"Or slandering the police," Seinfeld said.

Francisco shot him a sharp look. "The planet is in a very delicate state right now," he said, addressing Jackson directly. "We will not look with favour on anything that might tip us over the edge."

"With all due respect, Your Honour, we merely report the truth," Jackson said. "It is our duty to keep the public informed."

"That may be true," Francisco said. "However, by informing the public, you also make it impossible for us to deal with any...*problems*...quietly.

You have caused a great deal of disruption to the police force at the worst possible time."

Clarence gritted his teeth, half-expecting Jackson to say something that would make the matter far worse. It wasn't fair. It wasn't *remotely* fair. The police had been deeply corrupt long before Jackson—or Clarence himself—had been born. And everyone had known—everyone who lived outside the wealthy areas, at least—that the police could not be trusted. It was easy to argue that the police could have handled the matter quietly, but *would* they? No one in their right mind believed that the police would do anything. They'd been too corrupt for too long.

Jackson said nothing. Clarence allowed himself a moment of relief.

"You may go," Francisco said. "And don't let me see you back here again."

Clarence stood, nodded politely to the judges and headed for the door. Jackson and Jessica followed, collecting their coats and possessions as they left the building. Clarence felt an uneasy twitch at the back of his neck, instincts from the estates warning him that they were being watched by unseen eyes…the sense of *threat* was almost overpowering. It was all he could do to keep walking casually, resisting the urge to break into a run. The towering office blocks around them could easily harbour a sniper or two…

You're being silly, he told himself. *They're not going to have us assassinated in broad daylight.*

Jackson caught up with him. "That was close," he said. "I hadn't realised…"

"You've been playing with fire," Clarence said, flatly. He looked around. The crowds seemed harmless, as far as he could tell—no one appeared to be paying any special attention to them—but the sense of *threat* refused to go away. "And now the fire tried to burn you."

"You did brilliantly," Jessica said. "I was afraid they'd tear us to pieces."

"They still might," Clarence said. He sighed, inwardly. *Seeing Eye* needed a proper lawyer or two. But having a lawyer on staff might mean that all the really interesting stories would get cancelled before they hit the datanet. He'd seen it happen before, in the mainstream media. The editors didn't have to cancel stories—and make themselves the bad guys—when the lawyers would cancel the stories for them. "Welcome to the real world."

Jackson nodded, thoughtfully. "I think we should go to dinner," he said. He glanced at his wristcom. "And martinis. It has to be five o'clock *somewhere*."

"It's only three o'clock," Jessica said. "Shouldn't we be getting back to work?"

Jackson threw an arm across her shoulder. "As your editor, I say you can have the afternoon off at full pay," he said. "And Clarence too."

Clarence had to smile—it was impossible to imagine any of his other editors inviting him for a drink, let alone a meal—as Jackson led them down the street and into a large steakhouse. It was the kind of place the waiters would have taken one look at him, when he'd been working for the *Daily Truth*, and summoned the bouncers to evict him with as much force as they considered necessary. The men and women at the tables—comfortably spread around the dining room, rather than crammed so close together that it was impossible to eat without bumping one's neighbour—were all remarkably well-dressed. Maybe not the highest of the high, Clarence decided, but certainly members of the upper crust. The waiter checked Jackson's ID, bowed so low that merely *watching* him made Clarence's back hurt, and led them to a table at the rear. It looked so fragile that Clarence was almost afraid to sit down.

"Please, order whatever you like," Jackson said, as the waiter handed out menus. "My treat."

"Thanks," Jessica said. She gave the waiter a brilliant smile. "I'll order the chicken, please."

Clarence studied the menu thoughtfully. There were no prices, suggesting that anyone who had to *ask* the price probably couldn't afford it. He'd *heard* of restaurants that didn't have prices on their menus, but this was the first time he'd actually *seen* one. He hesitated, suddenly unsure what to order, then remembered that Jackson was a trust fund brat. He could probably afford to order everything on the menu without having to worry about the cost.

"I'll have the filet steak, medium-rare," he said.

"Thank you, sir," the waiter said. He took their drinks order, then bowed again. "That will be thirty minutes."

He departed. Clarence watched him go, then looked around the dining room. It was easy to pick out the staff—both men and women wore dark jackets, although the women wore knee-length skirts while the men wore trousers—as they moved from table to table, smiling in constant welcome. Clarence wondered, idly, if the staff had any reason to fear for their jobs, then dismissed the thought. The establishment attracted a very wealthy class of customer. They probably took enough money, in one day, to pay their rent for the entire month.

"You'll have to write up the entire affair for the newspaper," Jackson said, breaking into Clarence's thoughts. "I want a full article by the end of the day."

"I'll do my best," Clarence promised, as their drinks arrived. "But coming here isn't *that* conductive to actual work."

"You'll have plenty of time when we get home," Jackson said. He grinned. "Did they really think they could stop us?"

"Yes," Clarence said, flatly. "And they'll be watching, carefully, for us to make a tiny mistake."

"And then they'll jump on us," Jessica said.

"I'm afraid so," Clarence said. "We'll have to watch our backs."

He surveyed the giant room, studying the diners and trying to put names to faces. It was impossible. None of the *really* wealthy and powerful people would eat at a public steakhouse, even though the vast majority of the planet's population wouldn't be able to afford the bread and butter, let alone anything else. He thought he recognised a couple of faces, but he wasn't *sure*. They were probably important, even though he wasn't sure who they were, yet…

Clarence frowned. There was a thin aroma of *fear* in the room. He could *feel* it. But…he couldn't understand it. No one would come to eat *here* unless they were wealthy beyond the dreams of…well, anyone. Clarence would have killed, once upon a time, to be wealthy enough to spend money so freely. It had been hard enough going to a fancy bakery with Minnie, back when they'd been courting. That alone had nearly wiped out his wages for the month. They'd been too broke to call a hovercab when they'd had to go home.

"It feels curiously empty," Jackson said, thoughtfully. "We normally have to wait for a table."

"It doesn't *look* empty," Clarence said. He could only see a couple of unoccupied tables. It was possible, he supposed, that other tables had been stored in the backroom, but still…the place just didn't look empty. "What makes you say that?"

"There's normally a long queue of people waiting to get in," Jackson commented. "You're no one unless the waiter plucks you out of the line and takes you straight into the restaurant to eat. Now…we just arrived and we got a table on the spot, without waiting."

Jessica grinned. It was a surprisingly endearing look. "And you're not important enough to be allowed to skip the queue?"

"There *wasn't* a queue," Jackson said. "That's my point."

Their food arrived before Clarence could think of a response. His steak looked…*normal*, as far as he could tell, although there was a tiny note beside his plate explaining that the cow had been treated like a king…until it had been butchered, he supposed. It made him wonder what had happened to the Childe Roland, the heir to the Imperial Throne. Had he escaped Earth when the planet had collapsed into madness? Or had he been left to die as the Grand Senators made their escape? Clarence found it hard to believe that the Senators *hadn't* escaped. They wouldn't have had any trouble obtaining starships and fleeing into deep space.

"Tuck in," Jackson said. "You don't want to wait until it gets cold."

Clarence nodded and started to eat. The steak was cooked to perfection, although he found himself disliking the skin-on rustic chips and cooked vegetables. They were simply *too* upper-class for him. He silently kicked himself for not asking for fries instead, even though they weren't on the menu. The cook wouldn't have any trouble whipping up a batch if a customer wanted them. They'd probably add an extra thousand credits to the bill afterwards.

And that might not be a joke, either, Clarence thought. Most meat on Tarsus was vat-grown, these days. It was cheaper than actually breeding animals for the slaughter. *Real* meat was hideously expensive. *This little meal might wind up costing Jackson a bomb.*

"If they were willing to put us on trial," Jessica said, "what are they going to do next?"

"Good question," Clarence said. He took another bite of his steak. Truthfully, he couldn't tell the difference between real and artificial meat. "They may wait for us to break a law, if they're patient, or they may find another way to put pressure on us."

"Probably tell us to move out of the university," Jackson commented. "We *have* been turning a profit, after all."

"That will be expensive," Jessica said, quietly.

"Not if we rent buildings in the middle-class districts," Clarence pointed out. "There's no real *need* to have offices in the centre of town."

"Particularly as we don't need to be on the spot," Jackson said.

Clarence shrugged. There was little or no hope of having a reporter *everywhere* something newsworthy might take place. *Daily Truth* had thousands of journalists on staff and it hadn't been able to manage it. They'd just have to hope that they'd be able to catch up, once a story broke. The mainstream media would do everything in their power to stop them. God alone knew what they'd do next.

He frowned as he heard someone raising his voice. A red-faced man was arguing with the waiter, his voice loud enough to hear but too quiet for Clarence to make out any of the details. The portly man looked furious and embarrassed...a couple of additional waiters materialised out of nowhere and escorted him into the backroom. Clarence watched him go, wondering why the rest of the diners were studiously not paying any attention to the fracas. The man's companion, a woman who looked no older than Jessica or her friends, was staring down at her plate. Clarence couldn't help thinking that she looked as if she wanted to die of terminal embarrassment.

"Can we get the bill, please?" Jackson hailed the waiter. "And add a gratuity for the staff."

The waiter bowed, then held out a datapad. Jackson produced his credit chip and held it against the scanner. There was a pause, then a dull sound. Jackson blinked in disbelief and tried again. The datapad rejected the payment again.

"Your credit chip has been declined," the waiter said. His tone didn't shift at all. "Do you have any other means of payment?"

"Here," Jessica said. She held up her credit chip. "Try mine."

Clarence leaned forward, worried. Jessica's chip was rejected too. Had their credit chips been cancelled? He'd never heard of it happening, certainly not without warning, but it was technically possible. The government—or one of their other enemies—might have found a new way to bring them to heel.

"I have the money," a new voice thundered. An elderly gentleman was standing upright, waving a cane around as if he intended to brain someone. "I tell you I have the money!"

It isn't just us, Clarence thought. His blood ran cold. *What the hell is going on?*

"Try this," Jackson said. He pressed the company's credit chip against the scanner. It bleeped and accepted the payment. "That should be enough, right?"

"Yes, sir," the waiter said.

"We're not the only ones with problems," Clarence said, quietly. Unease was sweeping the dining room. "Do you use the same bank?"

"Of course," Jackson said. "Why wouldn't we?"

"Then I think there's a problem with the bank," Clarence said. "And that might be just the beginning."

"Yeah," Jackson said. He smiled, rather weakly. "Do you think there might be a story in it?"

"Probably," Clarence said. "But we have to get home to write it first."

CHAPTER TWENTY-FOUR

Nor was the military able to do anything about it. The officers on the ground might know the truth, but the (politically-appointed) officers back on Earth knew better than to meddle with the media. Their patrons, without whom there was no hope of advancement, would not have been happy if any restraints were put on the media by the military.
—**PROFESSOR LEO CAESIUS**
Crying Wolf: The Media and the Fall of the Empire

"WE SHOULD PROBABLY GO HOME STRAIGHT AWAY," Jackson said, as they left the steakhouse and headed down the street. "I need to get everyone on the case."

"Take Jessica and go," Clarence said. "I'm going to see if I can find out what's happening."

"Good thinking," Jackson said. He hailed a hovercab. It took a remarkably long time to arrive. "I'll see you back at the frat house."

"Be careful," Jessica said, as the hovercab landed. "You're our best reporter."

Clarence mock-saluted, then turned and walked down the street. It was lined with fancy shops, each one crammed with angry customers who were loudly insisting that they *did* have the money. *Some* credit chips were definitely working, Clarence noted, but at least two specific brands were not. Mega Bank and Interstellar Banking had apparently fallen out of the credit chip network completely. His blood ran cold as he realised just how many people kept their money in those two banks. The wealthy and powerful weren't the only ones getting a taste of what it meant to be living without access to funds.

And without access to credit too, he thought, as he stopped outside an automated bank machine and withdrew five hundred credits. The machine refused to dispense any more. *That* wasn't a good sign too, he thought. Normally, he'd be able to withdraw up to two thousand credits without problems. *What will happen when* everyone *starts withdrawing their cash?*

He kept walking, silently keeping track of developments. Large crowds were already forming outside the banking offices, even outside banks that hadn't—so far—dropped out of the credit chip network. Angry grumbles ran through the crowds as they grew larger, the people—including some very well-dressed people—demanding their money. Clarence had a nasty feeling that they were going to be disappointed. Bankers preferred to deal with electronic money these days, instead of paper cash. They probably didn't have anything like enough paper cash on hand to allow *everyone* to withdraw their savings. Clarence was no expert on interstellar banking, but he knew enough to be worried. If the credit chip network had collapsed, all hell was going to break loose.

A line of policemen appeared at one end of the street, their faces hidden behind masks as they started to deploy. Clarence winced, then forced himself to hurry past them and out of sight before the police sealed off the street completely. The police would probably be relatively gentle if a riot broke out in the shopping district, bearing in mind that anyone who shopped in the centre of the city would be rich or well-connected, but he doubted the police would take kindly to *him*. There were plenty of rumours about men who'd gone into a police cell and never been seen again. Clarence rather suspected he'd be unceremoniously deported if the police figured out who he was, *if* he was lucky. They'd be more likely to arrange an accident while he was in the cells.

He kept walking, noting the number of shops that were hastily closing their doors and bringing down the shutters. The shopping district rarely closed—it was practically open permanently—but it was closing now. Clarence shivered, even though it was a balmy evening. The relatively genteel chaos behind him was nothing compared to the oncoming storm when the *estates* realised that the credit chip network was on the verge of collapse. There were people there who were utterly dependent on borrowed money to remain alive…

And what will the government do, Clarence asked himself, *if the entire network collapses into a black hole?*

He stopped outside a bookshop—*real* paper books—and glanced inside. "We're closed," the owner said. He held a baseball bat in one hand, although it didn't look as though he knew how to use it as a weapon. "Go away."

Clarence held up his hands as he stood in the doorway. "I'm a reporter," he said. "Can I ask you some questions?"

The owner frowned. "Only if you don't mention me by name."

"I won't," Clarence promised. He stepped into the shop and looked around. The walls were lined with books, uncountable numbers of books. It felt like a quiet haven. He felt a sudden pang as he realised Minnie would have loved it. They'd never been able to afford *real* books. "I can write a story without mentioning you."

"Good," the owner said. "What do you want to know?"

"What happened?" Clarence leaned against the counter, trying to look interested and yet unthreatening. "All hell seems to have broken loose."

"I had a customer whose credit chip refused to scan," the owner said. "The payment just wouldn't go through. I checked the datanet and Mega Bank has apparently suspended operations completely…there was no way I could give him the book. So he stamped off in a rage and…well, the same thing happened to the next customer. Right now, I'm shuttering the doors until I know what's happening next."

"Riots, probably," Clarence said. "What does this mean for you?"

The bookseller wilted. "I don't know," he said. "I don't own this place, you see. If I can't make the rent, I get evicted. And then…I don't know. I don't bank with Mega Bank, but what if the other banks go too?"

Clarence asked a few more questions, but the bookseller was unable to shed more light on the situation. He thanked the man for his time and walked down the street, silently noting a handful of fights—and miniature riots—in a dozen shops. The security staff looked completely overwhelmed, unable to cope with so many problems. They were trained to intimidate potential shoplifters and help with the heavy lifting, not drive out so many rioters at once. And the police would be overwhelmed too. Clarence could hear something that *sounded* like a riot from the banking offices. It would be a long time before the police responded to a cry for help from the security guards.

His wristcom bleeped. Clarence checked it, frowning when he realised that it was nothing more than a message from Jackson asking if he was alive and well. There was no official message from the government, no reassurances that everything would be fine or dire threats to anyone who dared to threaten public order. Clarence wouldn't have put his faith in anything the government said, but it was worrying that the government had said nothing. An order to stay off the streets might have helped dampen the growing chaos.

And it's only going to get worse, he thought, grimly. *What happens when society starts to starve?*

Clarence did a handful of impromptu interviews, none of which shed any more light on the situation, then continued his slow walk towards the university. Almost all of the shops were shut by now, with their staff and owners nowhere to be seen. A couple looked to have been looted—he glanced into a shop and saw that the shelves had been stripped bare—but the thieves were nowhere in sight. The insurance alone was going to be a nightmare. He kept walking, carefully avoiding a small gang of teenage boys heading towards the riot. They didn't *look* to have grown up on the estates. Clarence felt a flicker of pity, despite the situation. They were going to get a lesson in how the *real* world treated rioters.

He reached the university gates, where he had to show his pass to the security officers before he was allowed to step onto campus. *Someone* had been smart enough to slam down the gates, he noted. It was uncommonly clever for the university staff—Clarence had heard that the Dean couldn't find his arse without holding a meeting with his entire staff—although he had his doubts about the security of the complex. The walls weren't strong enough to hold out a mob if it wanted in. He wondered, sourly, if he was walking into a trap as he made his way back to the frat house. There was hardly anyone on the streets.

Patricia met him at the door. "Clarence! Thank God!"

"I'm alive," Clarence said. "It wasn't *that* bad."

"The reports say that the entire city has been convulsed by rioting," Patricia said. "We've been ordered to stay on campus and wait for further instructions."

"The riots weren't *that* bad," Clarence said, although he had to admit that he'd only seen a tiny section of the city. Adana was *huge*, although far smaller than Earth's towering megacities. A riot on a lower-class estate—on *all* of the lower-class estates—would probably pass unnoticed on the university campus. "Methinks the mainstream media is exaggerating for some reason."

"No doubt," Patricia said. She fell into step beside him. "Anyway, Jackson wants to see you."

Clarence nodded and headed up the stairs. Jackson was in the common room, alternatively reassuring his staff and checking the datanet constantly. He looked relieved to see Clarence, as if he'd feared Clarence would meet a sticky end on the city's streets. Clarence thought he hadn't been in any real danger, but it was nice to know that his boss cared about him. It wasn't the sort of treatment that years of working for the *Daily Truth* had led him to expect.

"Good to see you again," Jackson said, as if Clarence had been gone for weeks. "What's happening out there?"

"Two banks have apparently failed," Clarence said, briskly. "And the entire city is going mad."

Jackson glanced out the window. "What can we expect?"

"I wish I knew," Clarence said. "I don't even know what's happened."

Patricia frowned. "Why would the banks fail?"

"They presumably can't meet their debts," Jessica said. She was sitting in a comfortable armchair, staring at nothing. "If a *person* can't meet their debts, they're screwed; if a bank can't meet its debts, everyone *else* is screwed."

"Everyone who trusted them with their money," Jackson said, flatly.

"Yes," Jessica said. "It will take days—perhaps weeks—to sort out the mess."

"And until then, we won't know what will happen to the money," Jackson said. "Or to our families or..."

Ouch, Clarence thought, as Jackson trailed off. *Your family might be completely wiped out by the bank's failure.*

"*Weeks* might be optimistic," Patricia said. "How long will it take to sort through every last credit and figure out what the bank owes?"

"I don't know," Jessica said. "I've never heard of a bank like Mega Bank failing. They always seemed too big to fail."

"But you can bet that the small customers will be the last to get paid," Clarence said. "And even if they do get paid, it will shatter their lives."

Jackson gave him a sharp look. "How do you mean?"

"People who live from paycheck to paycheck have no safety net," Clarence said. "If they lose their savings, such as they are, or simply don't get paid for a month or two...they're in deep trouble. Their landlord is unlikely to accept any excuses they may put forward because *he* needs his payment too. So the people get evicted and go...go where? There's nowhere for them to go."

Hellebore Estate? The thought entered his mind and refused to leave. *There are hundreds, perhaps thousands, of unoccupied apartments around the city.*

"But they will get paid again, won't they?" Patricia sounded stunned. "It's only temporary."

"It may prove lethal," Clarence said, flatly. "A bank failing could take hundreds of businesses down with it. They will lose their savings too. I hate to imagine what could happen when the shit *really* hits the fan. Millions of people will be out of work and on the streets."

"Go write it up," Jackson ordered. "And send it to me first, before you show it to anyone else."

"Yes, sir," Clarence said.

He walked back to his room, ignoring Patricia's unspoken offer to work with him, and sat down at his terminal. Hundreds of emails had flowed in over the last few hours, mainly tip-offs about problems in the banking industry. His lips quirked in annoyance as he scanned them quickly. If he and Jackson hadn't been at the so-called preliminary hearing, they might have realised that something was about to happen before it blew up in their face. A couple of prospective sources merited further investigation—he forwarded their details to Frank Wong, so he could check them out before Clarence replied to their emails—but the remainder weren't telling him anything he didn't already know.

And everyone else knows it too, Clarence thought, as he started to sketch out the story. It had been a long time since he'd done anything with economics, but that was hardly a hindrance. Indeed, it was something of an advantage. The economic writers he'd known at the *Daily Truth* had rendered their articles unreadable by extensive use of sophisticated technical jargon that was utterly impenetrable to the average layman. *I have to make what happened so clear that everyone can understand it.*

He divided his time between writing the story and checking the latest news updates from the mainstream media. Someone must have come down on them hard, because there were no more mentions of riots or anything beyond a few agitators. And yet…the government still hadn't said much of anything. There wasn't even a formal curfew! It made him wonder just what was happening, in the government's towers. The First Speaker might be on the verge of losing his post…

And we won't know about it until it's too late, he thought, as he finished the story. It was as simple as he could make it, although he had to admit the story was more complex than he'd wanted. *The government will tell us what's happening once it's made up its mind.*

He sent the story to Jackson, then stood and walked into the common room. Claudia and Jennifer Turner were sitting there, talking in low voices. Clarence hoped that Jennifer was listening to the older woman, even though he had to admit that *he* hadn't paid much attention to the old hands when *he'd* joined the *Daily Truth*. He'd thought too much of himself—and his journalistic skills—for that! It hadn't been until much later that he'd realised just how much he had to learn.

"Things were looking pretty grim out there," Claudia said, as Clarence put a burger in the microwave. "People were saying that the cash dispensers have run out of money."

"I wouldn't be surprised," Clarence said. "Where were you?"

"Following up a lead," Claudia said. "One moment, everything is fine; the next, all hell breaks loose."

Clarence took his burger when the microwave bleeped and sat down. "Things are going to be worse tomorrow," he said. "I know it."

Jennifer caught his eye. "How do you know?"

"The city doesn't produce its own food, right?" Clarence held up his burger to make his point. "Most of the food we eat comes from farms outside the city or orbital production facilities. What happens when people can't afford to buy the food?"

"But the government will step in," Jennifer said. "Won't it?"

"It may not matter," Clarence said. "If the government tries to…oh, I don't know…set the price of food, the supply will drop sharply. Farmers don't want to sell their food at government rates when they can make more money by selling it to smugglers. Even if the government manages to stop speculators like that, they're *still* going to have problems. And then there's the question of distribution. Are they going to force people to pay for their daily food? If so, what happens if they *can't* pay for the food?"

He frowned, remembering Neil Harran's comment about algae farms. "It could end very badly, unless someone thinks outside the box."

"True," Claudia said. "Very true."

Jackson entered, looking grim. "I read your story," he said to Clarence. "It'll be up tonight."

"Very good." Clarence couldn't help feeling that it would bring *Seeing Eye* more unwelcome attention. "I look forward to hearing what the readers have to say about it."

He finished his burger and stood. "If you don't mind, I'll get some sleep. I have a feeling I might need it."

"Good idea," Jackson agreed. He looked as tired as Clarence felt. Everything he'd worked for had been on the verge of falling apart, even before the *planet* had started falling apart. "It has been a long day, hasn't it?"

"Yeah," Clarence agreed. "The hearing alone was quite bad enough. And then…"

"All hell broke loose," Claudia said.

"But at least they won't have time to worry about us," Jennifer added. "They'll be too busy trying to keep rioters off the streets."

"You can go back out tomorrow," Jackson said. "I want you following up just *what* happened—and why. And what we might be able to do about it."

"Yes, sir," Clarence said. "I already have some ideas."

"The government won't listen," Claudia said, quietly. She sniffed as she took a sip of her drink. "Hasty action was never its forte."

"It was designed that way," Jackson said. "My ancestors helped build it. They just never expected…"

"Events," Clarence quoted. He'd learnt that at journalism school. Whatever happened, generally speaking, was rarely what people expected to happen. "Events, dear boy."

CHAPTER TWENTY-FIVE

Indeed, the powers-that-were that dominated the Empire, during its final
years, were seriously worried about a military coup. Prospective leaders
of such a coup—it should be noted that no plans existed, as far as we
have been able to determine—were often undermined by the media. It
made it harder for them to assemble the backing necessary for a coup.
—**PROFESSOR LEO CAESIUS**
Crying Wolf: The Media and the Fall of the Empire

"I'LL TAKE CASH ONLY," THE HOVERCAB DRIVER SAID. "If
not, you can walk."

"I have cash," Clarence assured him, as he clambered into the vehicle.
His tiny stockpile of ready money was shrinking fast. Hovercab drivers
weren't the only ones to realise that they could charge whatever they wished
for their services, now the credit chip network had been badly disrupted.
"And I'll pay when we reach the university."

He sat back in his seat and took a long breath, trying to relax. He hadn't
slept well, even though he'd been exhausted. Jackson had barely given him
any time to snatch breakfast and check his story's reception before sending
him out to conduct a string of interviews. It said something about their success, Clarence supposed, that *Seeing Eye* could now get interviews almost

everywhere, but it meant that *he*—and the other experienced reporters— were being worked off their feet. He wasn't sure when he'd have time to turn the interviews into a story.

And I'm not even sure we're getting paid this month, he thought. The students hadn't realised it—yet—but their families might have been wiped out by the banking crash. God alone knew what was happening to *Seeing Eye's* banking account. *What happens if we don't get paid?*

He gritted his teeth. He *loved* working for *Seeing Eye*. It was so much better than the *Daily Truth* that it wasn't even a contest, despite the amateurish aspects of the operation. Jackson genuinely cared about his employees, for one. Clarence was fairly sure that Jackson would never willingly throw someone under the bus for a simple mistake. That alone made him far superior to *all* of Clarence's former bosses. Clarence certainly wouldn't put himself on the line for *them*. They'd done nothing to earn his loyalty.

But if we don't get paid, he asked himself, *what then?*

It wasn't a pleasant thought. Imperial University would pick up some of the tab, unless…the university itself might have been wiped out too. The university got much of its funding from Earth, if he recalled correctly. No, the university *had* got much of its funding from Earth. Earth was gone. There would be no more interstellar bank transfers to keep the university open…and few benefits to be found by *keeping* the university open. Imperial University taught the Empire's elite, Clarence had been told, but what did that matter if the Empire no longer existed? Jackson's family might see advantage in moving their son to a home-grown university instead.

And most of the degrees are worthless anyway, Clarence reminded himself. *What will the graduates do when the shit hits the fan?*

His lips twisted in grim amusement. What would the elites do if they could no longer pay their staff? Their butlers? Their maids? Their security guards? Who would defend them against angry mobs if the shit *really* hit the fan? Clarence found it hard to believe that *anyone* would willingly stay with the elites, if they weren't paid. He'd met enough elitist students to be completely certain they treated their employees like crap. The maids might stab their mistresses in the throat as soon as they realised they no longer had to fear their revenge.

"Holy…" The driver's voice was shocked. "Hang on!"

The aircar rocked, violently. Clarence sat up, sharply. He'd been taking hovercabs for years and he'd *never* had a bumpy ride. Had someone flown too close to them? Or…he glanced around and swore, out loud, as he saw a plume of smoke rising up from an estate close to the centre of town. Not quite the upper-class district, but close enough. The shit might *really* have hit the fan.

"Take us there," Clarence said, leaning forward. A bomb. It *had* to have been a bomb. And he was close enough to get there before the streets were closed off. "Now!"

The driver looked at him. "Are you mad, man?"

"Get me there and I'll pay you double." Clarence's heart was starting to beat rapidly. This was it. This was the chance to be at ground zero of a *real* story. "Take us there and I'll pay…"

"I hope you know what you're doing," the driver said. He swung the aircar around, taking them out of their traffic lane. "If we get nicked, you're the one taking the blame."

Clarence kept his thoughts on that to himself as they approached the blast zone. Aircars were fleeing in all directions, trying to escape the scene of the crime. A handful of police aircars were heading towards them at speed. The driver swore as he dropped down into the street and landed neatly beside a looted shop. Clarence paid the bill without protest and clambered out of the car, his shoes crunching on the glass underfoot. The shop hadn't just been looted, he decided. It had been savaged.

He turned and ran towards the blast zone, ignoring the hundreds of people fleeing in terror as the smoke rose higher. It occurred to him, too late, that the bomb might have been designed to spread a chemical weapon as well as merely blow up the street, but…he shook his head and kept running. He owed it to himself to take some risks. Up close, it was all too clear that the bomb had reduced the Tarsus Pillar to rubble. Dead bodies lay everywhere.

It was no relief to know that, if the bomb had gone off before the banking collapse, the casualties would have been much higher.

Gritting his teeth, Clarence snapped his spectacles into place and looked around. It wasn't the first time he'd seen horror—growing up on the estates meant becoming hard very quickly—but there was something truly obscene about the devastation in front of him. The Tarsus Pillar was a planetary landmark, something that almost every schoolchild in the city was taken to see at least once. People came from all over the *planet* to see the Tarsus Pillar. And now it was rubble, surrounded by the dead and the dying. He glanced at a woman who was so badly wounded that she had no hope of survival, even if she was rushed to hospital, and silently recorded her final moments. The inhuman monsters who'd done this would *pay*.

He forced himself to think about possible suspects as the police and medical crews finally arrived in force, press-ganging passing civilians into helping with the wounded. Clarence had no qualms about helping, even though he wasn't a licensed medic. He recorded everything as he helped carry the wounded to ambulances, where stasis chambers were waiting to keep them in suspension until they could receive medical attention. The police and medical crews had responded with astonishing speed, part of his mind noted. But then, the riots had probably put them on alert.

Who did this? The thought ran through his mind, time and time again. *Who did this to us?*

He tried to come up with a possible suspect, but the list was very limited. Domestic terrorism was rare on Tarsus, simply because the police had wide-ranging powers to arrest and deport anyone they considered a threat. A lone operator *might* have managed to obtain explosives and set them off in the heart of the city, although Clarence had no idea *how*. The gangbangers who'd terrorised his estate hadn't carried—or needed—anything more dangerous than a knife or baseball bat. But why? A blow against the government? Or simply malice towards the upper-classes? He hated to admit it, but he understood the desire to make them *hurt* more than he cared to admit.

But the Tarsus Pillar wasn't in an upper-class area, he reminded himself. *Whoever blew it up was making a statement. They wanted to embarrass the government.*

It was nearly four hours after he arrived that the police coordinator finally declared that they'd recovered everyone who wasn't dead and ordered the remainder of the civilians out of the area. Clarence followed the others down the street to a corner, where an opportunistic stallkeeper had set up his wagon and started distributing mugs of tea and coffee. Clarence took one, then started to walk back to the university, heedless of the blood on his shirt. He would have to have it cleaned when he got home.

His wristcom bleeped an alert—finally—when he was nearly at the university. The government had declared a state of emergency and ordered everyone who wasn't in the emergency services to stay home. Clarence had no idea how the homeless would cope—he'd already heard reports of people being evicted from their homes, after the banking crash—but it hardly mattered. He reached the university, passed through the gates and walked down to the frat house. The entire complex seemed on edge.

"Jesus, Clarence," Claudia said, when he stepped into the house. "What happened to you?"

"I was helping at the bombsite," Clarence said. He took off his spectacles and passed them to Frank Wong. "That's pretty much everything I recorded."

"Go have a shower," Claudia said. "You can write your story afterwards."

"Will do," Clarence said. He glanced at Wong. "What did the police have to say?"

"Officially, nothing," Wong said. "Unofficially, I managed to hack the cameras covering the Tarsus Pillar. The bomb was carried in an aircar which broke out of ATC's control zone—quite easy to do if you know how to manipulate the system—and landed right next to the pillar. It exploded four seconds later. I'm still trying to trace the aircar itself. The police are probably way ahead of me."

"I'll be very disappointed if they're not," Clarence said, dryly. "Let me know what you find."

"Of course," Wong said.

"Get into the shower," Claudia ordered. "I'll bring you a robe."

Clarence felt his cheeks heat—remembering times when they'd shared a shower—as he turned and headed down the corridor. The students might be perfectly comfortable walking around naked, but *he* couldn't force himself to follow suit. Their perfect bodies were practically works of art—hell, they *were* works of art—while his had gone to fat long ago. He wasn't *that* unhealthy, he told himself firmly, but there was nothing like looking at a male student's genetically-engineered torso to make him feel inadequate. Normal men just couldn't compete.

Good thing intelligence isn't so easy to engineer, he thought. The upper classes liked claiming that they were the products of good breeding—and therefore had a right to rule—but he'd never seen any evidence suggesting that the upper classes were any smarter than anyone else. *We might be in real trouble if someone proved they* could *engineer a smart child.*

He undressed rapidly and stepped into the shower, silently grateful that it was empty. The university was surely rich enough to afford separate shower cubicles, but…instead, men and women showered together. It made him uncomfortable, not least because he knew *precisely* what would have happened at his old school if the boys and girls had used the same showers and toilets. God knew the sexual assault rate was through the roof with *separate* washing facilities. Maybe it was just something in the frat house's charter. Whoever had drawn it up might have thought he was emulating the lower orders.

Which is probably about right, Clarence thought, as he washed the blood away. *The upper classes don't have the slightest idea how we live.*

Claudia stepped into the room, carrying a woollen robe under her arm. For a moment, the years melted away and they were young again, no older than the students themselves. Clarence almost reached for her, to pull her into the shower, before he remembered himself and stopped. He was a married man. The thought cost him a sudden pang. He should email Minnie, just to make sure that his wife and son were alive. Minnie had made it clear that she didn't want to hear from him, but…he missed his son. Surely she wouldn't mind a single email. He hadn't quite lost everything, had he?

"The chief wants to see you," she said, looking away as Clarence dried himself before pulling the robe over his head. It was real wool, costing… Clarence didn't want to *think* about how much it had cost. "How are you holding up?"

"I'm fine," Clarence said. In hindsight, racing to the scene of the terrorist attack might have been a mistake. If there had been a second bomb—or worse—he might have been killed. Or arrested. God knew the police had no reason to love *Seeing Eye*. "I dare say I'll be fine."

"Just let me know if you want to talk about it," Claudia said. "You'll probably be better off talking to me than a counsellor."

"I'd be better off getting blind drunk than talking to a counsellor," Clarence muttered. The counsellors he'd known at the *Daily Truth* had been either idiots—it was hard to take them seriously after a reporter claimed to have been traumatised when her editor had corrected a couple of mistakes in her work and somehow earned medical leave—or spies for upper management, charged with rooting out discontented employees before they turned into problem cases. "But we can talk afterwards."

He walked up to Jackson's office and tapped on the open door. Jackson was sitting in his chair, watching the footage from Clarence's spectacles. Clarence winced, inwardly, as he realised that most of the footage would be put online. Journalists had always believed that '*if it bleeds, it leads*' but he'd never really liked it. There was something gruesome—and sickeningly voyeuristic—about watching wounded men and women take their final breaths and die. He would sooner have been one of the muckrakers who spent their time trying to catch celebrities in embarrassing—and exposing—positions than film horrors for public consumption.

Although the muckrakers do tend to get beaten up a lot, he reminded himself, dryly. No celebrity went out in public without a bodyguard who was more than willing to give a would-be voyeur a punch in the gut. And even if they survived the perils of the job, they found it impossible to get a press pass to…well, anything. *It isn't a job with good long-term prospects.*

"You did good work," Jackson said. He sounded pleased, but there was something in his voice that suggested he was more than a little distracted. "Guess what just happened?"

Clarence shrugged. He had no time for guessing games. "What happened, chief?"

"Well, the government has officially stated that the bombing attack was carried out by the Nihilists," Jackson said. "They claim that the remainder of the terrorist cell will be rounded up shortly."

"Really." Clarence wasn't so sure. His instincts were telling him that there was something wrong with the story. "They seem to have come to that belief remarkably quickly."

Jackson's eyes narrowed. "Do you believe them?"

Clarence shrugged. He'd never heard of any Nihilist activity on Tarsus. The Nihilists were a problem plaguing Earth and the innermost Core Worlds—or they had been, he supposed. Right now, the Core Worlds had plenty of other problems to worry about. But that didn't matter. The story was plausible. It was just…

"It shouldn't be possible to put together a determination so quickly," he said. He checked his wristcom. Barely six hours had passed since the bombing. "They would normally take longer to trace the aircar, even if the terrorists were stupid enough to use one that could be traced right back to them. This smacks of a story someone put together on the fly."

"The government *can* be efficient," Jackson pointed out. "Sometimes."

"It can't even lie quickly," Clarence said. It was quite possible that it *was* the Nihilists. Randomly bombing civilians—and aiming to kill as many as possible—was practically their trademark. But the government had pointed the finger too quickly for his peace of mind. "Maybe they're right. Maybe someone just jumped the gun. Or maybe the bombers had other motives than simple destruction."

Jackson shrugged. "We can discuss it later," he said. "For now"—he held out a datachip—"a press pass for the news conference tomorrow."

Clarence blinked. "News conference?"

"The First Speaker and the Security Secretary will be holding a joint press conference to discuss the banking crisis and the bombing," Jackson said. "They were kind enough to send us a press pass. Just one, but…at least they sent it."

"I see," Clarence said. It was remarkably cooperative for a government that had tried to shut *Seeing Eye* down. It made him wonder if something else was going on. But then, it wouldn't be the first time the government's right arm hadn't known what the left was doing. "And you want me to go?"

"Yes," Jackson said. "There's no way we'll get a scoop, but…we can make up for that with in-depth reporting. I want to know what they're saying—and your best guess at what they're *not* saying."

"Yes, chief," Clarence said. He'd have to be there early. Security around government press conferences had been tight even before the bombing. Now…he had a feeling he'd be waiting in line for hours. "I won't let you down."

"I know," Jackson said. "Good luck."

CHAPTER TWENTY-SIX

A further issue was that the media was part of the political wars.
Faction fighting was endemic. A media corporation was expected
to support its patron, mainly by running stories that boosted the
patron's prestige while attacking the patron's enemies.
—PROFESSOR LEO CAESIUS
Crying Wolf: The Media and the Fall of the Empire

CLARENCE HAD NEVER REALLY COVERED a political press conference, save—perhaps—for the First Speaker's hasty visit to Imperial University. He'd simply never been senior enough to join the reporters who were granted passes to press conferences, the favoured men and women who could be relied upon to put the right spin on events. Perhaps, he thought as he joined the line of reporters advancing towards the police checkpoint, that had been a blessing in disguise. He might have written the wrong thing several years too early and lost his job well before Seeing Eye had been conceived, let alone born. And that would have been the end.

He glanced around uneasily, watching the massed crowds as they shuffled towards the checkpoints. There were hundreds of policemen—and guardsmen—in view, but they didn't make him feel particularly reassured. The mainstream media had been blanketing the airwaves with horror stories about Nihilist atrocities on Earth. Gathering so many people together in one place struck him as a bad idea, even though the entire area was heavily patrolled. A single car or truck bomb could kill hundreds of reporters—and two of the most powerful politicians on the planet—in a single blow.

Not that everyone would consider that a bad thing, Clarence reminded himself. Journalists were one step below cockroaches, as far as the average citizen was concerned. Politicians were somewhere below even that. *The terrorists might make themselves very popular if they blew us all to hell.*

The line moved forward remorselessly. Clarence showed his press pass and ID to the policeman at the checkpoint, half-expecting to be told to leave at once. He hadn't expected *Seeing Eye* to receive a press pass to the Junior Vice Secretary's statement on culture and sport, let alone one of the most important press conferences in history. It was quite possible that their press pass had been decertified overnight…the policeman gave him a sharp look, then waved him through without comment. Clarence blinked in surprise. He *was* being allowed to attend?

Two policemen met him as he stepped into the male checkpoint and ran security sensors over his body. Clarence frowned as they confiscated his recording spectacles and terminal, putting them in a box for later recovery. The policemen were clearly determined to ensure that the government maintained a monopoly on information distribution. They were going to be disappointed—the mainstream media would *howl* if it was denied access to the complete recordings—but there was nothing to be gained by pointing that out. Besides, everyone knew that terminals could be used to coordinate terrorist attacks.

He left the checkpoint and walked into the giant media hall. A woman he vaguely recalled from the *Daily Truth* emerged from the female checkpoint, looking like a scalded cat. She probably hadn't enjoyed being searched very much either. Clarence made a mental note to file a story about the police returning to their old habits, although—the practical side of his mind noted—for once they might be justified in searching everyone thoroughly.

God knew there were plenty of ways to conceal recording gear in unchaste places. *Daily Truth's* lawyers were going to have a field day.

The woman stepped up next to him. "Clarence? It's Clarence, isn't it?"

"Yeah," Clarence said, trying desperately to remember the woman's *name*. She'd been a rockstar, as far as the editors had been concerned. Strikingly pretty, with long red hair and a smile that could move from warmth to ice in a second...they'd given her some of the most important stories in the city to cover. He was surprised she even remembered him, particularly after he'd been fired. "That's me."

"I'm Maddy," the woman said. She frowned as they walked into the press hall. "Have you ever seen such a mess?"

Clarence shrugged. The press hall was *huge*, almost as big as a stadium. Journalists—and media crews—were being herded into the upper levels, while the lower seats and stands were reserved for the party faithful. The walls were covered with banners, each one representing one of the planet's three main political parties; the stage, illuminated by brilliant spotlights, was empty. A low hubbub echoed through the room as reporters and party workers swapped rumours and lies about their doings. He couldn't help wondering just how long they'd have to wait before the speech actually began.

"It could be worse," Clarence said, finally. "No one was expecting a terrorist attack."

"I wasn't expecting to have my recorder stolen either," Maddy grumbled. "The old man is *not* going to be pleased."

Clarence glanced at her. "You *do* realise that a recorder could conceal a bomb?"

Maddy snorted. "No one could get a bomb into *here*," she said. "Have you seen the policemen outside?"

"I wish I shared your confidence," Clarence said. He admired her faith, but he questioned her judgement. The police only had to miss *one* thing for the entire conference to be blown to hell. "What's it like at the old place, right now?"

Maddy coloured. "The old man is in a bad mood, pretty much permanently," she said. "Is it…is it *good* to work at *Seeing Eye*?"

"It's better than the *Daily Truth*." Clarence wasn't sure what to feel. The sad truth was that Maddy, rockstar or not, was replaceable. Alistair Allrianne would have no trouble finding another rockstar—or someone he could groom into becoming a rockstar—if Maddy proved inconvenient. "Do you want to come work for us?"

"Perhaps," Maddy said. "Do you know how many stories have been killed over the past month?"

"Vaguely," Clarence said. Some of the best tips had come from disgruntled reporters. "And how many people have been fired?"

Maddy opened her mouth to answer, but a round of applause cut her off before she could say a word. Clarence winked at her, wondering if he should ask her out for a drink somewhere they could talk in private, then turned his attention to the stage. The First Speaker had stepped out of the sideroom, wearing a dark suit and tie. Clarence couldn't help thinking that he looked tired. The First Speaker had never really competed for office. He certainly hadn't been prepared to guide Tarsus through the maelstrom as the galactic economy collapsed.

Poor bastard, Clarence thought. He normally disliked and distrusted politicians, but he couldn't help feeling a little sympathy. *He reached the top and then everything went to hell.*

The First Speaker took the stand and waited until the applause had died away. Clarence watched, carefully noting who was applauding and who was conspicuously silent. It was hard to be sure, but it looked like only the Empire Loyalist party faithful were *actually* applauding their leader… it made Clarence wonder, suddenly, what was the point of being an Empire Loyalist if there was no Empire to be loyal to. The question nagged at his mind. If the Empire was gone, if Earth was no longer holding the Core Worlds together, what did it mean for Tarsus? What did it mean for the galaxy as a whole?

"These are the times that try men's souls," the First Speaker said. It was a quote from the past, although Clarence would have been surprised if more than a handful of people in the audience realised it. "Our world—our *galaxy*—has changed in a manner we did not expect."

He *sounded* tired too, Clarence thought, as the First Speaker droned through his speech as if he just wanted to get it over with and go back to work. It was hard—almost impossible—to convince himself that the party faithful would be inspired, let alone the rest of the audience. The First Speaker appeared to believe that things would go back to normal soon and it was just a matter of hanging on until the crisis was over. Clarence knew— he didn't think, he knew—that it was wishful thinking at its worst. Even if Earth was suddenly—miraculously—to be resurrected, there was no hope of repairing the damage the banking crash had inflicted on Tarsus. God knew that faith in the system had completely collapsed.

"Not a good speech," Maddy muttered. The droning had finally come to an end. "I wonder what the papers will say tomorrow."

"That it was the greatest speech in history," Clarence muttered back, as the First Speaker took his chair. He was entirely sure that Maddy would be fired on the spot if she wrote anything else. "And that it inspired us all."

He leaned forward as the Security Secretary took the stand to cheers from the Rebirth Party's faithful. Alfonse Drayton was a short man with an imposing presence, wearing a black suit as though it were a military uniform. He'd once been billed as the great hope of the Rebirth Party, although a combination of political incompetence and Tarsus's governing system had ensured that the Rebirth Party hadn't had a hope of actually reforming *anything*. Clarence himself had voted Rebirth, when he'd seen it on the ballot, but—cynically—he hadn't expected it to do any good. The system was designed to either absorb or destroy would-be reformers.

The cheering grew louder, the party faithful stamping their feet as they broke into a chant of "REBIRTH, REBIRTH, REBIRTH." The noise was deafening. Clarence glanced at the First Speaker, noting that the man looked physically ill. No doubt he hadn't *wanted* Drayton anywhere near his cabinet, certainly not in such a vital role, but the peculiarities of the system dictated that the ministerial positions had to be shared out among the major parties. It was a recipe for gridlock and stagnation. Clarence rather suspected that the planet's founders had wanted it that way.

Drayton raised his hands. Silence fell, instantly.

"Many years ago, we were cheated of our rightful place as sector capital." Drayton's voice was quiet, but he spoke with a conviction that echoed across the massive hall. "It was merely the start of the humiliations inflicted on us. We were an industrialised world, with a proud history, but we were constantly sidelined. The Empire dictated to us—the Empire set our laws—and, whenever we sought more freedom, we were punished. They tried to keep us down!

"But now the Empire is gone."

The words echoed in air. No one spoke. Clarence felt his breath catch in his throat. It was hard to believe that *any* politician could speak so bluntly, even now.

"The interstellar banks have collapsed," Drayton said, "and the galactic economy has been utterly shattered. The Imperial Navy, which has kept the peace for thousands of years, is fragmenting. There is fighting going on in the inner core, while the outer colonies have long since abandoned the interstellar unity…let us make no bones about it. Existence as we know it is over. Chaos threatens to overwhelm us.

"But let us not be terrified. Let us, instead, look to the future. Tarsus is not a weak and helpless world, cowering before the might of more developed worlds. Tarsus is strong, with an industrial base fully the match of any other world in the sector. Tarsus can reach for the stars, Tarsus can finally assume the position of leadership that she deserves. Tarsus can reach for a glorious future where her destiny will be decided by her people, not some distant Senate on a distant dying world. The future is ours, if only we reach out to take it!"

The party faithful started clapping and cheering, again. Clarence frowned as a handful of reporters joined them. The speech was an effective one, he supposed, but the cynic in him knew it wouldn't be *that* easy to take control of the sector. Tarsus would have to take control of its planetary system first and *that* wouldn't be easy either. He doubted the colonies on Argil, Agatha and Wormwood would happily subordinate themselves to Tarsus, even if they *were* having problems.

Drayton raised his hands again. The cheering died away so rapidly that Clarence was *sure* it had been rehearsed.

"No more will we be the puppets of off-world finance houses," Drayton said. "No more will our future be determined on Earth. No more…"

Clarence listened as the speech went on and on, punctuated by bursts of cheering from the party faithful. The First Speaker looked worse by the minute. Tarsus distrusted populism with a vengeance—the system was designed to make it difficult for anyone to ride a populist wave into power—but Drayton was *already* in power. And he seemed determined to rewrite the rules. Genteel political debate, in which nothing of any substance was decided, had been replaced…by what? Clarence could feel the energy, the demand for change, running through the room. It was only a matter of time, he thought, before it turned sour.

And keeping all of his munificent promises may be impossible, Clarence thought. The government had yet to find a way to cope with the banking crisis. *Seeing Eye* had received a tip-off suggesting that four *more* banks were on the verge of collapse. Their customers were already trying to withdraw their savings, even though paper money was rapidly depreciating in value. The planetary economy was in uncharted territory. *How is he going to pay for all this?*

Clarence's heart sank as the speech finally came to an end. The Security Secretary was making a bid for power at precisely the worst possible time. He didn't seem to understand what was *really* going on, let alone the misery being inflicted on millions—perhaps billions—of people on Tarsus alone. Clarence found it hard to care about thousand-year-old grudges when the entire planet was at stake. God! There was no point in moaning about which world had been selected as sector capital, not now! Drayton was merely digging up the past when he needed to look to the future and do something—anything—to help his people.

That's what he thinks he's doing, Clarence thought, sourly. He supposed there was *something* to be said for separating Tarsus from the interstellar economy, although it looked as though the interstellar economy had collapsed anyway. *But do we have the resources to build ourselves into an interstellar power when we have so many other problems we need to solve?*

He frowned, inwardly. Drayton had barely mentioned the Nihilists, let alone the bombing attack. He'd made vague promises of peace and security, but there was a worrying lack of anything *concrete*. It was hard to imagine what more, if anything, could be done…yet that wasn't the point. People were scared. They needed reassurance, even though anyone who thought about it would know that the reassurance would be worthless. There was no way to keep a determined terrorist cell from blowing themselves—and their targets—to hell.

And if they'd captured or destroyed the cell, they'd be telling everyone, Clarence reminded himself. *Instead, they're saying nothing.*

Maddy nudged him as the politicians filed out of the press hall. "What did you think?"

"I think that none of them are capable of solving our problems," Clarence said. He peered down into the lower levels. The party faithful were chanting again. "Do you want to get a drink somewhere?"

"I have to get back to the office," Maddy said, regretfully. "I'll send you my personal contact code. We can set up a meeting sometime next week."

"Of course," Clarence said, with the wry thought that Maddy might decide that meeting him was too great a risk. It was commonly understood that reporters had a right—and a duty—to meet with reporters who worked for rival media organisations, but Maddy's boss might decide that *Seeing Eye* was an exception. Maddy couldn't risk being fired, not now. She wouldn't have a hope of finding another job. "Let me know when you can make it."

They passed through the police cordon and walked down to the hover-cab rank. Clarence waved goodbye as Maddy climbed into a hovercab, then turned and walked down the street towards the university. The streets were eerily quiet, almost completely deserted. A chill ran down his spine as he noticed, for the first time, that everything was silent. The shops were closed and shuttered. There weren't even any security guards on the streets. He thought he saw someone peeking from behind a curtain as he walked past an expensive shop, but it was hard to be sure. It had just been a flicker of motion.

He looked up, silently noting just how few aircars were flying overhead. There were no shuttles at all. The spaceport was normally busy at all hours, but now...he wondered, morbidly, if Tarsus had been completely cut off from the rest of the galaxy. What would *that* mean for the planetary economy? He wasn't sure *just* how much Tarsus imported from the nearby worlds, but...

Clarence put the thought out of his mind as he kept walking. He'd have to write a story, when he got back to the frat house, but he wasn't sure *what* he was going to say. The First Speaker had sounded completely ineffectual, while the Security Secretary had promised sunshine and rainbows and...and too many other things, too many promises he couldn't keep. But Clarence knew that people would *want* to believe. They'd wanted—they *needed*—to feel that there was a light at the end of the tunnel. The problem was that the light might be an oncoming maglev train...

He was so lost in his thoughts that he didn't hear the groundcar until it was right beside him.

CHAPTER TWENTY-SEVEN

It was never easy to tell how much truth there was in any of the stories. A Grand Senator who made a gaffe was jumped on by his enemies, while his supporters either ignored or minimised the error. It wasn't uncommon for a politician to do something stupid, then have the story be mutated into something harmless or unrecognisable. The absence of independent reporting ensured that no one knew the truth.
—**Professor Leo Caesius**
Crying Wolf: The Media and the Fall of the Empire

CLARENCE LOOKED UP, ALARMED, as the black van pulled alongside him. It was rare to see a ground vehicle in the centre of town, unless it belonged to the emergency services and even they preferred to use aircars or flyers when they had to move from one side of the city to the other. But the van was completely unmarked. He barely had a chance to glance at the licence plate before the rear doors slammed open, revealing two masked men in black outfits and carrying shockrods. They lunged at him before he could do more than stare at them in horror, the leader jabbing him with his rod. Clarence screamed in pain—his nerves felt as if they were on fire—and collapsed to the ground, twitching. He could barely breathe. His entire body felt like a sack of useless potatoes.

"Grab him," the leader ordered.

Clarence struggled to move as the men grabbed him, lifting him up and throwing him into the back of the van. Pins and needles ran down his arms, making Clarence twitch uncontrollably as he struggled to move. His assailants grabbed his hands and yanked them behind his back, wrapping a plastic cord around them and drawing it tight enough to cut off the circulation. Clarence took a long breath, trying to understand what was happening. He'd heard of reporters being harassed, but someone being grabbed on the street and kidnapped was…it was new. Who were they? The police would have arrested him on the spot. They wouldn't have needed to hit him with a shockrod…

They might have wanted to hit me with a shockrod, he thought. The doors were slammed closed. A moment later, he heard the front door open and shut. His captors clearly had orders to leave him alone until they reached their destination. The vehicle lurched into motion a moment later, the whine of the badly-tuned engine assailing his ears. *Who are they?*

He forced himself to sit upright as sensation slowly returned to his body. The shockrod had probably been modified, if what he'd heard from protesters was true. Police shockrods weren't so unpleasant. He pulled against the cuffs, but the plastic was unyielding. There was no way he could break free with muscle alone. He looked around desperately, trying to spot a sharp edge. He *might* be able to open the rear doors from the inside—it was clear the van hadn't been *designed* to transport prisoners—but as long as his hands were cuffed escape was impossible. The people on the streets were more likely to mug him than do anything to help.

Assuming they don't think I'm on the run from the police, Clarence thought. The engine grew louder. He tried to guess where they were going, but came up with nothing. *Seeing Eye* had a lot of enemies. They'd failed to shut the newspaper down legally, so they were resorting to illegalities. Not, Clarence suspected, that anyone would care. The police would probably be quite relieved if *Seeing Eye* got a black eye. *Where are we going?*

He eyed the edge of the seat nervously—it looked too blunt to be of any real use—then turned and pressed the plastic cuffs against the edge, sawing with as much determination as he could muster. The plastic dug into his skin—he thought he felt damp, although he wasn't sure if it was sweat or blood—but he forced himself to continue. They'd made a mistake, he thought, when they'd used a plastic tie. Handcuffs would have been far harder to escape. But then, they would also have been harder to explain if the van had been stopped by the police. It was a surprisingly reassuring thought. The police weren't the ones kidnapping him.

Although they probably won't lift a finger to help, he thought. The plastic seemed to be weakening. He kept sawing, ignoring the aches and pains. The plastic seemed to be weakening. *They probably blame us for bringing their corruption to light.*

He let out a gasp as the plastic snapped. His hands came free. Clarence grinned to himself, then stumbled to his feet as quietly as he could. His legs felt wobbly—he'd been told that it could take hours to recover from being shocked—but he stumbled towards the rear door anyway. He wasn't sure how long it had been since he'd been snatched off the streets, yet—with the streets as empty as they were—the van could have travelled halfway across the city by now. The police had thrown up all sorts of checkpoints, but they weren't really concerned with vehicles *leaving* the city. No one would give a damn if terrorists blew up a hamlet somewhere outside Adana.

The door was locked. He cursed under his breath, then carefully removed the metal covering and fiddled with the lock, silently thanking one of his more disreputable childhood friends for the lesson. A groundcar could be stolen and hotwired quite easily, if one knew what they were doing. They were nowhere near as secure as aircars. The older models didn't even have control chips that linked directly to the city's traffic controllers. There was a loud *clunk* as the door unlocked. Clarence cursed again—the bastards were *sure* to have heard the sound—and pushed the door open. They'd left the upper-class parts of the city far behind. It *looked* as if they were somewhere in the estates.

Fuck, Clarence thought. *Here goes nothing.*

He braced himself as the vehicle started to slow down, then pushed the door open as wide as it would go and jumped. Someone shouted behind him as he pulled his body into a ball and landed hard. It hurt more than he'd expected—he'd never thought about jumping out of a moving vehicle before—but he forced himself to struggle to his feet and run for his life. A handful of people stared at him as he staggered off the road and down the nearest alleyway, too desperate to escape to care about the danger. It was probably better to be mugged than remain with the kidnappers.

The shouts grew louder as he hurried down the alleyway, looking from side to side for a place to hide. It wouldn't be safe, certainly not if he stumbled across a pack of gangbangers, but he was running out of options. The bastards weren't struggling with the after-effects of being hit with an over-powered shockrod. He stumbled past a gang of teenagers, male and female, then stopped. They stared at him in astonishment. He knew that astonishment would turn to anger—and worse—very quickly. But if he was lucky...

"The pigs are after me," he stammered. It was harder to talk than he'd realised. "Keep them off my back."

He shoved a hand into his pocket and produced a pair of hundred-credit notes. More money, he suspected, than any of the teenagers had seen in their lives. He shoved the money at them, then turned and ran down the street. His legs hurt worse than he cared to admit. He was running on pure adrenaline now, all too aware that he could collapse at any moment. It had been years since he'd been in the gangs himself, years since he'd been as fit as anyone on the planet...he forced himself to keep going, despite the growing pain. He didn't *dare* let the kidnappers, whoever they were, catch up with him.

A movement caught his eye. "Hey, man. You want some fun?"

He turned his head and saw a young dark-skinned woman standing by the door of an apartment building, wearing a short white dress and shirt that revealed more than they concealed. A prostitute, he realised. He'd never been anywhere near the brothels since he'd left the estates, even before he'd married. The brothels were cheap, but…he'd never liked them. He'd been all too aware that his sisters could easily have wound up in a similar place.

"I can do anything," the woman said. The desperation in her voice touched a nerve. "Ten credits for anything you like."

Clarence hesitated, then took the plunge. "Do you have a bedroom?"

"I do indeed," the woman said. She indicated the doorway. "What do you want?"

"Twenty credits if you take me there and give me some help," Clarence said. He tried not to think about Minnie. His wife would not be amused if Clarence visited a brothel, even if he had good intentions. "Please."

The woman nodded. Clarence felt a pang of guilt as he followed her through the door and up a creaking flight of stairs. Twenty credits wasn't *much* for the risk he was asking her to take on his behalf. He told himself that he had no choice as she led him into a small bedsit. If they caught him again, they'd make damn sure he didn't have a hope of escaping for a second time. It wouldn't be hard, either. They'd only have to keep shocking him every twenty minutes to keep him under control. They probably wouldn't give a damn about the risks of nerve damage either.

"So," the woman said. She took off her shirt with practiced ease, followed by her dress and underwear. "What do you want?"

Clarence had to smile. "A cup of tea and a quiet sit down."

The woman blinked at him. "What?"

"A cup of tea and a quiet sit down," Clarence said. "That's all I want, really."

"That's a very odd fetish," the woman said. "Why do you…?"

She shook her head as she turned away, heading over to the kitchen unit. Clarence watched her go, trying to ignore the bruises on the back of her thighs and buttocks. Her pimp had beaten her recently, probably for not bringing in enough money to satisfy him. It wouldn't be long before the bastard beat her to death or sold her to a brothel, once she was no longer profitable for him. She'd be dead before she reached twenty-five.

"Just tea," the woman said, wonderingly. "Do you want to watch me drink it?"

"No, thank you," Clarence said. He took the chipped mug she held out to him and sipped it gratefully. The tea was poor quality, but it was tea. "But you can drink some for yourself, if you like."

The woman looked bemused. "I can find you a boy, sir."

"I don't want a boy, or anyone," Clarence said. "I just want a rest."

He glanced towards the covered windows, wondering what he'd see if he looked outside. The kidnappers, hunting him? Or gangbangers, convinced that he'd brought the police into their neighbourhood? Or... or nothing? There was no way to know. The kidnappers could have been anyone. Clarence sipped his tea, considering the possible suspects. Simon Goldwater? Or someone in the police force? The kidnappers hadn't been policemen, but that proved nothing. It would be easy for someone in the police force to pay a gang of thugs to kidnap him and take him to a safe-house somewhere outside the city. He shook his head, grimly. There was no way to know. And no proof—he was sure—that would lead back to the person in charge.

It might even have been a random kidnapping, he thought, although he doubted it. The upper-class parts of the city were kept under extensive surveillance. Any criminal who operated there risked losing everything, once the police traced him back to his home. *They might have thought there were people who would pay for my safe return.*

He looked up at the woman, trying not to stare at her chest. "Where *am* I?"

The woman eyed him, sharply. "You don't know where you are?"

"I got a little lost," Clarence said. "Where am I? Which estate?"

"Remington Estate," the woman said.

Clarence blinked. Remington Estate? Right next to Hellebore? That could *not* be a coincidence. There were easier and safer ways to take a groundcar out of the city, ways that didn't involve driving through an estate crammed with poor and desperate people. The kidnappers might not have *time* to search for him, not if the gangbangers thought they were cops. It was quite possible that they were already dead...

But if they were taking me to Hellebore, he thought, *why?*

His mind ran in circles. What was so important about Hellebore Estate? And the other estates? Maxima Corporation had been so desperate to move ahead that they'd shelled out millions of credits in compensation...small change to them, perhaps, but corporate bosses rarely cared to spend money compensating people when they could keep a lawsuit going indefinitely until the claimants ran out of money. It just made no sense. He looked down at his hands, trying to think. There was no reason, as far as he could tell, for such haste.

Which means I'm missing something, he told himself. *But what?*

He finished his tea and looked up. The woman was very close to him, her bare breasts bobbling in front of his eyes. He felt his member start to stiffen, reminding him just how long it had been since Minnie and he had made love. It had been hard, so hard, to sleep together when they both had tiring jobs *and* a small child in the apartment. How long had it been? He tried to remember, but it was impossible. It was hard to remember his wife's *face*, let alone anything else.

She left me, he thought. He'd taken their marriage vows seriously, but now...they seemed so insubstantial. *I don't owe her anything.*

"The mattress is over there," the woman said. "How do you want me?"

"I don't want you," Clarence lied. He could have her. He could have her in any way he wanted, any way at all. She would do *anything* for a handful of credits. And yet, he didn't want to do it. His body wanted her, but his mind told a different story. It was just hard to put his reasons into words. "But I could do with more tea."

The woman eyed him for a long moment. "You're the strangest man I've met."

Clarence shrugged. He was fairly sure he knew her life story without having to ask. Her father would be a mystery, of course. Her mother had probably brought whole *armies* of stepfathers to her house, men who'd come and gone so quickly that the poor girl didn't remember their names. She'd grown up alone, probably losing her virginity very quickly…probably to the man who'd become her pimp. And then she'd spent the rest of her life servicing her clients, all too aware that if she failed to earn enough money she would be beaten or sold to a brothel. And…she'd be discarded anyway, once she grew too old and unattractive. Prostitution did not have a retirement plan.

Unless you work at a really high-class brothel, Clarence thought. *And there's no way they'd take someone from the gutter.*

"I'm too old to be interested," he said. "But I will pay you for your time."

He wondered, suddenly, if there *was* anything he could do. A dozen ideas flew through his mind, but they were all impractical. He couldn't find her an apartment in a better part of town. He couldn't find her a job. He couldn't even get her into a training college where she might learn a useful skill. There was *nothing* he could do for her and he knew it. Even giving her a major payment would be useless in the long run. Her pimp would probably take the cash off her as soon as Clarence was gone.

The woman poured him another cup of tea. Clarence stood, rubbing his aching arms and legs. The pain had largely faded, thankfully. He'd have to get a proper check-up at some point, just to make sure there was no long-term damage. *That* was probably going to be costly. The university had a medical centre, with free treatment for its students, but he had no idea if they'd accept him. He'd never been a student at Imperial University.

He drank the tea, then reached into his pocket and produced three credit notes. A ten, a twenty and a hundred. The woman's eyes went wide as he held them out to her, inviting her to take them. A hundred and thirty credits was *far* more than she'd expected. Clarence hoped she'd have the wit to hide most of the cash before her pimp came home and demanded the money. There was no way he could tell her what to do. God alone knew what she'd make of it if he tried.

She'd probably think I intended to take her away from her pimp and pimp her out myself, he thought. There were plenty of movies about good-natured prostitutes who fell in love and escaped the scene, but they had about as much in common with the truth as the average government financial statement. *Better to let her think I don't intend to come back/*

"Good luck," he said, quietly. He glanced out the window. The streets below were empty, but the sun was starting to set. He had to be out of the estate before darkness fell. "And goodbye."

The woman kissed him hard, her breasts pressing against his chest. "Thank you," she breathed, softly. "Whoever you are, thank you."

"You're welcome," Clarence said. A kiss wasn't so bad, right? "Goodbye."

CHAPTER TWENTY-EIGHT

Worse, the media's lack of experience told against them. It was often hard for them to understand what was really going on. A Grand Senator who had taken bribes to ensure that a particular bill was voted into law was not, in their view, any more or less corrupt than the rest of the Grand Senators. It was far from uncommon for politicians to take bribes. Business as usual, right?
—**PROFESSOR LEO CAESIUS**
Crying Wolf: The Media and the Fall of the Empire

"CLARENCE," JACKSON EXCLAIMED, as Clarence stumbled into the frat house. "What happened?"

"I ran afoul of some people who tried to kidnap me," Clarence said. It had taken him nearly two hours to walk back to the university. He'd barely managed to get out of the estates before sunset plunged them into darkness. "I had to find a way to escape."

He sat down and outlined the whole story, starting from the moment the van had pulled alongside him. Jackson listened, asking a handful of questions as Clarence glossed over some of the details. Clarence had the feeling that his boss didn't quite believe him, despite the marks on his wrists. Jackson lived in a world where kidnappings simply didn't happen, not outside bad movies. It had been an unpleasant surprise to Clarence too. He honestly couldn't imagine why anyone had kidnapped him off the streets.

Unless they want to scare us, he thought. The *Daily Truth* wouldn't give a damn if a star reporter was kidnapped, but *Seeing Eye* was younger. And Jackson was far closer to his staff than Alistair Allrianne had ever been. He might flinch at a ransom demand, instead of calling the HR department and ordering them to find another hotshot reporter to fill the missing man's shoes. *They might just have succeeded in scaring us too.*

"I see," Jackson said, when he'd finished. "We'll have to file a police report, of course."

"I suspect it will be pointless," Clarence said. "The police aren't going to listen to us."

"You were kidnapped," Jackson said. "You could have been *killed*."

"Perhaps," Clarence said. "But the police have good reason to detest us. And there's another problem we need to bear in mind…"

He briefly outlined his suspicion that the kidnappers had intended to take him to Hellebore Estate. He'd mulled it over time and time again, during the journey home, and concluded that there could be no other destination. The spaceport was, technically, in the same direction, but there was no reason to drive a groundcar through the estates if the kidnappers had intended to take him to a shuttle and send him off-world. He wasn't even sure there *was* a road leading through Hellebore that went to the spaceport. It was something he'd have to check.

"But there's no proof," Jackson said. "They could have intended to take you somewhere else."

"Yeah," Clarence agreed. "But where?"

He put the thought aside. "If you don't mind, I'd like to write the story and then see what I can dig up from the datanet," he said. "I've probably missed my deadline."

"I dare say we can overlook it, just this once," Jackson said, dryly. "Don't let it happen again."

Clarence nodded and hurried back to his room. His clothes felt damp with sweat, so he changed into a bathrobe before sitting down in front of the terminal. Someone had already put the two speeches online, spamming everyone's inbox with direct links to the videos. Clarence's lips twitched with annoyance. The judges had accused *Seeing Eye* of Grand Spamming, but the government had spammed *everyone*. He put the thought aside for later consideration and watched the two videos carefully. Nothing had been altered, as far as he could tell, but they'd been shot very carefully. The First Speaker looked as if he was on the verge of collapse, while Alfonse Drayton appeared young, resolute, strong and—above all—ready to take the helm. Clarence didn't need to see the production credits to guess that one of Drayton's partisans had spliced the video together. He'd done an excellent job of promoting his boss.

Clever bastard, Clarence thought. *It won't be easy to explain what you've done and why.*

He checked the mainstream media's reports. They were practically united behind the government, but…there was a subtle edge in some of the reports that nagged at his mind. On one hand, they were backing the government, yet—on the other hand—they were criticising the First Speaker and backing the Security Secretary. *That* was odd, to say the least. It was rare for the media to take *any* sort of stance against the government. Clarence skimmed through the lists until he found Maddy's report and read it carefully. Maddy, it seemed, had damned the First Speaker with faint praise and cheered Alfonse Drayton to the skies. There was nothing in the report that the Empire Loyalists could object to, not without making themselves sound like prats, but…they'd *know* what had happened. It might not be long before Maddy was unceremoniously fired from the *Daily Truth*.

They'll fire her even if someone else wrote the fatal words, if the First Speaker's office makes a fuss, Clarence thought. *There's always another rockstar just waiting in the wings.*

Shaking his head, he started to write his first article. It was easy enough to point to the problems with Drayton's vision, starting with a serious lack of concrete proposals for repairing the damage caused by the banking crisis. People who were on the verge of losing their homes because their savings had vanished into thin air had too many problems of their own to give a damn about Drayton's vision of galactic power. It would take years, perhaps longer, to stabilise the failing banks. Drayton might believe that the government could spend its way out of a crisis, but where would the money be spent? Clarence found it hard to believe that the people who needed help would be the ones who got the money.

He finished the article, sent it to Jackson for approval and started work on the second. It was harder to explain the media bias, at least without slipping into the kind of jargon that would make his words about as incomprehensible as the average economic statement. The average reader would notice if Maddy and her fellows had openly damned the First Speaker, but they'd find it harder to comprehend that he'd been subtly pushed aside in favour of Drayton and the Rebirth Party. Clarence had to work hard to put it into the kind of words everyone would understand. He wasn't entirely satisfied when he was done, but he sent it to Jackson anyway. The editor would be able to tell him if it was comprehensible.

And then we have to see what the rest of the world thinks, Clarence thought. *And perhaps update the article to address their questions and concerns.*

He put the thought aside as he started to trawl the datanet. It was no surprise to discover that information relating to Hellebore—and the other estates Maxima Corporation had claimed—had practically vanished from the net. His original article was hard to find, which he'd expected, but the puff pieces praising Maxima for compensating the former tenants were gone too. That *was* a surprise. Maxima had excellent reason for wanting them to be easy to find. Everyone knew that lazy searchers only read the first handful of articles that appeared in their search results and stopped there. The corporation could easily have paid the search engines to prioritise the puff pieces.

Curious, Clarence thought.

He kept digging through the records, trying to understand what had happened. Maxima had paid a great deal of money for something that seemed practically worthless. It made no sense and yet...his kidnappers had been taking him towards the former estate when he'd escaped. It *could* have been a coincidence—it wasn't as if there were a shortage of places in the estates where a captive could be held indefinitely—but Clarence didn't believe it. The estate just kept popping up, time and time again.

And they knew where to find me, Clarence thought. It was hard to believe that he'd been a random victim. No one would take the risk of snatching someone off the streets in broad daylight unless they were *sure* it would pay off. Either his kidnappers had gotten very lucky indeed or the whole affair had been planned from start to finish. *Why—how—did they know how to find me?*

He considered it for a long moment, scribbling notes to himself as he put the story together, piece by piece. The government had tried to shut *Seeing Eye* down, legally. That hardly suggested that the government looked upon them with favour. But, at the same time, the government had *also* given *Seeing Eye* a press pass...it made no sense. The easiest way to weaken *Seeing Eye* would be to *deny* the tiny newspaper the access it needed, ensuring that the reporters would always be working from second-hand accounts. Clarence wouldn't have known that the video footage had been carefully edited if he hadn't been there. It wasn't as if the mainstream media had pointed it out.

They would have expected us to send a reporter to the press conference, if they gave us a press pass, Clarence thought. It might not have been *him*, but he wasn't the only reporter who'd embarrassed powerful people. *Me or Jennifer or...well, anyone. They weren't after me in particular, just a reporter who worked for* Seeing Eye. *And once they had one of us in their power, who knows what would have happened next?*

He scowled, absently. It was easy, all too easy, to start believing his own theories. He'd been warned never to put the theories before the facts or he would start twisting the facts to fit the theories, rather than adjusting his theories to fit the facts. Conspiracy theories were attractive, his tutors had insisted, because they imposed imaginary order on chaos. People *looked* for order, rarely understanding that *some* things were nothing more than random coincidences. Correlation didn't always imply causation. A politician's speech might *not* be connected to something on the other side of the planet. And yet…

It was hard *not* to believe that there was a connection. Someone had set him—or another reporter—up. It had been clever, if it was true, and utterly deniable. There was no proof, he was sure, that the press pass and the kidnap were connected. He'd look a raving lunatic if he tried to make such a case in court. But then, most conspiracy theorists *looked* like raving lunatics. The government didn't need to discredit them because they did a wonderful job of discrediting themselves.

"But the whole affair doesn't make sense," he said to himself. "What are they doing?"

Gritting his teeth, he went back to the start. He'd reported on the Forsakers being evicted from their estate…and been fired. Simon Goldwater—or someone in his office—had taken exception to the report and ordered it suppressed. That was proof, Clarence was sure, that there *was* a fire somewhere in the smoke. No one would order a reporter fired when they could have killed the story, *unless* they wanted to make it very clear that further inquiry would not be welcome. And they'd probably succeeded. Clarence was, as far as he knew, the only reporter who'd bothered to even *try* to figure out what was going on.

He scribbled a note on his pad as he worked his way through the next step. He'd reported on Maxima Corporation ordering thousands of people to leave Hellebore Estate—*without* compensation. This time, the story *had* broken into the mainstream. And Maxima Corporation had folded. They'd paid out compensation at once, without making any attempt to fight. It suggested that there was something time-sensitive about the whole affair, but what? Clarence couldn't think of anything.

And at the same time, Goldwater attempted to buy us, he thought. *He offered to give us everything we wanted, knowing it would make us dependent on him. Why?*

Clarence sat back. It all seemed to come back to Simon Goldwater. Goldwater had fired Clarence from the *Daily Truth*. Goldwater had attempted to silence *Seeing Eye*. And...Goldwater's media empire had slighted the First Speaker while promoting the Security Secretary. In fact—Clarence skimmed through the records—it looked as if Maxima Corporation was one of the biggest donors to the Rebirth Party. *That* was odd—the original Rebirth Party had talked of breaking the corporate hegemony—but perhaps it was understandable. Goldwater had tried to bribe *Seeing Eye*. Why couldn't he try to bribe the Rebirth Party too?

I could just be imagining everything, Clarence reminded himself, sharply. It was impossible to be *sure*, damn it. Was he seeing the shadow of...*something*, a whale moving under murky waters, or was he just devising a conspiracy theory? *What if I'm wrong?*

He looked down at his notes. The pattern was clear, yet...yet what? It was easy to think there was nothing there. And he had personal reasons to dislike Simon Goldwater. One didn't have to be a socialist or a secessionist to think there was something wrong with a single man wielding so much power. Drayton had railed against distant puppeteers, but there weren't *that* many differences between Simon Goldwater and the Grand Senators. The Grand Senators had merely been more successful.

Maybe that's the point, Clarence thought, as he brought up a street map of the city and studied it. *Goldwater wants that sort of power for himself.*

There was a tap on the door. "Clarence? You there?"

Patricia, Clarence thought, as he concealed his notes. *Where's Claudia?*

"Come in," he said. There was no point in pretending to be asleep—or away. "What can I do for you?"

Patricia entered the room. "I heard you were injured," she said. "Shouldn't you go to the clinic?"

"I don't know if they'd take me," Clarence said, honestly. "I've had worse, believe me."

"That doesn't mean you shouldn't take care of yourself," Patricia said. She eyed his wrists doubtfully. "What happened?"

"I got kidnapped," Clarence said. "Luckily, the kidnappers didn't have the sense to use handcuffs."

"That's good to hear, I suppose," Patricia said. "Why...why did they kidnap you?"

Clarence hesitated. He would have confided in Claudia without a second thought—he could rely on his old friend to tell him if he was following a genuine trail or talking out his arse—but he wasn't so sure about Patricia. She simply didn't have the nose to be a good reporter. It took time to develop the right instincts and too many mistakes, too early, could blunt them permanently. But then, he supposed, blunted instincts might serve her well if she moved to a mainstream news organisation.

"I think they wanted to scare us," he said, finally. It might even be true, although he had a suspicion that something more had been intended. "I don't scare *that* easily."

Patricia shot him an admiring look. "Of course you don't."

"But everything just seems to lead back to Hellebore Estate," Clarence mused. "I think I want to go back there."

"When?" Patricia leaned forward. "I could go with you."

"Tomorrow, I think," Clarence said. "Or perhaps sometime in the next few days. I want to see the reaction to my last story before I go back there."

"I could go back for you," Patricia offered. "Just tell me what you want me to see."

"I'd have to tell you what I wanted you to *look for*," Clarence said, "and I'm not sure myself."

"But you'll know it when you see it," Patricia said. "Won't you?"

"I hope so," Clarence said. In truth, he was nowhere near as confident as he tried to sound. It was easy to miss a subtle clue when one didn't really know what was going on. Or, for that matter, see something that wasn't actually there. "I'll have to go in person and see."

"I can go first," Patricia said. She rested her hands on her hips. "I have a reputation to build."

"I wouldn't advise it, Patricia" Clarence said. "That's a rough area. You might wind up in trouble. Bad trouble."

"I'll be fine," Patricia said.

"No," Clarence said, flatly. She'd *seen* the estates. She should know better. "You could end up mugged. Or raped. Or murdered. I'll take you with me, when I go, but *don't* go alone."

Patricia gave him a defiant look. "You're not the boss of me."

"No," Clarence said. He reminded himself that he'd been just as determined to find the story when he'd been her age, never caring about the risk to life and limb as long as there was a chance to win fame and glory at the far end. Patricia was too young to share his cynical approach to life. "I'm warning you about the dangers. If you go there alone, without someone to escort you, you are taking your life in your hands."

"Fine." Patricia sounded petulant rather than angry, as if he were her father and he'd just denied her a treat. "I'll do as you say. But you *will* take me with you."

"Very well," Clarence said. If it was the only way to guarantee her safety—or at least *try* to keep her safe—he'd do it. "We'll go in a day or two."

And see what we can find, he added, silently. He had a feeling that they might need to climb over the barricade and sneak into the complex. *Who knows what might be waiting in that estate?*

CHAPTER TWENTY-NINE

But when the bill practically ensured—as a number of late-term political bills did—that there would be armed resistance...was it not treason?
—**Professor Leo Caesius**
Crying Wolf: The Media and the Fall of the Empire

"COLLECT YOUR DAYSTICKS," THE SERGEANT SAID, as the young men assembled in front of the blacked-out buses. "Remember what I taught you. Make me proud."

Colin Simpson swallowed, hard, as he took a daystick from the pile on the table and held it in his hands. It felt like a club, like the baseball bats he'd carried as a young man, but there was a solidity to it that he found reassuring. The sergeant had taught them how to use the daysticks for both offence and defence, pointing out that it was just as easy to smash someone's skull as it was to block an incoming blow. A thrill of anticipation ran through him as he realised they were *finally* going to put their training into practice. *Someone* was going to regret ever having crossed paths with him.

He smirked as he pulled on his balaclava and followed the others into the bus. This was it. Days—weeks, perhaps—of training and education, of endless lectures about how *they* were the great hope of the planet, were about to be replaced by action. He found his seat and sat down, glancing from side to side as the bus's engine whined into life. His comrades were hidden behind their masks, but he could tell they were as excited—and nervous—as himself. They all knew that they were about to face their first real test.

The bus shook, then rumbled forward. Colin took a long breath, and another, forcing himself to calm down. They had to be calm. Their instructions had been very specific. They were to get in, do as much damage as possible and, when the whistle blew, hurry back to the buses without delay. The sergeant had harped on that, time and time again. They were not to allow themselves to be bogged down—or to be caught by the police. *That would be disastrous.*

Although there's not much we can tell, Colin thought. He knew almost nothing about the resistance, from the location of its training base to the people directing operations from behind the scenes. The Captain and the Lieutenant had never bothered to share their names, let alone anything else that could be used to identify them. *They can knock me about all they like, but I can't tell them anything.*

He felt his heart starting to pound as the bus drove onwards. The windows were blacked out, of course, but…there was something odd about the journey. It took him longer than it should have done to put his finger on it. Ground traffic was controlled by streetlights, but the bus hadn't stopped once. They appeared to have kept moving from the moment they left the warehouse until…he glanced at his empty wrist, remembering—too late—that he'd left his watch at home. He didn't even know the *time*. It was hard not to feel offended that the resistance didn't trust him to keep their secrets, even though the sergeant had made it clear—time and time again—that trust had nothing to do with it. And, perhaps, to wonder if there really *was* anything above them. He'd met quite a few wannabes who'd claimed to have extensive connections with the gangs and criminal rings that infested the estates.

And none of them had any real connections at all, he thought, remembering a particularly slimy stepfather who—thankfully—hadn't lasted very long. The man had always been boasting about his connections, damn him, when he hadn't been peeking at Angelina and making spiteful remarks to Colin. *No one bothered to defend him when he got mugged in the park, did they?*

The bus started to slow down. "Get ready," the sergeant said. "On my command, form lines."

Colin braced himself. This was it. They were *finally* going to be tested. And they were going to strike a blow for their planet. They were going to teach the traitors a lesson they would never forget. He couldn't wait.

"Form lines," the sergeant ordered. He wasn't carrying a daystick. Instead, he was wearing a pair of boxing gloves. "When the doors open… you know what to do."

Colin stood, feeling the sergeant's eyes on him as he joined the line. He wanted—he *needed*—the man to be proud of him. It would be nice, perhaps, to have a *real* father figure in his life, instead of a line of seedy stepfathers. The sergeant was a *real* man. Tough, easily tough enough to put any of his trainees on the ground, but understanding too. Colin had no trouble believing the sergeant wanted him to succeed. He wasn't the kind of asshole who feared being replaced—or worse—by those he was supposed to teach. No, he was a man. Colin wanted to be just like him.

The doors crashed open. Colin had the faint impression of white buildings, so fancy that they *had* to be near the centre of town, before he spotted the marching crowd. The Empire Loyalists, the traitors who'd sold Tarsus to the Empire, were trying to put on a show of strength to keep the people from voting them out of office. It had been explained to them, time and time again, but Colin didn't need any encouragement to hate the bastards. The Empire Loyalists were the ones who'd inflicted the shitters on the estates.

He shouted a wordless challenge as the young men flowed out of the bus, charging right at the marchers. They were a curious mass of middle-class men and women, holding up banners that proclaimed their loyalty to the eternal empire. The march's stewards, the people charged with making sure that the marchers hewed to the party line, turned and stared in disbelief as the fighters bore down on them. They weren't ready for violence. Colin sensed, more than saw, the march waver. It gave him a vicious thrill. For the first time in his life, he had real power. He could make them *fear*.

They crashed into the marchers like the hammer of an angry god. Colin lifted his daystick and brought it down on a marcher's head, barely taking a moment to check that he'd been knocked down before he turned his attention to the next. A middle-aged matron stared at him, her mouth wide open as he lifted his daystick. Colin felt a surge of pure hatred—he'd seen too many women like her in school—and crashed his daystick down hard. The woman tumbled to the ground. Colin kicked her vindictively—perhaps she wasn't one of the idiots who'd talked down to the estate kids, but he found it hard to care—and moved on to the next target. A younger woman turned and fled, screaming. Her boyfriend...Colin expected him to *try* to defend the girl, but he was running away too.

Coward. Colin didn't bother to hide his contempt as he looked for another target. *You wouldn't last a day on the estates.*

The march had dissolved into hell. Hundreds of people lay on the ground, unconscious or dead. Blood stained the stones under his feet. A handful of resistance fighters were setting light to the abandoned banners, laughing as they caught fire with damnable ease. Colin turned slowly, feeling...he wasn't sure *how* he felt. He nearly tripped over a young woman—no older than Angelina—who'd been knocked to the ground by a mighty blow. Her skull was cracked and broken. Colin had no doubt she was already dead.

Bitch, he tried to tell himself. The girl had probably grown up sneering at kids who'd been unlucky in their choice of parents. She'd been one of the girls who'd laughed when a boy who didn't have a million credits in his trust fund asked her out. He was sure of it. And yet, looking at her dead body, he felt a flicker of guilt. *What have I done?*

He silently thanked the sergeant for the mask as he surveyed the horrors. The march had been smashed. Everyone had run, even the young men who could have put up a fight. It was vindication, almost, of everything he'd been told. The people in power were strong only as long as no one stood up to them. They'd folded at the slightest challenge. He remembered the fleeing boyfriend and snickered. That weakling wouldn't last a *week* in the brave new world. Without money and connections, what *was* he? Nothing.

The whistle blew. Colin hesitated, even as the rest of the fighters started to run back to the bus. It was tempting, very tempting, to just run the other way and lose himself in the crowded streets. He could mug a passer-by for his clothes, then run back to the estates…he shook his head. The resistance would know he'd deserted and hunt him down. They knew where to find him—and his family—too. He would have no hope of escaping them permanently unless he stayed well away from his old haunts. And besides, he didn't want to let the sergeant down. He *wanted* the man to feel proud of him.

He concealed his churning thoughts behind the mask as he ran back to the bus and clambered aboard. The sergeant counted the fighters, then snapped a command to the driver. Colin barely had a moment to sit down before the bus lurched back into motion, racing away from the scene of the crime. It wasn't a crime, Colin told himself, but…he tried not to think about the dead girl. Her face seemed to drift in front of his mind's eye, staring at him accusingly. He hadn't landed the fatal blow—he thought—but it didn't matter. He couldn't help feeling guilty. He'd thought of the Empire Loyalists as monsters, not people. And yet, they *were* people…

"Good work, all of you," the sergeant said. "You did very well."

They wet themselves the moment they saw us, Colin thought. Mob violence was a fact of life on the estates. It was better to kill someone who *really* crossed the line than risk a liberal lawyer getting the bastard off on a technicality. But it wasn't a reality in the upper-class parts of town. *They didn't even try to fight.*

It was impossible to sort out his feelings. The marchers had been Empire Loyalists. They'd supported policies that harmed the estate-dwellers. They deserved to know—to really *know*—that the estates would push back hard. He couldn't help feeling a little proud that he'd helped take the fight to the *real* villains. The shitters hadn't wanted to be moved to the estates, any more than the estates had wanted to take them. It was the corrupt politicians who were the real enemy, the enemies the estate-dwellers couldn't touch. But they'd been touched now. It felt good. It felt good to know that he'd *finally* hit back.

And yet, he felt a hint of guilt. The marchers had included women and children. And they weren't all condescending bitches. It was easy to *say* that the suffering should be spread around, that the people in charge needed to know that *their* relatives would be hurt by their policies, but it was harder to put it into practice. He looked at his daystick, noticing—for the first time— that it was covered in blood. It was suddenly very hard not to throw up.

The bus lurched to a halt. The doors banged open.

"Place your daysticks in the basket, then form up in rows," the sergeant ordered. "The Captain wishes to address you."

Great, Colin thought, sardonically. *What is he going to tell us?*

He stepped out of the bus, unsurprised to discover that they were back in the warehouse. He'd half-expected the other training groups to greet them as they returned, but the giant building was practically empty. The Captain was standing by the doorway, waiting for the trainees to assemble before he started his speech…Colin studied him, wondering—not for the first time—who was above him. Who commanded the resistance? And why?

"Into rows," the sergeant reminded them. His voice brooked no resistance. "Now, if you please."

Colin sighed, inwardly, as he hurried to obey.

• • •

Senior Constable Peter Quigley had been surprised when his suspension had been cancelled and he'd been called back to duty, although he supposed he really shouldn't have been. The banking crash had been quite bad enough, but the bombing—and the riots—had been considerably worse. Everyone with police and military experience had been called back to duty, even him. The other policemen might eye him with suspicion—as if he was the *first* policeman to claim the perks of rank—and he feared what would happen if a reporter recognised him amongst the throng, but…being called back to duty worked in his favour. It was a *de facto* statement that the charges against him could not be sustained.

He waited, with the other policemen, for the order to advance to Grantville Square. *Something* had happened, but what? The dispatcher had been very clear, ordering the policemen to assemble in force before answering the distress call. Peter had expected a handful of units to go ahead to make a preliminary report—and he'd also expected that Sergeant Grozny would volunteer him for the job—but instead he'd been told to wait for further orders. The policemen checked their weapons, drank coffee and swapped lies about what was waiting for them. None of them really knew anything.

Sergeant Grozny barked a command, his eyes lingering on Peter *just* long enough to make it clear that he, at least, didn't think Peter was off the hook. Peter sighed, snapped his protective mask into position and joined the other policemen as they began the march down to Grantville Square. Ambulances were assembling behind them, summoned by the dispatchers, clearly waiting for the police to secure the area before they collected the wounded. Another bombing? Peter had heard all sorts of rumours about terrorist cells being broken open, but none of them had been confirmed. It was impossible to know what to believe. Sweat trickled down his back as they marched onwards. They might be walking into a trap.

A rustle ran through the ranks as the policemen turned the corner and marched into Grantville Square. For a moment, Peter thought that there *had* been another bomb attack. Smoke was billowing up everywhere. Bodies—countless bodies—lay on the ground, some clearly beyond salvation. Rational thought asserted itself a moment later. Whatever had happened, it hadn't been a bomb. The pattern was all wrong. A bomb would have done a great deal more damage to the surrounding buildings…

He stumbled as the policemen spread out, hastily cordoning off the scene. He'd seen horrors civilians never saw—he'd seen battered wives and abused children and gang violence—but this was a special kind of horror. The marchers—they had to be Empire Loyalists—had been attacked, savagely attacked. It was all he could do to keep functioning as he started to check the nearest bodies. He'd never seen anything like it, not in the wealthy parts of town. Even the rioting, after the banks had started to collapse, hadn't been so brutal.

Sergeant Grozny glared at him. "Help the medical staff get the wounded into the ambulances."

"Yes, sir," Peter said.

His stomach churned as he found a wounded man and waved to the medical crews. He hadn't signed up for *this*. He'd seen being a policeman as a chance to finally get respect, even if it came at a price. No one really *liked* policemen, even other policemen. He hadn't realised just how far and how fast the planet could fall. He'd always assumed that things would never change. And yet…it was clear he'd been wrong.

He helped a young woman to her feet, careful not to do *anything* that might bring the sergeant's wrath down on his head. She was pretty enough, he supposed, but someone had given her a nasty gash on her face. The medics glanced at her, then told her to wait. She looked astonished, as if she'd expected immediate treatment, but Peter wasn't surprised. There were too many people who were on the verge of death. A black eye might be shocking, particularly to someone who'd never felt *real* pain in her life, but it wasn't the end of the world. She'd live.

"Sit down over there and wait," Peter ordered, quietly. He pointed at the handful of policemen who were taking statements. No doubt there would be a tidy little narrative in a few hours that bore little resemblance to the truth. "They'll want to talk to you."

The girl didn't argue, much to his surprise. She merely stumbled towards the policemen, leaving him behind. Peter turned and surveyed the scene as more and more senior officers arrived, command confusion starting to set in as it became increasingly unclear who was actually in charge. Tarsus had procedures for dealing with terrorist attacks, he'd been told, but they'd never actually been tested. The bombing attack should have been a wake-up call to senior officialdom. Peter wasn't surprised that they were still half-asleep.

And it might be time to start thinking about getting out, he mused, as Sergeant Grozny dragged him into a clean-up crew. He *really* hadn't signed up for this. *The planet is going downhill fast.*

CHAPTER THIRTY

It wasn't uncommon, either, for certain stories to be killed even when—in theory—the subject was on the other side of the political wars. The media publishers often covered up criminal acts that would have shocked the population, knowing that their patrons would be displeased. Senator Carder's depraved tastes were common knowledge amongst the elite, but nothing leaked out until after his death.
—PROFESSOR LEO CAESIUS
Crying Wolf: The Media and the Fall of the Empire

"THAT'S THE LATEST STATEMENT from our beloved Security Secretary," Clarence said, holding out a datapad. "It's pretty tough."

Jackson took the datapad and scanned it, carefully. "Do you have anything to add to the bare facts?"

Clarence winced. Four days had passed since the Empire Loyalists had been attacked by unidentified thugs, four days in which government statements had grown increasingly hysterical and—according to some of his sources—there had been a massive upswing in political violence and terrorism. Alfonse Drayton was the only politician who seemed to be rising to the moment, but his proposals for dealing with the crisis were draconian. The government seemed to be on the verge of a massive clampdown on just about everything, from free trade to press freedoms. Clarence had the feeling that it was only a matter of time before a full state of emergency was declared. *Seeing Eye* would probably be the first newspaper to be shut down.

"There aren't many actual *facts*," Clarence said, carefully. *Seeing Eye* hadn't been given a press pass to *that* speech, although—to be fair—only a handful of tame reporters had been invited to attend. "However, it is my considered opinion that the proposed counterterrorist measures will do more harm than good."

Jackson nodded. "Then write it up," he said. "I want the people to know the truth."

"It's opinion, not truth," Clarence corrected. "I may be wrong."

"You haven't been wrong before," Jackson said. "And I am prepared to back you."

Against the full power of the state? Clarence wasn't so sure about *that*. Jackson's parents might be influential enough that the government felt the need to tread carefully, but...once a state of emergency was declared, their opinions wouldn't matter. *We might all wind up in jail tomorrow.*

He put the thought to one side as he headed back to his room and started to work. It was easy enough to pull up a list of proposed security measures and explain how they would severely impinge upon freedom, although the cynic in him wondered if anyone would actually notice the difference. Tarsus had never been a particularly free world. The founders might not have wanted to give the government immense power—and effective separation from the people it was meant to rule—but they'd laid the groundwork for tyranny. In some ways, Clarence was surprised that Tarsus hadn't collapsed into fascism long ago. The major political parties had often had more in common with each other—and plenty of incentive to share power—than they had with the people they were supposed to represent.

And we don't even know if they can carry out their security measures, Clarence thought, as he finished writing his article. There were hundreds of thousands of policemen and security personal on the planet, but were there *enough*? Tracking down and questioning every idiot who posted something stupid on the datanet would require more police officers than Clarence thought were on active duty. *They might find themselves completely unable to actually enforce their new laws.*

He frowned. It was a simple rule of thumb that ninety percent of the crap posted on the datanet was nothing more than crap. People bragged, people made accusations…confident, so confident, that they could never be traced. It wouldn't be easy to tell the difference between someone who was speaking for the terrorists—the government had stopped talking about the Nihilists by name—and someone who was talking nonsense. Some poor kids were likely to find themselves hauled in for questioning—or simply detained until the police could find time to interrogate them. Clarence had a feeling that things were going to go down rapidly.

Too many people on the estates claimed to have connections outside of it, he recalled. *And most of them were talking bullshit, trying to build up a reputation that might save them when the shit hit the fan.*

Shaking his head, he checked the news reports. There was nothing particularly new, save for a claim that a police roadblock had stopped a terrorist cell from blowing up the spaceport by intercepting the bomber before he could reach his destination. Clarence rather suspected that the story had been blown out of all proportion, even though it didn't seem to have spread to the *rest* of the mainstream media. It was unlikely, perhaps, that the bomber had *really* been trying to reach the spaceport. Nothing short of a nuke would do more than minor damage to such a vast installation.

He stood and headed down to Frank Wong's office. The WebHead was looking frazzled, just like the rest of them, although he seemed to be having fun probing through the hidden sections of the datanet. He looked up as Clarence tapped on his open door, then pointed to a comfortable chair. Clarence sat down and waited for Wong to disengage. He'd always hated being interrupted at work too.

"I've been busy," Wong said. He spun the chair around until he was facing Clarence. "Our datanet node has been taking a *lot* of harassment lately. The bastards nearly took it down twice. Fortunately, I was able to deal with it by…"

He grinned. "Do you want the technobabble?"

"I don't think so," Clarence said. "Did you find anything interesting?"

"Oh, quite a bit." Wong grinned, savagely. "I'm not sure how *helpful* any of it is to you, but…you can be your own judge."

He swung back to the console and tapped a key. "The government tries hard to keep its systems isolated from the public datanet," he said. "Unfortunately, someone who didn't know what he was doing established a handful of links between their system and ours—the public system, I mean. I think the idiot thought they needed the connection to use their system to monitor *our* system. Their WebHead should have told them it was a really bad idea.

"So…well, eventually, I managed to hack the public surveillance system. The planet is fucking *covered* in cameras, right? Adana has more cameras in the centre of town than anywhere else. Big ones, small ones, ones so tiny that they're barely larger than William's dick…you can't see them. And it is very hard to escape surveillance if you don't know where the goddamned cameras are."

"I know the problem," Clarence said.

"One of the bastards in charge is a voyeur," Wong said. "A really disgusting one. I stumbled across an archive of…*recordings*…of men and women doing things better kept private. The asshole probably thought that no one would ever discover the evidence. I wonder if we should give his superiors a tip-off."

"That would also constitute proof that we were hacking the government's datanet," Clarence pointed out. He saw Wong's point, but he wasn't blind to the implications. "Surely, someone will find out sooner or later."

Wong shrugged. "Perhaps. Perhaps not. They'd have to audit the system pretty thoroughly to find the archive. I only stumbled across it through luck."

Clarence winced. He'd always known the government had cameras everywhere, certainly in the more upscale parts of town. And yet, he'd never realised just how extensive the network truly was—or how corrupt the operators had become. Who knew how easily it could be abused? A voyeur who controlled the cameras might be the least of the problems facing the people...

"That said, I found something very interesting," Wong added. "There are cameras everywhere, right? So there should be some footage of the march and riot, right? Well, there isn't. The camera network covering Grantville was turned off—completely deactivated—when the march began. There's no official footage from that moment until the police start to arrive, too late to do any damned good. Any hope we might have had of using the footage to track down the attackers is gone."

"...Shit," Clarence said. "Who shut the system down?"

"I don't know," Wong said. "I don't *think* a hacker could have done it. The surveillance system is pretty tough. I'd bet good money that it's actually hardwired. No one could take the system down from the outside—or even try to take the system down—without triggering all sorts of alarms. But someone on the inside..."

"Someone on the inside knew the attack was going to happen," Clarence said, coldly.

"I'm pretty sure of it," Wong said. "Whoever took the cameras down didn't just make sure there'd be no footage. They ensured there was no way to trace the attackers back to their hidey-hole. I cross-referenced the witness testimonial with the camera records, but...nothing. I couldn't isolate the buses the attackers used from the other buses driving around town. They could have gone anywhere."

Clarence cocked his head. "Could the police find something more?"

"They might," Wong said. "They have more people looking at the records than I do. I'm pretty dependent on analysis software and...well, it isn't always *right*. The programmers say it's perfect, but it isn't. God alone knows how many people have wound up in trouble because the program lumbered them with the blame for something they didn't do."

"I know," Clarence said. He'd once been accused of plagiarism because the software had misidentified his handwriting. It hadn't been easy to prove the wretched system wrong. "But...do you know what you're saying?"

"Someone in government—someone in the security services—knew that the attack was about to happen," Wong said, again. "And they cleared the way for the attackers."

He met Clarence's eyes. "It's worse than it seems, I think. I checked the police records, carefully. Very carefully. You know how the police operate? If something happens, something serious enough to require a major response, their standard procedure is to send a couple of units ahead to find out what's happening while the remainder of the force is assembled. Quick-reaction teams are mustered, linked up with street patrolmen and sent into the fray. This time...no one was sent ahead. The police were given specific orders to hang back until they were told to advance."

"Orders?" Clarence shook his head. "From whom?"

"I can't tell," Wong said. "They were relayed by the dispatchers, I think, but the dispatchers wouldn't be the ones issuing the orders. There's no way to trace them all the way back to whoever was actually in charge. However..."

He smiled, grimly. "If the dispatchers were bouncing a request for orders up the chain of command, going higher and higher as each successive command layer decided it needed to seek guidance from higher up, it should have taken a long time for orders to actually start filtering back down the chain of command. Right?"

"Yeah." Clarence had seen the same thing at the *Daily Truth*. No one wanted to go out on a limb for fear their superiors would cut them off in a heartbeat if their decision proved controversial. "I know what you mean."

"But in this case, the orders came down with astonishing speed," Wong said. "Again, someone *knew* what was going to happen and took steps to make sure the police would stay out of the affair. By the time they were unleashed, if the witness statements are correct, it was all over."

"And you don't know who issued the orders," Clarence mused. "I take it there was nothing written down?"

"Not in any database I've been able to access," Wong said. "Hackers believe that the police and security services have a number of completely isolated datanets, which cannot be hacked as long as they're not connected to the public system. The files we'd need to see would probably be kept there."

"And there's no way to get to them," Clarence mused.

"Not directly, no," Wong said. "We'd need access to a terminal linked to the isolated system."

"And they'd probably be behind layer after layer of security," Clarence said. A military officer he'd met once had told him that large military bases were rarely as secure as they looked, but Clarence didn't have the skills to take advantage of their weaknesses. Hell, he wasn't even sure what the weaknesses actually *were*. Sneaking onto a military base—or into a police station—was the stuff of legends, not real life. "I don't see how we could get to them."

"We'd need access codes too," Wong said. He smiled, thinly. "There's always the human element. Someone could be bribed—or blackmailed."

"It would probably be a bad idea," Clarence said. He'd once heard a cautionary story about a reporter who'd tried to blackmail a source into giving up vital information. The man had confessed to his superiors, the reporter had been arrested and his editors had sworn blind they'd never heard of him. "We do have certain ethics."

Wong pasted a surprised look on his face. "Reporters have ethics?"

"Yes, when they don't have a large organisation behind them." Clarence scowled, remembering all the moral compromises he'd had to make. "We don't want to make ourselves easy targets."

He leaned back in his chair. "So, let's recap. Someone knew the attack was coming. Someone made sure that the attack—and the perpetrators—would go unrecorded. Someone also made sure that the police would stay away, thus ensuring that the attackers wouldn't be caught immediately. That person is clearly a high-ranking police official, at the very least."

"To be fair, the police might not have been prepared for such violence," Wong pointed out, thoughtfully. "They spend most of their time harassing people on the streets and molesting women, not...not preparing for war."

"That might be true of the street patrolmen, but not of the tactical response teams," Clarence said. The tactical teams might have slipped over the years, given how little work they'd actually had to do...he frowned. They couldn't have slipped that far, could they? Their training was supposed to be first-rate. "They had a duty to help people."

He shook his head. Wong had uncovered another part of the puzzle, but—so far—Clarence had no idea how it went together. Or even if it fitted into his earlier theories. It *could* be just a coincidence...

"I did the work-up you wanted," Wong said. He picked up a datachip. "Rebirth has been getting a *lot* of funding from Simon Goldwater and a handful of other oligarchs. They'd paid out *billions* of credits over the last few years. I wondered if they were hedging their bets, just in case Rebirth won a clear majority, but neither the Empire Loyalists nor the Corporatists received anything like as much largesse."

"That's odd," Clarence said. He would have expected the Corporatists to receive much of the largess. But then, he supposed the Corporatists had no intention of rocking the boat. They'd been dominated by the big corporations for the last five hundred years. "And is there a *quid pro quo?*"

"If there is, it hasn't been written down." Wong shook his head. "I'd be surprised if Maxima Corporation didn't have its own private datanet. They'd be breaking the law by keeping it isolated, but who's going to go after them? They have too many friends in high places."

"True," Clarence agreed. He pocketed the datachip and stood. "How long do you think it will be until they try to shut us down?"

"Not long," Wong said. "I've been quietly backing up everything at an offsite storage facility—and using every trick I know to keep it hidden—but the government has vast resources. I think we should start planning for the worst."

"Jackson will need to be warned," Clarence said. "We *have* been planning to move out of the university."

"Which might be a bad idea," Wong said. "Imperial University has always enjoyed a special status. It's been treated as a diplomatic enclave..."

"And Earth is gone," Clarence reminded him, harshly. "Who's going to complain if the bastards shut the university down?"

He headed out the door, put the datachip in his room and grabbed his coat. He'd been putting off the visit to Hellebore Estate for too long. His instincts were telling him that there *was* something there, something he had to see for himself. He called Patricia, half-hoping she wouldn't come. He'd promised to take her, but he had a feeling it might be dangerous. She had far more to lose than him.

Patricia gave Clarence a bright smile as she joined him. "Are we going now?"

"Change into something less striking," Clarence ordered, flatly. He keyed his terminal, booking a hovercab. The service had been slowing down over the last few days as government restrictions started to bite. "And then we can go."

"I look fine," Patricia protested.

Clarence bit down the response that came to mind. For a student, Patricia was overdressed; for someone on the estates, she was terrifyingly *underdressed*. She would definitely draw attention—or worse. And there was nothing he could do to keep her safe if the gangs noticed her. Street harassment might be the least of her problems.

"You do not want to stand out on an estate," he said, trying not to remember his childhood and early teens. There had been a time when whistling at a woman had been...*normal*. It wasn't until he'd grown older that he'd realised how it had made the women feel. "Get into something that looks a little more conservative and then we can go."

Patricia glared. "Fine."

CHAPTER THIRTY-ONE

Even when the media focused on more mundane subjects, there were problems. Puff pieces were run about CityBlock girls who became celebrity superstars, but very few of those articles mentioned that the odds of superstardom were very low and, for every success, there were thousands of failures. They sold a dream that would almost certainly never become true.
—**PROFESSOR LEO CAESIUS**
Crying Wolf: The Media and the Fall of the Empire

"WE HAVE TO TAKE THE LONG WAY AROUND," the driver said, as the hovercab raced towards Remington Estate. "The police set up an aerial barricade over the river."

"That's fine," Clarence said. He could see a plume of smoke in the distance. Something was clearly happening, but what? A check of his wristcom revealed that there was no official story yet. The fire—or whatever it was—had gone unnoticed by the media. "We'll cope."

He grinned at Patricia and leaned back in his chair, trying to rest. It had been a long day, even though it was barely afternoon. There had just been too much work to do. He was almost relieved to be out of the office, despite a nagging sense that they were going into danger. It was a change from writing articles and browsing the datanet.

You wanted to be a reporter, he reminded himself. *Did you think you could spend your entire career behind a computer, plagiarising everything you wrote from other media outlets?*

He dismissed the thought as the aircar dropped into Remington Estate, landing neatly near the row of shops. Clarence had considered asking the driver to land along the southern edge, by Hellebore, but some instinct had told him that it was probably a bad idea. He clambered out of the hovercab, paid the driver and looked around with interest. The streets were almost deserted, save for a handful of elderly men shuffling towards the gambling houses. They were certain to lose, Clarence was sure, but he knew better than to point it out. Gambling was one of their few pleasures in a life that could be ended at any moment.

"This way," he said, leading Patricia down the street. "We'll be there in a few minutes."

The air felt uncomfortably hot as they walked, a faint hint of *burning* choking his nose and drying his throat. A couple of small houses had been burnt to the ground, sometime in the last couple of days. The fire service hadn't responded to the call in time to do more than quench the blaze before it could spread further, he noted. There was no sign of the former inhabitants. Migrants? Druggies? Or merely someone who had been very unlucky? There was no way to know.

He frowned as the barricade came into view. A pair of policemen were on duty at the guardhouse, despite the police force's desperate need for manpower. Clarence eyed them doubtfully, then led Patricia down an alleyway and through a maze of streets until they re-emerged close to the fence. The policemen shouldn't be able to see them, he thought. They certainly shouldn't be able to *stop* them—legally—unless they were actually trying to clamber over the fence.

"I can hear something," Patricia whispered. "Can you?"

Clarence peered through the chinks in the fence. Hellebore Estate was deserted, yet…he could hear a faint sound in the distance. It was too quiet for him to actually tell what it was, but it was there. Cheering? Or chanting?

He turned his head from side to side, trying to work out where the sound was actually *coming* from. It was hard to be sure, but he *thought* it was coming from the distant warehouses. They—and the rest of the estate—were supposed to have been demolished by now. Clarence remembered the people who had been ordered to leave and shuddered. Their homes were still intact, just empty.

He studied the fence thoughtfully, trying not to think about how useless he'd been at gymnastics at school. The fence would prove more of a challenge than the wretched climbing frame, he was sure, and the electric lines at the top suggested that trying to get over the fence and into the estate would be very dangerous. A couple of ideas ran through his mind, but neither of them were workable without special equipment and reliable help. He didn't really want to get Patricia involved with what was, effectively, breaking and entering.

Maxima Corporation wanted the three estates, he thought, *and they were willing to do everything in their power to move the former tenants out. But why? What did they hope to gain?*

The thought nagged at his mind—again and again—as they walked along the fence. He understood what a criminal hoped to gain, even if he didn't like it. A thief wanted money, a rapist wanted sex…they were understandable goals, if criminal. But Maxima didn't seem to benefit in any way from chasing out the inhabitants, then sealing off the estate. That made no sense. Just because he couldn't see how they gained from taking the estates for themselves didn't mean that *they* couldn't see an advantage…

Patricia nudged him as they crossed a small bridge. The stream might have been lovely—once—but it was now crammed with human waste and rubbish. No one in the estates cared if they lived in a shithole, Clarence recalled. In some ways, a bad reputation actually protected the people who lived there. It kept outsiders from wanting to move in and gentrify the place, something that inevitably drove the original inhabitants out. But Maxima Corporation hadn't cared. He couldn't help wondering how long it would be before they took Remington Estate too.

"There's no way to get into the estate," Patricia said. "Or is there?"

"Not that I can think of," Clarence said. In his younger days, he wouldn't have hesitated to try. It wouldn't be that hard to *accidentally* fly an aircar over the fence and land on the far side, despite the ATC zone. Or he could fake an in-flight emergency that just happened to strand him in Hellebore. But he was older and wiser now. "We might have to wait and see what happens."

"That's not good," Patricia said. "What if we cut the fence?"

"We'd set off an alarm," Clarence said, flatly. He rather suspected that parts of the lower fence would be electrified too. It wasn't as if anyone would care if estate-dwellers were shocked—or killed—by the fence. Everyone would say it was their own stupid fault and leave it at that. "I just don't get it. They go to all the trouble of getting their grubby hands on the estates, with a timetable so demanding that they pay compensation instead of screaming for their lawyers, and then they do *nothing*?"

"There's someone in there," Patricia said. The sound was slightly louder now. They were inching closer to the warehouses. "They're up to *something*."

Clarence nodded, slowly. Could it be that Maxima had wanted the *warehouses*? But if so, why bother to lay claim to the entire estate? It wasn't as if they had to buy the estate to purchase the warehouses. Were they up to something that had to be concealed? Was *that* why they'd cleared the estates? Where they so desperate to conceal what they were doing that they'd uprooted thousands of people and threatened to throw them onto the streets?

And it would have gone unnoticed, if I hadn't sensed a story, Clarence thought. None of the other newspapers had bothered to do more than copy the puff pieces, when they'd bothered to do anything at all. *And they went to a lot of trouble to try to silence us.*

"Hey," a voice shouted. "You there!"

Clarence turned. A pair of policemen were ambling towards them, their gait casual but deadly. Clarence felt his blood run cold. Here, miles from the centre of town—and any inconvenient witnesses—the police could do *anything* to them. Jackson knew where they were going, but…he wouldn't know what had happened, not really. They could simply vanish into an unmarked grave or police detention camp and…and that would be the end.

"Run down that street," Clarence ordered, sharply. "Don't stop for anything until you're at least a mile away, then call a hovercab and go straight back to the university. Go."

Patricia stared at him. "But…"

"Go." Clarence pushed her away. "Run like the wind!"

The policeman shouted as Patricia turned and ran. Clarence allowed himself a moment of relief that she'd changed into sensible shoes. He wouldn't have cared to try to run in high heels…he smiled at the thought, then turned and ran himself. The policemen might split up—he hoped Patricia could outrun the goon who went after her—but if they thought they had a better chance of running him down they might decide he was the better target. His back twitched as he sped up, reminding him that they might have guns. The police weren't normally armed with anything more dangerous than shockrods and stunners, but things had changed in the last few days. He'd heard all sorts of reports of gun battles all around the planet.

And none of those stories have been verified, he thought. His head started to pound as he crossed another bridge, keeping a wary eye out for possible hiding places. The police didn't seem to be here in force. They might give up if they thought he'd outrun them. *We don't know how many of them are true.*

He ran through an alleyway and down the street, hoping and praying that the policemen would stop. But they were still after him, their footsteps growing louder as they slowly narrowed the gap between them. Clarence glanced from side to side, hoping he could find someone to bribe into helping him—again—but this time there was no one in sight. His legs started to hurt, reminding him that he hadn't seen a proper doctor since the attempted kidnapping. There could be nerve damage that needed to be healed before it was too late.

Or it could be old age, part of his mind noted. He wasn't *that* old, but growing up on the estates tended to ensure that one didn't live long enough to collect a pension. He didn't have the genetic improvements that Jackson's family would have spliced into his bloodline long before he was even conceived. *I might not have long to live.*

A chill ran down his spine as the footsteps grew even louder. It would be a beating for sure, even if they didn't bother to check his identity. He knew how policemen thought. They were bullies, just like the bullies and gangbangers he'd known to fear during his childhood. They would blame him for forcing them to chase him down, for not taking his beating like a good little victim, and take their anger out on him. And if they *did* think to check who he was…Clarence allowed himself a moment of relief, just a moment, that Patricia had escaped. She had been spared their attentions…

And she knows where I am, he told himself. *She'll tell Jackson and he'd do…something.*

He winced. He was sure that Jackson would do something, but what? What *could* he do? A state of emergency could be declared at any moment. Jackson would be in deep shit if he *tried* to save someone who'd been sent to the detention camps, if the government chose to admit they had him. That unmarked grave was looking likelier and likelier by the second…

A groundcar pulled up beside him. The door burst open with a crash. "Get in," the driver snapped. "Now!"

Clarence hesitated, remembering the kidnap attempt, then gritted his teeth and jumped into the car. The policemen shouted, too late. Clarence yanked in his legs as the door slammed closed, the driver gunning the engine before the hatch had closed and locked properly. The force of the acceleration pushed Clarence back into his seat as the car rocketed down the street, leaving the policemen far behind. He forced himself to sit upright and take a look at the driver. He had a hard face, with bright blue eyes, grey hair and an unshaven chin…he was a complete stranger.

"Thank you," he managed. "Who…who are you?"

The man glanced at him. "Who are *you*?"

"Clarence Esperanza," Clarence said. If sharing his name was a mistake…well, he'd have to live with it. He'd be able to jump out of the car if the driver threatened to take him back to the estate and hand him over to the police. "You?"

"Nathanial Grozny," the driver said. "Why were they chasing you?"

"Good question," Clarence said. "I'm really not quite sure."

The driver shot him a sharp look. "You were poking around Hellebore, weren't you?"

Clarence looked back at him. "Who are you?"

"*Sergeant* Grozny, Planetary Police," Grozny said. "And you're the famous muckraker who got one of my subordinates in trouble."

He stuck out a hand. "Good to meet you at last."

Clarence shook Grozny's hand, numbly. "Why…why did you save me?"

"Those estates"—Grozny jabbed a finger towards the rear mirror—"we've been given orders to stay away from them. Imagine my surprise when Quigley and a couple of others with dubious records have had their suspensions cancelled, by order of someone so high up that my superiors jumped to obey, and were sent to guard the estate. In full uniforms. I got curious."

"And you were driving around in an unmarked car," Clarence said. He wasn't sure if he believed the story. "You took a hell of a risk."

"So did you," Grozny said. "I doubt they'd have taken you to the station if they'd caught you. Quigley…isn't the worst person on the force."

Clarence frowned. "Do you know who issued the orders?"

"No." Grozny's face didn't change, but Clarence could tell he was worried. "There's meant to be a paper trail of…well, everything. Who issued the orders, when and where the orders were issued, everything that Internal Affairs might need to carry out an investigation if things go horrifically wrong. This time, there was no official log. The entire estate has been declared off-limits to us and I don't know why."

"Interesting," Clarence said. He remembered Wong's exploration of the police datanet and smiled, inwardly. It was a pity he couldn't ask Grozny about the marchers directly. "Has this happened before?"

"Two years ago, I would have said it had never happened," Grozny said. "Procedure is procedure. An order that does not follow proper protocol is an illegal order. Full stop. I would be busted back to constable if I followed an order that was given improperly. But now…there have been quite a few orders with no discernible paper trail. And my superiors have followed them to the letter."

And you didn't object, because you knew you'd be fired, Clarence thought. He had a feeling that excessive paperwork probably accounted for the police force's problems. Why bother arresting someone if it meant spending hours filling in forms afterwards? *You just started your own investigation.*

He cocked his head. "Has anything else happened that concerned you?"

"Just rumours," Grozny said. "I try to discourage rumour-mongering amongst the men because they grow out of control so rapidly, but…I keep hearing vague whispers of trouble, hints that things aren't quite right. Nothing I can put my finger on, of course. Maybe I should have tried harder to be closer to my subordinates. But there are lines that one shouldn't cross."

"People don't share rumours with you," Clarence guessed.

"Not very often," Grozny confirmed. "And most of the time the rumours are obvious nonsense.

"But things have gotten worse over the past few months, even before your newspaper ran that damned video. Attacks on officers in the streets, entire estates turning themselves into no-go zones, fire-bombings and other attacks on migrants…the crime rate has skyrocketed and hardly anyone seems to care. They keep sending officers out, alone or in pairs, to places where they will be badly outnumbered if they're attacked. And some of the grumbling I've heard…"

He shook his head. "Things will get worse before they get better."

"I'll investigate," Clarence promised. He wasn't sure how far he could trust Grozny. "Do you have any clue who might be behind it?"

"If there is someone behind it," Grozny said. "Do you know what I was doing yesterday?"

Clarence considered it. "Terrorist hunting?"

"I was escorting a couple of bailiffs to evict a family who lost all their savings in the banking crash," Grozny said. "They weren't a bad family, either. Not the sort of nightmare neighbours who are hated by everyone else…they were good people. But I had to watch as they were turned onto the streets, their house and everything in it confiscated to pay their debts. They'd done everything right, yet…"

"They got kicked out," Clarence said.

"Yeah," Grozny agreed. "All the important things I could be doing and I was assigned to *that*, instead. The government doesn't know what the hell is really going on."

"No kidding," Clarence muttered. He wondered if he should write an article calling for a temporary ban on repossessions. It might help keep the chaos from spreading further. "How long will it be until bailiffs are greeted with lethal force?"

Grozny gave him a nasty smile. "Why do you think they screamed for an armed escort?"

He pulled the car over to the pavement and turned off the engine. "You can call a cab from here," he said. "Good luck."

"And to you," Clarence said. He hadn't made any progress towards solving the mystery—or had he? "And thank you."

"Thank me by reporting the truth," Grozny said. "That's all you can do."

CHAPTER THIRTY-TWO

It is unsurprising, therefore, that the media's blatant bias led to a profound cynicism running through society. If the media lied, who could be trusted? The vast majority of the population simply didn't trust anyone.
—**PROFESSOR LEO CAESIUS**
Crying Wolf: The Media and the Fall of the Empire

CLARENCE SPENT THE NEXT FEW DAYS EXPECTING the hammer to fall at any moment.

The policemen had seen him, he was sure. Grozny would keep his mouth shut—he would have to, unless he wanted to implicate himself—but the guards had every interest in reporting the near breach of security to their superiors. *And* they might have made a note of the car's number when Grozny had yanked Clarence off the streets before they could lay hands on him. Clarence told Jackson what had happened in careful detail, silently thanked the god of reporters that Patricia had escaped and added a handful of comments to his notes, all the while expecting policemen to arrest him at any moment. But, by the end of the week, nothing had happened.

"There's no arrest warrant for you," Frank Wong assured him. "They have to be listed online, if issued, and you're not mentioned."

"We'll see," Clarence said. He'd had Wong pull up Grozny's service record. The man was a straight arrow, too straight to ever see promotion above sergeant. His superiors probably felt they couldn't trust him to bend the rules if they felt it necessary. "Are there *any* mentions of me?"

"You're listened under a file marked 'wanted for arson, murder and jaywalking.'" Wong snickered. "No, like I said, your name isn't mentioned. The only one of us who *is* mentioned is Jennifer and *she* gave them the worst PR crisis in the planet's history."

Clarence wasn't convinced, but there was nothing he could do about it. There was no point in spending his days fretting either. Jackson kept him busy, alternately following up tips from his sources and interviewing people to put a human face on the growing crisis. It was surprisingly delightful to hear that his story on people who'd done everything right, only to be ruined by the banking crash, had gone all the way up to the First Speaker. The government had been leaning towards banning repossessions already, the First Speaker had said in a statement, but Clarence's article had pushed them over the edge.

And was that really because of me, Clarence asked himself, *or because the bailiffs have been coming under attack?*

He smiled, although it wasn't really funny. One pair of bailiffs had been tarred, feathered and forced to run for their lives by a howling mob. Another had been beaten half to death and left to crawl out of the estate. A third had simply vanished, with no one—including the police—showing much enthusiasm for looking for them. Or their bodies. Clarence was all too aware that the veneer of civilisation was wearing very thin. No one trusted the government—or the banks, or the police—and they were looking out for themselves. It wouldn't be long before no one in their right mind dared work as a bailiff. Or any bank would underwrite a loan.

"We've secured premises in Upper Dunsworth," Jackson told him, one afternoon. "The owner was quite eager to sell for a handful of guaranteed credits."

Clarence frowned. "Are we sure we own the land under the building as well as the building itself?"

"We do," Jackson confirmed. "I had the lawyers take a careful look at the title deeds. We own everything. We'll start moving there once we have the place set up."

"Good," Clarence said. He was growing increasingly convinced that it was only a matter of time before Imperial University asked—or ordered—*Seeing Eye* to move out of the frat house and go somewhere else. They *had* managed to turn the newsletter into a profitable business, although that might not last once their accommodation was no longer subsidised by a university trust. "I want a fancy office all to myself."

Jackson lifted his eyebrows in mock-enquiry. "Not an open-plan office?"

Clarence shuddered. "Whoever came up with that concept should be brutally tortured to death," he said. "Do you know how hard it is to hold a private conversation with your sources while the entire office is pretending not to listen?"

"Point," Jackson agreed. "It's a big building. There'll be offices for senior journalists like yourself."

He wasn't kidding, Clarence discovered the following day. The office block was huge, easily large enough to accommodate hundreds of journalists and their support staff. He'd looked up the records and discovered that the previous owners had lost everything in the banking crash, forcing them to fire their employees and sell the building merely to remain afloat. He hoped they didn't have debts to pay or they were going to be thoroughly screwed. But then, they'd probably been losing money anyway. There was something about the building that gave the impression of coats of paint splashed over serious structural problems. The building itself was fine, according to the surveyor, but the company might have been in a bad state even before the banks had crashed. And whoever was in charge had lost touch with how money was actually made.

Jackson and the others walked through the building, slowly working out what needed to be repaired or painted before the remainder of the staff

311

moved in. Clarence was impressed by just how *quickly* things were moving—the painters and decorators were already on call—although he had to admit that Jackson didn't have to satisfy hundreds of different departments before moving ahead. *Seeing Eye* was growing larger, slowly but surely. Clarence couldn't help thinking that *something* was going to be lost, once they passed a certain threshold. He just wasn't sure how to put it into words.

An innocence, perhaps, he thought. *Or a sense that we're all more than just cogs in some vast machine.*

The thought bothered him as Jackson showed him his office, with a bed and washroom in the adjoining compartment. The *Daily Truth* had regarded him as completely replaceable, no matter how hard he worked for them. There was no loyalty from the editors and—consequently—no loyalty offered to them either. But Jackson, on the other hand, chose to act as if he were merely first amongst equals. That would be lost, Clarence was sure, as more and more employees were hired. It would be hard for Jackson to be friendly with people he barely knew. He'd certainly have difficulties managing them.

And the more he loses touch with his people, the easier it will be to fire them for minor mistakes, Clarence thought. *And then we'll be falling into the same trap that killed the mainstream media.*

"We've already got hundreds of applicants for journalistic jobs," Jackson told him, once the impromptu tour came to an end. "I'll want your input on the more promising candidates. You may know some of them."

"That's not always a good thing," Clarence pointed out. What if one of his old co-workers had applied? He understood—perfectly—why they'd given him the cold shoulder after he'd been fired, and he was honest enough to admit that he would probably have done the same thing, but it still rankled. "You need people who don't know them."

"I have a bunch of bland references, where references were provided at all," Jackson countered. "I need someone to tell me if these people are problem cases or not."

Clarence nodded. It was hard to believe that Alistair Allrianne would dare provide a reference to *anyone* who wanted to leave the *Daily Truth* for *Seeing Eye*, even if he wanted to get rid of them. And if he did, it would be as bland and non-controversial as possible. The remainder of the mainstream outlets would go the same way. Who knew? They might try to unload their problem children on *Seeing Eye*.

Although they could just fire them at will, Clarence reminded himself. It wouldn't be hard to come up with an excuse to fire someone, if the editor was really determined to get rid of them. A competent editor could easily accuse someone of looking up porn on the datanet, in the certain knowledge that the charge would be impossible to disprove. *But then, if they want to sabotage us, they might find it easier to send the bad cases our way.*

He took the opportunity, once they returned to the frat house, to scan the files. They tended to fall into two categories, people with journalistic experience and people without. That didn't mean they were *bad* candidates, Clarence reminded himself—he'd spent four years at journalism school, although everything important could easily have been condensed into a single year—but it *did* mean that they'd have to be trained. It was easy to make a mistake—or cross the line into illegality—if one didn't know where the lines were. *Seeing Eye* still couldn't afford the small army of lawyers the other newspapers had on permanent retainer.

A handful of the more experienced candidates he dismissed at once, writing brief notes to Jackson to explain why. Two were prima donnas, so self-obsessed that they found it impossible to work with other people; three more were toxic personalities, the sort of people who kissed up to their superiors while dumping on their inferiors. Clarence knew one of them personally and he'd never quite understood why the asshole had never been fired. The boss couldn't be *that* blind to his flaws, could he? But then, the boss had probably liked having his ass kissed from time to time.

He blinked in surprise as he read a particular resume. "Maddy? Maddy is trying to work here?"

That was odd, he thought, as he prepared himself for bed. Maddy was a rockstar. She wouldn't give up her high salary from *Daily Truth* for what little *Seeing Eye* could offer, even if it did come with a bedroom of her own. Unless...was she a ringer? Someone whose *real* purpose was to spy on them? Maddy could do wonders for *Seeing Eye*, Clarence thought, but only if she was really committed. The only sign of any actual commitment on her part was the complete lack of a reference. Her editor had presumably declined to provide one. If, of course, he'd been asked at all.

It can be a mistake to let the boss know you're thinking of moving on, Clarence thought, coldly. *From that moment, you'll be automatically classed as disloyal.*

The following morning, he sat behind a privacy screen and watched the preliminary set of interviews. Jackson—and Elle and Jessica—had refined their interview technique, but not fallen into the trap of making the questions as difficult as possible. Indeed, there was a refreshing lack of trick questions with no right answer. Clarence silently blessed them for their common sense as the interviewees answered the questions, their relief plain to see. He didn't blame them. He'd met too many interviewers who were clearly on power trips.

Why do you want to work here? Clarence smiled at the question. *Money, of course. It's true, but it's not a good answer. Idiots.*

He put the thought aside as Maddy was shown into the interview room. She wore a professional black suit and tie, carefully tailored to deemphasise her femininity. A good choice, Clarence considered. Maddy was pretty, even with her long red hair tied back into a bun, but it could be harder to take a woman seriously when she dressed to emphasize her looks. Besides, Jackson and his fellows were surrounded by some of the most handsome men and gorgeous girls on the planet. Maddy was wise not to try to compete with them. She wanted—she needed—her interviewers to see her as a reporter first.

"Your record is a very good one," Jackson said, once the preliminary questions were over. "Why do you want to work for us?"

Maddy bit her lip, nervously. Clarence would have offered ten to one odds that it was an act.

"I've been a senior reporter for the last five years," Maddy said. "I've actually spent nearly ten years as a reporter. And in all of that time, I have never done anything like *real* journalism. I have achieved nothing. My stories have been spoon-fed to me or carefully rewritten to suit the prevailing narrative. I have never had the chance to dig up a story for myself, let alone publish it. And that is what I want."

"And *Daily Truth* didn't offer you the chance to do *real* journalism?" Jackson leaned forward, carefully. "Why not?"

A hint of bitterness entered Maddy's tone. "My role, after I was noticed by my first editor, was to look pretty and act dumb. That was all. I tried, time and time again, to carve out a role for myself, but it was impossible. The stories I wrote might as well have been written by someone else. Going to press conferences, the occasional private interview...that's all I did. I want a chance to be *real*."

Clarence frowned. He'd never had the impression that Maddy was so... bitter, although he knew from his own experience that it was hard to do *real* journalism when the editors and lawyers made it impossible. They'd blocked more of his suggestions than he cared to remember. It was why he hadn't told anyone he was going to watch the Forsakers being evicted and their campsite destroyed. He would have been told, in no uncertain terms, not to go.

He studied Maddy as Jackson dismissed her, wondering if she was telling the truth. It was easy to believe, but then...a good lie *should* be easy to believe. He certainly wouldn't believe someone who told him the moon was made of green cheese, or that Tarsus—not Earth—was the birthplace of the human race. If she was telling the truth...he made a mental note to suggest that Jackson took a chance on her. Maddy's desire to prove herself would probably lead to good stories. If nothing else, she had far more contacts in government than he'd ever done.

And we did say we'd meet up for dinner at some point, he reminded himself. *Perhaps we should go out somewhere and exchange notes.*

He put the thought aside as the next candidate was shown into the interview room. The man—Hamish Hawthorne, according to the notes—was another rockstar, although one with suspiciously few stories to his name. Clarence frowned as he read through the file, carefully noting just how little Hawthorne had actually *done*. There seemed to be an inverse correlation between his achievements and his promotions. If it had taken Clarence nearly ten years to become a senior reporter, with a solid collection of stories under his belt, why had Hawthorne done it in less than four?

Connections? There was no hint of connections in the file, but that didn't mean they didn't exist. *Or something more dangerous?*

Clarence studied Hawthorne thoughtfully as Jackson ran through the first set of questions. He looked young, with short blonde hair and pale face, but…there was something about him that Clarence didn't like. It was hard to put his finger on it, yet…it was there. Clarence told himself that he was being silly, that first impressions weren't always accurate, but he'd learnt to trust his instincts. And *they* insisted that Hawthorne was bad news.

"I have always been in awe of people who push the limits," Hawthorne said, when Jackson asked him why he wanted to work for *Seeing Eye*. "Your accomplishments are a matter of record. You changed the world. I wanted to be a part of it."

A lickspittle, Clarence thought. *That* explained Hawthorne's rapid promotions. Kiss up to the boss, kick everyone underneath…it made sense, he supposed. A boss would sooner promote someone he knew would support him than a person with solid achievements and a habit of independent thinking. *And quite possibly a snake in the grass.*

He felt a surge of sudden hatred. He'd always disliked the smooth-talkers who found it so easy to convince people to like them, despite their lack of any *real* qualifications. Hawthorne could be charming—he *was* charming—but there was nothing underneath it. *Seeing Eye* couldn't afford someone who didn't pull his weight. And *Jackson* didn't need someone telling him he was absolutely right, all the time, even when his policies were leading to disaster. *That* was how politicians and managers went bad.

Be fair, he told himself, as Jackson dismissed Hawthorne. *Some of them started out bad and got worse.*

"Maddy has potential," he said, when the interviews were over. "But Hawthorne...don't take him."

"He was nice," Jessica said.

Minnie would have pegged him at once, Clarence thought. He felt a pang of guilt that he'd barely thought about his wife and son over the last few days. *But then, a girl from the estates would know to be wary of anyone who tried to be charming.*

"That sort of person is always nice, as long as there's something you can do for him," he said, instead. Why did women like the smooth-talking charmers? It was something he'd never understood. "Or if there's something you can do *to* him. I bet he's terrible to waitresses."

"We'll consider all the candidates," Jackson said, firmly. "I..."

Clarence looked down as his terminal bleeped. "One of my sources wants a meeting," he said. He read the terse message quickly. "And I'd better go alone."

"You don't want to take Patricia?" Jackson looked concerned. "She needs something to do."

"Not with this guy," Clarence said. "To be honest, I'm surprised he's even got in touch with me. He has a lot to lose."

"Be careful," Jackson ordered. "And *don't* get kidnapped again."

CHAPTER THIRTY-THREE

*This was often reflected in voting tallies, insofar as they could be trusted.
The major political parties often found themselves competing against
extremist parties that genuinely were awful, but couldn't be effectively
painted as awful because the media had thrown its credibility away.
It is strange to realise that much of the media coverage of the Futurist
Party—a cover for the Nihilists, a terrorist group—was actually quite
accurate, yet hardly anyone believed the media until it was far too late.*
—**PROFESSOR LEO CAESIUS**
Crying Wolf: The Media and the Fall of the Empire

CLARENCE HAD BEEN TOLD, LONG AGO, that spaceports were
the same from one end of explored space to the other. A massive cluster
of hangars, terminals and warehouses, with a sizeable section devoted to
everything from shopping malls to brothels that was—technically—outside the planetary government's jurisdiction. Even the most heavily religious and restrictive planets were forced to host a spaceport where their
laws could be disregarded at will and spacers introduce their populations
to the joys of illicit pleasures. Clarence had half-expected it to be hard to
get into the spaceport—the police were still out on the streets in force—
but it had been surprisingly easy. He hadn't even had to bribe the guards.

But I'm not going into the terminals themselves, he thought, *and I'm not boarding the shuttles themselves. They don't really have to check anyone who isn't going anywhere dangerous.*

He put the thought aside as he strode down the street, silently noting that the effects of the economic crash had spread to the spaceport too. A handful of bars and shops—the latter selling overpriced crap that Clarence found it hard to believe anyone actually bought—were closed, while others were announcing that they were cutting their prices. The prostitutes were as numerous as ever—the spaceport was actually a safer place to practice prostitution—but it was clear that they were suffering too. They were calling out to everyone, not just passing spacers who had money to burn. Clarence politely turned down a trio of young girls as he reached the *Spacer's Suit* and walked inside. The bar had never been a decent place to go for a drink—it catered to tramp spacers, who rarely had enough money for decent beer—but it seemed to have gone downhill. Clarence had to breathe through his mouth as he made his way towards the rear of the building. The air stank of smoke and exotic drugs.

And the spacers who drink here will be lucky if they get a chance to go back to space, he thought. Tramp spacers were only hired by the most disreputable of shippers. No corporation would take the risk. *With interstellar trade starting to collapse, what are they going to do?*

He reached the rear compartment and stepped into a booth. Colonel Thomas Stewart—a tall dark man with hair cropped close to his skull—looked up with interest, then returned his gaze to his beer. A waitress walked towards them on high heels, carrying a menu under her arm. Clarence dismissed her with a wave, then watched her stride away. He had no idea how her dress even stayed on, unless it was somehow held up by the collective gaze of every man in the bar. It left absolutely nothing to the imagination. And anyone with enough credits, he thought ruefully, could convince her to take it off.

Stewart produced a privacy generator and put it on the table. "I thought about going to a strip club for background noise, but that would be too revealing," he said. "There just isn't enough noise in here."

"Be grateful," Clarence said. Stewart had been a friend, long before he'd become a contact—and a source. They hadn't spoken in years. "What's been happening to you?"

"I've been shit-canned," Stewart said. "Oh, I haven't been *fired*—I haven't been kicked out on my ass or dragged in front of a court-martial—but I've been stripped of all responsibilities."

"...Fuck," Clarence said. Stewart had done well for himself, particularly after an early life in the ghetto. Joining the military had been the best decision he'd ever made. "What happened?"

Stewart snickered. "I did nothing," he said. He took a swig of his beer. "But General Carlson got relieved of duty and everyone who worked directly under him has been moved to one side and told to stand in the corner."

"Why?" Clarence didn't understand. "Who's Carlson?"

"He is—he was—the officer in charge of planetary security," Stewart told him. "The senior uniformed officer, at least. He used to command everything from the rapid-reaction squads to the planetary defences. Everyone thought he'd finish his career with a couple of years as *the* senior officer, if he didn't go into politics. He had the connections to make it work."

"I see," Clarence said. "And now?"

"Well, the bombing took place." Stewart held up his glass, considering the brown liquid inside. "And, in the aftermath, Carlson was relieved of duty. Bad news for me and everyone else who considered Carlson a patron. We didn't get sacked, but we might as well have been. I have no hope of getting another command, let alone a position of power, even if I do stay in the army."

"I'm sorry to hear that." Clarence meant it, too. "I haven't heard anything about this."

"That's the least of it," Stewart said. "Quite a few officers have been relieved of duty in the past few days. Others have been reassigned. General

Tailor, who used to command the First Regiment, was dispatched to an isolated training base and replaced by some dickhead no one's ever heard of. Lieutenant-General Polanski has been sent to the South Pole…yep, *lots* of officers have been shuffled around. And everyone is uneasy as hell."

"I don't blame them," Clarence said. "Why…why now?"

"Officially, they were relieved because the planet's military needs new leadership in the face of a growing crisis," Stewart said. He shrugged. "It might be true, you know. God knows it's been fucking *years* since we did any actual fighting. We were supposed to send a regiment or two to the clusterfuck on Han, but the politicians kept stalling until Earth got tired of repeating the demand and gave up. I was CO of a company for a couple of years and the most dangerous thing that ever happened was some idiot accidentally falling off an ATV and breaking his leg.

"But unofficially? I don't know."

Clarence leaned forward. "What do you *think*?"

Stewart snorted in bitter frustration. "I don't know *what* to think. Point is…the people who are being shoved in as replacements are as ignorant of *real* fighting as the people they replaced. There aren't many people on Tarsus who *have* seen the elephant. Frankly, most of the lads who *really* want to test themselves join the Imperial Army or the Marines or sell themselves to a mercenary outfit. And then…

"When I was in command, there was a clear chain of command, a clear understanding of who would be in charge if I got shot by the enemy or something. If I'd been relieved, someone from my cadre of officers should have been promoted into my shoes. That's basic common sense. Officers are *meant* to know how to take command if necessary. My second knew the company as well as I did. But the newcomers? They're from outside the regular chain of command. No one under their command—now—knows them."

"I don't understand," Clarence admitted. "They're not army officers?"

"Imagine you're still working for that worthless rag, the one that doesn't even have the decency to make itself soft, strong and totally absorbent," Stewart said. "Imagine…"

"It is a little hard to use an eReader to wipe one's bottom," Clarence said, dryly.

Stewart ignored him. "Imagine that you're still working for them. And your editor—oh happy day—gets fired. And *then* whoever's in charge of the useless lie-factory puts in someone you don't know. Maybe he's got the right qualifications, on paper, but you don't know him. You have no personal relationship with him. You have no idea if he really knows what he's doing or if he's the sort of useless officer who has to be worked around if the sergeants want to keep the men alive. Is he brave? Is he going to need a pair of brown pants when all hell breaks loose? And can you count on him in a crisis?"

"I don't think I could have counted on *anyone* in a crisis," Clarence said, after a moment. "No one supported me when I was fired."

"Of course not," Stewart said. He finished his beer and waved to the waitress for another one. "And that's in a newspaper office, where the worst thing that can happen is you get fired. In the military...a lack of trust can prove disastrous. It takes time to build up the sort of personal relationships you need to make a military unit work—or prove, beyond all doubt, that the officer needs to be circumvented as much as possible. I mean, if you were interested in improving efficiency, wouldn't you put the people who knew what they were doing in charge?"

"You mean the sergeants," Clarence guessed.

"Unit efficiency *would* double, I suppose," Stewart said. "Point is, the government seems to have decided to take steps to *reduce* efficiency at precisely the moment they need to *improve* it. And the results have been pretty bad."

"It's only been...how long?" Clarence studied the tabletop for a long moment. "Four days?"

"Yes," Stewart said. "I've heard rumours—all kind of rumours, from people I know and trust—about all kinds of screw-ups. Military units going the wrong way because someone forgot to steal the lieutenant's map. Sergeants and other NCOs being relieved for objecting to impossible orders. Damn it, you *don't* want military officers learning on the job. A unit shouldn't be working up as it tries to pull security detail all around the city. By thunder, Clarence. It makes no sense!"

Nothing about this makes sense, Clarence thought.

He considered it, thoughtfully. Alfonse Drayton was clearly *the* rising power on Tarsus. It was quite possible that he—and his supporters—were relieving officers who'd supported the wrong party and replacing them with loyalists. Why not? Tarsus had never had to fight a real war. It was an open secret that promotions—in the police and security services as well as the military—depended more on patronage than actual competency. Drayton would hardly be unique in taking advantage of his position to strengthen his patronage network as much as possible. *Everyone* did it.

My editors certainly did it, Clarence thought. It was hard not to be bitter, sometimes. *Better to promote your clients than someone who might actually do the goddamned job.*

He shook his head, slowly. Alistair Allrianne had been given to hysterical exaggeration, but the *Daily Truth* had never been in danger of complete collapse. Simon Goldwater and Maxima Corporation could have made up any shortfall—if the newspaper hadn't been profitable—and ensured that the organisation had never had to reform. But the military was different, especially now. This was no time for business as usual. The entire planet was in crisis. Why play patronage games when it put the entire planet at risk?

Maybe they don't care, Clarence thought. *Or maybe they're up to something.*

He looked at his old friend. "Do you have any idea how extensive it is?"

"Vaguely," Stewart said. "Thirty-seven officers who worked under Carlson, including myself, have been effectively placed on someone's shit list. That might change, if Carlson is returned to grace, but that will probably take years. Beyond that...I know at least seventeen officers who have been relieved or reassigned and, in all cases, replaced with people from outside their formations. Pretty much all of them were in positions of extreme responsibility."

Clarence's eyes narrowed. "In what sense?"

"I told you about the regimental commander." Stewart glared at his beer as if it had personally offended him. "Another relieved officer commanded a garrison on the outskirts of the city. Two more commanded tactical squads. Others...the only one who *didn't* have a position where he might go from total calm to complete chaos at a moment's notice was a supply officer at the commissariat. The guy who took the job was suspiciously thin. Never trust a thin supply officer. He's incompetent or stupid or both."

"I suppose that explains a lot," Clarence said, absently. "What do you *think* is going on?"

"I don't know," Stewart said. "But it scares me."

Clarence made a mental note to check into the relieved officers—and their replacements—once he got back to the office. Frank Wong *might* be able to dig up their files and see who, if anyone, had taken them as clients. Perhaps there was an innocent explanation, but he doubted it. The government might have relieved the officers and insisted that they were doing *something* about the chaos, yet...why wouldn't they have told the entire planet? It wasn't as if they'd have any difficulty convincing the mainstream media that relieving the officers was good for planetary security. No one at the *Daily Truth* would know any better.

"I'll look into it," he promised. "What are you doing later this evening?"

"I'm *supposed* to be on base," Stewart said. "But no one will give a damn if I stay out all night. They probably wouldn't care if I stayed here for the rest of my life."

Clarence had to smile. "They won't shoot you for desertion?"

"I'd be surprised if they noticed I was gone," Stewart said. "An officer without responsibilities has no friends or family. No one dares be friendly for fear that it might rub off."

"I know," Clarence said, quietly. "No one called me after I got fired."

"At least you made a clean break," Stewart told him. "I'm still being paid, but what for?"

"You're being paid," Clarence pointed out, dryly. "And you have free accommodation and food."

"But I'm also waiting for a call I know is never going to come," Stewart said. "And where would I go, if I got kicked out?"

He grinned, suddenly. "There's a brothel down the road. Want to come?"

"Not really," Clarence said. "Minnie left me after I got fired, taking Henry with her. I still miss them, you know."

Stewart cocked his head. "I'd say that you and Minnie were having problems well before you got fired," he said. "It isn't *that* easy living today, is it?"

"No," Clarence agreed. It was true, even though he didn't want to admit it. They'd both had to work to maintain their lifestyle and pay their debts and arguments over money had been fairly frequent even before he'd been fired. He hated to think of what they'd been doing to their son. What lessons had Henry been learning from watching his mother and father arguing all the time? "And…maybe we did have problems. But I still miss them."

"Give her a call," Stewart said. "Or…go find Henry's new school and claim visitation rights. You're his father. You do have a legal claim."

Clarence sighed. "I didn't want to give him a life like mine, you know. I wanted it to be better."

"You haven't failed yet," Stewart pointed out. "But you probably should make contact before she finds another man."

Clarence looked down at the table. "Is that going to happen?"

"You're asking me?" Stewart snorted. "How many stepfathers did *you* have when you were a little boy? How many men wandered in and out of your life while they fucked your mother? And how many of them actually stuck around after they got what they wanted?"

"None," Clarence said. A couple of his stepfathers—none of them had actually been *married* to his mother—had been kind to him, but most had simply ignored him. The hell of it was that he knew he should be grateful. There were kids who were plunged into a nightmare when their parents remarried. The evil stepparent trope probably dated all the way back to Old Earth. "I don't want to think about it."

Stewart pointed a finger at him. "I know why you let her go. You were fired, you were shocked, you were effectively emasculated. It might have been better for her—and the kid—if you let them go. Your failure might taint them if you didn't. But you know? You're not a failure any longer. You're one of the most famous reporters in the world. The only one who is *more* famous is the girl who captured footage of the police being assholes. You can go back to her now and see what happens."

He tapped the table, firmly. "Maybe she'll come back to you too. Or... if she doesn't, you damn well should make arrangements for your son. You have a responsibility to him, you know. You can't rely on the state to keep supporting him."

Clarence nodded. "Particularly as the social welfare net is starting to collapse."

"It'll be gone in a few weeks," Stewart said. "Go see your son. Or come with me to the nearest strip club. I don't care."

"I think I'd better get back to the office first," Clarence said. "You've given me a lot to think about."

"Just keep my name out of it," Stewart said. "I don't want them remembering I exist long enough to fire me."

"Understood." Clarence let out a long sigh. "I'll keep my lips sealed."

CHAPTER THIRTY-FOUR

It was also reflected in how the general population responded to crisis. An announcement that food deliveries had been delayed, but would be resumed as soon as possible led to immediate panic-buying and hoarding, both of which were technically crimes. An announcement that refugees from one CityBlock would be housed in another led to immediate riots. No one believed that the media was telling the truth.
—PROFESSOR LEO CAESIUS
Crying Wolf: The Media and the Fall of the Empire

IT WAS ALL FALLING APART.

Thomas Wycliffe, First Speaker of Tarsus, sat in his comfortable chair and stared down at the latest set of reports. Riots on the streets. Gang violence, directed against everyone from bailiffs and policemen to government officials. Two more banks on the verge of collapse, threatening to drag down the remainder of the economy with them. A constant liturgy of disaster, most of which they'd managed to keep out of the news. Thomas had no faith in their ability to keep secrets any longer. They couldn't hide the growing economic and financial chaos. They might as well try to classify the sunrise or lie about which moon was in the night sky.

He reached for his glass, wishing for something stronger than imported—and expensive—wine. He'd never wanted to be First Speaker, not really. He knew, deep in his heart, that he'd been a caretaker candidate when the Empire Loyalists had staked their claim to government. No one had expected him to have to make the *really* big decisions, let alone have to act fast to save the entire planet. The crisis had caught him and his staffers by surprise, even though they should have seen it coming. But they were Empire Loyalists! It was disloyal to even *think* that the Empire might be coming to an end.

It just wasn't *fair*, he told himself, time and time again. He was the planetary leader, the most powerful person for five or six light years, but he could do nothing to avert the growing crisis. His subordinates—his cabinet secretaries—were already manoeuvring for position, preparing themselves for the power struggle they knew would come when Thomas lost a vote of no confidence. It wouldn't be long before Drayton, damn the man, called for a vote and to hell with the consequences. The bastard had been sniping at Thomas ever since the crisis had begun, snidely pointing out the flaws with everything Thomas proposed. Damn him. Damn him to hell. Drayton wasn't the First Speaker. *He* wasn't the one who would be blamed for the crisis, was he? He could snipe from a position of perfect safety.

Unless he wins the election, Thomas thought. *What will he do if he finds himself charged with fixing the problem himself?*

He smiled at the thought, even though he knew it wasn't likely to happen. Neither the Empire Loyalists nor the Corporatists *wanted* to call a general election, not now. They both knew the risks of Rebirth winning a sizable majority. Instead, there would be wheeling and dealing, haggling over minor points until a new First Speaker was put in place. And then...the crisis wouldn't go away. It would probably have become a great deal worse while the politicians argued over who should be in charge. They might as well be fiddling while the entire planet burned to the ground.

Thomas sighed to himself. The political system had been designed to make it impossible for *anyone* to act quickly. Better to balance the planet's competing interests—the founders had said—than risk them fighting for supremacy. Thomas understood the logic, even though it was a major head-ache when the government *needed* to take action. The Empire Loyalists might *want* to rule the planet, but they understood the dangers of a power struggle that might leave them—and not their rivals—defeated and destroyed. But Drayton? The man didn't seem to play by the rules. He was undermining the system that would legitimate him if *he* became First Speaker.

He wants to solve the crisis, Thomas thought. He'd never doubted his rival's patriotism, merely his judgement. *But everything he wants to do will be utterly disastrous.*

He stood. It was late, too late, and his eyes ached from reading and signing an endless stream of paperwork. Everyone had proposals for deal-ing with the crisis, from establishing algae farms to feed the population to mass deportations of useless members of the population. And *none* of them seemed to realise that their ideas would have unpleasant side effects. And...

There was a knock at the door. Thomas blinked in surprise. There were people who had the right to see him without an appointment, but even *they* had to call ahead. His secretary would have warned him. She would have called him if someone had arrived unannounced, just to give him time to prepare. And...he turned as the door started to open, without permission. Who would dare...?

His heart sank as Drayton stepped through the door, followed by two men in black suits. The Security Secretary had the right to demand audience at any moment, but...even *Drayton* would have called ahead...wouldn't he? And he'd brought an audience? Thomas glanced at the two men, wondering who and what they were. Drayton had a secretary, but...who were they?

"First Speaker," Drayton said. "I'm afraid you're going to have to come with me."

Thomas stared at him. "What...what is the meaning of this?"

Drayton's voice was surprisingly gentle. "My people are in control of this building," he said. "Government House belongs to me now. I also have control over the garrison, the police and the internal security services. There is no point in trying to resist."

"Resist what?" Thomas reeled in confusion. "You…you've seized the government!"

His legs buckled. Political violence was almost unknown on Tarsus. The politicians preferred genteel manoeuvrings to naked violence. It was better to outwit an enemy—and give the enemy room to retreat—than start a civil war they might not win. But Drayton had thought outside the box. Thomas had never imagined that he would actually launch a coup…

"Yes," Drayton said. "If you cooperate, your life will be spared. You can go into comfortable retirement with your family. If not…well, I'm sure you can guess."

"You *bastard*," Thomas said. "Do you know what you've done?"

"I'm saving the planet," Drayton said. "Take him away."

His companions moved forward. Thomas offered no resistance as they searched his body, then marched him out of the room. There was no point in trying to fight. Armed men occupied the antechamber, their eyes flickering from side to side as if they expected to be attacked at any moment. Thomas knew they were safe. If Drayton had control of the security services, it was unlikely that anyone outside the building would realise what had happened in time to do something about it. The bastard had gambled and it had paid off for him.

And he'll soon find that it's harder to rule a planet than it looks, Thomas thought, vindictively. *What will he do when he realises that he doesn't have as much power as he thinks?*

He shrugged. He would probably never know.

• • •

Colin felt his heart start to beat as the blacked-out bus drove out of the warehouse and onto the city streets. The briefing had been surprisingly short, but it had covered all the important parts. The resistance had seized control of the government and they—the trainees—had a vitally important part to play in *keeping* control. They'd been issued with uniforms, helmets and daysticks and given some basic instruction before they'd been ordered into the buses and told to sit. Colin could hardly believe it. The resistance had *already* taken control of the government?

The bus picked up speed, rattling uncomfortably. Colin tensed, then told himself to relax. They'd be there soon enough and then…he wasn't sure. They were pretending to be soldiers, with the promise that they would *be* soldiers soon enough. And yet…they'd been sent out, time and time again, to spread chaos. Why? Why did the resistance even need them if it could—and had—taken control already?

He put the thought out of his mind as the sergeant strode past him, nodding in approval before moving on. The sergeant looked so calm and composed that it was hard to believe that they were going to war. If, of course, they *were* going to war. The Captain had made it clear that their *real* purpose was to convince anyone watching that the government was under their control…and, more importantly, that resistance was futile. Colin understood the importance of a show of strength—anyone who grew up on the estates knew that it was better to look strong than weak—but he still wondered. What was *really* going on?

Perhaps it doesn't matter, he thought. He'd done too much. Everything he'd done had seemed right and necessary, but now…he couldn't back out now. *All that matters is making myself so useful that they don't throw me out.*

He picked up his daystick as the bus lurched to a halt, the doors slamming open moments later. It was dark outside, but there was enough illumination—barely—for him to make out the looming towers of Government House. He'd never been there, of course, but everyone knew what the building looked like. He glanced up at the towers as they hurried out of the bus, forming up in lines. The streets were dark and deserted, save for a handful of guards at the checkpoints outside Government House. They were holding weapons, *real* weapons. Colin wondered, absently, when *he* would be allowed to carry a real gun.

"Form up in squads, then prepare to march out," the sergeant said. "Keep your daysticks at the ready."

Colin hurried to obey. The uniform itched, slightly, as the squad started to march, advancing down the street as if they were going into combat. But there was no one waiting for them, not even a single solitary protester. The luxury houses, homes to the rich and powerful, were dark and silent. Row upon row of shops were firmly shuttered, as if the crime and criminality of the estates had moved to the inner city. He couldn't help noticing that half the shutters looked new and strikingly out of place, as if the shopkeepers hadn't expected rioters on the streets and thieves in the night. Perhaps they hadn't. The inner city was supposed to be the safest place on the planet. Colin had known pickpockets who'd gone into the inner city, expecting rich pickings...and never been seen again. The police might have caught them before they'd managed to take more than a handful of wallets.

The balmy night air felt odd as they reached the edge of the inner city, where the police had set up a roadblock, and started to turn away. Colin half-expected the police to say something—anything—but nothing happened. It was...odd. The police were the enemy, right? But they had strict orders not to provoke a fight. Any questions—from the police or anyone else—were to be directed to their superior officers. He caught a number of policemen looking at them warily, as they made their way down the streets and frowned. Why...?

They believe we're soldiers, he thought, suddenly. *That's why they're so concerned.*

The night wore on. Colin and his squad were directed to man a barricade, then resume their patrols. Dozens—perhaps hundreds—of vehicles moved in and out of the complex, some crammed with military and police officers. The luxury houses were secured, the occupants told to remain indoors until they received further orders. Colin heard a whispered rumour that the *real* owners had departed long ago, to country estates or orbital habitats well away from the madding—and dangerous—crowds. The occupants were their staff, left behind when their masters fled. Colin couldn't help wondering if they were engaged in a little looting. He'd have been tempted himself if the sergeant hadn't made it clear that looting would be severely punished.

But it doesn't matter, he thought, as the first hints of sunlight glimmered over the distant hills. *We won. Didn't we?*

. . .

Senior Constable Peter Quigley ignored Sergeant Grozny's quiet disdain as Captain Blair Young issued orders. The police had expected a state of emergency to be declared for quite some time—preparations had been underway as soon as the politicians had realised that the planet was infested with terrorists—but it had taken longer than anyone had expected for the government to take the plunge. Perhaps they'd been struggling desperately to integrate the reservists with the regular military. The soldiers on the street were an odd mixture of trained professionals and clowns, the latter showing bare traces of military training. They hadn't been trusted with guns either, Peter noted. It was a wise decision. He rather suspected the half-trained fools would start shooting at the slightest hint of enemy attack.

"You have your orders," Captain Young finished. He was a decent officer, fully aware of the stresses and strains facing his men. *He* had no patience for Grozny's by-the-book policing when there was *real* work to be done. "Go to your cars."

Peter felt a hand fall on his shoulder. "You'll be riding with me," Grozny hissed. "And behave yourself."

"Yes, Sergeant," Peter said, obediently. He'd behave, in public. And, in private, he'd file a complaint about the sergeant that would see him transferred to some godforsaken hamlet in the middle of nowhere. Sandford, perhaps. Peter had heard it was the most boring posting on the entire planet. "Shall we go?"

Grozny glared at him, then led the way to a police groundcar. Peter climbed into the passenger seat, clicking on the radio automatically. The regular program of music, one that had helped keep him awake on many a boring night shift, was gone, replaced by a constantly-repeating emergency broadcast. Peter rather suspected that most people weren't going to listen, at least at first. It would take some time for them to realise that the police—and the military—were serious about keeping the streets cleared.

And anyone who causes trouble can be marched straight to a detention camp, he thought, grimly. The stadiums were already being converted into makeshift holding facilities. They were designed to seat tens of thousands of people. They'd have no trouble hosting a few thousand suspects until they could be tried and sentenced. *This time, we have the power to keep the streets under control.*

The dispatcher was oddly quiet as they drove though the city, only passing on a handful of updates and orders addressed to other units. It was almost creepy. Peter had more than enough experience to know that the dispatchers rarely shut up, even in the wee small hours before dawn. But the streets were empty, the shops were boarded up…everyone with any sense, he was sure, was fast asleep in bed. He smiled to himself as Grozny stopped the car outside a mid-sized house. He was—finally—back in the game.

"Behave yourself," Grozny repeated, as he climbed out of the car. "And let me do the talking."

Peter nodded and followed Grozny as he walked up the garden path and knocked hard on the door. A long moment passed, then he heard someone shuffling inside the house. Had they woken the owners? Or did the owners have a maid? The house wasn't *that* big, but it was expensive enough to be well beyond his limited salary. Judging by the gardening, the owners had lived in the house for decades. It might even have been passed down from a time when housing hadn't been quite so expensive.

The door opened. A dark-skinned man peered out, blearily. His gaze sharpened as he saw their uniforms.

"David Craddock?" Grozny's voice was firm. "I have a warrant for your arrest."

Craddock stared at them. "What…what for?"

"You'll be informed of the details when you reach the station," Grozny said. The warrant was a formality. A state of emergency had been declared.

The government could detain whoever it liked without charge. "Please inform your wife, then come with us."

Peter smirked, wondering if Craddock would try to run. Grozny could hardly complain if Peter used his daystick to knock a fleeing suspect to the ground. Peter had no idea what Craddock was supposed to have done—he was sure his superiors would think of something in time—but it hardly mattered. All *he* wanted to do, right now, was take his frustrations out on a convenient target.

"I'm coming," Craddock mumbled. He shuffled, uncomfortably. "Just let me call my lawyer…"

"No lawyers," Grozny said. "Come with us now."

He didn't sound pleased. Legally, a suspect had the right to call a lawyer before he was handcuffed and taken to jail. Peter had never bothered to tell his suspects that they had the right, but a straight arrow like Grozny would. Maybe Grozny would resign in protest. It was the sort of grand gesture that would appeal to a man like him.

"If you wish." Craddock was very pale. Perhaps he knew why he was under arrest. Or…perhaps he'd thought he was immune to arrest. Who knew? Who cared? "I'm coming."

"You'll be back home soon enough, I'm sure," Grozny said.

Perhaps he was trying to be reassuring. Peter didn't care. But he had the feeling—for all sorts of reasons—that Grozny was wrong. This arrest was just the beginning.

There were many more to come.

CHAPTER THIRTY-FIVE

*Indeed, there was good reason to believe the media wasn't telling
the truth. The gap between the truth, as seen by a person's eyes,
and what they were being told was simply too large. Matters weren't
helped by pointless pontificating from talking heads; an overweight
announcer telling city-blockers that they should take advantage of
food shortages to diet did not go down well with the general public.*
—**PROFESSOR LEO CAESIUS**
Crying Wolf: The Media and the Fall of the Empire

CLARENCE JERKED AWAKE. Someone was banging on the door.

"Clarence," Patricia shouted. "Get up! Now!"

Clarence rolled over in bed and stood, one hand grasping for his robe. He hadn't had time to shower when he'd finally returned home, after his meeting with Stewart. He'd simply undressed and fallen into bed. He pulled his robe on, then picked up his terminal and checked the time. It was barely six o'clock in the morning. No wonder he felt so terrible, even though he'd refrained from drinking the highly-suspect beer. He'd barely gotten four or five hours of sleep.

"I'm coming," he mumbled. He pulled open the door. Patricia was standing outside, wearing a pair of silk pyjamas that concealed nothing. "What's happening?"

Patricia caught his arm. "Come with me," she said. "There's an emergency broadcast."

She pulled him down the corridor and into the common room. Jessica was standing by the coffee machine, brewing a large pot of black coffee, while the rest of the staff were watching the terminal. A talking head—Clarence remembered a number of reporters trying to prove that the man was nothing more than CGI—was pontificating about *something*. He rubbed his head as Jackson caught his eye. A headache was pounding at the back of his skull.

"Listen to this," Jackson said. He held up his terminal. "It's on all the channels."

"*...Is an official broadcast,*" a harsh voice said. "*A state of emergency has been declared. Martial law is in effect. All members of the public are to remain off the streets and await orders. All public services have been suspended. All businesses, schools and places of worship have been closed. Anyone found on the streets will be arrested and detained. Remain in your homes. Remain calm. This ends this official broadcast.*"

Clarence sucked in his breath as the message started to repeat. "This is real?"

"It's not just on every radio channel, it's *everywhere*," Frank Wong said. "They've pushed it out to every terminal and email account on the planet."

"Fuck," Clarence said. He had to sit down. "What do you have?"

Jackson jabbed a hand at the screen. "According to him, the First Speaker has been taken ill and the cabinet is in control. But we don't know what's actually happening."

"I can tell you that there's a shitload of official traffic passing through the city's nodes," Wong said. "Everyone is involved, somehow."

"Somehow," Clarence repeated. The First Speaker had been taken ill? *That* sounded unlikely. The First Speaker would have access to the latest and greatest in medical technology. Tarsus was hardly a primitive stage-one colony world on the far side of explored space. Any illness would have been defeated long before it threatened his career. "Do we know *anything* for sure?"

"Just that the population is being told to stay home and off the streets," Jackson said. "The emergency broadcast is everywhere. So far, people seem to be listening."

Clarence frowned. He could see the value in shutting schools, gym halls and everywhere else people might congregate, but work? Telling people to stay home from work might put the final nail in the economy's coffin. Or, perhaps worse, get a lot of people fired. He'd known managers who wouldn't give a shit about the government's instructions when there was work to be done. They'd expect their workers to sneak through the police and military and get to work—or else. God knew it wasn't as if most workers could afford to sue their employers.

Maybe the managers will stay at home too, Clarence thought. He was lucky. His place of residence was also his place of employment. Very few people slept at their workplaces. He certainly wouldn't have wanted to sleep at the *Daily Truth*. The hours were long enough without making them 24/7. *I wonder what they're thinking over there...*

He watched the announcer babbling on and on about the state of emergency, reassuring the population that everything would be completely fine. It sounded as though he was reading a set of Rebirth Party talking points, speaking in vague generalities and carefully avoiding any specifics that might cause his listeners to stop suspending their disbelief. Clarence rather suspected that things weren't going to move as smoothly as the talking head suggested, particularly as the state of emergency dragged on and on with no end in sight. The economy would go downhill—downhill *faster*, he supposed—and eventually hit the ground. And what would happen then?

Clarence shuddered. There had already been food riots in the estates, if the tipsters were to be believed. Two reporters had been sent out yesterday to discover the truth, but neither one had returned. Clarence hoped that meant they'd been caught and detained by the police, instead of being crushed in the riots or beaten to death by the gangs. The estates had been on a knife-edge for years. Now, they might have decided to fight for survival despite the risk of being arrested or killed. What did they have to lose?

Jackson caught his eye. "What do you think is going on?"

"I'm not sure," Clarence said. He didn't *want* to put the pieces together. It was unthinkable, the conspiracy theory to end all conspiracy theories. And yet, the evidence seemed irrefutable. "I think this is a coup."

"A coup," Jackson repeated. "What do you mean?"

"I think that the First Speaker has been removed from power and Drayton has taken his place," Clarence said, flatly. The talking head had named Drayton as the head of the cabinet during the First Speaker's indisposition. "That's what they're doing."

Jackson looked stunned. "But..."

Clarence didn't blame him for disbelieving. Not really. Jackson had grown up in a genteel world where everyone had known the rules and played by them. Defeat was never the end of the world for the upper classes. There might be some embarrassment, there might be a loss of power and influence for a few short decades or so, but they wouldn't be killed by their rivals. They could afford to surrender, instead of fighting to the death, because defeat wasn't really so bad. A loser would still have a large mansion, a fancy car and a vast bank account...

...But Clarence had grown up on the estates, where wars between drug lords and gangbangers were waged to the death. He'd watched desperate young men wager everything on a single throw of the dice, gambling their lives—and their family's lives—that they could outwit their opponents and secure supreme power. It never lasted, not really. A successful gangster rarely had a moment to take a breath before he faced a new challenge, one that would crush him if he didn't crush it first. The stability Jackson took for granted had never been known on the estates. Clarence had struggled so hard to escape because he'd known it was only a matter of time before his life was cut short in the gang wars.

"The military would never allow it," Patricia said. "They'd overthrow the plotters, wouldn't they?"

"They don't know it's a coup." Clarence remembered Stewart's words and shuddered. The coup plotters didn't *have* to subvert the entire military to win. They just needed a few conspirators in key places. The soldiers would follow orders, completely unaware that they were on the wrong side. No one would think anything about a state of emergency being declared. Everyone had been expecting it for weeks. "That's why they're telling everyone the First Speaker is ill. They don't want to alert potential enemies until they've secured control of the levers of power."

"If you're right..." Jackson shivered and started again. "If you're right, what do we *do* about it?"

"Tell everyone," Jennifer said. "We can get the word out, can't we?"

"But what if you're wrong?" Patricia took a step forward. "What if...what if this *isn't* a coup? We would end up with egg on our faces, for nothing."

"It's certainly very odd," Jackson agreed. "But..."

"It might be worse than that," Claudia commented. "They'd arrest us for spreading rumours and undermining the government and they'd be *right*."

"If they weren't launching a coup," Clarence said. He was *sure* of it now. The pieces were starting to fall into place. "We'd be right to tell the world about the coup..."

"But we don't *know*," Patricia said. "This could get us shut down!"

Clarence gave her a sharp look. A nasty thought was forming at the back of his mind. "How do you know they won't shut us down anyway in the next few days?"

"They wouldn't," Jackson said. "The law..."

"To hell with the law!" Clarence stamped his foot, hard. "This is not a debate in a courtroom, with points and counterpoints and twisted legal arguments that bend the law into a pretzel until one side gets what it wants. They've thrown the law out the window! They can silence us—or tell the university to silence us—any time they like."

"The university would refuse," Jackson insisted. "They *have* to maintain their independence from the planetary government."

"And then what?" Clarence jabbed a hand towards the window, towards the university buildings in the distance. "The university tells them to take a sexual travel package, then what? So you think, for one moment, that the proctors could stand up to an army? The police could storm the gates at any moment, if they wanted. Resistance? What resistance? A single police squad could kill or capture every proctor on the campus without breaking a sweat. The proctors don't even carry weapons!"

Elle snorted. "Earth would..."

Her voice trailed off. "Earth is gone," Clarence said. "All the old certainties are gone now. Last year, no one would dare lay a finger on the university; now...now there is no one who would give a damn if the government arrested everyone on campus, demolished every last university hall and sowed the ground with salt. Do you have any idea, any idea at all, how much students like you are hated? Your threats of riots and campus unrest were always backed up by Earth's big stick. No one was scared of *you*. They were scared of the Imperial Navy."

Jackson swallowed, hard. When he spoke, he sounded as though he didn't believe his own words. "Our families would raise hell."

"Your families might be in trouble too," Clarence said. "And even if they weren't...the cops are unlikely to care. They hate and resent you—they hated and resented you *long* before Jennifer exposed their brutality for all to see. The cops won't be gentle if they come here, believe me."

He lowered his voice. "Playtime's over. You're in the adult world now."

"Shit," Jennifer said, quietly. She was the only youngster who seemed to understand. But she'd felt the power of the state. She'd been arrested by someone who *hadn't* known who she was. The others...the others didn't really believe it, not yet. They hadn't felt what it was like to be helpless, to be at the mercy of the state. "What do we do now?"

Clarence sighed. "Good question," he said. "How far are you prepared to go?"

Jackson met his eyes. "Are our families in real danger?"

"If I'm right, Drayton has just mounted a tiger." Clarence looked back at him, evenly. "A savage tiger. And the problem with riding a tiger is that you can't get *off* the beast or it will have you for dinner. Drayton has smashed every political norm this planet has developed for the last thousand years. He can't stop now or he'll be crushed. He *must* secure power and if that means co-opting or destroying your families, he'll do it. He has no choice."

"You sound as if you think like him," Patricia observed, snidely.

"You don't have to like someone—or agree with them—to understand how they think," Clarence countered, sharply. "I can tell you why someone wants to do something awful or stupid without actually wanting to do it myself."

He snorted in bitter memory. One of the first stories he'd covered, as a cub reporter, had featured a group of teenage boys who'd been killed on the maglev tracks. Everyone had been looking for answers, and someone to blame, but the truth had been terrifyingly simple. The young idiots had talked themselves into playing on the tracks because their peers had been playing on the tracks. Clarence knew that it was stupid—he would have known even if the affair *hadn't* ended in tragedy—but he also knew that it was hard to stand up to one's friends.

And we weren't allowed to write that down, he remembered. It had been the moment when cynicism had started to set in. *The editor said it smacked of victim-blaming.*

"Then we have to warn them," Jackson said. "Tell them...what do we tell them?"

"You can't call them, not legally," Wong told him. "The datanet telecommunications network is down. They're saying it's reserved for military and police operations, but there's next to no traffic on the system. I think they're trying to make it harder for the outside world to realise what's going on."

"Probably," Clarence said. The coup plotters probably had control of every vital installation by now. Even if they weren't under their *direct* control, they held the communications and relay hubs. It was funny, he reflected sourly, how something that was meant to improve efficiency could be weaponised if someone was prepared to think outside the box. "Can you send a message through the deep net?"

"I think so," Wong said. "But they'd know what we'd done."

"I thought they couldn't monitor the deep web," Jackson said. "You assured me..."

"They'd know when the message surfaced in your father's inbox," Wong said. "They may even be able to wipe it before he sees it. I can do some fiddling, and perhaps get the terminal to sound an alert as soon as the message arrives, but there's a good chance it won't go through."

Jennifer looked pale. "So we're alone?"

Clarence nodded, slowly. "I think we need to get out of here," he said. "They'll be coming for us soon enough."

"But..." Jackson stared at him, wildly. "We can't just *go*."

"We don't have a choice," Clarence told him. He mentally catalogued everything in his emergency bag. He'd only need a few minutes to grab his terminal, a few pieces of equipment and the photograph he'd pinned to the wall. "Grab your stuff and get ready to go."

"The streets are swarming with soldiers," Patricia said. "They'll be watching for us."

"They can't guard everywhere," Clarence said. Sure, the police *could* throw a ring of steel around the university, but they'd have to pull men away from just about everywhere else. He had a feeling the university wasn't considered *that* important. "Once we get out of the university, we should be able to hide."

"Where?" Patricia didn't sound convinced. "There are cameras everywhere. Where can we hide?"

"There are ways," Clarence said. The nasty thought was growing stronger. "The camera network isn't so extensive outside the inner city."

"We can go to the new offices." Jackson sounded pleased with himself, as if he'd solved a problem. "That would take us away from the university, at least."

Clarence nodded, although he knew it would be worse than useless. The government wouldn't need more than five minutes to track them down. They'd just have to check the records to see which building *Seeing Eye* had purchased, then send the police to arrest the reporters and their support staff. Or send their gang of bullies. If Drayton—or someone—had been prepared to order an attack on a political march, taking the risk of showing their hand openly, they would have no hesitation in sending the same thugs to burn *Seeing Eye* to the ground. It wasn't as if they'd be in the university any longer.

And they might want to burn the university anyway, Clarence thought. The police weren't the only ones who resented the students. It was easy to imagine a mob of estate-dwellers marching on the university with blood in their eyes. *Drayton might lose control as old hatreds and resentments continue to surface.*

"Get dressed and grab your bags," Clarence said, firmly. How many of the students had packed an emergency bag? Claudia would, of course, but who else? He would be surprised if any of the students had bothered. "Don't take anything more than the bare necessities. And money."

"Untraceable cash," Jackson said.

"They might have frozen your bank accounts by now," Clarence said. Electronic cash was convenient, but it gave the banks and governments far too much power. Thankfully, paper cash and coinage had never *quite* gone out of fashion. They could move without attracting attention until they ran out of money. "We have to assume the worst."

And hope we can get out of here before it's too late, he added, silently. Drayton was not a man to let the grass grow under his feet. The mere fact that he'd had the imagination to launch a coup proved *that*. None of his rivals—or Clarence, for that matter, had seen it coming. *They might be coming for us by now.*

He eyed Patricia thoughtfully. *And what*, he asked himself, *are you up to now?*

CHAPTER THIRTY-SIX

By the time the Empire fell, therefore, the population was primed not to believe anything from the media—or anyone else, for that matter. Civil servants, from basic repair functionaries to military officers, were regarded as completely untrustworthy.
—**PROFESSOR LEO CAESIUS**
Crying Wolf: The Media and the Fall of the Empire

SENIOR CONSTABLE PETER QUIGLEY allowed himself a terse smile as he joined the remainder of the assault squad outside the university gates. Sergeant Grozny hadn't wanted him there—the sergeant probably hadn't wanted to be there himself—but the orders had been clear. They couldn't be spared, let alone reassigned somewhere else. The police force was pushed right to the limits. It had never had to arrest so many people in so short a space of time.

Peter felt the smile grow wider as Captain Young briefed them on the mission. It was relatively simple—enter the university campus, go to a particular frat house and arrest everyone inside—but it held special meaning for him. The frat house was the headquarters of *Seeing Eye*, the newspaper that had screwed his career. He didn't know if the other constables had realised it—the sergeant's constant presence meant that he couldn't ask—but he would have been surprised if they weren't relishing the chance for some payback too. The university students had been spoilt little brats before they'd started a newspaper and set out to change the world. Now...

What they need is a damn good thrashing, Peter thought. He touched the daystick on his belt, smiling at the thought of bringing it down on a student's head. The police had had to put up with a *lot* of indignities from the little brats. Teaching them how the *real* world worked would be sweet. *Their parents can't protect them now.*

He snapped his mask into place as Captain Young led them down the streets, towards the university gates. Imperial University was meant to be secure—an enclave near the heart of the city—but the walls were so low that Peter found it hard to believe that they kept intruders out. The gatehouse looked impressive, like something out of a pre-technological romance flick, yet it wouldn't stand up to a determined assault. Peter rather hoped the university staff *would* put up a fight. He'd *love* to watch as a Manta Assault Vehicle crashed through the gate, squishing the guards under its treads. Only a complete idiot would dare to stand in front of an assault vehicle. Peter had seen them crush groundcars into pancakes.

The proctors eyed the police nervously, their eyes flickering from side to side like suspects who knew the policeman knew *something* even if they didn't know *what*. Legally, the proctors were the law on campus; practically, they couldn't cope with anything more challenging than a legion of girl scouts armed with cookie boxes. Peter smirked unpleasantly at the thought. The proctors also had their hands cuffed by their superiors, he suspected. A proctor who laid hands on a student, even a drunken idiot who was on the verge of getting someone killed, would be lucky if he was merely fired. Imperial University might as well be a lunatic asylum run by the inmates. Student demands got more and more absurd every year.

Captain Young spoke quickly to the proctors, who folded at once. Peter was almost disappointed as the policemen were waved through the gates. He would have liked the chance to smack a proctor or two with his daystick too. Instead, he followed his commander down a long road that looked surprisingly nice. The students practically lived in paradise, he thought, as envy waked in his breast. It was like entering a small town. The apartments looked bigger than anything he could afford on his salary and...and they had *gardens*, of all things. Why the hell were they complaining all the time? He clutched his daystick's hilt tightly. Any student who got in his way was going to regret it.

The frat house came into view, a blocky structure with a statue of some idiot in an academic gown in front of it. Peter felt his smile grow wider and hastily schooled his face into a grim expression, feeling the sergeant's eyes lingering on the back of his neck. The frats were the worst of the worst, as far as he was concerned. They sent their prospective members out to harass the police, then hid behind their university membership when angry policemen sent complaints to the authorities. One of the silly idiots had even tried to steal Peter's cap when he'd been a junior patrolman. Oh, he was going to enjoy teaching the smug little bastards a lesson. This time, they couldn't hide behind their parents or the university staff.

Captain Young knocked on the door, hard. Peter drew his daystick, ready to follow his commander into the belly of the beast. Sergeant Grozny moved up beside him, carrying a shockrod in one hand. Peter suspected the sergeant intended to shock him, rather than a student, if he did anything stupid. He kept his face under tight control, wondering if he dared arrange an accident for the bastard. A frat house was supposed to be private. There were no cameras in the rooms and halls. It wouldn't be hard to crack his daystick on the sergeant's head and blame it on a student...

But he's wearing his helmet, Peter reminded himself. *And if I failed to knock him out, he'd kill me.*

"They must have seen us coming," someone muttered from the back. "They're not opening the door."

"What a shame," Captain Young said. "Knock the door down."

Peter stepped forward, gladly. "Yes, sir."

• • •

"They're here," someone shouted. "The cops!"

Clarence cursed and snatched up his bag. They should have been gone by now, but the wretched students didn't have the slightest idea how to pack an emergency bag. It was something that, in hindsight, they should have practiced. Clothes and toiletries were one thing, but what sort of idiot packed an evening dress for going on the run? Did she think they were going to attend a party while they were hiding from the police? Clarence found it hard to believe. They were going to have too many other problems to attend *parties*.

"We need to go out the back," he snapped. A dull *thump* echoed through the frat house. The door was solid—Clarence had checked it when he'd first arrived—but it wouldn't stand up to the police for very long. A battering ram or a shaped charge would be more than enough to bring it crashing down. "Grab your bags and move!"

"They could be outside," Jackson said. He was starting to panic. "What do we do?"

"We hope," Clarence said. The police *could* have surrounded the building. If they had...the game was up. But if they hadn't...he shook his head. There was no point in worrying about it now. They had to move. "Let's go."

He glanced back as they hurried down to the fire escape. It was *just* possible that the police hadn't realised that the university had installed a gravity chute. The technology had been mainstream for hundreds of years, but builders on Tarsus had always resisted suggestions that it should be made mandatory, even on towering apartment blocks. They found it easier—and cheaper—to install metal ladders and staircases instead. Clarence had always found their attitude to be incomprehensible, but it might just have worked in his favour. The police might have checked the frat house's appearance and decided that there was no way for anyone on the upper floors to escape.

Unless we jump out the windows, he thought, wryly. The frat house was surrounded by grass, but he doubted it would be a soft landing. *We'd be lucky if we only broke our legs.*

Another crash echoed through the building. Clarence cursed under his breath. They'd broken down the door. How long would it take them to get upstairs? The frat house's plans were a matter of public record. The police might take the time to secure the two stairwells first before moving up to the upper levels. Or they might charge up the stairs in hopes of snatching evidence before it could be deleted or destroyed. They were going to be disappointed, Clarence thought. Frank Wong had already unleashed a computer virus that would wipe everything on the frat house's computers.

Jackson opened the chute and stepped to one side. "I'll go last," he said. Sweat shone on his face. "Everyone else, go."

Claudia stepped forward and jumped into the chute. There was a pause, then a faint thud from the lower levels. Clarence glanced at Jennifer, then followed Claudia into the chute and slid down to the bottom. His stomach twisted unpleasantly as the gravity field caught him, slowing his fall an instant before he was thrown out of the tube. Claudia was already on her feet. A red-faced Jennifer followed, holding her skirt firmly in place. Clarence had to smile at her expression. It would have been wiser for her to change into a pair of trousers before jumping down the chute.

And I would have been wiser to sleep in my clothes, he told himself, as the others dropped down the chute. *In hindsight, there are a lot of things we should have done.*

"This way," Jackson said. "There's a way to get over the wall over there."

Clarence followed him, hoping and praying that the police didn't realise they'd escaped until it was too late. The police might not have a complete list of everyone who worked for *Seeing Eye*, but they'd certainly know the major players. Jackson, Elle, Jessica, Jennifer...Clarence promised himself, silently, that he'd do everything in his power to keep Jennifer out of a police cell. He wouldn't give a forged credit for her chances if the police got their hands on her. She'd embarrassed and humiliated them. They wouldn't forget her in a hurry.

They scrambled over the wall and dropped down on the far side. A handful of vehicles—all aircars—were parked there, but there was no point in trying to steal them. Clarence was sure of it. Frank Wong *might* be able to hack their onboard systems and take control—if they were lucky—but the police would track them down in a heartbeat. The ATC system would track them wherever they went. A groundcar would be easier, but there wasn't one in view.

Jackson caught his arm. "Where do we go now?"

"This way," Clarence said, picking a direction at random. If what he was starting to suspect was true, they needed to find somewhere to hide. "We have to hurry."

"Yeah," Jackson said. "But where do we go?"

"Trust me," Clarence said. He didn't *really* have a good idea, beyond a seedy hotel on the edge of the estates, but right now the only *real* priority was getting away from the police. "I have a plan."

And hope we can get it to work, he added, silently. It was only a vague idea, but it was also the only one he had. *Too many things could go wrong.*

• • •

The door crashed open, coming off its hinges and smashing to the ground. Peter barely noticed as he threw himself inside the building, glancing around with interest. He'd had a vision of a frat house as an endless party, with the walls covered in the sodden remains of alcohol, sex and vomit—where they weren't covered with pictures of dubious legality—but the interior looked more like an office building than student accommodation. A pair of students—both boys—stared at the police in horror as the frat house was stormed. They were knocked down and cuffed before they had a chance to do more than stare.

"Get up the stairs," Captain Young snapped. "Find the bastards!"

Peter leapt to obey, running up the stairs as if the devil—or Sergeant Grozny—was right behind him. The second and third floors appeared to be bedrooms—he caught a glimpse of a third student retreating in horror—but the fourth was a large collection of offices. He smirked as he saw the sign on the door—*Seeing Eye*—and shoved it open. The common room was empty, but the signs of a hasty retreat were everywhere. A kettle sat on the stove, rapidly coming to the boil; a handful of clothes lay on the floor, including a selection of flimsy underwear that probably cost more than he earned in a year. He ignored the urge to pick it up as he ran into the next room. It was crammed with computer terminals, but all of them were blank. A thin wisp of smoke hung in the air.

Shit, Peter thought. It looked as if someone had not only wiped the terminals, but taken the time to physically destroy them as well. That wasn't good news. Peter was no expert, but he was fairly sure it was impossible to recover information from a destroyed terminal's datanodes. *The boss is not going to be happy.*

He put the thought aside as he heard a scream up ahead. Someone was in trouble. He kicked the door open and plunged into the next room. A young woman stared at him in horror—and recognition. Peter gave her a sharp smile—this was going to be fun—and then felt his heart sink when the sergeant followed him into the room. He sighed and watched as the sergeant cuffed and searched the woman with consummate professionalism. What sort of man ignored the chance for some fun and games with a criminal suspect? It wasn't as if anyone gave a damn about them…wasn't it?

Grozny will be gone soon, Peter told himself, as they searched the rest of the floor. The staff seemed to have vanished, but how? Betrayal? It seemed unlikely. No one had *known* the frat house was going to be searched until the police had received their orders and no one had had the chance to make a call after they'd heard the news. Perhaps Grozny had found a way to alert the students. Even if he hadn't, it might be possible to plant evidence suggesting he had. *The Captain is going to want a scapegoat if a mountain of shit starts rolling towards him.*

Peter contemplated the possibilities, then put the thought aside for later as they walked their captive down to the ground floor. A couple of dozen students sat on the floor, one nursing a nasty-looking black eye. Peter felt no sympathy for the rich kid. He just wished he'd had the chance to land a blow himself. Instead, he let his eyes linger on the woman as Sergeant Grozny made their report. The frat house had been seized, but all the *real* targets had fled into…into where? They could be anywhere by now.

"We found an escape chute," Constable Mathews reported. He sounded as if he expected to be summarily demoted—or executed—on the spot. "They jumped down it and fled."

Captain Young gritted his teeth. "Then we'll have to search the rest of the university."

Ouch, Peter thought. There were only ten men in the assault squad. Enough to seize a frat house, particularly given the lack of effective resistance, but nowhere near enough to search the entire campus. Imperial University was *huge*. *We'll need to draft in more men to search for the bastards.*

The Captain had a different idea. He turned and peered at the captives. "You know where they've gone," he said. "Tell us where and we'll let you go."

Peter hid his amusement with an effort. No one outside the campus would believe anything a policeman said, certainly not a promise of freedom. A captive would either be transported to a holding facility or forced to work—he smiled in happy memory—for her freedom. But here? In a university where the students—until recently—had been coddled and protected by their families? Maybe—just maybe—one of the students would break.

And if they don't break, there are other things we can do, Peter thought. A state of emergency was in effect. They could break fingers, if their commander thought it necessary, or beat their captives halfway to death. No one would complain. *I wonder if they realise just how little safety they have, now.*

One of the students looked at him, then down at the floor. "They were going to the other offices," she said. She sounded broken, as if she was utterly unable to defend herself. "They…they thought they could hide there."

Peter nodded to himself. He'd been on the streets long enough to develop a sense for when someone was lying or deliberately trying to mislead him. Witness statements were inherently unreliable—a problem no one had managed to solve since the first police departments had been founded—but…he was almost disappointed. The girl had broken without hesitation, without more than the merest hint of pressure. There was no need to force her to talk.

"Get the van up here, then hold the captives until further notice," Captain Young ordered, curtly. He ignored the girl's splutter of protest. "And then we'll go to their other offices."

Sergeant Grozny nodded. "Yes, sir."

And we know precisely where to find them, Peter thought. Hiding out in their offices was a dumb move, but it was what he'd expect from a pack of idiotic students. Everyone knew a degree from Imperial University was worthless as anything more than toilet paper. *We'll catch them soon enough.*

CHAPTER THIRTY-SEVEN

This ensured that all efforts to prevent the Fall of Earth—or at least mitigate the effects of the collapse—failed. Attempts to secure 'safe zones' for a tiny fraction of the general population, or recover skilled personnel, were futile when large numbers of the population believed that they were simply going to be killed. It was rare for any of them to follow orders.
—**PROFESSOR LEO CAESIUS**
Crying Wolf: The Media and the Fall of the Empire

THE HOTEL WAS NOT, CLARENCE THOUGHT, the seediest place he'd ever visited. It was lacking in luxury, but there was hot water, clean sheets and a landlady who took paper cash and refrained from asking any awkward questions. He'd been in worse places. Hell, he'd lived in worse places. But Jackson and his remaining staff had never slept anywhere that wasn't a mansion or five-star student accommodation. The beds were small, the sheets were itchy, the food was cheap and nasty and the toilets were unspeakable. He would have found their shock amusing if they didn't have too many other problems.

And it beats being out on the streets, Clarence told himself. They'd been lucky the hotel was even *open. And it is way better than a prison cell.*

He checked his terminal, once again. Frank Wong had promised that it was untraceable, but Clarence had his doubts. The government might be looking for them…no, the government *was* looking for them. He'd expected to run straight into a police patrol as they'd fled the university and he was all too aware that, even though they'd seen nothing, that they could be under surveillance. The police might be hanging back, hoping the fleeing reporters would lead them to the rest of the conspirators. They were going to be disappointed.

Not that it matters, Clarence thought. He'd given strict orders that no one, save himself and Wong, was to do so much as *touch* a terminal. *If I'm right, we may have a serious problem.*

He put the terminal to one side and stood, peering out the grubby window. The river had always been discoloured, after the original settlers had used it to dispose of industrial wastes, but now it looked different. Beyond it, flames and smoke were rising from the distant estates and industrial wastelands. Hellebore and Remington were both on the far side of the river. He wondered, morbidly, what the inhabitants of Remington were doing. Were they fighting each other? Or attacking the police, if there were any policemen in sight? Or…or doing nothing. He found that hard to believe. A time of chaos was an excellent chance to settle old scores.

Someone tapped on the door. Clarence turned as the door opened, revealing Jackson and Patricia. He'd told Jackson to order the rest of the crew to go downstairs for dinner, then bring Patricia to him. It had taken longer than he'd expected. No doubt the students were complaining about the food. Clarence hoped they'd have the sense not to complain to the landlady. If they were annoying little bastards, the lady could assure herself of a reward by betraying her customers to the police. The students just didn't understand what had happened to them.

Claudia is with them, Clarence told himself. His friend had the kind of common sense that came from experience. *She'll keep them under control.*

He put the thought aside as Jackson shut the door. The student looked tired, as if he were on the verge of collapse. Jackson—and the rest of the staff—were stronger than the average student, physically and mentally, but their world had been turned upside down in less than a day. The real world had reached out and touched them and…Clarence hoped that they'd come to terms with it, before it tore them apart. A couple of staffers had openly wondered what would happen if they turned themselves in to the police. Clarence knew it wouldn't be anything good.

He glanced down at his terminal as his guests sat down, Jackson on the bed and Patricia on an uncomfortable-looking wooden chair. He'd started scanning for bugs as soon as they'd reached the hotel. There was no outgoing signal, as far as he could tell. It wasn't a *perfect* bug detector—military and intelligence technology was often more advanced than the critics realised—but they didn't seem to be under surveillance. And yet…

"A couple of odd things happened," he said, quietly. The walls were thin here. A person could stand outside the door and eavesdrop, without any technology that might set off an alarm. "And when I thought about them, I realised that they were part of a pattern."

He tapped on his fingers as he spoke. "I went to Hellebore and wrote a story, that very evening, about how an evil corporation was cheating the tenants out of the compensation for their homes. And that corporation folded, practically at once. A little later on, I went to the estate again and nearly got caught by the police. I only escaped through sheer dumb luck."

"You never said how you escaped," Patricia said.

"I ran." Clarence met her eyes. He'd thought he was saving her, but if he was right she'd been in no real danger. "And then—now—we had to run from the office."

"We know," Jackson said, dryly. "I still have the bruises."

"Yes," Clarence said. "And, all the time, Patricia was trying to slow us down."

He kept his eyes firmly fixed on Patricia's face. "You tried to spend a lot of time with me," he said. "You even tried to seduce me. And you were very insistent that I take you when I went to the estate, where we were nearly caught and arrested. Who are you working for?"

Patricia tensed. "You. I mean…*Seeing Eye*."

"You—well, you and Jennifer—have good reason to know and fear the power of the state," Clarence said. "And yet, you were the one who kept urging us to slow down. We would all have been caught if we hadn't already started making preparations to run. I think you're working for someone else."

He tapped his terminal, meaningfully. "I checked your file," he said, "and then I traced your family tree. Your family has links to Goldwater… you were one of the people who thought we should accept Goldwater's offer. You're working for him, aren't you?"

Jackson frowned. "Clarence, she was one of the original reporters for *Seeing Eye*…"

"That's right," Patricia flared. She slapped her hands together, her face reddening with anger. "He's just…pulling together threads to make an imaginary story."

"I checked the records," Clarence said. "The frat house has been in existence, under its rather unusual charter, for fifty years. In that time, it has given birth to thirty-seven small businesses, nineteen of which became and remained profitable after they moved off campus. I believe that the big corporations eventually bought up eleven of them. It's not out of the question for Goldwater to ask someone to join *Seeing Eye*, just in case it became profitable or a genuine rival to his media empire."

"I joined because I wanted to make a difference," Patricia snapped. "I thought we *could* make a difference."

"And he might have found a way to bring pressure to bear on you," Clarence said, quietly. "I think he could and he did."

"You kept insisting that we should hire more people," Jackson said. He sounded like a man who was coming to some very unpleasant conclusions. "But that would have forced us to take a loan, becoming dependent on…"

"You can't prove anything." Patricia stood, one hand reaching for her handbag. "And I don't have to stay here."

"Yes, you do." Clarence stood too, hoping and praying that Patricia was *just* a university student who'd gotten in way over her head. He knew from experience that a man was generally stronger than a woman, but military and police training—and biological enhancement—could go a long way towards evening the odds. And it had been a long time since he'd had to fight anyone. "I don't want to hurt you, but I can't let you leave."

Patricia swung her handbag at him. Clarence caught it, instinctively. The force of the impact nearly broke his hand. Patricia had either hidden a brick inside the bag or, more likely, purchased one that had been designed as an emergency weapon. He yanked it out of her hand, ignoring the pain, and shoved her to the ground. Patricia struggled desperately as he landed on top of her. But she didn't cry out...

"Behave and we will let you go, once this is over," Clarence promised. He motioned for Jackson to pass him the duct tape. It wasn't as easy to gag someone as the movies made it look, but he managed. "If it doesn't end in a hurry, we'll leave the hotel and tell your family where to find you."

He ignored her angry sounds as he taped her arms and legs, then searched her as dispassionately as possible. She had a tiny terminal—no larger than a lipstick tube—concealed in her underwear. Clarence nearly felt his heart stop before he realised it wasn't transmitting. He shut it down and checked carefully to make sure it really *was* shut down, before finishing the search. She wasn't carrying anything else.

"She was recording us all along," Clarence said. In hindsight, they'd been very lucky. If Patricia had risked activating her terminal, she could have had the police crashing into the hotel within minutes. Thank *God* he'd told them that he'd detect a stray signal at once. "She must have been gathering evidence for the bastards."

Jackson looked pale. "What do we do with her?"

"Leave her here, for the moment," Clarence said. There was no point in confiding in the rest of the staff. They didn't have enough evidence to convince *everyone* that Patricia was guilty as sin. It was possible—unlikely, but possible—that they'd made a terrible mistake. "She can stay here while we plot our next move."

He picked Patricia up and carefully laid her on the bed. She'd been a good spy, he thought sourly. He wouldn't have suspected her if she hadn't been doing everything in her power to keep them from running for their lives. Even so...he supposed he should have realised *something* when she'd tried to seduce him. A university student wouldn't try to bed a man fifteen years older than her unless he had millions of credits in the bank. And Patricia would *know*, beyond a shadow of a doubt, that Clarence was practically penniless.

Jackson caught his arm as they left the room, locking the door behind them. "What if she needs the toilet?"

"That will be very unfortunate," Clarence said, flatly. It would be unpleasant, but they would have to cope. Claudia could take care of attending to Patricia, after dinner. It wouldn't be pleasant for either of them, but it would be better than the alternative. "We can tend to her needs later."

"And what if you're wrong?" Jackson stopped, dead. "Or what if there are other spies?"

"We'll just have to hope we caught the only one," Clarence said. There was no way to be entirely sure that they *had* caught the only spy. He'd read horror stories about conspiracies where every last member was actually a government plant. "One way or the other, we're in deep shit."

"I know that," Jackson said. "They violated the university!"

"Existence as you know it is over," Clarence intoned. "Prepare for a brave new world."

Jackson looked down as they stepped into the next room. Frank Wong was seated at the desk, working on his terminal. He'd sworn blind that he couldn't be traced, but Clarence couldn't help feeling nervous. If a security monitor noted that the level of datanet traffic going in and out of the hotel had tripled in the last few hours, someone might draw the correct conclusions and send the police to arrest them. Or merely to ask questions. Too much of the civilian datanet had been shut down or suspended for his peace of mind.

"We're not going to make it, are we?" Jackson sat down on the bed, looking and sounding as though he wanted to give up. "They're going to catch us and kill us."

"They haven't caught us yet," Clarence said. He'd been considering the possibilities himself, but none of them were good. The only real hope was to get out of the city, but he doubted that was possible. All public transportation had been suspended. Besides, without money, they wouldn't last long in any case. The best they could hope for was finding a friendly farmer who'd be happy to shelter them in exchange for work. "Where there's life, there's hope."

But perhaps not for us, he thought, silently. The girls might find hiding places, if they had to sell themselves to do it, but him...? He knew, all too well, just how easy it was to leave an electronic trail. The police might already be on the verge of tracking them down. *We can't hide forever.*

"I think I understand now," he said, quietly. "They must have been putting the plot together from the moment they heard about Earth. The estates...they were only purchased, those they didn't already own, after they knew a crisis was coming. We must have put an unexpected spoke in their wheels."

"Bully for us," Jackson said, stiffly. "We cost them a little money and in exchange they destroyed our lives."

"Given the odds, perhaps we should be grateful we accomplished anything," Wong put in, without looking up from his portable terminal. His fingers never creased tapping on the keyboard. "At least we gave them a fright."

"And now they're going to kill us," Jackson said. He put his head in his hands. "Was it worth it?"

Clarence shrugged. "Frank, can you publish a newsletter? I mean... can you get it everywhere? *Without* getting it scrubbed out of the datanet?"

"I think so," Wong said. "I could get a few other WebHeads to help. Spamming is illegal, but...right now *we're* illegal. I could make it look like an official government broadcast, if you want. It wouldn't be hard to hack the mainstream media and get the message out through their datanodes too. Yeah, I could do it."

"And then they would kill us," Jackson said. He looked up, briefly. "They would track us down easily."

"They might," Wong admitted. "There are fewer datanodes out here. I can obscure the trail to some extent—more if I get help from the rest of the hacker community—but a dedicated WebHead might be able to trace the message back here. Then…well, they'd have us."

"Yeah," Jackson said. "They'd kill us."

Clarence cursed under his breath. Jackson was starting to come apart at the seams. It was hard to blame him for failing to realise what was going to happen, not when he'd never understood that his life wasn't typical… seeing a friend exposed as a spy couldn't have helped either. The students generally didn't need to worry about informers in their ranks, not when most of them wouldn't be arrested for anything less than murder or grand larceny. A good lawyer could probably make sure the charges were dropped in exchange for a suitable amount of compensation.

But there was no time for Jackson to have a breakdown. Clarence met his eyes.

"Do you want to hear a story?"

He went on before Jackson could say a word. "There was a man—a ruler—in a state called China, one of the semi-mythical countries on Earth from the time before the planet was united under a single government. This man believed firmly in the virtues of capital punishment, to the point where *everything* was punished by death. All crimes were equal. A child molester might be beheaded next to a man who neglected the proper honorific when talking to his social superiors."

"He sounds just like our politicians," Jackson said.

Clarence smiled, humourlessly. "So—one day—a team of farmhands were making their way down to the farm when one of them turns to his mates and asks them what is the penalty for being late? Death, they chorus.

And what's the penalty for revolution? Death, they say again. And the man smiles and tells them that they're *already* late."

"So they might as well rebel," Jackson finished. "Did they win?"

"I don't know," Clarence said. Truthfully, he knew very little about pre-space history. The story had been a cautionary tale, not a historical lecture. He wasn't even sure where China had *been*, before the land had been covered with megacities and the oceans turned into a poisonous nightmare. Britain? America? What *were* they to him? "But they had the choice between walking calmly to their deaths and fighting for their lives. They had nothing to lose by fighting. Did they?"

"No." Jackson sat upright. "And your point is that *we're* dead, so we might as well rebel? With what?"

"With the truth," Clarence said. "If we have nothing to lose, we might as well go out with a bang. I'm going to write a story, I'm going to tell the world what happened, and Frank is going to put it online. And then…I'm going to go to Government House."

Jackson gave him a sharp look. "Why?"

"Because I want to be there," Clarence said. In one sense, Jackson was right. They were going to be caught, sooner or later. It was suddenly easier to take a great many risks. "One way or the other, it will be the story of the century."

CHAPTER THIRTY-EIGHT

But then, this was not their fault. They had grown up in an environment where they were lied to—constantly—and knew they were being lied to. Why should they believe what they were being told now?
—**Professor Leo Caesius**
Crying Wolf: The Media and the Fall of the Empire

SENIOR CONSTABLE PETER QUIGLEY gritted his teeth in annoyance as the sun started to set. The day had started out well, but it had turned to shit the moment they discovered that the wretched reporter-students had fled the coop. Their offices had been deserted, save for a pair of builders who'd claimed to know nothing about their employers. Captain Young had marched the police back to Government House, where they'd been assigned to man a checkpoint along the barricades. There had been barely any time for a quick rest and a meal that tasted like crap.

He sighed, wondering when they'd have a chance to go on patrol again. It was hard to see, in some ways, if they were actually doing *anything*. The streets were quiet, anyone in the nearby homes were *staying* in the nearby homes and he was bored. It was all he could do to keep from falling asleep as he stood on watch. Only the sergeant's dire warnings kept him from sneaking off for a nap.

They have to relieve us soon, he thought. He'd seen countless police—and *real* soldiers as well as goose-stepping reservists—moving in and out of the compound. Surely, *some* of them could take over. *We're going to be falling asleep on our feet before too long.*

He frowned, one hand gripping his daystick, as he caught sight of someone walking down the road towards the checkpoint. He was walking in the middle of the road, careful to keep his hands in plain sight; Peter tensed, bracing himself for either an unconvincing explanation of *something* or a potential attack. *Smart* people were careful when they approached the police, but his entire career had been a lesson in the *lack* of intelligence shown by the general population. Peter had never expected to stand at a checkpoint where the threat of a car bomb was more than a paper threat, but...his eyes narrowed as the newcomer came into view. He was short, trending to fat, with dark skin and short dark hair...Peter felt a jolt that had him standing upright, grabbing for the terminal on his belt. Clarence Esperanza. It *was* Clarence Esperanza. The reporter the police had failed to nab on the university campus had walked right into their arms.

"Stay where you are," Peter boomed, as Sergeant Grozny hurried to join him. "Keep your hands in the air."

The reporter stopped. He was trying to look unafraid, as if walking into the lion's den was something he did every day, but Peter wasn't fooled. He'd made harder men wet themselves when he'd been patrolling the estates. And yet...he eyed the reporter's dark suit, wondering what it concealed. The man could easily be carrying a bomb under his clothing. Or—Peter's eyes sharpened as he remembered the wretched girl who'd got him suspended—he could be carrying a wire.

"He's mine," Peter muttered. There was a reward on Clarence Esperanza's head, but Peter didn't give a damn about *that.* Bringing in a man with a price on his head would *finally* allow him to put the suspension—and the threat of being fired—behind him. No matter that the bastard had simply walked into their hands. Peter's career was safe again. "Mine."

He raised his voice. "What do you want?"

"Take me to Drayton," the reporter said.

Peter snorted. "Do you think he wants to see you?"

"Tell him that Clarence Esperanza is outside, demanding to see him," the reporter said. He had the same smug assurance as the never-to-be-sufficiently-damned bitch who'd ruined Peter's career. "He'll see me."

"You're going to vanish into a detention camp," Peter said. There was no bomb. The reporter had nothing, but misplaced self-assurance. "No one will ever see you again."

Sergeant Grozny tapped his terminal, muttering into it. Peter cursed under his breath. Grozny wasn't the kind of person who would *normally* steal credit for collaring a wanted criminal, but now…Peter knew Grozny hated him. And the sergeant needed to look to his career too. His cherished ambition to become a supervisor might be granted if he, not Peter, was credited with capturing Clarence Esperanza. The man was wanted, dead or alive.

"We're to take him upstairs," Grozny said. There was something in his voice Peter didn't like. "Search him first, if you would."

Peter gritted his teeth, silently promising himself that Grozny would get everything he deserved sometime in the future, even if Peter had to put his career at risk to make it happen. He advanced towards the reporter, half-hoping that the bastard would do something—anything—to resist. A police officer had the right to search anyone—anywhere, anytime—if he had the slightest suspicion that a crime had been committed. Resistance was *de facto* proof of criminal intent. But Clarence Esperanza offered no resistance as Peter searched him thoroughly, checking everywhere a weapon or a recorder might be concealed. The man seemed amused, damn him. He'd be laughing out the other side of his face after he'd been transported to a detention camp.

The reporter lifted his eyebrows as Peter stepped back. "I trust you *are* going to buy me dinner afterwards?"

Peter felt a hot flash of anger. It wasn't the first time he'd heard that, but it never failed to get on his nerves. He didn't *like* searching men. It was just part of the job. The suggestion he might be doing it—putting his hands where the sun didn't shine—because he *enjoyed* it was appalling. He didn't get his jollies by searching *men*.

He lifted his hand, fully intending to slug the reporter in the face, but Sergeant Grozny cleared his throat loudly. Peter forced himself to calm down, despite the growing urge to murder the pair of them and blame it on...on someone. He was sure he could come up with a convincing story, if anyone cared enough to ask. Clarence Esperanza was a reporter and Sergeant Grozny was an embarrassment. No one would care much if their bodies were pulled from the river or found half-buried on one of the estates...

"This way," he growled. "And then you're mine."

The reporter, wisely, didn't rise to the bait.

. . .

It was not the first time Clarence had been searched—he'd been frisked as a teenager, then strip-searched when he'd visited secure compounds as a reporter—but it was easily the most unpleasant. The policeman—it hadn't taken long for Clarence to place the man's *face*—hadn't enjoyed it any more than Clarence himself, yet he hadn't allowed that to get in his way. Clarence had known, intellectually, how horrible it had been for Jennifer to be searched and groped by the asshole, but he hadn't really believed it. He knew better now.

He was careful not to say or do anything to Sergeant Grozny as the two policemen marched him towards Government House. The walls were lined with armed men—policemen, soldiers, youngsters wearing ill-fitting uniforms—and a handful of armoured vehicles were parked outside, ready to repel attack. Clarence felt a chill running down his spine as he was escorted through a second checkpoint, wondering if he'd made a terrible mistake. It would be the last mistake of his career, if so. There was no hope of rescue, let alone escape. The cops hadn't bothered to cuff him—they'd even let him keep his belt and shoes—but Clarence had no idea how he could escape. A super-soldier from an action flick could take the entire police force, Clarence thought, yet *he* had the scriptwriter on his side. Clarence doubted he could outrun the guards even if the police gave him a head start.

It was the first time he'd been to Government House and he couldn't help looking around with interest as he was escorted up the stairs. A dozen offices, all empty; a pair of communications suites, crammed with men and women wearing headphones and talking into microphones in hushed voices. The corridors were lined with paintings of First Speakers, from the first elected head of government to Thomas Wycliffe himself. Clarence couldn't help thinking that they all looked remarkably alike. They'd come from different parties, the position rotating with monotonous regularity, but they'd all been the same. None of them had been anything more than a party hack.

Which suited everyone fine, until it didn't, Clarence reflected. *The system wasn't designed to produce men who could take action in a crisis.*

He pushed the thought out of his mind as the policemen shoved him into the First Speaker's office. It was massive, decorated in an elegant style that told him the occupant had no need to show off his wealth and power. An immense wooden desk—the wood had come from Earth, if Clarence was any judge—was positioned in front of a towering bookcase. It was lined with books—old-fashioned paper books—but Clarence would bet good money that none of the office's occupants had ever bothered to read them. The lone window offered a spectacular view of the city. Crisis or no crisis, Adana was lit up like a Christmas tree.

"Mr. Esperanza," a familiar voice said. "How…*nice*…of you to join us."

Clarence stood straighter. There were two men in the room, sitting in comfortable armchairs: Alfonse Drayton and Simon Goldwater. Clarence wondered, as the policemen let go of his arms, which one of them was actually in charge. It was easy to believe that Goldwater was the mastermind, with Drayton as his puppet, but Clarence had his doubts. Drayton had too much…*personality*…to be a mindless puppet. Besides, he was much younger than his backer. Goldwater could afford the best enhancements money could buy, but he wouldn't last forever. Death came for everyone, in the end.

His mouth was suddenly dry. "Thank you," he said. "Can I trouble you for some water?"

Drayton looked up at him. "Why did you come here?"

No water, Clarence thought. He wondered why he felt a little surprised. Perhaps Goldwater's kindly old man persona had made more of an impression than he'd realised. Or, if what he suspected was true, perhaps it had something to do with his work. *I put a spanner in the works long before I even started to suspect that something* big *was going on.*

"The First Speaker isn't ill," Clarence said. "You launched a coup."

Drayton didn't bother to deny it. "Why did you come here?"

"Because I want to know what's happening," Clarence said. "And because I want to interview you."

"Really?" Drayton sounded as if he wanted to laugh. Behind him, Clarence heard the cops shuffle uncomfortably. "You came here to *interview* us? *Us?*"

Goldwater held up a hand. "What do you think you know?"

Clarence took a breath. He had to keep talking. He had to keep them focused on him. But if he said the wrong thing…the building was full of Drayton's supporters. He could be carried to a window and thrown out at any moment…or worse. *Clarence* might not have known what was going on until the coup was mounted, but it was unlikely either Drayton or Goldwater knew it. From their perspective, he'd been causing them inconvenient problems for months. They had to wonder if he'd known the truth right from the start.

"I didn't understand at first," he said, laying out the pieces one by one. "You fired me—you had me fired—for reporting on the Forsakers being deported. It made no sense at all. There was nothing to be gained by deporting them or by firing me. It would have been cheaper to drop them on an island somewhere, if one really wanted to get rid of them, or simply kill the story if you didn't want it to run. Instead, you fired me. Why?"

"The Forsakers were using up good oxygen," Drayton rumbled.

"You spent more money to deport them than it would have cost to keep them," Clarence pointed out, coldly. "Hell, if you intended to *exterminate* them, there were cheaper ways to do it. Why waste so much money on something so pointless?"

"Perhaps we simply wanted to give them a better home," Goldwater said, smoothly.

"You could have done that here," Clarence said. He tapped his chest. "And then you fired me. You could have had the story killed, and no one would have thought anything of it, but instead you fired me."

"You *were* poking your nose somewhere you didn't belong," Goldwater said. "And you were making a nuisance of yourself."

"I would hardly be the first reporter to do both." Clarence felt a flicker of pride. It was nice to be acknowledged, even if it was unlikely he'd see another sunrise. "You crushed me. You practically destroyed my life."

Goldwater looked, just for a second, as if he were bored. "And your point is?"

Clarence ignored the sudden urge to strangle the old man. "It made no sense."

"Perhaps we just wanted to make an example of you," Drayton said.

"Perhaps," Clarence agreed. "You certainly terrified everyone at the *Daily Truth*."

He took a breath. "And then there was the affair of Hellebore Estate. It made no sense either. You force thousands of people out of their homes, with a PR campaign telling the world that you are paying compensation, but the moment *Seeing Eye* calls you on your bullshit you fold. You fold so quickly that the story barely had time to go around the world before you were already ahead of it. You tell a sob story about estate agents cheating the proles, you pay a remarkable amount in compensation...and you get the estate. And you tell us you plan to demolish it, but...you don't.

"I checked the records. You only laid claim to the estate shortly after we heard that Earth was gone. Normally, it takes *months* to get planning permission, even for a big corporation like yours, but...this time, you got the permissions in less than a week. And then you surrendered and paid compensation, again far too quickly for it to be believable."

"You don't think we *might* have been screwed by an estate agent?" Goldwater leaned back in his chair. "Shifty buggers, those agents. Everyone who grows up on an estate knows not to trust them."

Clarence ignored the dig at his origins. "No, because it makes no sense. You might have been as pure as new-fallen snow, but you would still have had to figure out what *really* happened before you started accepting liability and paying compensation. I think you had a contingency plan in place all along. And I think you only did *that* because whatever you were doing was time-sensitive. Better to pay out the compensation than put your timetable back a few weeks. It still made no sense.

"And that estate kept coming up on my radar! You were so quick to kick the tenants out, but slow to actually demolish the buildings. I was kidnapped and, when I escaped, I was close to the estate…close enough to be fairly sure that my kidnappers were taking me there. When I visited again, I could see signs that people were still inside—behind a secure fence, patrolled by policemen. What was so important about the estate? Why?"

He took a breath. "Here's what I think happened. You heard that Earth had fallen. You probably had some inkling it was going to happen before it actually did. And so you started planning to take control of the government. You bought the estate and used it to house your army of thugs while creating a state of unrest that could be used to justify a declaration of emergency, moving military officers and units around and—eventually—taking control of the government. There were no terrorists! You were in control right from the start."

Drayton's face darkened. "You're committing treason!"

"You're the one who mounted an illegal coup," Clarence countered. "Why didn't you just wait for the next election?"

"Why should we?" Goldwater's voice was very calm. "And why should we expect the *people* to vote in their own interests?"

"People generally act in what they *see* as their own interests," Clarence said. "And you could have explained your position to them…"

"The system was never designed to deal with a crisis," Drayton said, flatly. "By the time we took office, assuming we did, it would be too late. We took desperate measures to save our world from complete collapse. And you, you selfish bastard, tried to get in our way."

"You killed hundreds of people," Clarence said. Drayton had a point, but his methods were despicable. "And you fired me."

"A mistake, clearly," Goldwater said.

"It doesn't matter," Drayton said. "You'll go into one of the detention camps. When we're in complete control, you'll be deported or simply dispatched to a penal island. I trust the *interview* was worth it. You walked into our hands and we will never let you go."

Goldwater's eyes sharpened. "What did you hope to achieve by coming here?"

"It doesn't matter," Drayton said. He spoke as if Clarence wasn't in the room. "Just another young fool, so convinced of own righteousness that he doesn't see the danger."

A sharp tap echoed through the room. The door burst open. "Sir," a young man said. "There are people on the streets!"

"Disperse them," Drayton snapped.

"Sir…there are *thousands* of people on the streets," the man said, desperately. "Hundreds of thousands. Millions! The whole city is on the streets!"

Goldwater's voice was very cold. His eyes bored into Clarence's face as if they could see into his very soul. "What have you done?"

"I told the people the truth," Clarence said, evenly. "And now they are on the streets."

CHAPTER THIRTY-NINE

Indeed, the problems facing the media were a microcosm of the problems facing the Empire itself. On one hand, it had too many problems caused by half-assed attempts to fix earlier problems; on the other, it had simply grown too large for effective government. And its governors were unwilling to do the only thing they could— give up power—to fix the problem. The results were inevitable.
—PROFESSOR LEO CAESIUS
Crying Wolf: The Media and the Fall of the Empire

THE PATROL HAD SEEMED SO SIMPLE. And then it had turned into a nightmare.

Colin stared in disbelief as hundreds—no, *thousands*—of people advanced towards him, looking ready to fight. The mob was *huge*, larger— far larger—than any crowd of rioters or marchers he'd seen on the estate. Men and women, young and old…they were striding towards him, driven by…what? He didn't know what had happened or why, let alone why there were so many people on the streets. The command net was filled with section leaders like himself requesting instructions, but there were no answers.

The daystick felt reassuringly solid in his hands, yet…he knew it wouldn't save his life. He might brain a handful of people, he might *kill* a handful of people, but the remainder of the crowd would tear him into bloody chunks. He'd seen it happen, back on the estates. A person might push the crowd too far and then…and then he'd die. It took him longer than it should have done to realise what had happened. The people on the streets were no longer afraid of him. His uniform didn't make him a big man any longer. It made him a target.

Magus caught his arm. "What do we do?"

Colin glanced around for the sergeant. Or someone—*anyone*—who could give him orders. But there was no one within eyeshot. He was alone, in command of ten young men…he didn't know what to do. He'd been told that he'd be supported, whatever he did; he'd been told that he would no longer be alone, that he would no longer have to tamely accept whatever happened because he was no longer alone…he was alone. The sergeant would have known what to do, but Colin…? Colin didn't have the slightest idea what to do.

"We move back," Colin said. Heading back to Government House might be dangerous—and he had orders to stay on the streets—but it was the only thing that came to mind. "Inch backwards, carefully…"

The urge to run was almost overpowering. Sweat poured down his back as the crowd started to sing the planetary anthem, thousands of voices blurring into one. It was all he could do to keep moving backwards, all too aware that the crowd was steadily gaining in confidence and power as they weakened. His section was alone and isolated, completely outnumbered. He wanted to turn and flee. But a display of weakness would be fatal. It wouldn't take much to spur the crowd into running his team down and crushing them underfoot.

It would have been a different story if they'd had guns, he told himself. They could have mown down the crowd…the thought was terrifying. The crowd wasn't composed of thugs, gangbangers or even migrant shitters from the countryside, but decent men, women and children. They were…they were the sort of respectable people Colin wanted to be, the sort of people who grew up in safety and never knew how hard life could be on the other side of the river. Colin wanted to scream at them—*we're fighting for you, you idiots*—yet he knew his voice would be lost in the song. Who would have thought that the planetary anthem could be so threatening? Years ago, people had joked that the composer had bribed the founders to select his work as the anthem. The joke wasn't so funny now.

His legs started to buckle as he saw a groundcar driving down a side-street, trying to escape the mob. Who was it? Had it been stolen in the chaos? Or...or was it one of the leaders, trying to make his escape before the mob came for him? Colin didn't know. All he knew was that the crowd was getting bigger and bigger. The alleyway was teeming with people, some flowing out to join the heaving mob. Colin had to force himself to keep moving slowly as the song grew louder. It was pounding into his skull, deafening him. The command net was silent. He couldn't tell if there were no orders or if he simply couldn't hear them.

Magus shouted something incoherent and broke into a run. Colin wanted to shout at him, to curse him for not standing his ground, but then the panic began in earnest. The crowd howled and lunged forward, picking up speed as the rest of the section started to run. Colin felt hot liquid trickling down his legs...he swallowed hard, then started to run himself. The crowd was growing louder and louder...

Colin tripped and fell, hitting the pavement hard enough to knock the wind out of him. He tried to get up, but the mob was already on him. He had a moment to realise that he'd tripped over Magus's daystick—and to wonder, perhaps, if he'd been on the wrong side—before a foot came down hard. There was a brief flash of pain, a sense that something had broken, and then there was nothing. Nothing, but darkness.

• • •

Drayton stood and ran to the window. "What are they doing?"

"I told you," Clarence said. "They're coming to tell you that they don't *want* you."

Goldwater remained calm. "What did you do?"

"I wrote the story," Clarence said. It was hard not to gloat, even though he was pretty sure he was about to die. "And we made sure that *everyone* got a copy. I'm surprised you didn't realise it was happening before it was too late."

"It doesn't matter," Drayton said. He didn't look away from the window. "We have the guns. That crowd out there is unarmed."

Clarence smirked. "Are you sure?"

Drayton turned to face him. "What do you mean?"

"You were replacing senior officers—in the police, the military, the civil service—with your own people," Clarence said. He silently blessed Stewart for the tip-off. "But you couldn't subvert every last soldier, could you? You couldn't even subvert a majority of them! If you'd had control of the military, or even a small percentage of it, you wouldn't have needed to raise an army of thugs in the first place. You thought you could take control by putting your own people in place."

He smiled. "But we sent the story *everywhere*. Soldiers on the streets, spacers in the Orbital Guard, policemen and civil servants and everyone else…we told them what you did. We told them what you were doing. And we asked them if they really *wanted* to be part of it."

"They will obey orders," Drayton snarled.

"Are you sure?" Clarence met his eyes, evenly. The room was sound-proofed, but he could hear the faint sound of the planetary anthem. He hated to think how loud it must be outside the building. "You're not ordering them to defend the planet. You're not ordering them to fight a bunch of rioters. You're ordering them to gun down innocents, thousands of innocents. Do you think they'll obey?"

"We pay them," Goldwater said. There was a faint hint of unease in his voice. "They'll do as they are told."

Clarence shrugged. "Are you sure? How much are you worth these days? The economic crisis must have hit you pretty hard."

Goldwater started to speak, but Drayton spoke over him. "It doesn't matter. We didn't do this because we wanted power for our selfish reasons. We did this—we took control of the planet—because the planet *needs* us. Half the banks have been wiped out. The rest will be gone in mere days, if they can't staunch the bleeding. Most of our industries will follow them into oblivion. Harsh measures were necessary—*are* necessary—to save the planet."

He glanced out the window. The singing was growing louder. "We can do it. We can still do it. We can make Tarsus a power to be reckoned with, once again. Yes, there *will* be problems. Yes, we will have to work hard. But we have an industrial base that we can turn into the keystone for rebuilding our power in the sector and…"

"What does it matter," Clarence asked quietly, "if half our population starves to death?"

"They won't starve," Drayton said.

"Yes, they will." Clarence kept his voice under tight control. "You're reaching for the stars, but the ground below your feet is crumbling. Do you believe that you can train all the newly-unemployed to become shipyard workers and starship technicians and everything else we might need? Do you even think we have the resources to do it?"

"You're an ignorant reporter," Drayton scoffed. "What do you know?"

Clarence winced. A year ago, that would have been true. It was still true of the vast majority of reporters. But Clarence…? He'd had to read up on his subject, just to put everything he reported in proper context. He didn't claim to be an expert in anything, certainly not economics or spaceship maintenance, but he knew enough to be fairly sure that Drayton couldn't wave a magic wand and rebuild the economy. Drayton would have done it by now if he could.

"I have common sense," Clarence said. "That's all I need."

"A very uncommon attitude," Goldwater said.

Drayton looked at his assistant. "Give the order," he said. The young man turned pale. "The crowds are to be dispersed, using whatever means are necessary. And yes, that includes lethal force."

Clarence swallowed, hard, as the assistant started to speak into his terminal. If he was wrong, thousands of people were about to die. And it would all be his fault. He'd been the one who'd written the story. He'd been the one who'd encouraged Frank Wong to make sure it went *everywhere*. Copies of the story were probably on their way out of the system by now, on their way to a hundred worlds that had never heard of Drayton or Goldwater or Clarence himself. If he was wrong...

"This uprising will be crushed," Drayton said. "We'll teach them a lesson they'll never forget."

"And then what?" Clarence asked. He could still hear the singing. "Do you think that fearful people can build a whole new world?"

He looked at Goldwater, wondering—grimly—if the older man *did* believe it. Goldwater was far from stupid, but he'd grown up in a world where he had always known he was going to inherit vast wealth and power. It was possible that, at some level, he saw everyone below him as interchangeable, with no more individuality than a cog in a machine. Perhaps *that* had been why he'd fired Clarence, back when everything had begun. He hadn't really believed that Clarence would find a way back.

And I wouldn't have done, if Claudia hadn't come for me, Clarence thought. *It could have ended there, in my apartment, and no one would have known what was really going on until it was too late.*

The assistant looked up. "Sir...the police are refusing to fire!"

Drayton sucked in a breath. "Tell them, damn it!"

"They're not responding," the assistant said. His terminal bleeped. "Sir, we just lost control of Boylston Garrison! General Levy has been relieved of command and detained by his men."

"Those goddamn traitors," Drayton snarled. "Get on to the Orbital Guard. Tell them to blow Boylston off the map before this spreads!"

Clarence kept his face under tight control. Drayton was losing control. No matter what he did, he was losing control. Ordering the Orbital Guard to bomb a garrison was a sign of desperation. Clarence wondered, idly, what *that* would do? Would the Orbital Guard follow orders, probably starting a civil war? Or would the spacers refuse to take orders? There was no way to know.

"We've just lost Dawlish Garrison," the assistant reported. "The officer at Fordham Garrison reports a firefight on the grounds and…he thinks it will only be a matter of time before the HQ building is stormed."

"Never mind them," Drayton ordered. "Get on to the Orbital Guard!"

"Sir…the Orbital Guard isn't responding." The assistant looked terrified. "There's no response at all."

Goldwater stood. "I believe it might be time to negotiate," he said, smoothly. "The First Speaker is downstairs. Perhaps we can come to some arrangement."

"No, damn you." Drayton spun around. "We've come too far to be stopped now!"

"We're also losing," Goldwater said, evenly. "If we've lost three of the six garrisons, civil war becomes inevitable even if we maintain control of the rest. The Orbital Guard is refusing our calls. If they join the other side"—he shot an unreadable look at Clarence—"the situation becomes hopeless. We need to start negotiating now while we have something to negotiate with."

Drayton shook his head. "You won't sacrifice me to save yourself," he snapped. He glared at Clarence. "You"—he pointed a finger at Quigley—"kill the reporter."

Clarence turned and saw the policeman already holding his pistol. There was no time to try to jump him, or to evade a bullet. It felt like the end. He took a deep breath and closed his eyes, silently wishing he could have seen his son one final time. A shot rang out…

…And he heard a body falling to the floor.

His eyes snapped open. Sergeant Grozny was holding a smoking pistol in one hand. Peter Quigley was lying on the floor, blood leaking out of a hole in his head. Clarence felt sick. It wasn't the first time he'd seen a dead body, but…he'd come so close to death. Quigley would have shot him without a second thought. The man had no future if Drayton lost and he'd known it. Clarence felt a twinge of regret that the policeman would never face trial for his crimes—Jennifer was far from his only victim—and then shoved the thought out of his head. One way or the other, the bastard would never hurt anyone else again.

Sergeant Grozny cleared his throat. "I believe you should tell the people downstairs to calm down before some idiot pulls a trigger," he said. He jabbed his gun at Drayton when the man tried to speak. "We're not out of the woods yet."

"Do it," Goldwater said.

Clarence met his eyes as Drayton's assistant went to work. "Do you really think you can buy your way out of this?"

Goldwater looked pensive. "Perhaps," he said. "But that isn't the point. We did this for the good of the planet…"

"And a hell of a lot of greed," Clarence injected.

"…And there's nothing to be gained by prolonging the agony when we can no longer win," Goldwater said. He turned and peered out the window. "I would never have expected the people to rise up against us."

Clarence joined him. The streets below were *jammed* with people. It looked as if the entire city had joined the protest. There were no stewards, as far as he could see; there was no one telling the people which way to march, or what they should chant, or *anything*. It was no staged march, no genteel protest designed to let people vent rather than effect lasting change…it was the people on the streets, *demanding* change. Clarence wondered, grimly, if anything would *really* change, after the protesters went home. It was hard to believe that things could change so rapidly, if at all.

They will, he promised himself. Behind him, the assistant was telling the remainder of Drayton's people to stand down and surrender. *The world will never be the same.*

"I don't understand it," Goldwater mused. "Why did they come onto the streets?"

"They're idiots," Drayton said. "They're scared of change."

"No," Clarence said. "They knew—yes, they knew—that most of what they heard from the media was nothing more than lies. They wouldn't have believed the *Daily Truth* because they knew, all too well, that the *Daily Truth* lies. But us? They know we have a reputation for telling the truth because we *do* tell the truth. We built up our credibility by telling the truth, by openly admitting our mistakes, by being unafraid to confront issues that the mainstream media refuses to admit even exist. And when we told them that you were mounting a coup, that you were going to reshape the world, they believed us."

"Fools," Drayton snarled.

"People have been too scared to speak up for too long," Clarence said. "Too many little resentments, too much fear of what will happen if they dare speak up; their careers destroyed, their lives pulled apart for the pleasure of the mob...they're not scared now. They know they're not alone. And you will never terrify them into submission again."

"Damn you," Drayton said. He yanked his hand out of his pocket. He was holding a small gun. "You...damn you."

Clarence sighed. *I'm getting too old for this.*

"Put the gun down," Sergeant Grozny said. He was covering Drayton with his gun, but Clarence knew it was already too late. "Now!"

"Damn you," Drayton said. It wasn't clear who he was addressing. Clarence or Grozny or Goldwater or himself. "Damn you to hell."

And then he pointed the gun at his head and pulled the trigger.

CHAPTER FORTY

The media had cried 'wolf' too many times. And so,
when a real wolf arrived, no one believed them.
—**PROFESSOR LEO CAESIUS**
Crying Wolf: The Media and the Fall of the Empire

"IT DOESN'T LOOK AS THOUGH he's really going to get away with it," Claudia said. "Does it?"

Clarence shrugged. A month had passed since the coup, a month since the entire planet had been turned upside down. Nothing was the same anymore, including the position of the once-great corporations. Maxima and her fellows were still too large to be easily dismantled, or even brought to heel, but they were no longer in a position to dictate to the government and its courtrooms. The trial of Simon Goldwater was probably the most honest—and transparent—trial in the history of Tarsus.

"We will see," he said, as they walked down the steps and onto the road. The trial hadn't been delayed as much as he'd been expecting, something that had surprised him despite the First Speaker's promise that Goldwater would be tried as soon as possible. "But I wouldn't be surprised if he does manage to buy his way into a reduced sentence."

He sighed. The week following the coup had been chaotic. A considerable number of Drayton's people had committed suicide, sometimes with a little help, or been arrested and unceremoniously deported. Given the chaos engulfing the Empire—or what had once been the Empire—Clarence had no idea where they might have been sent, although it was hard to care. Others had resigned and been allowed to slip back into the general population. It was astonishing to see just how many policemen had resigned in the last week alone, once they'd realised that the people had had enough of their bullshit. *Inspector* Grozny had told him that it would take months—perhaps years—to retrain the remaining policemen and hire replacements for the departed. But no one had much sympathy for the policemen who'd left their jobs. Too many people believed they'd gotten away with it.

"I suppose it depends," Claudia agreed. She grinned, humourlessly. "I heard from Patricia yesterday, by the way."

Clarence snorted. He didn't really *dislike* his former partner—and he didn't blame her for being used by her relatives—but he didn't want to think about her either. "How's she doing?"

"She says the *Daily Truth* is changing," Claudia said. "They're actually developing journalistic ethics."

"Hah." Clarence rolled his eyes in disbelief. "*That* will be the day."

"She was quite confident of it," Claudia said. "Now the monopoly is broken, it's getting harder for the media to find an audience. They're starting to improve."

"We shall see," Clarence said. There were thousands upon thousands of new media organisations now, from one-man operations to small businesses like *Seeing Eye*. He was fairly sure that most of them would collapse fairly quickly, or fail to build a large audience, but the survivors would be in a stronger position to challenge the mainstream media's dominance. "I doubt the *Daily Truth* can really save itself."

"Who knows?" Claudia looked pensive for a moment. "The world is a different place now."

Clarence nodded in agreement. The old laws were still on the books—a problem he suspected would come back to haunt them, sooner or later—but no one was paying any real attention to them. Earth's dominance was gone too. The start-ups were manufacturing and selling whatever the hell they liked, allowing the free market to pass judgement on their products and services. There had already been a handful of minor problems—and Clarence was fairly sure that it was only a matter of time before there was a *major* problem—but it was kick-starting the economy. The public demand for…just about *everything* was insatiable. It probably helped that the new terminals—Neil Harran's work—were designed to be impossible to turn into surveillance devices.

They paused outside a stall selling algae-based food. Neil Harran again, Clarence noted; the slop tasted awful in its pure form, but cooks were already finding ways to give it some flavour. Chicken-flavoured glop couldn't compete with *real* chicken, yet a man didn't have to be starving to eat it. The base foodstuff was provided free too. A street-seller would make a tiny profit, but a profit none-the-less. And that too would help boost the economy.

And keep people from starving in the streets, Clarence thought. The laws forbidding squatting hadn't been repealed either, but that hadn't stopped people from opening up the abandoned housing estates and turning them into homes. It would be a serious problem, he was sure, when the time came to see which estates really *were* abandoned and which still had living owners, yet…for the moment, it helped keep people off the streets. *Things are getting better.*

"Elle was talking about opening a rival newspaper of her own," Claudia said. "Did she approach you?"

"No," Clarence said. He had been very busy over the last few days. The trial had been consuming all of his time. He'd barely had a chance to sleep. "Do you think she can make it?"

"She watched *Seeing Eye* from the inside," Claudia reminded him. "And she does have shares to sell. I dare say she can get some investment too."

Clarence shrugged. There had been no official announcement, not yet, but Imperial University wasn't going to be open much longer. The combination of a major funding shortfall—thanks to Earth falling into chaos—and a simple lack of utility in the real world had damaged the institution beyond repair. He'd discussed it with Jessica, when they'd tried to think of a way to salvage something from the wreckage, but nothing had come to mind. The people who had the money to save the university had no particular interest in doing so—and nothing, the cynical part of his mind added, to gain from such a vast expenditure. He wondered, idly, what would happen to the university's grounds. Perhaps they could turn the frat house into a museum.

"If you're joining her, good luck," Clarence said. "And if you're not...I look forward to working with you in the future."

Claudia elbowed him. "And if I hadn't thought of you," she said, "where would you be now?"

Dead, Clarence thought. He had no reason to doubt it. He would have drunk himself to death, either in his apartment or on the streets. Or he would have been killed for his heavy coat. He shivered, despite the warm air. He'd come so close to death. *She saved my life.*

"Thank you," he said, seriously.

"You're welcome," Claudia said. "How does it feel to be famous?"

Clarence hesitated, unsure how to answer. He was—now—the most famous journalist on Tarsus. He might even be the most famous *person* on Tarsus. It was easy to believe that everyone knew his name, although only a handful of people had recognised him on the streets. The combination of articles lionising him as a hero—and his own, *completely* factual account of the final showdown in Government House—had made sure of that, although some of the article writers seemed to believe that he had muscles on his muscles. There was even a proposed miniseries that would have Clarence—or, more accurately, an actor playing Clarence—storming Government House at the head of an army of heroic soldiers, big-breasted women and innocent children whose only purpose, as far as he could tell from the script, was to die so the audience would feel...*something*. Clarence had refused to give the producers his blessing, but he had a feeling the production would go ahead anyway. The mythmaking had already begun.

"It feels...*hollow*," he said, finally. He had arrived. He had made himself so famous that he could set his own terms, wherever he wanted to work. There was enough cash in the bank—and hidden away in a couple of places—to keep him going for quite some time. And yet, he couldn't help feeling there was something missing. "There's nothing else to do, is there?"

Claudia elbowed him. "There will be more stories to write," she said. They turned the corner and walked towards the new headquarters. "And you know it."

Clarence started to reply, then stopped himself. Someone was standing outside the gate...no, *two* people. He felt his heart start to pound. Minnie and Henry were waiting for him.

"I'll go inside," Claudia said, quietly. "Come and talk to me later, if you wish."

"Thanks." Clarence wanted to run to Minnie and embrace her, tightly. He also wanted to turn and flee as fast as he could. "I'll see you later."

Minnie hadn't changed *that* much, he thought, as he walked towards her. She wore a simple black dress—a *teacher's* dress. It made sense, he supposed. Minnie would have had to get a new job, just to escape the stigma of being married to a man who'd lost *his* job. And *teacher* was an easy job to get, if one had the right certificate. He wondered, absently, who she'd bribed to get the paperwork in order. School authorities were notoriously corrupt.

And they keep talking about cleaning up the schools, Clarence thought. *I wonder how that is going to work out for them.*

"Clarence," Minnie said. "I wanted to talk to you."

Clarence looked past her, at Henry. The boy was standing there, looking as unsure of himself as Clarence felt. God alone knew what Minnie had told him—or, for that matter, what her *mother* had told him. Better for Henry to think his father dead than unemployed. It was stupid—everyone knew a boy needed a father to grow up properly—but understandable. The shame of being unemployed would last forever...

Unless the unemployed man gets another job, he reminded himself. *And I did get another job.*

He looked back at his wife, unsure of his feelings. If he'd been younger, he would have shouted and screamed at her...or even just turned around and left. But he was a mature adult. He didn't really *blame* her for leaving him, or for coming back. He knew too much about the way the world worked to waste time screaming about it. Minnie had done the best she could for her son—and herself. And what Clarence felt about it didn't matter.

"We can go down the street to the coffee shop," he said, finally. "And there...we will talk."

EPILOGUE

FROM: *A Childish Trick*. Clarence Esperanza. *Seeing Eye*. Tarsus. Year One, Post-Empire.

THERE IS A TRICK WE PLAY ON OUR CHILDREN.

As they grow up, as we send them to school, we tell them stories and bombard them with images of children who change the world. How many of us were forced to read the *Tremendous Timothy* books in Junior School, where the titular character saves the universe time and time again; how many of us devoured the *Susan and the Adventure of [insert title here]* in High School? How many of us read *Emperor Theodore*, where the hero becomes a child emperor who is deferred to by the adults in his life? How many of us claim never to have read *Theresa and Harriet*, where two teenagers in love defy their parents and win their right to be together? Our children leave our schools convinced that they can change the world.

But, as we learn when we become adults, it is rarely as simple as books make it seem. The real world would be very cruel to *Tremendous Timothy*, who would rapidly discover that an innocent child might be right...but would also be ignored by the adults in his life. Book V, in which Timothy puts an end to a sectarian war that has gone on for centuries, is simply fanciful. *Susan and the Adventure of the Missing Heir* has the two characters solving all the empire's problems in a single book, causing a Golden Age that—we are told—will last for a thousand years. *Emperor Theodore* would discover that his advisors would run the empire to suit themselves. And *Theresa and Harriet* would find that the path of true love does not run smoothly. Happily ever after rarely comes as easily as we think.

And so, when our kids leave the schools, it is easy for them to become jaded. Very few problems can be solved without a great deal of toil, trouble and *real* work. So few kids are even taught the underlying *causes* of the problems, ensuring that their attempts to fix them are—at best—misaimed. The antislavery campaigns that dominated large swathes of the political discourse for the last two hundred years were not misguided, by any reasonable definition of the term, but they were certainly misaimed. Slavery did not exist, by and large, because the people who bought the slaves were *evil* (although some of them clearly *were* evil). Slavery—more accurately, indentured and involuntary colonists—existed because economic conditions made slavery profitable. To paraphrase the words of a long-forgotten savant, the activists have attributed conditions to malice that have been caused by economic necessity.

Activism, therefore, is a force for both good and evil. It can change the world—sometimes. It can also make the problems it sets out to solve a great deal worse. If the people in charge understand what they're talking about, if they understand why the problem exists, they may be able to do something about it. But if they're merely screaming and shouting nonsense, with no true understanding, they will—at best—just make themselves look like kids. And the real world has no true respect for kids. Most people, no matter how much they deny it, believe that children should be seen and not heard. The same is often applied to know-nothing teenage activists.

As another savant put it, "know the enemy and know yourself and you will win a thousand battles."

And I was asked if we really *did* manage to change the world. Did we?

Seeing Eye was dreamed up by a teenager, someone young enough to be idealistic and old enough to make his concept a reality. He was lucky enough to be wealthy and well-connected, ensuring that his dream could get off the ground. And his early hires were much the same, giving *Seeing Eye* a clout—and a presence—that many other start-ups couldn't hope to match. His later hires—including me—were chosen more for journalistic experience than connections. It made us vulnerable, but it also made us daring.

We did, in some minor ways, have an effect on the world before the coup. We exposed Maxima Corporation's misdeeds and ensured that the corporation paid for them. We exposed a long-standing tradition of police misconduct and made it impossible for the police—and the government—to bury the details in the fields. And we boosted the other start-ups, giving them the publicity they needed to flourish. We asked questions, and sought answers, that no one else wanted to ask. Yes, we had an effect on the world.

But, before the coup, our effect was very limited. We did not change everything. Nor did we have any lasting effect. Do not believe anyone who says otherwise.

And yet, during the coup, we *did* have a lasting effect. Or did we?

Systems—and *government* is a system—need constant maintenance to work. Yes, we shook up the government. We told people that something was badly wrong. We encouraged them to go onto the streets and protest, to make it clear that we would *not* surrender to the plotters and their dreams of a very different world. The people had had enough…and, because they trusted us, they believed us when the time came to protest. But how much did we really change?

I can't answer that question. No one can, not yet. The government may backslide—now, a year from now, a hundred years from now—or we may face a crisis from outside our star system. We may lose our new freedoms as quickly as we gained them…or we may see them weakened slowly, over time, as the government slowly claws back its power. We must never forget—not now, not *ever*—that the laws that suffocated us were not signed into law because the writers were evil. They sincerely believed they were doing good. But the laws became tools of evil—and of the bureaucratic mindset that forbids its workers from thinking about the reasons behind the laws, then putting them aside if they no longer applied.

The heroes and heroines of children's novels never have to think about the long term. We—us adults—must think about the future. We must understand that getting what we want in the short term may not be good in the long. And the consequences that appear at once may not be the consequences that appear in the future.

Did we make a difference? Yes, we did.

But did we do good? Time will tell.

It always does.

• • •

The End
The Empire's Corps **Will Return
Soon.**

AFTERWORD

You cannot hope to bribe or twist, thank God! the British journalist.
But, seeing what the man will do unbribed, there's no occasion to.
—Humbert Wolfe

THERE'S AN OLD JOKE FROM THE DAYS of the Soviet Union
that goes a little like this.

One day, in New York, the British and Russian ambassadors had a race.
The British ambassador won. The British newspapers reported "*the British
and Russian ambassadors had a race and the British ambassador won.*" The
Russian newspapers reported that "*there was a race between ambassadors in
New York and the Russian ambassador came second.*"

You'll notice, if you read the second statement carefully, that it is *technically* accurate. There was indeed a race between ambassadors and the
Russian did indeed come second. However, it is also deliberately misleading.
It carries an implication, cunningly disguised, that there were more than
two ambassadors in the race, which leads to a suggestion that the Russian
did not *lose* so much as simply come second. And, if anyone should happen
to call the writer on the statement, the writer can simply point out that it
is technically accurate.

Which it is. It isn't a lie. It's just misleading.

It is difficult to argue that there was ever a point where the media was a paragon of honesty and truthfulness. Journalists are human; it would be strange indeed if they were to remain above the fray. Nor were editors and publishers ever above pushing their own views; William Randolph Hearst, for example, pushed the narrative of Spanish atrocities on Cuba that helped fuel the Spanish-American War. It was discovered, afterwards, that many of his stories were lies, but—his defenders argued—lies told in a good cause. Hearst's determination to aid the Cuban rebels in their struggle against Spain led him to do everything in his power to urge American intervention. He may have meant well, but he set a dangerous precedent for the development of future journalism.

A journalist can—obviously—suffer from a conflict of interest. Hearst certainly was torn between his responsibility to report the news and his sympathy for the rebels. However, a journalist cannot allow his work to be tainted by such a conflict. Abraham Rosenthal (1922-2006) once fired a reporter for having an affair with (and accepting gifts from) a political figure she was meant to be covering. When he was challenged by his staff, he responded with "*I don't care if you have a romantic affair with an elephant on your personal time, but then you can't cover the circus for the paper.*" There are at least two versions of this story, as far as I am aware, but the point remains the same. A reporter cannot allow either a conflict of interest or the *appearance* of a conflict of interest.

To a large extent, I think, the rot within Anglo-American journalism started to set in after Watergate and Vietnam. On one hand, more and more reporters were leftists; on the other, there was clear evidence of governmental (presidential) misconduct and serious problems within the military. There were ample grounds to be sceptical of the official line, be it government or military. However, it went too far. The journalists effectively assumed, deliberately or otherwise, that everything that came out of a government's spokesperson's mouth was a lie. And then, when they discovered a tiny inconstancy, they would treat it as proof of more government misconduct, rather than considering it in isolation. Therefore, President George W. Bush's apparently genuine belief that Iraq had WMDs was transformed into deliberate malice. There was no attempt to consider that Bush might have had good reason for believing, if wrongly, that Iraq had WMDs.

What made this worse was a growing habit of accepting statements from *enemy* powers (however defined) as the truth, rather than questioning them. The left-wing journalists refused to see the evil of states like the Soviet Union (a prison camp above ground, a mass grave below), Communist China and North Vietnam. They simply lacked the experience, let alone the willingness, to accept that they were (at best) being shown a Potemkin Village, a fraud carefully designed to convey the wrong expression to a bunch of 'useful idiots.' Thus, when the North Vietnamese claimed that the Tet Offensive had been a communist victory, their claims were accepted without question. The simple fact that American and South Vietnamese forces had won was ignored. It may not be an exaggeration to say, as many did, that the American media was a *de facto* enemy combatant.

This problem became more pronounced as the Cold War came to an end. On one hand, reporters were increasingly inexperienced and unable to tell the difference between truth and lies. Fewer reporters had the background necessary to understand what they were actually seeing (in the sense, perhaps, that a newbie writer wouldn't see anything wrong with a contract from a predatory agency.) Worse, perhaps, the reporters were largely born within liberal cities—New York, in particular—and lacked the understanding of life outside what came to be known as the media bubble. And, on the other hand, the media had shifted to a point where it was unwilling or unable to challenge most left-wing figures. A vast amount of damage was done to the media's reputation, for example, by the refusal to subject Barack Obama to the same degree of scrutiny the media aimed at George W. Bush and Donald Trump. Their bias was painfully obvious.

Indeed, the 2016 elections may have done irreparable damage to the media's reputation for fairness, decency and honesty. Their original decision to treat Donald Trump's candidacy as a joke accidentally, one assumes, gave Trump a great deal of free publicity and helped him cement the nomination.

At that point, the media went mad with rage. Trump was attacked savagely, time and time again, while Hilary Clinton was largely given a free pass. There was no attempt to understand why Trump was so popular, at least in part because Trump's popularity came from his gritty determination to stand up to the media (which had been subjecting Republicans to similar attacks for years). The media turned Trump into the underdog and his supporters loved him for it. Indeed, they have learnt nothing from the experience. They are *still* tripping over themselves in a desperate bid to get Trump.

In some ways, they are unable to understand how and why the world has changed in the past two decades. The internet has enabled the rise of hundreds of independent news services and thousands upon thousands of bloggers, each one offering their own take on developing situations. When Trump was lambasted for using tear gas to defend America's borders—and the fact that reporters had to ask *why* the borders should be defended says a great deal about them—it didn't take long for bloggers to reveal that Obama had *also* used tear gas to defend the borders. Their bias was painfully clear. They are no longer the undisputed masters of the media sphere and they hate it.

Trump may be a bad President. His supporters may have been conned. But why should anyone listen to the media who cried wolf? The media that treated them with scorn, if not outright hatred? The media that went easy on Hilary Clinton and overlooked Obama's scandals? The media that practically dropped the presidency into Trump's lap?

The long-term effects of media malpractice started to take their toll long before Trump and will continue to pervade American (and Western) politics long after Trump vanishes from the political scene. On one hand, the constant nagging questioning of everything the government does will constantly force the government to be on the defensive, rather than acknowledging that *nothing* is perfect and there are no perfect solutions to anything. Alternatively, the failure to question governments the media actually *likes* will deceive the government into believing that it *is* perfect. Trust in the media—and the government—is steadily being undermined, not least because the media's mistakes are increasingly obvious.

And, on the other hand, it will increase cynicism throughout the population. A failure to put forward a nuanced approach, acknowledging that there are two sides to every issue, will make it impossible to believe anything. An either/or approach to life cannot fail to cause backlash. Distrust of the media will ensure that, in the event of a genuine fascist trying to win election, no one will believe the media. Why should they? The media had a lot of pleasure pointing out the mote in their enemy's eyes. But they chose to ignore the log in *their* eyes.

The sensible thing for journalists to do, right now, would be to clean up their act. A reporter who hates Trump (or Clinton or whoever runs against Trump in 2020) should not be allowed to report on him. Reporters should be hired, by and large, from people who have genuine life experience, including life outside the big liberal-ruled cities. There should be a clear willingness to subject *all* candidates, not just the conservatives, to scrutiny, with the results put forward without spin. Reporters who lie, or mislead, or have obvious conflicts of interest should be sacked. The media, in short, should not play favourites.

I doubt, however, that they will make *any* attempt to clean up their act.

• • •

I wrote this a while ago, but it still makes sense.

This is a story of two villages.

Once upon a time, in two villages—we'll call them Alpha and Beta—there were two teenage boys who were charged with guarding the sheep. Only one boy from each village could be spared for this very important duty because it was a hardscrabble life—every man, woman and child needed to work to ensure the village could survive the winter. And it was an important duty because everyone knew there were wolves in the mountains. If the wolves killed the sheep, the villagers would starve.

One day, those two boys—in their separate fields—decided to play a joke. They cried WOLF!

There was instant pandemonium! The villagers dropped their tools, grabbed their weapons and ran for the fields. And when they got there, the villagers each found the boy laughing at them. He showed no remorse at all for his little joke.

In Alpha, the boy was severely punished. He was thrashed by his father, scolded by his mother and shunned by the rest of the village. No one would talk to him, his friends abandoned him, no girl would consider marrying him. Eventually, he left the village in disgrace and was never seen again. The rest of the villagers took note.

In Beta, the boy was feted as a hero. Most of the villagers thought the joke was funny—"boys will be boys"—and the ones who didn't were accused of lacking a sense of humour. He was surrounded by friends; he had no trouble finding a girl willing to marry him. His life seemed perfect. And the rest of the villagers took note of that too.

Over the next few weeks, the mountains surrounding Alpha were quiet. But the mountains surrounding Beta constantly echoed with the cry of WOLF! At first, the villagers would rush to arms the moment they heard the dreaded cry and hurry to defend their flocks; later, they would ignore the cry, reasoning that it was just another young boy trying to cement his position amongst his peers. A handful of villagers swapped homes—some thought that Alpha had been too harsh, others that Beta had been too lenient.

And then, one day, the cry of WOLF was heard in both villages.

In Alpha, the villagers rushed to arms—they raced to the field, caught the wolf and killed him. The sheep were safe.

In Beta, the villagers ignored the cry. The wolf ate the shepherd, the sheep and slunk away happy. Eventually, when someone realised that the shepherd hadn't come home and went to check on him, they discovered the truth. But by then it was too late.

The Alpha villagers lived happily ever after.
The Beta villagers starved to death.

Christopher G. Nuttall
Edinburgh, 2019
PS—Keep reading for a free sample of *Fenris Unchained*…

Out now from Henchman Press:

FENRIS UNCHAINTED

BY KAL SPRIGGS

The Wolf is Loose

TEN YEARS AGO, AFTER HER PARENTS WERE KILLED in a terrorist attack, Melanie Armstrong walked away from a military officer's career to raise her orphaned brother.

Since then she's been captaining a tramp freighter—shuffling from world to world, scraping to barely get by, but content that she's made the right decision.

But when her ship crashes, authorities make her an offer: take a fifteen-year sentence on a prison world where the average lifespan is a third of that.

Or take part in a mission to stop an ancient, and until-now forgotten, robotic warship, the *Fenris*, from completing its hundred-year-old task of destroying a planet, killing millions.

CHAPTER 1

Time: 0815 Local, 01 June 291 G.D.
Location: Dakota, Dakota System

A YELLOW LIGHT BEGAN TO FLASH on the control board.

That was nothing new, not aboard the *Kip Thorne*. Warning lights lit up half the panel. It was a Christmas display of yellow caution lights, flashing priority lights, and red danger lights that gave the board an aspect of impending doom.

The pilot didn't look over to the panel to see what was wrong. One of the red lights indicated a malfunction in the auto-pilot system. That meant that the tall, blond woman had to bring the *Kip Thorne* down by hand.

Not a difficult a task for an experienced pilot. She enjoyed flying, enjoyed it more than anything else, really. She didn't enjoy thirty six hours of flight time spent awake on stimulants while flying a ship that needed far too many repairs.

She shot a glance at the panel, and then flipped on the intercom. "Rawn, take a look at the starboard thruster." She shook her head. Tried to push thoughts through a mind that seemed turned to mud.

The intercom crackled and hissed, his voice difficult to make out. "Uh, Mel, we might have a problem."

The light ceased flashing. She sighed in relief, "No, it cleared up here, good job whatever you did."

The ship bucked. The alarm light flashed red. A moment later, so did six or seven other warning lights. "What the hell did you just do, Rawn?!"

Mel fought the control yoke, eyes wide, as she swore to herself:

"Rawn, was that the starboard pod going out?"

The ship yawed over as she overcompensated and she fought it back under control.

"Rawn, you'd better get that thruster back online."

She heard a squeal from the hatch as it opened. It had always reminded her of a ground vehicle's brakes screeching just before an accident.

She tried not to apply that metaphor as some sort of warning to her current flight. Her brother spoke from behind her: "I'm going to pack the escape pod. Anything you want me to throw in?" he asked.

"What?" Mel craned her neck to look at him.

The ship spun sharply and threw her against her straps and tossed her brother into the wall hard. She bit off a curse and struggled with the controls for a moment. It seemed to take an eternity to fight the ship back under control.

The radio crackled, "Freighter *Kip Thorne*, this is Dakota Landing Control, you broke out of your landing queue, return immediately, over."

"We're going to lose the other thruster. The port thruster is in worse shape. What do you want me to put in the pod?" her brother asked.

His calm voice made her clench her teeth.

"We're not abandoning ship," she told him sharply. "I can land this thing." It would be hard, though, with just one thruster. They couldn't engage their warp drive in atmosphere, not without disengaging safeties that were there to prevent that. *Even if we had time,* she thought, *it would be a stupid thing to do.* The warp drive field would tear the atmosphere around them and if they hit anything in warp, the difference in relative velocity would not only kill them but quite possibly wipe out Dakota's biosphere.

She forced her mind to focus. When she spoke, her voice had the calm tone that she emulated from her father: "Dakota Landing Control this is

Freighter *Kip Thorne,* we just lost our starboard thruster and are requesting immediate assistance, over."

"Freighter *Kip Thorne,* is this some kind of joke?" The speaker's nasal, officious tone suggested she wasn't amused.

Rawn snorted. "I know the safe combo, I'll grab our cash and some keepsakes. I'll clear out your desk too." He pushed his way back off the bridge.

"Get back here—" Mel clamped her jaws shut. *One thing at a time.* "Negative Dakota Landing, this is no joke, our starboard thruster— "

Her voice broke off as another yellow light began to flash, the warning light for load limit on the other thruster. "Our starboard thruster is out and we're about to lose our port thruster, requesting assistance, over."

"Negative, *Kip Thorne,* you'll have to break off your descent and return to orbit," the nasal voice answered. "A repair craft can be sent to you there."

"Dakota Landing, this is an emergency. We lose our port thruster, there won't be anything keeping us up here." Mel snapped. "We don't have enough thrust to get back into orbit, and you don't have time to—"

"*Kip Thorne,* break off your descent or you will be intercepted by our customs cutter. Over."

"Dakota, I hope they got a tractor," answered. "Because—" The ship shuddered and the other thruster went dead. "We just lost our other thruster. *Kip Thorne,* out."

She turned off the radio and sat in the chair for a long moment as the small freighter bounced. Soon it would begin to tumble, she knew, without the guidance from the thrusters.

"Six years, six years I kept her goin'. Dad, I did my best."

She wiped her eyes; now was not the time to cry.

The ship fell now, without anything to slow its descent besides atmospheric friction. Superheated air flashed across the hull and cast glowing flames across the cockpit glass.

Mel sighed. She kissed her fingertips and touched the control yoke one last time, then unbuckled and left the bridge. She didn't look back.

• • •

Time: 1720 Local, 1 June 291 G.D.
Location: Dakota City Detention Center, Dakota System

Marcus looked over at his companions.

"Don't be so gloomy. They're not nearly so angry with us as they are with whoever crashed that freighter." He ran a hand through his brown hair and gave them a shaky smile.

Brian didn't lift his head out of his hands. "You were carrying ten kilos of rex. Do you know how illegal that is? We'll be lucky if they only confiscate our ship and give us a few years in jail."

Strak spoke from where he sat, cross-legged on the floor. "That's overly optimistic really; rex dealers don't get good treatment in jail. Most of the inmates know someone who's OD'd on it."

Marcus winced, looked away.

"Look, I'm sure I can get us out of this."

Rex was a performance drug, and it was the most illegal and the most common illegal drug in known space. Rex's addiction was both chemical and psychological because it gave a person something that was priceless.

A rex junkie didn't act like any other druggie, because rex didn't distort your senses or give you a euphoric feeling. People on rex were confident, their thoughts were clear, they were able to make quick, well thought-out decisions. The most shy, nervous youth could become the self-assured center of activity with a single dose of rex.

Tertius was the third level, the cheapest. It only affected brain activity. Secundus and Primus Rex chemically modified the body.

Primus was the highest level, the most addictive. Secundus heightened the senses and stimulated the central nervous system, giving a person greater control over their body. Primus did all that and also lent strength, streamlined metabolism, and heightened reaction speeds.

Of course, if Rex's benefits were heaven, its side effects were hell.

They sat in silence for a while and Marcus studied his two companions. He'd signed on as crew aboard their ship, the *Varqua*, six months ago. A crew of five, including these two. The *Varqua* was a tramp freighter, a Stout-class, one of thousands that plied the edges of Guard Space, serving the smaller colonies.

Brian Liu was the owner of the ship. Apparently he had a good head for business or good contacts. The *Varqua* had been a profitable ship, unlike most that plied their runs. A short, stocky man, clearly of Asiatic origins, Brian was a decent enough boss, if overly picky about the law most of the time. Marcus couldn't fault him that, though the man's arrogance grated at times.

Strak was something of an enigma. Calm and collected where Brian was loud and arrogant, overweight and slow where Brian was muscular and bird-quick. He had held a sort of general maintenance job aboard the *Varqua*. In reality, he served as an adviser for Brian, and a watchdog over the rest of the crew. Getting anything past the old man was more than difficult, it was damn near impossible. He seemed remarkably loyal to Brian, and Marcus got the feeling that they shared some kind of history.

Marcus hadn't ever felt unwelcome…just the outsider.

"Everything would have been fine except for those damned pirates," he muttered.

The door at the end of the cell block clanged and then groaned open. Two prisoners led the way, followed by two guards. The first prisoner was in his late teens and he wore a ragged set of coveralls. An unruly mop of blond hair hung above a face covered in dirt and oil.

The other prisoner was a tall, statuesque blonde, with dark brown eyes. She wore an equally ragged cut of clothing. As they came past, Marcus blinked in surprise. "Mel?" He asked as he moved close to the bars.

She turned, hearing his voice. Her eyes went wide in recognition.

Then her fist snapped out, slipping between the bars to strike him full in the face.

Marcus dropped like a stone. She kicked through the bars, hitting what she could, punctuating each word with a kick, "You owe me ten thousand dollars, you free-booting piece of—"

One of the guards cuffed her to the ground and then drew her to her feet and pushed her into the cell opposite the other three prisoners.

Both the guards and the other prisoners laughed.

Marcus sat up, touching his nose and wincing, "You bwoke my mose!"

Mel shook her head, jaw clenched in rage, "Too bad I didn't break your neck."

Strak laughed, "Sounds like she knows you fairly well, Marcus."

Marcus sat on his bunk, holding his nose with one hand. "Well, mow that 'ou've gob ib' ou' of yo', you want to talk?" he asked in a calm tone. He felt hot blood run down his face and the salty copper of it in the back of his throat. Well, he'd tasted worse things before.

Mel shook her hand, flexing it a bit. "Sure. You still owe me ten thousand dollars. You're still a piece of shit." She took a seat on one of the bunks in her cell. "So what more do we have to talk about?"

Marcus stared at her for a long moment. There was something more here besides his theft. Granted, Mel had a tendency to overreact at times. "Five years ain't been enough to cool your anger?" He asked. She didn't answer.

Brian looked up, "This bastard screwed you lot over as well?"

The boy spoke, his voice was calm, but his eyes were cold. "Marcus Keller is not a man to be trusted."

"A little late to tell us that." Brian's voice filled with bitterness. "He had ten kilos of rex stashed in his room."

"Wow, I knew you were a bastard," Mel said, "but dealing rex? That's sick, that's really sick." She smiled sweetly. "I hate to think what they'll do to you in a prison."

Marcus held his nose, feeling the blood run down his face. He didn't say anything. There wasn't anything he could say. He looked away from her angry dark eyes and met those of her brother Rawn. *She has every reason to hate me,* Marcus thought grimly, *and her brother, too.*

* * *

"Hey, boss, got a couple possible recruits."

Agent Mueller looked up from his paperwork, "Not interested. I wouldn't even want to pick up the other two to get our man if it weren't for the package deal."

"One of them is a pilot. Her brother is certified engine crew."

"Oh?" Mueller raised an eyebrow, "that could be useful, but this is a recruitment mission—"

"Both of them lost their parents to a GFN terrorist attack."

The Agent picked up the file, he browsed both folders quickly. He began to smile slightly, especially as he read the note from the investigating officer. "Interesting...All right, you've convinced me. Tell the magistrate I want them."

• • •

"The accused will step forward."

Mel stepped forward into the courtroom. The only occupants were a pair of guards and a man in Guard Fleet uniform. "Sir, I want to—"

"You will be silent or you will be held in contempt of this tribunal," the uniformed man cut her off. "The tribunal is now in session."

There was a faint hum as recording equipment turned on.

"Certified Pilot and Ship's Owner Melanie Armstrong of the Century System is charged with Criminal Negligence, Reckless Endangerment, and Willful Disobedience of Traffic Control Commands." The tribunal officer sounded bored. "How do you plead?"

"Uh, sir, that is—"

"Accused pleads guilty to all charges. Evidence is amended to tribunal recordings."

"Hey, I didn't say—"

"The tribunal finds the accused guilty of above crimes and also for contempt of the tribunal. Sentence for conviction is fifteen years hard labor. Convicted is remanded to Guard Custody for duration of the sentence."

The officer flipped a switch. The hum cut off.

"Hey, wait, you can't do this!" Mel shouted. "That wasn't even a trial! I demand to see a lawyer—"

One of the guards grabbed her by her collar and dragged her out.

· · ·

Time: 1100 Zulu, 11 June 291 G.D.
Location: Female Block, *Justicar* Prisoner Transport

The cold, dark ship's sole purpose and design came from the need to transport the maximum number of prisoners with minimal difficulties. Cells were just that, cells of solid steel that ran down the length of the ship, each door secured by a digital lock whose combination changed every time the guards opened it.

They separated Mel from her brother and put her in the female block. There were only three other women in the block. Apparently the Guard didn't get many prisoners on this run.

She didn't talk to them. They didn't talk to her. The silence was almost companionable. Her food arrived via a tray slid under her door, twice a day, delivered by a female guard who never spoke.

On the third day, her door opened.

There were two female guards. One of them gestured. "Come on out."

They took her out of the cells, past the security checkpoint and into a clean, sterile room. "Shower's there," one gestured to a door.

"Clothing's there." She gestured to a neatly folded pile of clothing on a table.

"When you're clean and dressed go through that door." She pointed at a second door.

Then they left.

It was the first moment of privacy Mel had had in days. She wanted to cry. Instead, she went to the shower. It was an experience she wanted to savor, but she also didn't want to be dragged out of it. She suspected that or worse would happen if she lingered too long.

She hurried and then got dressed quickly. It was normal, comfortable civilian clothing; it even fit her fairly well, though it was bland and unremarkable. It felt alien after the prison smock she'd worn for what seemed forever. A part of her mind whispered that it had only been a week. She didn't want to imagine the longer period of imprisonment ahead of her.

The second door opened into another sterile room.

A long mirror covered one wall. A man sat behind a table with a slim folder on it.

"Have a seat," he said without rising.

Mel sat. She knew this was some kind of game, knew she was being manipulated. It should have made her angry, but somehow it only made her feel more helpless. Over his shoulder she saw her reflection. Her face looked pale, blonde hair lank, eyes shadowed.

The man opened up his folder. "Melanie Armstrong, born 266 to Anne Marie and Hans Armstrong on the planet Century, of the same system."

His voice was empty and cold, "Your aunt and uncle were archeologists on Century, they and their youngest child were killed in a pirate attack on Century, leaving only your cousin Jiden Armstrong alive. Your grandmother, Admiral Victoria Armstrong of Century's Planetary Militia is something of a local war hero. You got your pilot's license at fifteen, qualified for entry into the Harlequin Sector Fleet Academy at seventeen, rather than joining Century's Military Academy. You were in the top five percent of your class for three years. Then your parents died in a Guard Free Now terrorist attack two months before graduation. You resigned and took guardianship of your younger brother. In the six years since, you managed the *Kip Thorne* as captain and owner until a week ago when it broke up above Dakota."

"I suppose you even know my calculus test grades from my plebe year," Mel joked weakly, "So what is this about?"

The man smiled thinly, "You got excellent marks, your teacher put in a recommendation that you be sent to further schooling in higher level mathematics." The man stood "Do you know what your sentence is?"

"Penal colony I'd guess." Mel answered.

"Fifteen years on Thornhell." He stood up and looked down at her. He wasn't tall, probably ten centimeters or more shorter than Mel, but he seemed to loom over her.

Mel gulped, "I heard there was a war on there." What she'd heard of the planet left her feeling faintly sick.

The man shook his head, "Not anymore. Not that it matters much. You'd be working in the mines. Fifteen years is ten years longer than the survival rate on that planet."

"It's not fair!" Mel snapped. "I did the best I could, I didn't even get a fair—"

His voice cut across hers like a knife, "No, it's not fair. The universe isn't fair." He smiled a cold, reptilian smile. "Think on this though. How fair would it be if your freighter had landed on someone, rather than smashing into some wilderness on a backwater planet?"

He smiled wider as she shook her head stubbornly. "No, it didn't. But your next stop was Salvation. Think for a moment what would have happened if your thrusters went out there. Something similar happened on Expo just last year. Over fifteen hundred dead when one battered freighter crashed into a residential block in the middle of the night. No warning; definitely not fair to them, eh?"

Mel looked down at her hands. "If we'd made that run, we could have paid for the repairs we needed."

"No, if you'd made the run, you would have needed to make several more to pay for the repairs you needed. We reviewed your logs and analyzed your cargo versus your maintenance bill. Even with some kind of loan, you weren't going to pay for it all." The man answered.

Mel looked up, anger in her face. "What's this about? I'm going to die on some crappy, worthless world, I failed my brother and I failed myself. Is that what you want to hear?"

She gestured at the mirrored wall, "Is that what they want to see?"

The cold man smiled. "What do you know about the Second Sweep?"

Mel's jaw dropped at the complete change in subject. She shook her head while she tried to get her bearing. Finally, she answered, "Started a hundred years ago. Bigger war than the War of Persecution. We almost lost."

"We very nearly were *exterminated*." The cold man spoke softly. His eyes seemed distant and there was a tone of reverence to his voice. "The Culmor were at the front gate. Fifty million soldiers and sailors died. Over three billion civilians wiped out. The entire Sepaso Sector razed; half of Harlequin sector exterminated."

He caught Mel's gaze with his own cold and calculating eyes.

"That certainly wasn't *fair* to them. That didn't stop it from happening. You wrote a paper about the automatons." He paused. "Tell me about them."

Mel stared at him for a long while, "Uh, the Preserve and Triad ran low on trained personnel. They made fully automated vessels for the fighting." She frowned.

"Most had small crews to run them, some were controlled entirely by computers: Artificial Intelligence, supposedly limited by programming to think only within tactical orientations. They weren't supposed to think outside of the mission parameters."

The unknown man picked up a copy of her paper, she could follow along as he read the instructor's comments scrawled on the top, "A decent paper, excellent research but you didn't touch very much on the reasons the ships were discontinued."

Mel shrugged. It seemed a strange topic of conversation, but... "They behaved erratically in combat. Mission parameters were vague in many cases. They were amazingly effective as rear-area raiders, or serving as suicide attackers against Culmor bases. While in formation with human ships, though, they sometimes targeted friend and foe, went berserk. Some took damage and went haywire."

She was slightly surprised at all she remembered after several years. Then again, it had been an interesting topic in history. The subject had been all the more intriguing for the fact that most people didn't like to talk about it.

"And then the war turned, we didn't need them any more. So the ships were discontinued, most of them were scrapped."

Mel nodded impatiently, "Right, they weren't designed to carry crews, the weapons, plants and engines had little shielding, the ships didn't have life support. It was easier and cheaper to scrap them than to refit them for human use."

"Don't worry, this all has a purpose." The cold man smiled, took his seat. "That history is something of a fascination of mine; also, it's part of my job."

"Which would be?" Mel asked.

The man removed a wallet from within his suit, "Guard Intelligence."

Mel pushed back from the table, as if he'd transformed into a venomous snake.

He grinned broadly, "No need to fear, I'm not hunting you or even here to harm you. As bad as it may sound, I'm actually here to help you."

Despite his words, he clearly enjoyed the effect he'd had on her, Mel saw. The light to his eyes and the smirk on his face marked him as someone who cultivated the persona.

Mel knew that she should stay quiet and shouldn't provoke him. Even so, she couldn't help but snort in derision, "Right. As in 'I'm from the government, I'm here to help you.'"

The spook's smirk vanished and his eyes narrowed in irritation. "Some agents believe that coercion is sufficient to gain service from those they need. I do not believe so. Believe me, I will lie to you, I will use you, but I understand that I must give you some incentive if I want you to assist me."

He stared at her in silence for a long moment, almost as if to suggest that he were reconsidering whether he were going to offer Mel anything at all.

Good job, Mel thought to herself, *piss off the guy who holds your life in his hands.*

Even so, she couldn't help a spurt of irritation with the man. He wanted her to feel this way, wanted her to second-guess herself. He was building towards something and he wanted her off balance and uncertain. She fell back on the fire that had gotten her through the Academy and she felt her back straighten, even as she clenched her teeth on the spike of anger at this continued manipulation.

"What do you know about the Wolf-class battlecruisers?" He demanded.

Back to the games, Mel thought with a sigh. She took a moment to think. Part of the Academy had dealt with ship identification, with a basic overview of every Human military ship made in the past three hundred years.

"The class was designed for heavy combat. Fully automated, some self-repair capabilities. Only ten or twelve of them even begun in construction, I don't think any of them ever saw combat."

It was the sum of all her knowledge. She'd been far more fascinated by the smaller ships while at the Academy. *I wanted to be a fighter pilot,* she remembered. That part of her seemed very distant, in many ways as dead as her parents.

"Three Wolves commissioned, two of them went on missions, the third went to the breakers within a month of completion," the agent stated flatly, all emotion gone from his voice.

"The *Romulus* went against a Culmor dreadnought squadron at Baker in order to delay its attack on Harlequin Station. That mission cut the war short by an appreciable margin. It destroyed three of the squadron's four dreadnoughts, and the fourth was destroyed in a follow-up run."

Mel blinked. A *battlecruiser* destroyed three dreadnoughts?

"The other ship, the *Fenris,* departed on a separate mission three weeks later, in March of 193. It first attacked a troop transport convoy, sighted at Bell, then a captured deep-space station serving the enemy as a raider base. Its final target was to be the center of the Culmor advance in this sector, Vagyr."

Mel frowned, "Wasn't Vagyr captured intact nearly a year later?"

"It was, by 'auxiliaries' that were, and are, little more than pirates," the agent replied.

"The *Fenris* never arrived at Vagyr. It intercepted and destroyed the convoy, scouts confirmed the destruction the raider base, and that was it. Guard Fleet presumed it destroyed in the fight at the raider station. Significant debris clouds suggested a significantly larger raider force at the station than intelligence had suggested." He shrugged. "Logic, therefore, suggested the autonomous ship was destroyed in combat."

"I assume we're having this conversation because it wasn't?" Mel snapped, her patience at a ragged end. The history lesson grated, particularly given the fact that her future seemed tied to this random bit of history.

"Indeed." The agent smiled. "In fact, you are quite right."

"Two weeks ago, a merchant ship suffered a minor warp drive failure. Their FTL warp drive kicked off in what was supposed to be an empty, barren system. While undergoing their repairs, they spotted activity in the inner system. They also detected military transmissions in the system. Like any merchant with something to hide, they quietly got their ship repaired and left. Someone aboard talked and one of my colleagues collected their sensor data as a precaution."

"And it was this missing ship?" Mel asked.

"That took confirmation by a cruiser squadron we sent to investigate. They were extremely fortunate: the *Fenris* queried them for identification and accepted their modern codes."

"So the ship was damaged and hid in some backwater system. What's the problem?" Mel asked. Some part of her whispered that she would be better off trying a more helpful tone...but everything about this Guard Intelligence agent made her back go up.

The agent closed his eyes, sighed slightly. "I've had to tell this story twenty-seven times. Do let me finish at my own pace." He opened his eyes and peered at her somewhat inquisitively, "I don't think you want to make me angry."

His gaze reminded her of a snake that had just eaten, regarding a mouse it might make room for. Mel shivered.

"Guard Fleet dispatched a courier ship with the proper clearance codes and query data to order the ship to power down. Upon receiving the query codes, the vessel replied that repairs were 98% completed, and that the mission would continue. Upon receiving the codes to power down, the ship did something it shouldn't have. It ignored the codes and replied that the mission would be completed. Then it engaged it's strategic warp drive."

"And you have no idea where it went." Mel sat back.

"On the contrary. We know exactly where it is going."

• • •

Time: 1500 Zulu, 11 June 291 G.D.
Location: Solitary Confinement, *Justicar* Prisoner Transport

Agent Mueller stepped up near the bars and dropped a chair outside. He settled into it backwards, arms crossed over the back, "Leon, you look like shit."

The prisoner didn't look up from where he sat, huddled in the shadows at the rear of the cell.

"Trying to ignore me? You got pretty good at ignoring many things, Leon, but you never could ignore me." Mueller entwined his fingers and rested his chin on them.

"What do you want?" The voice was only a whisper.

"My friend, my mentor, what do you think I want? I want you, the famous agent, I want you working for us again." Mueller let the sincerity drip through his voice. It was easy enough, after all, because it was the truth. They needed him, and men like him, especially now.

"That will never happen," Leon hissed back.

"Come now, never is an awful long time." Mueller replied. "I know you've still got family back on New Paris. For that matter, I'm sure I can find someone a little closer to... focus your mind."

422

He hated to use threats, not because they weren't effective but because it seemed so dirty. *Why do people continue to make me threaten them,* he thought, *just to do what needs to be done?*

"What do you want?" The whisper was faint, difficult to hear. It was enough.

"I need you on this one. It's bad, I won't lie. Has the potential to be extremely bad. Entire planet annihilated, not a good thing to have happen on my watch, you understand." Mueller shrugged, as if to say it would be an unavoidable tragedy.

"I get the point, what do you want me to do?"

"Don't cause problems. I've talked your friends into helping us. Go along with it. They'll come through this fine; you'll come through this fine. Maybe I can even get you some treatment—"

"No. I have my own ways for dealing with my demons."

The agent shrugged, "Have it your way. It's a shame you left. Yours are hard boots to fill."

"What, the killing, destroying and murdering boots, or the scheming, plotting, manipulating boots?" The prisoner scoffed. "I'm sure you're doing just fine."

"Thanks, Leon, you always knew just how to cheer a fellow up," Agent Mueller smiled. "I must say though…I did learn from the best."

"Get out of my sight bastard, before I kill you," the voice of his former mentor showed some echo of real anger. That surprised him a bit, he thought it would take more than that to break through the man's shell of self-pity.

"Oh, you wouldn't want that to happen, Leon. If I die, well, let's just say you wouldn't want certain other deaths on your already heavy shoulders." Despite his languid words, the man rose quickly and left. He'd already set the hook, no need to further bait the tiger.

CHAPTER 11

Time: 0800 Zulu, 12 June 291 G.D.
Location: *SS John Kelly,* Expo System

MEL LOOKED THE UNFAMILIAR COCKPIT over with a critical eye. She'd seen a couple of these ships before, though never from the inside. The Lotus Blossom class were somewhat infamous. A far fancier name than was entirely necessary, she thought. The ungainly and actually rather ugly ship had little in the looks department to compare to most small freighters. It wasn't really a freighter at all, more of a military light cargo transport.

Marcus stepped in the door behind her, "Should have known I'd find you here, already. Studying a bit early aren't you? We still got six hours before departure."

She didn't answer him at first. It took her a few seconds to squash her anger so that she didn't erupt from her chair to attack him. He would expect that, she knew from the overly relaxed tone in his voice. He wanted to provoke her. "You're a manipulative son of a bitch, you know that?"

"Mel, I'm hurt…*really.*" His innocent tone didn't fool her. Marcus took a seat in the copilot seat behind her.

"Don't you have something else to do?" Mel asked.

"Why? I'm only familiarizing myself with the systems, just like you," Marcus said. She didn't have to look over her shoulder to see the insolent smile on his face.

She sat there for a long while, concentration broken by anger. She hated this man, hated him with every ounce of her body. "Why'd you do it?" She asked finally.

He didn't answer for a moment. She expected another off-handed joke. Instead, when he finally spoke, his voice was gruff. "You wouldn't understand."

"You're right. I probably couldn't understand how a betrayer thinks." She answered. "I don't think I'd want to anyway."

"Things aren't always what they appear, Mel." His voice was sad, somehow. "Keep that in mind when you work with Agent Mueller. Sometimes things aren't what they appear to be."

"And sometimes things are exactly what they look like," Mel snapped back instantly. She didn't want to think he'd had any motivation besides self-interest. Those thoughts robbed her of her anger, left her only with pain.

His seat creaked as he leaned forward to speak softly in her ear. "Don't trust anyone on this ship."

With that he rose and left.

• • •

Time: 1400 Zulu, 12 June 291 G.D.
Location: *SS John Kelly*, Expo System

Mel completed the undocking procedure and drew away from the prison ship. She looked out the canopy distastefully, gazing with distaste at the decrepit vessel. "LMV *John Kelly*, clear of your drive, *Justicar.*" She couldn't find it in her to wish them a good journey.

She heard a dark chuckle from behind her. "I'd love to be able to take all the prisoners off and blast that bastard out of the sky."

"I'm sure you would, Marcus, but you won't be doing that." Agent Mueller said from behind them both. Marcus muttered something about who he wished was aboard the prison ship when he did it.

Mel smiled in spite of herself.

Her smile broadened as she looked across the indicator panels and saw only two yellow lights. She took her time as she swung the bow around and inserted the coordinates for the warp engines. There was joy in a ship that responded.. There was happiness to be found at the yoke of any vessel, even if it wasn't home. *I have no home now,* she thought, her joy darkened with sorrow. She had lost the last thing she had left of her parents.

"Warp coordinates uploaded. Strategic drive active in thirty seconds," Marcus acknowledged.

Being reminded of his presence killed the smile. It didn't hurt nearly as much this time, but it certainly didn't feel good.

She watched the countdown timer. Most such maneuvers were routine; the good thing about warp drives was that they worked or they didn't. The drive rings that circled the ship did their job unless they suffered actual physical damage, at which time the ship reverted immediately to normal space. *Though they can function at lower levels of capability,* she thought.

Watching a ship go into warp was a sign of how well a ship worked. A ship in top shape engaged smoothly, because its drive was properly aligned. Most civilian ships were slightly misaligned, not enough to cause damage, but enough to cause slight nausea to those unfamiliar to the experience. Local space warp drives, often called 'tactical' warp drives utilized only one ring so noticing any motion was difficult. The faster than light warp drive, often called strategic drive by the military, utilized both drive rings on a ship and so any issues with alignment were more easily detected.

As she'd expected, the drive was very smooth. "Minimal misalignment."

"She goes down like a drunken—"

"If you finish that statement, you're going to wish we had a doctor aboard." Mel stated flatly. She'd heard the phrase before; the last person she wanted to hear it from now was him. She opened the intercom to the engine room. "Rawn, how are things down there?"

"No problems, sis." She could almost hear his shrug. "Strak's monitoring the power plant, and that Giran guy is keeping an eye on the control panel."

"Thanks, Rawn."

She heard the door slide closed, and flipped on one of the internal cameras to watch the Guard Intelligence agent walk down the corridor, toward the hangar bay.

She felt Marcus looking over her shoulder. "Getting a little suspicious of our good friend and boss?"

"I got less reason to trust you. Shut your trap." She spoke without force, though. Why the Guard needed to rely on seven convicts to do this job she didn't know. But she didn't trust it one bit.

She flipped on the receiver for the hangar bay intercom. Two of the other crew members were there, Brian, the third and last member from the *Varqua*, and Stasia, who seemed to be a hacker of some sort. The hacker seemed to have a large number of boxes to sort through and as Mel watched, the woman opened up a box, drew out some computer components and then checked them off an inventory.

"Everything good down there?" Agent Mueller was asking.

"Da, seems good." Stasia was a short, skinny woman with mousy brown hair. Her face had a pinched look and she seemed to squint at everything nearsightedly. Mel had spoken to her briefly; she'd seemed very distant, as if her mind was elsewhere.

As Stasia returned to sorting through her boxes, Brian gestured toward three black crates. Each was long and narrow, roughly the size and shape of a coffin, banded with metal strips. The security camera didn't have a good angle, but Mel zoomed in and was able to read bright orange numbers written on the top of one of them.

"Three crates arrived for you just before departure." Brian spoke. There was an unspoken consensus by the crew that no one would refer to the agent as 'sir'. He hadn't earned any kind of respect, and he gave them that minor victory. That they followed his orders seemed good enough for him.

"Only three?" the agent asked.

Brian held out the inventory list, but Mueller waved it away. "Have them put outside my cabin."

"That crate is carrying MP-11s," Marcus said from behind her. He pointed at the first crate. As the agent turned, the other two crates were clearly visible. "That one is a case for a MG-144, and that is a—" He cut himself off, looking at her.

Mel stared at him for a long moment, the obvious question unasked. Marcus was a smuggler, a thief, and a general scumbag. There was no reason for him to instantly recognize the coded label on a military weapon crate.

Movement on the screen caught her attention and she saw that the Guard Intelligence agent was headed toward the bridge. She cut the camera feed and brought up data on the warp drive just as the door opened.

"I trust everything is well in hand?" He asked.

Mel didn't trust herself to face him without revealing too much. Marcus saved her by unbuckling. "Everything's good here. We can probably go to autopilot for the rest of the trip. Damned good computers – equipment, too – for a freighter. Where'd Guard Intel come up with it?"

"There will be a briefing in five minutes in the lounge. I trust you'll both be there."

The agent turned and left without saying anything.

"Fishing for information?" Mel asked.

"Trying to distract him. Agent Mueller is a very perceptive man. I thought it best to give him some false lead as to what we were doing in here during his absence."

"His name's Mueller?" Mel asked.

There was a moment of silence. "Yeah, Adam Mueller. I caught his name when he flashed his badge."

That sounded a little weak to Mel, "Sounds to me like you know something about this GI agent."

He snorted, "Sure I do. *I* know *he'll* know we're up to something if we aren't on time for his little briefing."

Mel opened her mouth to retort, but too late. He had slipped through the hatch before she could come up with something suitably acidic.

"I *hate* that bastard," she growled. Even she wasn't sure which bastard she meant.

• • •

The eight of them met in the lounge for the first time.

Agent Mueller stood next to a holo-projector. Brian and Strak had taken one couch, Mel and Rawn the other. Marcus, Stasia and Giran were seated at the lounge's lone table.

"As most of you can easily guess after our conversations, we are going after the *Fenris*." The agent smiled. "I believe we can dispense with the pleasantries and get straight down to business."

He had a smirk on his face, as if he expected them all to laugh at his turn of phrase. When none of them responded with so much as a smirk, his face went cold. "First: payment." The agent ticked off his fingers as he addressed each item. "All of you will be pardoned for your crimes. Easy enough for me to arrange, I assure you." He shrugged. "Second: each of you receives a bonus for completion. In addition to your freedom, each of you will receive ten thousand dollars."

The seven ex-prisoners eyed each other. Mel judged from the suspicious looks she received that the others trusted her as little or less than she trusted them.

"Each of you has talents that I may find useful." The agent spoke on, "Stasia is our computer expert. Hopefully she's learned her lesson regarding illicit hacking and will not stray. Melanie and Marcus can serve as pilots, Brian and Strak as general crew, Giran and Rawn as engine crew. All of you have other abilities that may come in handy. And all of you were conveniently present when I needed volunteers." He said the last in a light-hearted tone.

Mel didn't feel any surprise when no-one laughed at his joke.

The holo-projector came to life, where it displayed an external view of a ship. "This is the *Fenris*. You all know what it is. So do some others who didn't make the screening process. We are going to shut the vessel down, before it strikes Vagyr. A task force is preparing to meet it in orbit, should we be unable to stop it."

No one looked at him; they all had good ideas what the price of failure would be: a digital pardon was very easy to 'misplace.' *For that matter,* Mel thought darkly, *he could easily have us all killed or marked as escaped prisoners.*

"What should happen is that we catch up to it at one of its navigational stops, and we shut it down via external command. If that proves ineffective, we have to board it. That will not prove to be an easy task." The projector changed, flashing through a deck-by-deck overview. "The entire ship is covered by a security system, which allows the AI to send in security robots, close out sections of the ship, and do all sorts of nasty things."

"So you're giving us all this, just for playing taxi?" Rawn asked.

There was a long, empty silence. The GI agent was silent, his face impassive.

Strak said, "He's using us because we're a cut-out. If this doesn't work, the Guard won't take the blame." The old man stood slowly and shrugged his shoulders, "Probably lots of evidence will point to a salvage ship, us, having activated the ship in the first place."

Everyone looked from him to the agent, Mueller smiled. "A clever idea, but one that is entirely excessive. The Preserve built the *Fenris.* The AI system was produced on Triad, ten decades ago. The forces we're positioning in Vagyr show that the Guard is doing our best to avert tragedy. We don't need any kind of cover-up."

"So," Mel asked, irritated by the agent's smug attitude, "Why do you need us?"

"Because you are expendable," he shrugged. "No reason to send highly trained professionals to deal with a semi-berserk battlecruiser, not when a handful of criminals can do the job just as well. Also, you were easy enough to recruit, whereas mercenaries or professional agents capable of the job would take longer to gather."

"You said this wouldn't be dangerous." Stasia said. Muscles in her right cheek twitched nervously as she spoke.

"I also said I'd be paying you ten thousand in Guard dollars and giving you your freedom. If you're looking to question the terms, by all means, we can discuss any changes right now." They all rapidly got the impression that changes would include first, removing the payment and second, putting them back in their cells.

He's all by himself, Mel thought. *It should feel like an empty threat, but who knows what resources he can call on?*

"Excellent. The *Fenris* needs to drop its drive field in three locations to make navigational checks on the course we believe it is taking. The ship has an older version of our warp drive, meaning our ship has twice its speed. So we have sufficient time to catch it at its second navigation check."

"What command will we be sending?" Stasia asked.

"I've got the authorization codes and copies of its core programming. There wasn't time to put together a program to do the job before we left. That will be your job, Stasia."

Agent Mueller pointed at Rawn and Giran: "You two will be checking her code and making sure that it has no flaws. Our trip should take twenty six days, including two navigational stops, one at Expo and the other at Salvation. Our rendezvous is located in the Crossroads system, two light years west of the Bell system. We should arrive between twenty and thirty-six hours ahead of the *Fenris*. Data on the ship is in the computer. Disabling that ship is our objective, through any means necessary."

Mel shivered at his words. She wondered if she'd have been safer on Thornhell.

• • •

Time: 1900 Zulu, 12 June 291 G.D.
Location: Crossroads System

There were many star systems which could be classed as high value. Harlequin Station was one such, with two life-bearing worlds, three metal rich asteroid belts, and gas giants to provide hydrogen for power generation.

If Harlequin Station was high value, then Crossroads was definitely low value. Its only value was to serve as a way-point for ships on their way to bigger and better places.

A number of small, icy rocks orbited the cold, tiny star…along with one large starship that emerged from warp exactly where the Guard Intelligence Agent had said it would be.

Mel felt a tingling along her spine. Reading about all the firepower that ship had was one thing. Knowing it might be aimed at her was quite another.

"It's *Fenris*," Marcus stated. "Right on time."

"Unidentified craft, transmit identification codes or be fired upon."

Everyone started at the voice. It was the voice of a man, gruff and gravelly. It didn't sound like the soulless machine they'd all expected. The sound was dangerous and slightly sinister, but somehow also carried the overtones of irritation at the interruption and perhaps even a sense of boredom.

Agent Mueller nodded at Mel, "Transmit the codes, prepare the upload."

Mel did so and then waited for what seemed to be an eternity.

"Identification codes accepted, *John Kelly*." Perhaps it was Mel's fears talking, but the voice of the AI sounded slightly disappointed that it couldn't open fire. "Transmit your data upload when ready."

"Do it." Mueller said. He had a smile of triumph on his face.

"Transmitting." Mel said.

She watched as the laser transmitter made connection with the receiver on the other ship. As it began downloading the program, she released a sigh of relief.

"Orders have been updated. Receiving programming update." The voice modulated, changed. There was no boredom in its next transmission, only pure hostility: "Security protocols have been engaged. Primary programming cannot be compromised. This vessel will *not* be hijacked."

"Detecting the warp drive powering up." Marcus yelped. "We're being hit by targeting sensors."

Agent Mueller looked around frantically, "Did the upload go through? What happened?"

Mel brought up the communications system on her screen. Her eyes widened as she realized someone else had also accessed the program from the engine room. The other user began to delete the upload as she watched.

She saved the file to a drive on her console, then opened the intercom to the engine console. "Rawn, someone's trying to delete the program, stop whoever it is!"

"What?" he answered. "What's going on up there?"

"Just stop them, lock the console."

She brought up the security camera for the engine room, caught a sight of Rawn yelling something to Giran, and then Agent Mueller stepped in front of her view. "Was the upload complete?" he demanded.

"It wasn't. I can't tell how complete it was either, because whoever tried deleting the file wiped the record of the transmission from the computer first." Marcus said angrily. "It got the opening packet for certain, but I'm not sure beyond that." He looked up from his console. "The *Fenris* just went into warp."

Mel pushed Agent Mueller out of the way of the screen. She felt her stomach sink and her throat seemed to constrict as she forced the words out of her mouth, "We've got a bigger problem. Does anyone know where Giran got a gun and why he has it aimed at my brother?"

• • •

For more, find it online now!

Printed in Great Britain
by Amazon

84585069R00257